COMMENTS OF CRITICS

THE WARPED JUDGEMENT (Novel)
The Warped Judgement is a tale of societal hypocrisy the games destiny plays in human's life, the complex human relationship and the quest for finding the perfect love. Though quite sad and poignant at times, the fiction is a lovely read.
** The narrative is gripping and the reader can relate to the dilemma of the protagonist. ** Metaphor and the mundane are weaved together to show the loneliness of the protagonist and the fight with the self to come out of his past. ** An intelligent and thoughtful piece of writing that pulls at the heartstrings but not so much as to become depressing. ** The book makes every possible attempt to entertain, enthrall and shock the reader out of his wits. ** the digressions are few and it holds tightly to the plot giving it a racy character which makes it hard to put down**

Soma Chakraborty
BUREAUCRACY TODAY

** Neither too brutal nor transcending barriers of reality, The Warped Judgement provides an excellent account of Kapoor's journey. His character is an outstanding one encompassing all shades. Yet it has a rare blending of melancholia and reason which makes Kapoor an even more interesting personality. ** a praiseworthy effort by Chadha to paint life in print with a touch that really

deserves appreciation. He shows enough promise as an author and his forte is combining imagination and reality with the ideal doses.

Ranjan Das Gupta
THE STATESMAN

IN TURMOIL (An anthology)

They say life is short but living each day, surviving situations and making choices that may or may not lead to a happy conclusion makes life one long journey and a constant turmoil. Author Sushil Chadha captures this churning turmoil in an anthology of short stories — In Turmoil published by Unicorn Books. Chadha unlatches his treasure trove of wisdom and what emerges are 14 tales with complexities of human emotions. ** The anthology comes with a strong storyline that unravels complications of relationships ** the overtly simple approach and an uncomplicated writing style make it an easy read. The author neatly packs life stories and emotions into an anthology and presents it to the readers to see life play out in words.

Reya Mehrotra
THE FINANCIAL EXPRESS

CLIPPED WINGS

SUSHIL CHADHA

F-2/16, Ansari Road, Daryaganj, New Delhi-110002

☎ Ph.: 011-23262683, 23250704, 45644782

E-mail: info@unicornbooks.in • *Website:* www.unicornbooks.in

ISBN 978-81-7806-579-3

Edition: 2023

Type set: Font Name: *Minon Pro,* Font Size: *12pt.,* Font Leading: *15pt.*

This is a work of fiction. Names, characters, organisations, places, events, and incidents are either products of the author's imagination or are used fictitiously. Any resemblance to actual persons, living or dead, or actual events is purely coincidental.

Printed at : Param Offsetters, Okhla, New Delhi-110020

To Sushma

Only those survive,
Who forgive or seek forgiveness.

The Monsoon

(AUGUST 2000)

Built by the British in 1920s and 1930s, Lutyens' zone in central Delhi, is the heartland not only of the capital, but of the country. The ceaseless activity in this area is the pulsation that breathes life into the nation. Stretched over less than 2% of Delhi's area, it houses the Parliament, North and South Blocks, other spacious office buildings and landscaped residences of those who exercise power in the country: politicians, bureaucrats, top brass of the defence forces, judiciary, the super rich and chosen journalists. Anyone wielding some authority tries to squeeze into this region. It is in the well guarded offices or residences of the PM, Cabinet Ministers, and the elite that important decisions affecting the future of the nation are taken. Be it the declaration of war or changing diplomatic relations with a superpower or a neighbour, or the toppling of State Governments of rival parties or matters relating to security, financial and commercial policies. Often, names of loyalists and celebrities are picked up for governorship, ambassadorship or national awards and rewards in the late garden parties over drinks, and rarely a dash of opium. Above all, it is the seat of the President symbolising glittering pageantry, and awesome solemnity. At the periphery of this belt is the proactive Supreme Court delivering, sometimes, landmark judgements turning the government uneasy and changing our way of life. Lutyens' Delhi is the nerve centre that controls and monitors all the happenings within the country and beyond its waters.

The thick green cover lends the area a dignity and quiet aura. The traffic drops: even the monstrous DTC buses are cautious not to pollute or honk. The neem, tamarind, and blackberry trees on both sides of wide roads with generous pavements, filter the blazing May, June sun, and turn the heat wave that zips through the rest of Delhi into a waft of cool breeze. In winter, a hazy mist settles down over the treetops reminiscent of the English weather. As one drives down from The Ashok Hotel to Aurangazeb (now called Abdul Kalam) and Shahjehan Roads, the branches of the trees across the road appear to entangle with one another and provide a picturesque view.

Deepak Chopra, one of our main protagonists, stays at Akbar Road, and has his office in Dholpur House, the former residence of the Ranas of Dholpur, Rajasthan that now houses the UPSC (Union Public Service Commission) complex on Shahjehan Road.

On hearing the rumble of clouds, Deepak Chopra, Chairman, UPSC rose from the swivel chair, and looked out of the window. Rain lashed the trees, shrubs and the little garden at the back of his office. Suddenly, there was lightning followed by a cloudburst, and the windows of the building rattled. Pelting down of rain was an auspicious omen for him. He had got the news of his topping in matriculation in the U.P. board when half the town was flooded in unseasonal rain. It was no different in graduation, post graduation, and the IAS (Indian Administrative Service). All his children were conceived when there were explosions in the sky. But rain had played truant on his wedding day even in July, and at night when the rituals were performed, the sky glittered with stars. No wonder, his marital graph was marked with prominent dips.

Impulsively, he stretched out his hand and liked the feel of water spray formed by the rain hitting the side-window projection. It transported him to school and college days when he along with his friends, ran in the open fields ignoring the reprimand of his mother or played football at the college grounds in rain. "What days!" he murmured to himself.

The monsoon mesmerized him: the roaring clouds, the sheets of rain and all-pervading dampness. It washed away all the bitterness of his life and filled him with a frisson of happiness. He saw joys where none existed. His nostalgia was momentary, and misplaced; his childhood had been miserable and lonely. He had come a long way from that distant hazy past and had fulfilled the promise he had made to his mother more than five decades back that one day he would attain the pinnacle of glory in the government. Now, he wanted to make sure that all his four children were equally successful in their careers.

The buzzer interrupted his thoughts. The PA informed him that the Home Secretary was on the line.

Because of his financial constraints, Deepak wanted some assignment after his term expired in the Commission. According to rules, Deepak could try only for an office of governor. Last month, he had called upon the Home Minister, and he was given a patient hearing. Deepak's term was to expire in about one and a half years, and he had set the slow government machinery in motion.

"Good morning, Trevedi. How is the country?"

"Everything under control, sir!" He laughed, and confided that Deepak was likely to be considered for the Governorship of Rajasthan on completion of his term in the Commission. "Incidentally, a Padma Vibhushan is also on the cards."

Deepak blushed slightly. "Thanks, and keep in touch."

Supriya, the officiating Secretary of the Commission, breezed in with a "hello" and looked at her boss. Fair complexioned, and with an aristocratic demeanour, Deepak Chopra looked attractive though he was over sixty-two years old. Admiringly, she looked at his tall persona and smiled. Supriya had a crush on him even before she had joined the IAS, and their relationship had blossomed and matured over the years. He maintained an unbridgeable distance from everyone and was reputed to be reticent in bureaucratic circle. But she had a hypnotizing effect on him, and the dykes of resistance crumbled under her smiles and laughter. There were few recesses of his heart where she had not peeped in. Without any mental reservation, they shared their delectation and sorrow; the more she got to know him, the more she adored him. They discussed everything, from Gide, Sartre, Madhubala, Dilip Kumar to politics and the state of the economy, and felt that the best part of the day was the time spent in each other's company. Her idolization of him amongst her friends was spontaneous, and she missed no opportunity to glorify him whereas he never mentioned her in any gathering as if it was almost a taboo. Often, she talked of her love in the privacy of his room and with great intensity; he refused to admit it though he loved her with equal fervour.

Deepak told her about Trevedi's call. She smiled smugly and commented that the offer was apt for a former Cabinet Secretary, and the Padma Vibhushan was overdue.

She inquired about his wife's health. Lost in her thoughts, one day, Vaishali crossed the major roundabout near her house. A speeding car driver tried to save her, and swung the car on the other side, and rammed into a truck. All the five occupants of the car were killed instantly. The truck did not stop and made away. The car had hit Vaishali's buttocks, and she had collapsed on the road. She was lucky to have survived after spending two weeks in the hospital.

"Oh, she is much better and is in complete command of the house. Her survival was nothing short of a miracle."

"It was," she said solemnly. "But if God had willed otherwise, would you have married me?"

Deepak froze. He stared at her in disbelief as if she had gone crazy.

"I would have divorced my husband for your sake."

"I am at least 15- 20 years older to you. What do you find attractive in this old man?"

"I have loved you from the day I saw you the first time at Mangalore beach. I've worshipped the very earth you walk on."

"I don't deserve so much Supri," he said, and shook his head. "I have infinite failings. Ask Vaishali."
"You are dodging my question: if God willed otherwise, would you have married me?"
He rose and peeped outside; the clouds thundered.
"No, Supri, I'll not marry you. I have never thought of marriage with you."
His voice was hoarse, unlike his own.

(2)

On the third floor of the seven-storey building of the Indian Institute of Technology (I I T), Delhi, Dr. Vinay Chopra was taking the postgraduate class when the cloudburst followed by rain disturbed his thought process. He stopped abruptly and looked uncomfortably outside. Twenty-five students of MSc Physics (final) huddled on the first two benches looked at the famous physicist with admiration and devoured every word he uttered. He frowned, and continued discussing the Heisenberg Uncertainty Principle according to which you cannot measure the position and momentum of a subatomic particle simultaneously. Later, he concluded his lecture, and threw the tiny bit of chalk in the waste-paper basket. Two students desiring clarification on some issues followed him to his room. Enthusiastically, he moved towards the small white board fixed on the wall, scribbled the equation and spent another fifteen minutes with them.

To his horror, Vinay realized that the table, chair, and some of the important papers were spoiled by a blast of rain from the open window.
"Bloody rain!" he cursed. "How I hate it?"
The euphoria of a satisfying lecture evaporated. He

disliked the very sight of clouds. The three months he had spent in the gloomy cloisters at Oxford under cloudy skies were awful. Down with bronchitis, he was frustrated and depressed. He escaped to Cornell, US; there too, the wintry days made him miserable.

But Madhulika, his wife, loved the rain. The first downpour of the monsoon exhilarated her. She forcibly dragged him into the rain, and he ended with a bronchial problem. This year, she had mercifully spared him as she had her fill of it with a colleague while walking down from University Library to Miranda House in a thunderstorm. She had gone gaga while narrating the experience and it had made him envious of her. Perhaps, she would be wading through the puddles at this hour with sandals in her hands.

He picked up the ringing phone and was delighted to hear his wife's crisp voice.

"What coincidence! Just now I was thinking about you, Madhu."

"Were you? I had a feeling that physics is all you need. There is no place for me in your life."

"Please, Madhu."

"I called to inform you that there is some function and I'll be late."

"But at what time would —" he muttered, but she had already slammed down the receiver. It dismayed him.

They were in love when they married and had a great time in the first year of marriage in US. Gradually, they had drifted away from each other and now after four years of marriage, had little to say to each other. On return from the US, she had refused to stay in the joint family and Vinay was forced to opt for I I T, where residential accommodation was easily available in comparison to Delhi University. He missed the free academic environment of a university, though.

When he got a message that the Director wished to see him, he turned timorous as his previous meetings with him had not been pleasant. His every move was a covert operation, and the faculty members were wary of him. Prof. A N Sinha welcomed him with a broad smile and gestured him to take a seat on a sofa and continued talking on the phone. Vinay liked the room: its expansiveness, décor and the view below where fountains were playing. It had an air of status, style and grandeur. 'One day, I shall occupy this room,' he promised to himself. But he was aware it was not easy. The engineers were highly monopolistic in taking all the key positions in the institute, and the chair of Director was the holiest of the holies.

"Sorry," Sinha said, and walked over, and sat down next to Vinay.

"I hope I have not disturbed you," he added placing an arm on Vinay's shoulder. Sinha was known to keep an eye on the faculty members.

"No, no, I am free for the day."

In a roundabout way, Sinha sought his help in running the institute. "Would it be possible for you to take over as the Dean, Faculty of Sciences?"

Vinay was surprised. It was a prestigious position reserved for the senior professors in sciences, and he was too junior in the hierarchy.

But what did he want from him? Vinay contemplated.

"You are wondering why I am offering it to you."

As if chastised by his schoolteacher, Vinay was ashamed

of his inability to control his emotions.
"I met Prof. Maheshwari of TIFR (Tata Institute of Fundamental Research) last week at Stanford. He rated you as one of the three physicists in the country whose understanding of the subject could be matched with the best in the world."
Vinay was grateful for the compliment.
With a flourish, Sinha handed him an envelope containing the letter. One of the privileges of the post was a bungalow attached to the post.

Vinay was congratulated by a few colleagues; the seniors resented his rise and protested to the Director.
"The days of seniority are over," Sinha said. "I go by merit."
Vinay called his father and was congratulated by him.
"I have still better news for you. You have been selected for the post of Deputy Scientific Adviser to the Minister for Defence. The file has gone to PM. But I think it is a formality," Deepak Chopra told him. It was a distinguished position equivalent to Additional Secretary in the Ministry of Defence.
"You have pulled it off, papa."
"You deserve it on merit, son."
Suddenly, Vinay thought of Stella, his roommate, and lover, and felt a stab in his heart.

(3)

The thunder and lightning in the sky, the pouring rain, the approaching squall, and the peak hour traffic in the late evening on Bhishma Pitamah Marg slowed down the motorcade led by Kranti Chopra, Deputy Commissioner (East), Delhi Police. The storm was upon them in all its fury when they turned towards the Ring Road, known for its traffic snarls. Wild with rage, Kranti continued to

swear turning the driver jittery.
"Please sir," Sudha Verma, Assist Commissioner, Police said. "Hoshiar Singh is doing his best."
Hoshiar Singh was the best driver they had in Delhi Police.
"They are all a bunch of —" he answered and glared at Sudha. Kranti was behaving like a hungry lion that had scented blood. "Stop the car Hoshiar Singh," he shouted. "I'll take over."
In such a chaotic situation, Sudha was the only phlegmatic member of the team. Often, she interceded effectively but today Kranti was past listening, and had grown reckless.

Time was of utmost essence. Kranti had been checkmated once by the criminals; all the witnesses had disappeared. It was a godsend opportunity, and Kranti could not afford another slip. The honour of Delhi Police, and his future was at stake. Known for his courage, he could convert an iota of opportunity into a winning situation. The car swirled to 100 Km per hour sloshing through water, skidding, and creating chaos in the traffic. The visibility was poor, and Inspector Chowdhary Rattan Singh guided his boss. Once on the Jaipur expressway, Kranti pressed the accelerator on full throttle, and the car zoomed into the dark night rushing through the elements gone berserk. Chowdhary Rattan Singh hollered at the traffic in the near vicinity warning of dire repercussions.

Against the wishes of DS Krandhikar, Delhi Police Commissioner, Kranti had manoeuvred to go for a two- week training program at the Police Academy, Hyderabad. Kranti's father-in-law, a retired Supreme Court Judge, had suffered his third cardiac attack at Hyderabad, and Kranti wanted to be by his side along with his wife. Justice Kapoor survived; unfortunately, his condition deteriorated about the time Kranti's training program was over, and he was forced to extend his leave by a week. Krandhikar blew his top, and with a reason.

Immediately after Kranti's departure, three teenage girls of J J Cluster at Pushta Buland Masjid were kidnapped, and gang raped. They escaped from their kidnappers after 7-8 days, however, committed suicide after being maltreated by their parents. The residents of the colony with over 2000 dwellings were shaken by the ghastly tragedy. The media lapped it up, and the story appeared for 3-4 days on the first page in all the major dailies. Some TV channels also repeatedly televised it. Police were blamed for the breakdown of law and order in the capital. Worse, the local SHO had refused to register the case for a week, and the opposition parties found an opportunity to rap the government. When police were unable to apprehend the culprits, the issue was taken up on the floor of Parliament. Cutting across party affiliations, the government was severely criticized by all the political parties. Krandhikar came under heavy fire from the Home Secretary. Later, he was summoned by the Home Minister.

"I give you a week and no more. I want results."

The tone was soft but menacing. For the first time, Krandhikar feared the Minister.

On return from leave, Kranti had barely taken the seat when Krandhikar walked in brusquely and exploded.

"So, you have found time to attend the office?"

Unlike other Police Commissioners, Krandhikar believed in having direct interaction with the field officers in-charge of the districts.

The presence of the Commissioner in Kranti's office sent shock waves around the complex. Kranti explained about his father-in-law's worsening condition.
"To hell with you and your father-in-law!" Krandhikar shouted. "The country is on fire because of you."
Kranti felt the earth shake underneath him. Over 6ft 4" tall, and with the build of a boxer, Krandhikar looked dangerous. Kranti was petrified and apologized. Gnashing his teeth, the boss explained the details of the case.
"It is a blot on my thirty years of service." He roared. "If I get pulled up for it, you will get the sack. I give you five days to crack the case and not a day more."

The girls had been lured away with the inducement of a late-night movie, and costly gifts. They had slipped away from the colony between 8-9 pm; most of the residents were indoors due to the incessant heavy rain, and local shops had closed. Two people had seen the driver, and they had insisted he was an outsider. Subsequently, on being intimidated by police both disappeared, and did not resurface.
The Commissioner was wild. "Mentally, you are still at Hyderabad. Don't you understand its war! Why didn't you arrest them?"
Kranti didn't have the courage to correct him that he was not on duty but on leave.
"Sorry, Sir." Sudha, directly responsible for the slip, interceded hoping her womanly charm would mollify the old man; she had done it successfully in the past.
His rage turned on her. "Turn Delhi upside down and get me the results otherwise I will strip you of your uniform."
"The bastard!" Kranti said sotto voce after the boss had

left the complex.
Sudha retained her calm. "I'm aware he doesn't mean it."

High tempers, sniping at one another, and rampant use of abusive language was the hallmark of the third day. The police got their first break on the fourth day with the return of Radhu, who ran a tuck shop and was away to his village in Saharasa, Bihar. A special team had been sent to get the information from him. Radhu was able to give the number of the Omni used for kidnapping. The driver lived in Hauz Kazi, the heart of old Delhi. He spilled the beans that Shera, a wily underworld don, was involved in it. Shera was into illegal trafficking of young girls to Middle- East. Simultaneous raids in six different locations in Delhi proved futile. An unexpected, forced entry by a sub inspector into a bungalow in the posh residential area of Golf Links gave them the clue: Shera was in hiding at Behror on the Delhi -Jaipur expressway. With a posse of three Jeep loads of police jawans, Kranti and Sudha were heading towards Behror. Everyone was tense and prayed that Shera should stay put at the place.

At about 10pm, they arrived in Behror. Kranti paced the room in the Circuit House planning his strategy. The prospect of a shoot-out thrilled him, and he rubbed his hands with glee.
"We attack at 3(am)," he told Sudha. Though all the men were flaked out, Sudha knew if Kranti had made up his mind, no argument could change it. She picked her best dozen men, and in the pouring rain, under cover of darkness, the team moved towards Shera's hideout. He was well guarded, but the surprise attack dazed him. In a fierce battle, most of his men were killed. Through a secret door, he slipped away with his aide, and hid in

the fields. Kranti and Sudha tracked him down; and in a close-range shoot-out, arrested him. The police lost a cop, and Sudha was slightly injured. After a prolonged interrogation, Shera admitted to kidnapping of the girls but showed total ignorance to their rape.

Krandhikar was in a press conference at Police Headquarters when Kranti and Sudha reached his office. "Here come the conquering heroes who have always brought glory to Delhi Police force!" he said.

"It must have been under your direct guidance, sir?" One of the journalists inquired.

"No. It is all their doing." Commissioner smiled.

Both were euphoric.

Unable to reach Kranti on the mobile, Deepak was anxious. When he heard of his success story from Trevedi, he breathed a sigh of relief and felt immensely proud of his son.

The Home Minister called Kranti. "Well done my boy and continue to be at the top."

(4)

Vivek Chopra was an early riser and liked to see the sun glide out of the eastern horizon. From the second storey of the only concrete structure for miles in Lehriya village, he could have a panoramic view of the outstretched fields. At times, when he rose before dawn and strolled in the fields, he felt he was intruding into the privacy of Mother Nature and was a little embarrassed. On other days, with his long strides, he walked 6-7 miles through the fields touching the crops of wheat or sugar cane, talking to them and sharing his mundane thoughts with them. His movement had a leisurely ease, and he wanted to live each moment of the morning. It filled him with vitality. The zest for the morning walk was the one thing he had in common with his father, Deepak Chopra, with whom he was invariably at logger heads. Vivek abhorred authority of any kind, and Deepak Chopra was the symbol of authority in the government and at home.

Unlike his parents and other siblings, he interacted with the locals, be it a labourer, servant or farmer. His family was too snooty to even ask the names of the lower class, and if they ever were gracious enough to inquire (on occasions when they expected more out of them), they often mixed up their names. But Vivek remembered even their nick names and could talk to them for hours inquiring about their problems, ambitions and dreams. He had the natural skill to strike a conversation with them and could gossip on non-issues in order to understand their psyche. The rapport he had established with them was rewarding; he could feel the pulse of the country better and appreciate its heartbeat.

Vivek peeped outside the only window of his two rooms-set. It was pitch-dark. He could hear the continuous drizzle on the terrace but was unable to peer through the hollows of darkness. Possibly, the fields were flooded with water. It was pointless to go out for a walk in such weather, though he felt slightly claustrophobic inside the room.

Branded as a nonconformist by the family, he had disappointed them in every walk of life. With a first class in History (Honours) from St. Stephen's, his parents expected him to take the civil services examination after post graduation. He befuddled them by disappearing in MA (Previous) and working in the slums of Mumbai. For the last ten years he had not earned anything substantial and worse, according to his parents, had no such plans to improve his earnings in future. Mostly, he lived off the doles from his mother, and to the surprise of the siblings, was not ashamed of it. Dubbed as a parasite in the family, he took their snide comments in his stride.

Convinced that the benefits of development of the country had been gobbled by the middle and rich classes, and had not reached the poverty-stricken masses, he had decided to devote his life to improve their lot. Five years back he planned to uplift Lehriya and other neighbouring villages, and had laid the foundation of Vaishali Development Project, an NGO (Non-Government Organization). He had sent the project report to the Ministry of Social Justice and Empowerment two years ago and was still unable to convince the ministry officials to clear his ambitious project of extending his welfare schemes to the entire Meerut district, and later to the whole of UP. For the present, he was managing with a meagre grant from the State Government.

Sheila, his live-in companion, shared his views and vision, and had cast her future with him. Love had brought them together. She gave up the conveniences of life and settled down with her lover in this godforsaken place that was over thirty miles from the Delhi- Haridwar expressway and had no running water and electricity or toilet facilities. The only offspring of a broken family – her mother was Spanish, and father an Indian settled in New York – she was against the institution of marriage, whereas Vivek was under pressure from his mother to solemnize the marriage.

He moved towards her and dropped a kiss on her cheeks suffusing them with colour.

"Sharma called at the post office yesterday, and wanted you in his office today," she said. (Neither of them had a mobile.)

RK Sharma was the Deputy Secretary in the ministry whom they had met at least 2-3 dozen times to get the project cleared. The message did not excite Vivek; nonetheless, he agreed to go when the drizzle stopped.

Sheila was lightly built and had striking features. Dressed in light blue jeans, and a dotted white top, she looked attractive. On the backseat of his motorbike, she caught him possessively, tightening her grip over his waist. "Romance is in the air," she shouted over the noise of the old bike, and the whizzing of the wind. The rain was upon them in torrents before they made it to Sharma's office.

"Congrats Vivek," Sharma said. "Your cheque is ready."

Dumbfounded, both said in unison, "I don't believe it."

Sharma opened a file and handed him the cheque. "Now you can fulfil your dreams."

The initial grant was for Rs 50 lakhs, the remaining amount of 1.5 crores was to be paid later in three instalments.

"Last week you were so sceptical — how did the miracle happen?" Sheila was still under shock.

Sheepishly, RK Sharma blurted the truth. "Last week your father turned up in the office and blasted our Secretary. He has personally sanctioned the entire amount."

Noticing that the cheque was about to get crumpled in Vivek's hand, Sheila, with a swirl of her fingers, snatched it, and rose. "Thanks a lot Mr. Sharma." She offered her hand; it was virtually grabbed by him.

The cheque disappeared in her purse.

Kicking the bike, he muttered, "But I never told papa."

"He knows what you want." She caught his waist affectionately and told him to turn in a bye lane.
"Stop," she said, and kissed him passionately. Impulsively, she asked, "Will you marry me?"
"Of course, I will." He reciprocated the kiss. "I've been anxiously waiting to hear this news for the last one year."
"Your dislike of your father is uncalled for. And you were about to ruin the future of many."
He apologized for being carried away. There was cloud burst, and lightning in the sky.
"Let us go to ma." He suggested, and she acquiesced.

(5)

Showered with compliments from his superiors, Kranti was on cloud nine when he left Krandhikar's room. About to sit in the car after 9.30 pm, he noticed two missed calls on his mobile from Dr. Amit Bhardwaj. He recalled that Amit had invited him for a party where some foreign VIPs were expected to turn up. Kranti returned the call and assured him that he would attend the party but Prema, his wife, refused to join at such a short notice.

An International Conference on Cancer was held at Vigyan Bhavan, Delhi. Amit was the joint secretary of the conference, and he had thrown a party in honour of the foreign dignitaries at his home in GK-I. Kranti and Amit were great pals; they had been together at school. Amit's wife Kavita belonged to the Customs &Excise Service and was Kranti's batchmate, and it had strengthened the bond.

Amit was delighted to see Kranti and introduced him to the distinguished gathering.
"And finally meet Mrs. Jean Simpson, the world-famous oncologist tipped to receive the Nobel Prize this year."

Jean smiled and offered her hand.
Kranti looked up at the exceptionally tall, well-built Jean Simpson who towered over him. She had a long, beautiful face, and her fluttering golden hair sparkled in the garden lights. Infatuated by her beauty, he caught her hand, and pressed it affectionately. Jean had a warm, pleasant disposition whereas her husband was rather snobbish. More than a year back, she had visited India for a month, and now she planned to stay for a longer period.

Keen to oblige Jean as he needed her help for a scholarship abroad, Amit asked Kranti to invite the couple for dinner. Already floored by her appearance, he agreed.
"My wife will be delighted to meet you. Why don't you two join us for dinner tomorrow?"
Mr. Simpson wanted to visit Agra again. It made her hackles rise. "How many times will you see Taj?" She snubbed him.
She smiled at Kranti, and graciously accepted the invitation. Kranti continued to monopolize Jean; the host and hostess did not approve of it as they were aware of his weakness for flirting with fair women.

Sameer, Amit's son, collided with a Spanish guest who shrieked and created a scene as her plate slipped from her hand spoiling her dress. Annoyed, Amit asked his wife, "Where is Julian?"
A young, pretty woman with typical north-eastern features ran in. "Sorry sir, Sameer is getting very difficult tonight."
Kavita apologized to the Spanish lady, and Sameer was chaperoned away by Julian.
Kranti stared at Julian, and asked Kavita, "Who is she?

Her face looks vaguely familiar."
Amit explained that she was their maid- cum- governess and was with them for more than a year.
"You are getting impossible?" Kavita reprimanded Kranti. "That's what happens to men if they turn up at parties alone."
"I'm dead serious." Kranti was grim as he glanced at Julian trying to cajole the little boy.
"You always are where pretty girls are concerned." Amit smirked. "Don't I know you since school days?"

During the twenty-minute drive to home, Kranti thought more of Julian than Jean Simpson, but he could not place her, and it perplexed him.

On reaching home, when he mentioned about the dinner invitation to Jean and her husband, Prema admonished him for not consulting her before inviting the couple. Vaishali rescued her son from the awkward situation. "Let us invite the Simpsons on Sunday at Vivek's engagement ceremony."

At one inconspicuous corner of the spacious lounge sat Kanupriya, the only daughter in the family, unhappy and worried about her future. Dark, plump, and a divorcée with a five-year-old girl, she had just completed her MBA from I I M Kolkata and was lucky to manage a job at Mumbai in the campus interviews. She had requested for a change to Delhi and was tense how she would cope if her request was rejected. She was the only one in low spirits.

(6)

The engagement ceremony was held on the second Sunday of August in the extensive gardens of Deepak's bungalow on Akbar Road amidst a gathering of about a hundred guests, mostly from bureaucratic and political circles. The gate festooned in bright yellow marigolds, the soothing lights filtering through the bushes and trees, soft background music, the grass still wet from the previous day's downpour, mistiness in the air, and a fuzzy crescent moon looking down from heavens: it was a dreamy, romantic setting for the couple. "It's perfect," Sheila whispered to her fiancé surveying the ambience with a sweeping glance and rested her eyes on the lawn swathed in mercury lights. Clandestinely, Vivek moved her to a dark area, and kissed her lightly, and she responded.

Jean Simpson felt privileged at the invitation to a private religious ceremony and was immensely grateful to Vaishali and Prema. The invitation was also extended to other foreign delegates though only four couples attended. The Western ladies accoutred in flowing evening dresses of different hue and daring décolletage added glamour and colour to the occasion. In a white gown studded with tiny Swarovski crystals, Jean looked dazzling. Not only the men, but even the women were bowled over by her charm. However, Mr. Simpson had preferred Taj Mahal to the party.

After the priest solemnized the engagement, the guests scattered across the lawns. Jean made it a point to be with Prema and Kranti and chatted endlessly about the unspoiled natural beauty in India. She wished to visit the remote spots not on the tourist map. When Prema was called by Vaishali, Jean told Kranti, "I have a very personal agenda during this visit," and furtively glanced at him.

With a flirtatious chuckle, Kranti said, "I am a cop and can be useful." He took a step closer to her. Appreciating

her blue eyes and striking profile, he added, "Try me."
She looked at him for a long time debating how far to trust a cop, then made up her mind, and told the truth. "I am searching for one Dr. Vinay – Vinay Chopra. He is a famous physicist and a celebrity."
"Why do you want to meet him?" Abruptly, his tone and manner changed.
"He was my sister's boy friend and had a live - in relationship with her for about 2-3 years. I want to know certain facts about my sister before her death. I had not met her for over a year before she died."
"But that must have been many years back. What is the urgency now?"
"Some matters relating to property need to be settled."
Unconvinced, he looked at her minutely; he was certain it was a cock and a bull story. What had Vinay to do with her sister's property?
Jean gave him one of her charming smiles.
"And Vinay can help?" he asked.
Jean nodded, clasped his arm, and whispered conspiratorially, "I have his photograph," and showed it to him.
Though enchanted by her beauty, Kranti was on his guard. Removing her hand, Kranti moved to a corner and was about to caution his brother on the mobile, when he saw Vinay and Madhulika making an entry from the wicket gate of the garden. Due to some emergency, the couple could not make it on time. Vinay waved at Kranti, walked over and embraced him. Kranti looked at Jean from an acute angle and observed that she was comparing the photograph with Vinay's profile. For an instant there was a flicker of anger on her face, but she recovered swiftly,

and smiled back at the two brothers. It made Kranti uneasy. Now, he was sure that the charming oncologist was here to settle some old scores. He acted fast.

"You don't need to study the photograph, Jean. Meet Dr. Vinay Chopra." He introduced them. "And he is my elder brother."

Unconsciously, his polite voice had changed to a command; there was a slight hint of warning. It did not go unnoticed.

"Your face is vaguely familiar, have we met in US earlier?" Vinay inquired.

"Did you know Stella — Stella Fisher Stone at Cornell?"

"Of course, I knew her very well, even her younger sister Steffi."

"I am the oldest of the three – Jean." Her tone was flat. "I have heard a lot about you but never met with you."

Memories of Stella hit Vinay, and he turned sad.

"Jean has come all the way from US in search of you; the conference appears to be only an excuse." Kranti made the situation transparent for Vinay.

"I am flattered that someone should fly all the way from US to see me. I didn't know I was such a celebrity." Vinay grinned. "What can I do for you?"

Jean was flummoxed at the ease and aplomb with which Vinay had handled the situation.

"I was not in touch with Stella for many months before her death. I need to know a lot about her. Just nostalgia — you know."

"It's been a long time." Vinay drawled.

"Eight years and ten months," she replied sharply. "But this is hardly a place to converse."

"Tomorrow 7 pm at Taj Mansingh. I'm in room no 406,"

Jean added. "And please come alone."

Looking at the happy, cheerful faces of the guests, she wondered how they would react if she suddenly disclosed the secret of Vinay's famous research work to them. She was certain that they would be shocked, and the gathering would melt in a few minutes.

Animatedly, the bureaucrats and politicians discussed the cons of coalition politics, and sniggered how poor Atul Bihari Vajpayee, the PM and a chronic bachelor, was harassed by not one or two, but three single -women politicians. Kranti introduced Jean to his father. Shaking hands with him, she narrated that at a banquet thrown by the US Ambassador she had met Dastur, the Foreign Secretary. "He appears to be a great admirer of you," she said.

Deepak Chopra felt embarrassed.

"But Shekhar Srivastava, the Indian Ambassador to China, was quite critical of you. Does he hate you?" Her tone had turned abrasive.

"I don't think so," Deepak muttered uneasily.

Jean stated that Srivastava had hinted about corruption in high places; even those who had an excellent image had manipulated to form cooperatives and got land at throw away prices. She continued her tirade against the Indian bureaucracy displaying her animosity. Honesty and corruption were a question of relativities, she concluded.

"The world depends upon the glass one looks through." Deepak quoted from Alexandre Dumas Junior's novel 'Camille' and moved away from her. Though he dismissed her comments as fatuous, when he turned, he collided with a guest. Amidst turbulent situations in office or stormy Cabinet Meetings, Deepak was unruffled, but the slightest aspersion on his integrity could upset him.

Jean had studied the conduct and behaviour of all the family members including the daughter and was somehow sceptical of Vaishali. Though she had turned a little skinny with years, still she was attractive, and seemed to control the entire activity of the evening. The firmness in her demeanour expressed through a little movement of eyes or a gesture or soft words worried Jean. The husband and sons were bound by rules and ethics but circumventing her would not be easy. She could go to any length to protect Vinay.

Attired in a spangled evening dress, and a lapis lazuli pendant, Sheila had looked resplendent at the betrothal ceremony. As the hours slipped by, she was rather exhausted getting introduced to close relatives and friends. She chatted for a long time with Jean Simpson. They made an incongruous pair: Sheila looked pale and fragile in contrast to Jean who was bursting with vitality and had an overwhelming presence. Amit commented on her poor health. Jean observed her minutely, and asked, "Do you have a medical history?"

Sheila nodded and told her that for last one month she was having a mild temperature in the evening, and slight pain in the throat. On the spur of the moment, Jean decided to examine her, and told Amit to bring the medical kit from the car. Sheila protested as she did not want to spoil the festive air.

"For me, the patient has the first priority, the bride can wait." Jean placed her arm on Sheila's shoulder, and added tenderly, "My dear, marriage is a very serious business. You must be physically strong to endure it."

Inside the house, the newly engaged Sheila was examined

by Jean and Amit. Sheila needed a thorough medical check up, and Jean told Vivek to bring her next day to Amit's clinic.

Vivek nodded.

"Do you suspect something?" Amit asked Jean taking her aside.

"Yes, throat cancer," Jean whispered. "I hope I'm wrong."

The appearance of Deepak's father in the apparel of a sadhu created a flutter of excitement amongst the guests. Handsome and majestic, Ram Narian stole the hearts of all the guests particularly the foreign ladies.

Aware that Vaishali did not like him, he said with a playful smile, "I hope I am not unwelcome in your house, Vaishali."

"How can you say such a thing bhapaji?" She touched his feet and explained that the betrothal ceremony was decided only four days back. "It was so sudden that we forgot to invite you." She apologized, and he smiled condescendingly at her. Deepak took his own time to pay his regards to his father and folded his hands on seeing him.

Ram Narian gave Sheila an indulgent smile and placed his hand on her head. Then he warmly hugged Vivek, his favourite grandson. He frowned perceptibly on seeing Jean. The Western ladies bombarded him with questions on karma, next birth etc., which he deftly avoided, and went inside the house. He called Vaishali and told her, "Keep that woman Jean away from your home. She is a bad influence on our family."

After talking to all the grandchildren and their families, the old man departed.

□□□

II

Unfolding Of A Secret

Amongst scores of intelligent students at Calvin Talukdar School, Lucknow, it was the unanimous opinion of the school faculty that Vinay was exceptionally brilliant and would excel in sciences. Vinay protested. He did not like physics, chemistry and mathematics; the mathematical equations and the chemical reactions made him uneasy. Humanities attracted him, and he wanted to opt for it in 9th class. His father was understanding but advised that the future was in sciences. Noticing his son was unconvinced, Deepak asked which course he wanted to pursue.

"Music," he said, and beamed at his father. "I want to play the piano; the symphonies of Beethoven."

Deepak had taken Vinay to a musical concert at Delhi last year, and his son had gone into raptures at the end of the 9th symphony.

"Music is not much of a career, son. Take it up as a hobby. I'll buy you a piano whenever I have some spare money."

Unwillingly, Vinay gave in, and continued in the science stream. The expectation of playing on his own piano helped him sail through the school years. However, Deepak could not spare enough money to purchase a piano.

Following his father's footsteps Vinay topped in the U.P. board. "All the bright ones go to Physics (Hons)," was the consensus of the Calvin Talukdar faculty as Vinay was a Science Talent awardee. Since he disliked mechanical drawing, engineering had been ruled out. In the meanwhile, Deepak had moved to Delhi. Appreciating that something was bugging his son, Deepak spent some time with him, and probed.

"Papa, can't I take up History or even English Hons? I don't like the maths in physics, I really don't."

Surprised, Deepak said, "But son, your marks don't show it. You are a ninety percentager."

Deepak patted him affectionately, and added, "Once you are in it, you'll love it."

Confused, Vinay looked at his father. He didn't have the spine to argue and obeyed.

Vinay liked the ambience of the Delhi University campus, the St. Stephen's College, and the physics department. He felt most comfortable in the coffee house; it was the only place that encouraged the clash of minds without fear. The smell of masala dosa and the aroma of South Indian coffee invigorated his cells and sharpened his brain. But there was not a single day when he didn't detest maths, and he slumped to tenth position in the class. He joined a newly opened orchestra group and practised late in the evening. With the increasing pressure of academics, he was forced to give it up in second year.

It astonished him that most of the physics teachers began the lecture by jotting down long equations on the blackboard without giving any explanation. And the students scribbled them hurriedly, their eyes glued on the notebooks, worried that the teacher would erase them before they were able to copy them. There was no time to understand, and somehow it seemed least important to everyone. Often, he wondered whether this was the only way to teach the dull subject, and why such a methodology was handed down from one generation to the other. Could it not be made more interesting? To make matters worse, a few teachers, whose confidence bordered on arrogance, changed the notations everyday completely confusing the students. Most of the teachers were over enthusiastic; some of the short ones hopped around in front of the blackboard like frogs and looked rather comical with their dark suits smeared with chalk dust.

Whenever he stared at the equations covering the entire blackboard, the notations turned into monstrous serpents chasing him in his nightmares, and daytime reveries. The thought of living with them all his life gave him goose pimples in the class. At times, it occurred to him whether the complicated Lagrangian and Hermitian polynomials would ever be of any use in his later life. Despite his dislike of the subject, he topped in Honours.

In MSc (Previous), he was told by his professor to install the Wilson Cloud Chamber in the yearly science exhibition with the help of a research scholar. The Cloud Chamber was out of use for last many years, and both spent over a week working late into the night and made it operational. When Vinay demonstrated the experiment to the visitors in the dark room, he was thrilled to the marrow of his bones. It was repeated every half an hour, and all the visitors applauded the young scientist. One afternoon, a young South Indian girl with long flowing hair, and a short skirt attracted his attention. Vinay explained what she had just seen was the trajectory of electrons.

"Oh, that's fascinating," she said, her eyes popping out. "Physics is a wonderful subject."

That one casual remark by an unknown girl slightly altered his attitude to the subject.

One day, while going to the university in the bus, he was amazed to see the same girl sitting next to him.

"Oh, hello! Are you not the Cloud Chamber scientist?"

He grinned and nodded. He learnt that she was Sunaina Iyer and was doing Chemistry (Hons) instead of Physics (Hons) because she had not been able to make the grade. He liked her company and made it a point to catch her after the classes. She envied him for being in physics, and frequently mentioned that it was great to study the nature of physical matter. Vinay disagreed, and felt physics was rather drab.

"I wish I could swap places with you," she said, and confided that she would do her post graduation in physical chemistry. On another occasion, she told him that she admired him for his intelligence.

"I am not intelligent; actually, I mug up everything including the equations. But don't tell anyone."

"You must be kidding," she answered, and looked minutely at him. "And you are the limit of humility."

Gradually, under her influence, he started believing in

his brilliance, and infinite potential. The dread and the phobia he had of the subject melted under the warmth of their stolen kisses. He no longer disliked physics and accepted it as a subject suitable for his career. He also noticed that only two or three students in the class were passionate about the subject, and none of them was among the first ten in merit. He broke the university record in Previous and gave all the credit to her.

Sunaina's sudden disappearance from his life in the beginning of MSc (Final) gave him a rude shock, and he was unable to rationalize why she had not taken him into confidence before leaving the campus. Without her emotional strength, he felt lonely and lost; however, he managed to retain his position in the university.

His father inquired of him if he wanted to take the civil services examination. To spite him, he refused. Again, against his father's advice of going to Oxford for higher studies, Vinay signed up for research in Delhi University hoping to get the doctorate in 2-3 years instead of spending 4-5 years in the U.K. But the guiding force was the thought of opposing his father.

Unfortunately, it backfired.

His guide, the suave, distinguished Prof. Raina turned out to be a sham. His primary motive was to get his son coached by Vinay. On refusing to oblige, Raina systematically demolished his confidence by passing snide comments on his intelligence. Vinay could not publish any research paper for two years, and deep down in the pit of his stomach, he started doubting his decision of pursuing research. There was no Sunaina Iyer to allay his fears and cheer him up. At the end of the third year, Prof. Ranganathan, Head of Physics Department, summoned Vinay and told him to quit research, and take up teaching in one of the affiliated colleges. Point-blank, Vinay rejected the offer as he didn't want to ruin his future in a college.

Ranganathan said, "Raina thinks you are incapable of any research."

Vinay argued that his guide disliked him on personal grounds.

"I don't believe you, and I agree with Raina," Ranganathan answered.

Vinay volunteered to work with Prof. A. Roy, but Head of the Department was categorical that he would not get any scholarship.

Vinay confided in his father about his problems. Deepak, then Senior Joint Secretary, Ministry of Home, volunteered to intervene and meet the Vice Chancellor. Vinay vetoed it as it would be counter productive in the long run.

"Treat it as a bad experience and move on," Deepak told his son, and within a few months arranged for him to fly to Oxford. The inclement English weather was hostile to him, and within four months he moved to Cornell, USA, where Prof. Anand, Deepak's friend, was the Dean.

Frustration, and subsequently depression awaited him at Ithaca. His performance in most of the semesters was below average, and he was in danger of losing the teaching assistantship. Three years slipped away, and he was nowhere near getting an MS. Prof. Anand warned him. "I give you six months more, if you don't show results, I'll have you thrown out of the campus."

"Hi! Why are you so glum?"

Vinay raised his downcast head, and looked at the smiling face of Stella, his new classmate he had been dating for the last 5-6 weeks. With hands in the pockets of the short coat, and a twinkle in her eyes, she looked bewitchingly pretty. Fully aware of the background — Prof. Anand's reprimand was common knowledge in the physics department — she gestured at the sky above where some clouds moved languidly across the sun, and said, "It will pass like the clouds." The forlorn, handsome face of the Indian, and the vulnerable air around him touched her heart. She invited him to her room and made love.

"What you need is a woman," she said. "You are too obsessed by physics."

She was soft, considerate, and a great company. Stella had the natural ability to solve complex polynomials and use them in her research; she helped him out in his weak areas in maths. A fortnight later, she asked, "Why did you take up physics? Your heart is not in it."

He thought for a moment, and then told the truth.

"Poor Vinay?" She kissed him lightly. "How many years have you wasted and how many more would you sacrifice to physics?"

"I don't know."

"Do you have courage?"

Unsure, he fidgeted on the bed.

"If I were you, I would chuck physics, and take up Music."

It was not possible for Vinay to discard physics as he had given the last six years to the subject. However, he joined evening classes in music.

Whenever he was down in the dumps, she encouraged him. "Your foundations are weak in maths, but your understanding of physics is quite sound." In the next few weeks, empathy turned into love, and he moved into her pad.

His relationship with women at Cornell lacked ease till he met Stella. He had been trying to search a surrogate Sunaina Iyer in them and was sadly disappointed. Unlike the coy Ms Iyer, they were more direct and forthright in their approach. He had had sex with two of them, but they refused to get involved emotionally. Stella was in love and was as lusty as he in the bed.

Finally, Vinay managed to obtain MS in four and a half years; Stella completed it in one and a half. One night, he said to her, "I've had enough of physics. I am planning to take up a job in industry."

Thoughtfully, she studied the lines on his forehead and palms. Her gut feeling was that physics was in his stars and told him to go ahead and complete the doctorate.

"You advocating it!" he said. "You - who know everything about me."

"Music and sex will do the wonders," she said, and laughed. They decided to get married after getting their doctorate.

Spurred by Stella's faith in the lines of his palms, Vinay had the audacity to inform Prof. Anand of his wish to pursue research for a doctorate.

"Going by your track record, you will take at least another 6-7 years."

"Just two years."

"Will Stella write your thesis?"

Vinay ignored the sarcasm and persisted.

"Sorry, Vinay, it is not possible to help you any further."

Fortunately for him, Prof Anand got a lucrative offer from Stanford, and his departure made things easier for Vinay.

Another year passed. As expected, Vinay's progress was tardy despite Stella's help in maths. In contrast, Stella had made rapid strides, and was on the threshold of completing her thesis astounding her guide Prof. Tse Tung, a Chinese known to be a hard task master. "You are a little genius," he told her in Vinay's presence twisting his heart, as he was the butt of all the jokes on the campus.

Stella departed for a visit to her younger sister, Steffi in Canada. Vinay was alone, and in a bad humour. He realized he had made a mess of his career, and it had something to do with his parents' relationship with each other. On the surface, his parents seemed a compatible couple, but he alone knew that in the privacy of their bedroom they often sparred with each other and slept in separate rooms. He could not rationalize why his parents quarrelled so much though he had a vague feeling that it had something to do with Gandhiji and brahamcharya. The fear that his parents might divorce haunted him. It was therefore not surprising that out of all the siblings, he was the only one who felt emotionally insecure. Though he was fond of his mother, her views did not count in decision making. Once in Honours, he had confided his problems regarding physics to his mother, and she had discussed with Deepak also. Unfortunately, in those days Deepak was under intense pressure from his own Minister. Worse, he had unwittingly rubbed the Prime Minister on the wrong side. The danger of his repatriation to U.P cadre - the second time - loomed large over Deepak, and he could not spare any time for his son. Vinay could not muster enough courage to go back to his mother, instead he squarely blamed his father for coercing him into physics. With years, he started detesting him. In fact, he himself was thinking of taking the IAS examination to get rid of the subject, but once the suggestion came from his father, he opposed it. Had he explored another career, he might not have felt so suffocated and shackled? Now, he didn't know how to break free.

Stella brought bad news. Steffi, a mentally unstable younger sister, had undergone a divorce, and decided to stay with Stella as she had no other option. Whimsical, and given to throwing tantrums, she was very difficult to live with. Earlier, such emergent situations were handled by Jean Simpson, the eldest of the three sisters. Unfortunately, Jean had moved to Europe last month with her husband, and Steffi was forced to shift to Ithaca with Stella. Reluctantly, Vinay agreed to move out; Stella was equally unhappy at the thought of missing his company.

"Hey! I am Steffi."

A young girl barged into his room. She was a younger and more beautiful version of Stella. Vinay offered his hand; instead, she pecked him on the cheek stating that he was going to be her brother-in-law. He took her for coffee and found her sensitive, and highly emotional. Stella was fiercely independent whereas Steffi wanted to be pampered. Witty and mischievous, Steffi made him laugh all the time he was with her. Later, she told Stella that she was lucky to find a man like Vinay.

Suddenly, Prof. Tse-Tung flew to China as his son and daughter-in-law had been thrown behind the bars due to a political upheaval. Before departure, he told his prodigy Stella that if he did not return in six months, she could submit the thesis with the help of Prof. James Smith, the Head of the Department.

Seven months passed, and Stella's guide did not return from China. Neither was there any news from him. Stella had completed her research and decided to write the thesis, and then approach Prof. Smith. At the crucial stage of writing, Steffi made Stella's life hell. She sought Vinay's help.

"Take her off my back for 5-6 weeks, Vinay."

He reminded her that Steffi could be very demanding.

"I know," she said trusting him implicitly. "If necessary, kiss and fool around with her a little — she'll be all right."

Confused, he looked at her. He had yet to get a break in his research topic with the third new guide, and Stella was about to finish her thesis. Of late, he had developed a phobia that on completion of her doctorate, Stella might kick him out of her life. After all, in contrast to her, he was a failure. And failures had no place in the hearts of successful men or women in the US. To take on the onerous responsibility of looking after Steffi and indulging her seemed to be a foolish idea. But he loved Stella and could go to any lengths to help her out of the messy situation. A bundle of contradictions, he was a pathetic sight.

"I know she can be bitchy. Tolerate her for my sake, love." She pleaded.

Suddenly, she had a brain wave. Throwing her arms around his neck, Stella said, "Okay, we will get married immediately after I submit my thesis without waiting for your doctorate."

The bait worked. Her assurance lighted up his face; he kissed her and left the room cheerfully.

Transformed on hearing that she would be spending most of her time with Vinay, Steffi was on her best behaviour. Often, she was at his place: cleaning the room, making breakfast, cooking meals, washing, and ironing his clothes. The pretence of kissing and fooling around ultimately led to sexual intercourse.

One morning, when she was on top of him, the phone rang, and Stella said excitedly, "I have finished my thesis, Vinay."

Caught in the act of cheating, he mumbled incoherently, "Congrats."

"Why are you not thrilled? Are you okay? You sound troubled."

"No, no. I — I - was sleeping." He lied.

Later, turning to Steffi, he told her to get out.

In the evening, Stella handed him a draft copy of the thesis, and asked him to go through it, and suggest changes if required. "My professor felt that my research was really very good, and we might bag an award. But don't tell anyone - you know how secretive the old man is!"

She thought for a while and handing over the second draft copy to him said, "Steffi, at times, can get violent and destructive; it will be safer with you."

Vinay told her that he had had enough of Steffi.

"You don't have to worry about her anymore." Stella assured him.

He wanted to tell her about his relationship with Steffi when something urgent interrupted him.

At night, Ted Compton, a common friend of his and Stella's, called to inform him that Stella and Steffi were involved in a major car accident, and were in the hospital. He rushed there and learnt that both were killed when their car collided with a truck. Numbed by the shock, he spent the entire night in the hospital corridor mulling over the years he had spent with Stella, and the last few weeks with Steffi. Both the sisters had showered their love and warmth on him. Without Stella's love, he might have been shattered or perhaps committed suicide. While interacting with Steffi, he had feared that his concupiscence would get the better of him; if he wanted, he could have stopped Steffi, but her youth and beauty had pulled down the weak barriers with which he had fortified himself. He felt ashamed that he had been disloyal to Stella and didn't have the decency to apologize.

Vinay told Ted Compton to inform Jean Simpson, but she did not turn up at the funeral.

Unashamedly, Vinay cried.

With the help of Ted, he packed everything, and shipped the boxes to Jean along with a letter.

'My dear Jean,

We have not met but Stella often talked about you. I am sending four briefcases; one of them contains Stella's research papers, and the original thesis. Please have it published. I am sure she will be famous posthumously.

Yours
Vinay Chopra

Lonely, despondent for weeks, Vinay was at breaking point. Accidentally, he ran into Prof. Hudson, his guide, who gave him a mouthful. "More than seven long years into research and a worthless MS only? I should stop your assistantship and have you thrown out of the campus. Do you have sufficient money to buy a ticket for India?"

Vinay had been through such dire straits earlier – he was excoriated 3-4 times by Prof Anand and other guides —

and his strategy in such eventualities was to keep quiet, and nod or fidget.
"I'll work harder, sir." His throat was choked.
Rated as one of the most brilliant physicists in the country, Prof. Hudson was now past his prime, and had been served notice to show results otherwise his contract would not be renewed. He had incurred heavy debts to please his third wife (newly married) who was 30-35 years younger than him. The joke going around in the campus was that scholars learnt more from her in bed than physics from the professor.
"Girls! Girls!! That's all you young men are after."
Hudson had seen Vinay talking to his wife the previous week.
"Damn it, you are the most stupid scholar I have encountered in my life. Change your topic if you can't handle it. Sit down in the sun and scratch your bloody grey matter, if you have any left."
Hudson carried on using foul and almost abusive language for another fifteen minutes. "The bottom line is that you are a duffer, a dunce, and you can never complete your thesis."
He had seen the worst of the old man. Vinay was advised by his seniors not to take him lightly and give serious thought to his suggestion.

Ted Compton brought a letter addressed to Stella and left. Vinay was so lost in his gloomy thoughts that he entirely forgot about it.

Vinay pondered over the words of Hudson till late in the night. Humiliated by all the guides for the last ten years why had he stuck to physics? Just because his autocratic father believed that he had the brilliance to shine like a star in physics. What was so great about his future in physics that Stella too had told him to carry on research? Would he be a world-famous physicist one day? Supposing, both were wrong? A duffer! A dunce! Ten long years and a lousy MS? It was high time that he gave up research and settled down in life with a stable job in industry. Maybe, Raina was right: he lacked creativity? Without Stella's support how would he move ahead in research? Throughout his academic career in India — both in school and college — his marks in all the examinations were overrated. They did not reflect his actual potential, and intelligence. His father had hoped that he would improve upon his (Deepak's) performance in life, but he was likely to be at the bottom of the ladder amongst all his siblings.

He cried and cried.

It was the cumulative effect of years of frustration accentuated by Stella's death. Tears trickled down his cheeks for a long time till they dried up.

A young cat, a pet of the previous occupant, frequented his place, and often disturbed him at night. He hated the sight of the kitten but could not get rid of it. Spotting the feline in a corner of the room, he threw a slipper at it. It jumped on the table, and Vinay hurled one of the clodhoppers with all his force. The cat squeaked, dived, ran towards the kitchen, and disappeared from a broken glass window. In the confusion, the wine bottle tilted, rolled over the table splashing the contents, and crashed down on the floor. Stella's draft copy of thesis that had been lying at one end of the table for weeks got spoiled.

"Oh, hell!" Vinay was distraught. "I am really stupid in all things." He shook his head in desperation as the copy of the thesis was partially stained; he had wanted to keep it as souvenir in his beloved's memory.

He caught his head in his hands, and wondered why he was such an idiot? Hudson's words 'duffer', 'dunce' resounded in the room mocking at him. And how ironical that he was the topper of Delhi University?

He prepared a cup of black coffee, and slowly sipped it. The contemptuous epithets continued to make him miserable. Suddenly, he stared at the copy of Stella's thesis, and whispered, "I need not be an idiot."

An idea germinated in his brain.

It was past four in the morning. He jumped from the bed and tore open the letter addressed to Stella.

It was a letter from Prof Tse- Tung's daughter-in-law informing that she had escaped from prison, but the professor was being tried for high treason, and may be hanged or if he was lucky, sentenced to life imprisonment. The professor wished that she should get the thesis published. It was sure to bring her fame and glory.

Vinay read the letter twice and burnt it.

Two weeks later he ran into his professor again in the parking lot. With his pretty wife leaning on his arm, and whispering sweet endearments to him, Hudson had a slight swagger in his gait, and was unusually cheerful which he wanted to share with the world.

"Sorry, young man, I lost my cool the other day."

"It's okay, sir." Vinay smiled back at him.

"Did you give it a thought?"

Vinay nodded and explained Stella's subject.

"Sounds interesting; go ahead." Hudson patted him

affectionately on his back. Vinay turned towards his car, and Hudson said indulgently, "Sweet young man."

No one on the campus knew of Stella's subject as the Chinese professor was very secretive and distrusted everyone. Hudson was astounded at Vinay's progress in the next four months.

"One scolding and I am getting the results." Hudson confided to his wife, a little surprised. "I should do it more often with my scholars."

With little finishing touches from Hudson, Vinay's doctorate created ripples of excitement in the world of physics. It was hailed as one of the most fundamental researches of the last decade.

Once, Vinay overheard Hudson telling a colleague, "I didn't know Vinay had it in him."

Vinay kicked away the indolence out of his life and grew as passionate about research as he had seen Stella. His research was still being evaluated in the scientific world when he told Hudson that he had started working on the data collected from other clusters of galaxies.

**A few months later, a team of top scientists unanimously declared that it was indeed a work of genius. Vinay and Hudson's stocks soared, and both reaped the benefits. Hudson's contract was renewed with a much better package, and a special chair of professor was created for Vinay. His subsequent papers on the subject added to his stature.

Music was the only casualty: now, he didn't have the time for it, and neither did he miss it.

"How wrong I was?" Hudson often told his wife. "But how could his grey matter suddenly explode to such brilliance

---

**Please see Appendix for Stella and Vinay's research

after six long years with only one scolding!"

Doubts persisted among other senior faculty members too; however, the result had been approved, and endorsed by the top scientists of the US. All the apprehensions of brilliant physicists of Cornell were swept under the carpet, and at the most, remained in the confines of their secret discussions, and did not spill out into the corridors or at any formal gathering.

Vinay was fully aware of the undercurrents and was privy to the opinion of various faculty members including his guide. He took the precaution of destroying Stella's thesis. His attitude to life underwent a metamorphic change, and he worked for 12-13 hours a day, and improved upon his understanding and depth of knowledge.

Some of the senior professors of physics were a little disappointed whenever they discussed the subject with him but were indulgent towards him and felt that he was still young and would blossom with the years.

No girls, he promised himself. Hudson was right; they sap away man's strength and intellect.

Safely ensconced in his newly acclaimed honours, awards, and the luxuries that money could buy, Hudson was on the top of the world. Unfortunately, his life was cut short by a massive heart attack.

But Vinay was on a roll, there was no stopping him. In the next 3-4 years, he continued to add laurels, and glory and gave everything he had to physics. Aware of his limitations, he chose his scholars carefully, and made them do all the research. Now everyone looked up to him; his name was taken with respect, and admiration.

Despite all the accolades he had gathered from the

scientific community, he could not face himself at night. Stella's ghost tormented him. He had cheated on her in love, and research. To get rid off his ex- lover's apparition, he married Madhulika. But it did not help. Unable to stand it beyond a point, he decided to go back to India, and settle down there.

Vinay returned to India as a celebrity.

(2)

What did Jean Simpson want from him and that too after about nine long years? Vinay was agitated. Had she smelt a rat? Vinay had prepared himself for such an eventuality many years ago, and he had just managed to survive in the first encounter amidst a distinguished gathering. All of a sudden, he remembered the original thesis he had sent to Jean on Stella's death? His heart skipped a beat, and he panicked. Had she now retrieved and read it? If the secret leaked out, what would happen to him? His doctorate would be annulled, he would lose the professorship, be thrown out of IIT, and his whole world would shatter. He may even land up in jail. He felt his head explode, and he tried to reach out to his wife, and nestled closer to her. She rebuffed him and turned her head towards the wall. Terrified, he could not get a wink of sleep.

When he got up in the morning, Vinay was tense and disoriented at the thought of meeting his nemesis in Jean Simpson.

"Why are you feeling so jittery since morning?" Madhulika asked when she found Vinay in the kitchen. "Don't hover around me. I've to prepare for the afternoon lecture."

Timidly, he went back to his room, and turned the pages of a magazine. Madhulika entered with a coffee tray, and

asked, “Why are you looking death-pale? Are you going to lose your job?”
He clarified that he didn’t have any sleep in the night.
“Tell me what is bugging you.”
“I am feeling a little restless.”
She wanted to call Dr. Kulshresht, the family physician; he rejected the suggestion.
“One shouldn’t take it lightly. Mama told me that you never had a strong heart.”
Irritated, he gulped the coffee, and was about to go to the library when she said, “Kranti told me that you have a dinner date with Jean Simpson.”
“Yes, she and her husband.”
“Can I make the foursome?”
Vinay remembered that Jean had asked him to meet her alone.
Seeing the confusion on his face, she asked, “Is there something confidential, which I can’t share?”
“She wants to talk of Stella.”
Madhulika had heard a lot about Stella from him.
“Why can’t I hear something more about my husband’s great girl friend?”
“You may be uncomfortable?”
He was afraid of losing his cool if she carried on with her questioning.
“You and not I will be embarrassed.” She was emphatic. “But considering your poor health, I’ll not impose myself on you.”

In the evening, he dressed meticulously for the dinner date, and looked his best in the blue three- piece suit. It restored his colour and self-esteem. With his looks and reputation, he could charm even the formidable Jean

Simpson. Unfortunately, the circumstances were against him. He was apprehensive of her. A little slip and she could ruin him.

His car was in the garage, and he sent for a taxi. He called Jean from the reception of Taj Mansingh.

"Give me five minutes I'll be in the lounge." Her cold, sharp voice was disconcerting. He chose a seat from where he could have the advantage of seeing her walk down from the elevator.

Dressed in black and red, she looked devastatingly pretty and severe, almost like royalty. He inquired if her husband was going to join them.

"No. I packed him off to Jaipur." She was brief and curt.

Her continuing hostility perturbed him; he wondered how he would stand her for the next one hour or so.

She led him to the restaurant; the pastel blue sofas and matching curtains had a soothing effect on his nerves.

"I trust only the salads in India," she said, and told him to order whatever he wanted. Vinay settled for chicken and garlic bread.

"What do you want to know about Stella?" He was direct; he considered it to be the best strategy.

Opening her purse, she took out a letter, and tossed it to him. "This is from Stella's Chinese professor."

Her manner was so intimidating that for the first time Vinay glared at her. "I don't know him."

"You don't know Prof. Tse-Tung?"

"No. I didn't know him at a personal or official level. I only knew that he was guiding Stella."

Ignoring his protest, she ordered him to read.

Suddenly, he became aggressive. "How am I concerned?"

Exasperated, she raised her voice. "Read, man — read.

You don't want me to shout from the rooftops."

Subdued, he went through the contents.

'I hope your sister would be a world-famous physicist. Her research was fundamental – should have got an international award. I wrote letters – she did not reply. I live in a small village – no touch with world. I read about your contribution – remarkable work. I was released from jail on mercy petition. Tell her to write.'

The letter was addressed to Jean at the US Embassy, Beijing. Vinay read, and memorized the address of the village where the professor was residing.

Vinay returned the letter and smiled at her.

"What happened to Stella's thesis?" Jean asked.

"I sent you four brief cases out of which one contained all her research papers, and the original thesis."

"Are you sure you sent me the thesis?"

"Yes, I am sure," he replied. "In fact, Ted Compton and I had done the packing together, and the four pieces were booked by him. He had given me the receipt which I kept for many months."

Jean Simpson had got the intimation from the shipping company and had purposely not collected the pieces as she was residing in a small flat in Paris that had no storage place. On getting the Chinese professor's letter she had tried to retrieve them, but it was too late. The shipping company had disposed off the belongings as per their procedure.

"I got the brief cases but not the thesis." She lied. "Where is the thesis?"

Confidently, he replied, "I am sure I had sent the thesis to you in one of the four briefcases. If necessary, you can cross check with Ted."

"But how is it that you got your doctorate immediately after Stella's death and became famous. Though according to this letter, Stella was entitled to all the awards posthumously."

"I worked with Hudson; he guided me well. Whatever I achieved was on my own efforts and has nothing to do with Stella."

Jean again persisted that she had not received the thesis, and he repeated the same reply verbatim.

Vinay concentrated on the chicken, his body and mind controlled.

"The Vinay particle should have been called the Stella particle," she said.

"Stella was my friend. I would have been too happy to share everything with her. Fame, glory! Unfortunately, she died. She never told me what she was working on."

"But you slept with her."

He nodded. "I loved her. Even now I love her. She was the only one who gave me love and warmth."

She reminded him that he had slept with Steffi too. He did not respond, and instead wondered how she knew it.

"You loved both of them."

"No, only Stella."

"And you stole her work."

"You are talking through your hat, Jean."

His restraint was snapping. He had rehearsed diligently for the interview at night, and he was doing well. He understood that Jean was trying to wear him down.

"I know what I am saying." She rebuffed him again.

He retaliated by pointing out that she was getting emotional.

"I have a right to it; she was my real sister."

"You didn't find any time to attend her funeral - no, funeral of both your sisters - the only relatives you had."

"I had my own commitments."

"Possibly, but are you aware that Stella and I were planning to get married?"

"She never mentioned it."

"Did she ever mention anything to you?"

Cornered, she replied slowly, "No, we were never close."

"In her death, I am the one who lost the most. You were indifferent to her in her life, and in her death. Now, suddenly you appear on the scene after so many years and are trying to dramatize everything."

She insisted that she wanted her sister to have her due.

Vinay played his calculated move. "If it pleases you, I can declare to the world that the research was hers. We shared everything. But she never shared her research with me though she taught me maths. And I am grateful."

Taken in by his emotional outburst, Jean was fooled, and felt that perhaps she was in the wrong. Maybe, the Chinese professor had gone crazy; prisons can have such an effect. She looked at him for a long time as if reviewing her next move.

"Stella was the brightest of the three sisters. Whenever I bag an award, I remember her. My father, who taught maths at Princeton for thirty years, often said that Stella would get the Nobel one day. She had the sparkle of a genius. That's why I think she wrote the paper and not you. This letter of Chinese professor is an additional proof."

"Do you know that I was the topper of Delhi University throughout, and my father had broken all the records from school onward?"

"No, I didn't know but I do know that you took 9-10 years for your doctorate."

"My bad luck," he answered.

Later, he inquired of her if she wanted more salad. She shook her head.

"But maybe nature had something better for me, those years were rewarding in the end."

She dropped a bomb. "I spent a day with Prof. Anand."

"I wish you could meet Prof. Hudson." He retorted.

"I am told you were his favourite student."

"You have made a lot of inquiries about me."

"Yes, I have. I got the Chinese professor's letter about four months back and since then I am confused."

Vinay paid the bill though Jean protested.

"I have to get to the bottom of it," she said slowly. "I may discuss this with our ambassador."

"You are trying the wrong end. Start from Ithaca."

The touch of sarcasm did not escape her.

"Certainly, I would," she said. Her tone was menacing.

"If you need my help, I will pitch in."

"No thanks. I can handle it." She glowered at him as if she would chew him up.

"As you please," Vinay said and rose; she remained seated in her seat, lighting her tenth cigarette.

"If you succeed, please do let me know. And —" he stopped for a while and stretched himself to his full height — "remember, I am always ready to help. For Stella's sake."

Jean refused to answer, and Vinay left.

"I will teach this thief a lesson," she muttered to herself. If she had the original thesis, this man would have been behind the bars.

She ordered a large whisky and sipped it slowly. She might have to fly to China to meet the old professor. But she knew it was not easy to meet him as he had a charge of treason slapped on him earlier. Consumed by revenge, something flashed across her mind, and she overturned the contents of her bag on the table and went through all the papers. "The bastard!" She hissed to herself. "The bloody vinay particle." The eponym hurt her.
Sitting for over an hour, she finalized her strategy to fix Vinay.

(3)

Vinay's façade of courage and innocence broke down in the taxi, and he sobbed like a child. The driver slowed down the taxi and asked him if he was unwell. Not getting any response, he said, "Sahib, it appears somebody has beaten you."
"No." Vinay was gruff and told him to drop him at Chanakya.
In a way, the driver was right, he reflected. He was badly mauled by Jean, and worse was to come.

He went to the rest room at Nirula, refreshed himself, bought a cola and occupied a table. He needed to collect himself before facing his wife. A group of I I T students, three boys and two girls, wished him, and it restored his confidence. He wondered how they would react if they learnt that he was a plagiarist, or a thief. He had put himself in such a precarious position that he had to play-act with Jean and was again going to do the same with his wife. Cheating, cheating all the time. He felt ashamed of himself. Lost in self persecution, his glass slipped from his hands, and spilled on the table. In the process, his best suit was spoilt. Nothing was sailing smoothly in life and all because of his own doings in the past. He rose. One of the girl students at the adjacent table smiled at him, and he smiled back peevishly, and again escaped to the washroom to clean up.

He decided to have a long walk to I I T under a moonless sky covered with dark grey clouds. It was sultry and still. After a while, he was soaked to the skin in sweat, yet he continued to walk, and did not hail an auto. He needed time to think.

This was the moment he feared; his goose was cooked. Though it was Stella's idea, her focus was limited to one galaxy cluster only. He had gone far ahead and examined the data from twenty-one other galaxy clusters. If he had included her name, it would not have made any difference. Now she was no more, and all the kudos would have been his only. But during the crisis, he was so confused and engrossed in guilt complex that he was unable to rationalize the situation. It was too late in the day to make amends. Maybe, Jean had misplaced the thesis or destroyed it without being aware of its significance. If she had it and was teasing him like a seasoned matador with a muleta before administering the coup de grace — it was catastrophic! The thought of the police handcuffing him and taking him to Tihar jail made him shiver.

Under muted lights, a freshly bathed Madhulika, reclining against the cushions and flipping the pages of a fashion magazine, was waiting for him. Her slender arms, the glowing body in the provocative negligee, and the long fluttering hair in the breeze of the ceiling fan heightened her femininity. Perhaps, the thought of Stella had egged her to push the envelope of sensuality a little further.

But all her effort was wasted on the sullen husband.

"How did it go? It was a long dinner chat," she said.

Exhausted, he explained that his taxi had broken down, and he had to foot the distance.

"Didn't Dr. Simpson miss me?"

"He preferred Jaipur to a dinner date with me."

"Very wise of him, otherwise he would have been bored."

He did not respond and looked glumly at her.

"Eh? So, it was a quiet twosome. You knew about his Jaipur visit."

"Honestly, I didn't."

"Is Jean as beautiful as Stella was?"

At Vivek's engagement ceremony, she had rushed to meet Vaishali and had not met Jean. She had a glimpse of her from a distance talking to her husband.

"Stella was thin and delicate whereas Jean has the build of an athlete."

"I hope you didn't find out the difference in bed." She had a dig at him.

He informed that he had not gone to her room.

"Shabbily disposed off in the restaurant?" Madhulika chuckled. "She must have been wary of your company."

"I am not such a bore as you think."

Looking at the sinewed body of her husband who was changing his dress, she realized that he would have spent many hours in the gym in the US. He looked handsome, and girls would have fallen for him.

"Yes, you can be charming if you want to, especially with strangers." She had a quick glance at him, and again asked, "So, what did you discuss? Stella or Steffi or both."

He realized it was stupid of him to have confided in his wife about his past love life. He felt that marriage was based on trust, and he had told her of all his affairs; her trying to get at him through his past or ridiculing him upset him. But why did he believe in such high-sounding principles when he had cheated on Stella? Slowly, he raised his head, and stared at her angrily.

"Why the hell are you prying, probing as if I have committed a crime, just because I told you everything about Stella and Steffi? Incidentally, Stella loved me as you have never done."

"I never said you have committed any crime, it's your perception."

Suddenly, she felt his throat choke as if he was undergoing turmoil within. Something was amiss; her banter had brought him near the threshold of a collapse. She rose and went up to him.

"Vinay, I've always loved you and no one else."

The assertion of her love mellowed him. "I had forgotten Stella; she was in the past and dead. Jean's presence has again brought her alive."

Slowly, she undressed herself, and relieved him of his pain through her love.

Later, he whispered, "It was out of this world."

"Why can't we capture such moments more often?" She kissed him tenderly.

Under the waterfall of her sweet endearments, Vinay forgot Stella, Steffi and even the devilish Jean Simpson.

(4)

In the dead of the night, the phone rang, loud and clear. To Vinay, it seemed like the bell of justice. Madhulika picked up the receiver, and said, "Yes."

"Can I speak to Vinay Chopra?"

"At this time! Are you crazy?"

"Are you, his wife?"
"Yes. Who is it?"
"I am Jean Simpson."
With a start, Madhulika was jolted out of her sleep.
"Do you know you have married a thief?"
"Shut up, you bitch!" Madhulika banged down the phone. Vinay inquired who had called, and why she had abused the caller.
"It was Jean and she called me a thief's wife. I would have chopped off her tongue if I could." In a fury, she went to the toilet, and slammed the door.
The ominous phone rang again.
"Yes." Vinay was gruff.
"Jean again. How are you Mr. Thief?"
"Shut up!"
"For your information, I have a copy of the thesis and I am going to call a press conference tomorrow."
"Thank God! Now, you can appreciate the difference between her and my work."
"You are a hardened criminal!"
"Use your head, and don't be dictated by your heart, Jean. And don't dare to disturb me again otherwise I'll call the police."

Jean was shocked. The pronounced relief in his 'Thank God.' took the wind out of her sails. He knew she had a copy of the thesis, and still had the cheek to declare as if all his problems were mitigated by this discovery. She relied more on her intuition and sixth sense rather than the Chinese professor's letter. "But how can I be wrong?" She made a large drink. Maybe, he was not phoney or had nerves of steel. She could not beat him in psychological war, but she could get him through his wife; she appeared a normal person.

Back from the washroom, Madhulika harshly questioned her husband. “Why has Jean called you a thief? How have you wronged her?”

“She is behaving like a mad woman.”

“Maybe, but what have you done?”

Vinay did not react and looked at the clock. It was past 3am.

“I have a suggestion. Let us catch some sleep, we will talk in the morning, and I’ll explain everything.”

“No, I can’t sleep with the charge of being a thief’s wife.”

He caressed her bare arm, and she revolted. “Don’t touch me till you are cleared of the charge.”

For an instant, he was lost in the past. When he was in his teens, his mother had hurled similar words at his father. Out of nowhere, it became clear to him — something which had disturbed him for more than two decades — why his father had taken the brahamcharya vow.

“Where are you lost, Vinay?”

“No where,” he said, and handed a tranquillizer, and a glass of water to her. “Take it, we will discuss in the morning.”

In a fit of anger, Madhulika threw away the tablet.

“Why do you need time to think? I want facts, and not fabricated stories.”

“Don’t you trust me?”

“I trust my husband but not a thief.”

Vinay kept on reminding himself that he should continue to be calm. He had pulled it off with Jean; he could do the same with his wife, and maybe the rest of the world.

“For god’s sake say something!” She spoke in exasperation. “Your coolness frightens me. You give me an impression as if you are talking to yourself and I don't exist."

"Jean has been talking idiotic things since evening, and I don't want to be rattled."

"That's what I dislike about you: your lack of reaction. If Kranti were in your place, he would have smashed something or driven to her hotel and bashed her up. But you sit here and philosophise over it."

"I am Vinay and not Kranti. You married the wrong man!"

"Consciously, you are going off on a tangent, and I stupidly give you the opportunity. I should not have mentioned Kranti; it was more of an example rather than any fondness for your brother. And you know it."

She had two glasses of water, and said, "Now, I am not emotional. I am as cool as Vinay. Tell me everything and don't hide anything. Remember, I am your wife and not Jean Simpson. You might have bluffed her but if you try the same with me you had it."

Throwing a bed sheet over her husband's legs, she nestled close to him, caressed his hands affectionately, and said, "Love demands faith and honesty. Lying beside one's nude wife, I am sure that no man can tell a lie."

He understood her strategy. In a way, he was more scared of her judgement than Jean Simpson's.

He was quiet for a long time, and she wrapped her husband's legs with her body. She was aware that he did not like the cold. "The truth, my love," she said.

Coerced by the pressure of her body warmth and love, he laid bare the facts he had hidden from the world. When the truth burst out from him after being bottled up for nine long years, it was broken in bits, incoherent, fuzzy, harsh and ugly. She had to ask many questions before she was able to piece the answers together to verify the authenticity of facts. He took a long, long time to reach the present spelling out his past frustration in life because of his subject, his treachery to Stella, and his guilt. Her body responses told him what she felt about him.

"Are you finished?"

He nodded and felt more naked than his wife. She was beautiful in the nude, whereas he felt he looked despicable. She dressed quietly, and said, "I am a thief's wife all right, but perhaps not as rotten as Jean thinks."

III
Approaching Disaster

The euphoria of the betrothal ceremony evaporated when Vivek overheard Jean whisper to Amit that she suspected Sheila had throat cancer. In the last decade no party had been thrown in his honour. At times, he had felt that he was given a subaltern status in the family, and his views were not taken seriously. The glamour of the festivities in which the entire focus was on him, and his fiancée had boosted his spirits: he felt he had taken the penultimate step and had risen to be an equal amongst the siblings. On witnessing the betrothal ceremonies of his brothers and sister, he had wished that his should be the best with all the embellishments, and trimmings of a Hindu engagement ceremony: his mama had lived up to his expectation.

Though an altruist, he was not opposed to wealth and the comforts associated with it. Like a normal young man, he wanted all the good things in life. But how could he have them without taking substantial sums of money from the NGO? Some of the NGOs paid their staff and top executives better than the corporate sector, but Vivek did not pay them much and neither allowed himself and the executives any luxuries or benefits as a matter of principle. When Sheila joined him, he was forced to take a small amount. Somewhere along the uneven journey, his image got overlaid with one who loathed money. He lacked the courage to correct it, as it was in sync with his mission in life.

Initially, when he had thought of the project, he was a vagabond without any commitment, and was unaware of the hard work needed to accomplish it. Insouciant in his attitude to life, he simply wanted to extract as much joy from life as he could. However, the people around him — the sociologists and especially the bureaucrats — had pumped into him the spirit of dedicating his life for the downtrodden. "We are tied down by rules and procedures, but you can do wonders for the poor," they told him, and he started believing in them. The two years he had spent in the Mumbai slums had opened his eyes to a strange new world with which he was unfamiliar, and he had considered doing something for them at some stage of his life. His earlier life comprised flitting like the firefly, from one momentary passion to the other: painting for six months, photography for three months, street plays for a year during which he acted and directed two of them, modelling for nine months, and so on.

Once he took up the project, there was no turning back. Multiple doors of new opportunities were thrown open. He established a handicraft centre in the village, and a shop in Meerut that sold the products made by the villagers. A school and degree college were set up subsequently. A new tailoring centre for two dozen women was established and its new building planned in the adjacent village. Last month, he had got a small computer centre inaugurated by the Collector. Twice in a month, he was in touch with the Block Development Officer and called upon the collector once. He ran special classes for the students of classes 10 to 12. One of his students had made it to the National Defence Academy, Kharagvasla. He promised them that one day students from the village would make it to the IAS. He was accessible to everyone, and they approached him for advice on all matters. Out of seven to eight hundred families in Lehriya village, many of them were indebted to him in some way.

Girls, he had avoided; the drivel they talked irritated him. He did not want to waste his life cocooned in one relationship. Girls meant money, time and responsibility. In principle, he avoided taking up any responsibility of any kind. And he was always short of money, and time.

Sheila's entry in his life had changed his attitude to the other gender. Active and sporty, she matched her steps with him, and was of immense help. She had more experience of the world, and her judgement about individuals, and situations was sound. She gave him so much of love and sex that he turned more caring and didn't mind being saddled with more duties.

But nature had erred. At the culmination of his happiness, the news of Sheila's ailment of throat cancer had stunned him. How could a girl who was even more active than him have cancer? It was sheer coincidence that on that very day she had felt the exhaustion and nausea.

Seated on an empty bench in the corridor of AIIMS in the late evening, Vivek was tense. Sheila had undergone a battery of tests in the hospital. The Director of the institute had personally met Jean Simpson and thrown open all the facilities for her. After four hours and plus, Sheila was exposed to the first session of radiation of an electron beam. Kranti and Prema had paid a short visit.

The first time Vivek had cast his eyes on Sheila was ten years back when he had returned from Mumbai after staying in the slums. On a hot May afternoon, he was walking in the corridors of Connaught Place (C P) when she asked him the location of the Thomas Cook office. Perspiring in a thick cotton top and baggies, she had the innocence of a teenager, and the curiosity of a tourist. He volunteered to show her the office as he had to go in the same direction. He learnt that her father was Indian, and mother Spanish, and they stayed in New York. It was her first visit to India, and she was totally disgusted with her trips to Agra and Jaipur. Smitten by her red cheeks, and bursting vitality, he turned chivalrous and volunteered to show her Delhi. Gratefully, she accepted the offer. Jama Masjid, Red Fort, Qutab Minar, Lodhi gardens, the Lotus temple, and the Old Fort. Mesmerised by his tall figure, she forgot that she had to meet her father for dinner at The Oberoi, and instead had her dinner with him in one of the well-known eatery joints of Pandara market. But she felt that he was rather lukewarm to her as he had not paid a single compliment to her since they met.

"You have not looked properly at me even once since last 7-8 hours," she said greatly disappointed.

"I observe everything —" his eyes sparkled mischievously — "and whatever I don't see, I imagine."

She laughed.
His gaze surveyed the room where young men and women were toasting to one another or attacking the chicken or mutton. Amongst the din of garrulous Punjabi diners, he slowly sipped the iced lassi and talked to her of illiteracy, poverty of millions in India, and confided to her of his plans for their uplift. It was done perhaps more to impress her with his zeal than actual commitment to his grandiose plans. He asked her to be a part of his dream.
"You are a dreamer. Dreams are dreams, they don't materialise into reality."
"And you want to be a successful girl?"
"Yep! Why not?"
"But the whole world has been made by dreamers only."
Sheila shrugged her shoulders. Peeved by the dismissal of his proposal, he asked her what she had liked the most in India.
"You," she replied looking frankly into his dark grey eyes.

She disappeared from his life (his attempts to track her down failed) and reappeared suddenly four years ago. She was in a hotel at Paharganj and needed help.

She had had a live - in relationship for a year with one Dr B B Kathuria and got engaged to him. He went to see his parents in India and did not return for two years. She had traced him to the Indian Institute of Sciences, Bengaluru and learnt that he had married, and had a three-month-old daughter.

Vivek helped Sheila by borrowing money from Prema. He cajoled Sheila to join his dream project to which she agreed stating that she was no longer afraid of failures. When Vivek managed a grant from the State Government and rented a house at Lehriya village, she moved to his place. For more than three years they had shared their joys and sorrows with each other, and their lives with the villagers. With the background of a practising nurse, Sheila had opened a small dispensary for emergent cases, and the locals felt grateful to her.

Last year, they had set up a small handicraft centre-cum-outlet near the expressway, which was doing better than the one at Meerut. Now, they were exploring markets for the products in Delhi and other commercial cities of U.P. With the approval of a major grant by the Central Government, Phase II of the project of replicating the Lehriya model in the rest of the tehsil, and later the district, had begun.

At about 9pm, Jean Simpson walked out of the glass door, her severe countenance showing strains of exhaustion after a gruelling day. Her mouth widened to a prominent smile on seeing Vivek. Assuring him that his fiancée would be okay, she turned to her pale patient, and added, "My dear, you need to postpone the marriage by at least 5-6 months."

She gave detailed instructions to Sheila and Vivek and warned that she should not go to Lehriya village and stay put at Delhi.

"Shall we go Amit? I am already late for my dinner appointment with the ambassador."

Dr. Goel discussed with Vivek and Sheila and told them to come for the next session of radiation everyday for three weeks.

(2)

Waiting for her husband who had gone to attend a meeting in his capacity as Dean of Sciences, Madhulika was absorbed in her contemplation. "Somehow, I always expected something of this kind," Madhulika muttered to herself, "Vinay lacks creativity." She did not doubt his scholarship and understanding of the subject but was sceptical of his capability of discovering the Vinay particle. Whenever he had assisted her in her thesis, she had noticed that he was confused if confronted with something new or not in print.

Vinay was back in less than two hours. In light cream trousers, and a chocolate-coloured shirt, he looked handsome. Over cold coffee, she wanted to know if Jean had a copy of the thesis.

"If she had it, she would have gone to the police," he said confidently, and explained that he had sent her the original thesis, which probably was lost in transit.

"If you had remembered about sending her the thesis, would you still have stolen Stella's research work?"

"No." He was emphatic. "I would not have dared it. It's surprising that I entirely forgot about it and instead went about planning so that no one could find out the truth."

"The resurfacing of the Chinese professor has been our undoing," she said.

Touched by her usage of 'our', he felt that she was with him, and he was forgiven for the crime.

"What should I do, Madhu?" he asked, throwing all his troubles on her shoulders.

She suggested that one option could be to admit everything.

"All hell will break loose," he said. "And I'll be jailed for cheating."

She reminded him that he too had contributed quite a lot. He turned irascible. "But then it would not be called Vinay particle. It would be termed Stella - Vinay particle."

Madhulika winced. She did not like Stella's name associated with her husband, and especially preceding his. Vinay noticed it.

"And then how do I prove what I did and what Stella did?"

"Did you really do what you are claiming?"

The hurt in his eyes was so transparent that she felt she had transgressed her boundaries. "I'm sorry, I shouldn't have said it."

"When you are down, everyone tramples you."

"I'm sorry, I really am."

"I am not saying only about you, I'm generalising."

Impulsively, she said, "You are good at generali—" and then hurriedly regretted it — "I am getting bitchy. I apologize."

Vinay rose. "You are entitled to it."

"No, I am not. But to be frank, the epithet of thief's wife hurts. It really does."

"I know you deserved better from life."

Without looking at her, he left the room.

(3)

In the evening, Vinay preferred a game of tennis to his wife's unpleasant company. Madhulika was planning to visit her neighbour when the phone rang.

"I am Jean again."

Agitated, Madhulika screamed at her. "What do you want from me?"

"I want to talk to you about your husband."

"But I don't want to talk to you."

"Your husband stole my sister's research work and became famous."

"Shit. I don't believe in this crap."

But she lacked in conviction and had to make the most of

the rotten situation.

"Give me half an hour — I'll convince you."

Uncertain whether Vinay would approve of it or not, Madhulika turned down the request, and Jean again insisted.

"All right, you can come to my place tomorrow evening."

"No." Jean was categorical. "I don't want to run into your husband again. Any other place in Delhi would do."

"Tomorrow 6pm, at York."

Madhulika gave her the directions.

Without informing her husband, when Madhulika reached York restaurant on Connaught Circus next day, Jean was already settled in her seat upstairs with a wine glass, and a Havana cigar secure in her mouth. York was the favourite restaurant with the physicist couple; Madhulika liked the soft décor, and most of the waiters, and the steward knew her well.

"Hello!" Jean rose, and offered her a rich smile, and a warm handshake. Jean looked beautiful in a cream-coloured skirt and black top.

Madhulika waved at the waiter, ordered lemonade, and mutton cutlets, but Jean refused to take anything.

Jean was about to initiate the discussion when Madhulika interceded. "Please don't waste your time; I know all the facts, perhaps even better than you."

Ruffled a little by the intervention, Jean had a sip of the red wine, and said, "Don't you think, my dear, that your husband usurped all the fame and glory, which rightfully belonged to my sister."

"I concede that the new particle should have been named Stella - Vinay particle. Vinay made a positive contribution; he worked on the data from 21 galaxy clusters and generalized the whole concept. Without his contribution, Stella's research would not have been hailed as such a path breaking discovery."

"How can you say that?" Her tone turned offensive.

"Because I know the facts."

Lucidly, Madhulika explained the contributions of Stella and Vinay.

"Stella's work would have been of little consequence if Vinay had not given it universality," Madhulika said at the expense of repetition.

"I didn't know," she muttered, and looked minutely at Madhulika wondering whether she was telling the truth or bluffing her.

"How do you know so much of physics?"

"I teach physics at Miranda House."

"Oh!"

Full of consternation, Jean had a long sip, and her face turned grave.

"Supposing I go along with you, can Vinay make a statement to that effect?"

"I don't know." Madhulika was unsure. "Vinay may not agree; it may ruin his future."

"That's what I intend to do."

Madhulika's drink arrived.

"If you have already made up your mind, why have you called me?" Madhulika shrieked at her.

Many heads turned towards the two women.

"I had a feeling you could help me to change Vinay's mind."

Controlling her rising temper, Madhulika said, "Listen Jean, Stella is no more. She is dead and gone. No amount of effort on your part can bring her back. Vinay is alive, has a big future, and he is my husband. Let the dead rest in peace and let the living live."

"If Vinay does not make a statement to the press within a week, I'll certainly ruin him."

"What proof do you have?"

"I have the original thesis sent by Vinay to me."

"If you really had it, you would not have been surprised at what I told you."

Caught on the wrong foot, Jean was dumbfounded.

"I only want Stella to have her due." Jean clarified her intention.

"What do you expect of me?"

"I'll not settle for anything less than a press statement."

"Knowing Vinay, I don't think he has the guts to do it. He may break down or commit suicide."

"That's exactly what I want. To finish him," Jean said.

Smouldering with anger, Madhulika hissed. "You bitch! Vinay is my husband and I'll not allow it."

"Go away." Jean snapped her fingers at her. "Go away — you — the wife of a thief!"

Boiling with rage, Madhulika dramatically flung the half-finished lemonade in Jean's eyes, and marched away defiantly through the hall.

Livid, Jean muttered, "I swear by Stella that I'll finish both the husband and wife."

The interview with the awesome Jean Simpson revitalized Madhulika. Her triumphant act of splashing the lemonade laced with black pepper in her enemy's eyes was icing on the cake. It had cooled the bursting volcano inside her as she negotiated the rush hour traffic through Connaught Circus. Now, she was sure that Jean didn't have Stella's thesis, and that was a big relief.

Excitedly, she blurted out all the details to Vinay. He did not share his wife's enthusiasm; he was worried about the consequences of her insulting Jean personally and fuelling her wrath.

"I am doomed," he said slowly preparing himself for the worst.

Madhulika emphasized again that Jean had no proof, but he continued to be distressed.

"If Jean decides to visit China, how can we stop the Chinese professor from telling the truth?" she asked.

A little indecisive in how far to trust his wife as she had the habit of taking control of things, Vinay looked at her doubtfully. Madhulika touched him lightly on the arm to encourage him to confide his misgivings in her though at the back of her mind, she was sure her feelings were misplaced. He was a crook, and a hardened one at that.

"2-3 options are available," he said. "First, we can go to China, explain everything to the professor and plead for mercy. In old age, people tend to be forgiving. Second is to put pressure through our ambassador who is a friend of papa's. Third could be to leave it to nature; it has its own peculiar ways of sorting out the complexities. Maybe, the old man is too foggy in the head to remember anything. And the fourth —?"

Uncertainly, Vinay looked outside the window. It was a bright moonlit night. He was quiet for a long time.

"What is the fourth option, Vinay?"

"Have him killed," he whispered. His soft words were menacing.

'Did he do the same to Stella and Steffi?' The unholy thought flashed across her.

Her face reflected her feelings so vividly that Vinay replied spontaneously, "No, I didn't."

Unsurely, she asked aloud, "What?"

"I repeat. I didn't do them in." His hands were shaking.

Gravely, she looked at him, rose, and returned with drinks.

"If you are planning on those lines, would it not be easier to handle Jean here rather than the Chinese professor in China?"

Vinay did not respond and toyed with the glass.

"Kranti could be of some help," she added. Sheila had confided in her that once when she and Vivek had run into trouble with local goons on the expressway, a phone call to Kranti had helped: two highway patrolling vehicles had reached in less than fifteen minutes and rescued them.

Intuitively, Vinay perceived that he had made a mistake in confiding his inner most thoughts in Madhulika. Quietly, he finished the drink, and left the room.

(4)

At the dining table, Vaishali was agitated, and admonished anyone who was slightly out of sync with her. She had been earlier unhappy that Vivek had fallen for Sheila, a foreigner, and that too of mixed Hispanic blood. A girl of English origin would have been more cultured and civilised; at least the English girls knew how to control their emotions.

From the moment Vaishali learnt that Vivek had sponged on his sister-in-law to render assistance to Sheila, she had not approved of her. Now, she was saddled with throat cancer. What kind of progeny would she give the family? Disgustingly weak children who would not be able to stand the heat wave in summer, and she would run away to the cooler climates of Europe or America. Afraid that she would lose Vivek to a foreign country, Vaishali barely touched the food, and her eyes wandered uneasily from one end of the table to the other; Sheila was resting in the guest room with Vivek.

"The whole thing is very sad," Deepak said. "The marriage will have to be postponed to next year."

Vinay and Madhulika's not turning up at the hospital was briefly hinted. "They must be stuck with something really important." Vaishali defended her eldest son.

In the privacy of the bedroom, Kranti told Prema that he had tried to speak to Vinay, but could not reach him, and Madhulika was slightly distressed. "Something is bugging her, I think she appeared tense," he said. Prema didn't approve of his sympathy and concern for her sister-in-law. Intuitively, she felt he was getting attracted to her after the Puri trip.

About two months ago, Vinay had to attend a conference at Bhubaneswar. Madhulika suggested to Prema and Kranti to join them as she would be bored when Vinay would be in conference. Vaishali assured them that she would take care of the children. Kranti booked the circuit house at Puri, and the foursome had a great time on the beach. At the weekend, the women turned exuberant in the wild sea. Madhulika, known for being a malcontent in the joint family, was excited, and laughed a lot. Dressed in a flimsy red and white two piece, her long fair legs shining in the bright sun, she looked ravishingly pretty. "I want to chew you up," Vinay said. Full of coquetry, she answered, "Do so," and slipped away merrily from him.

Kranti looked adoringly at Madhulika; to him she looked devastatingly beautiful. He could not take his eyes off her appreciating her fair, lithe body. Prema had a voluptuous figure, and a flawless olive complexion, but she was not fair. Prema glanced at her husband and saw the mounting desire in his demeanour. "I wish I was as fair." She sighed.

Kranti turned, and said, "I like you the way you are, Prema."

Sadly, she smiled, and walked back to the place where they had kept their belongings and covered her legs with a towel.

Again, in the afternoon, she caught Kranti staring blatantly at Madhulika's semi-nude figure, and chose not to comment. While the four of them were playing with a ball, a powerful wave hurled them towards the shore. When the waters receded, Kranti's leg was on Madhulika's and Vinay's hand was on Prema's breast. All of them were terribly embarrassed. To get over the awkward situation, the women giggled making the men look rather stupid.

At night, after Kranti and Prema made love, she said, "Today you loved me with the thought of Madhu," Prema said.

"Is it necessary to dissect each and every thought of your husband?"

"I don't like your loving me while thinking of Madhu or any other girl." She repeated. "I know that Madhu has two advantages over me. She is younger and fairer. And you have a weakness for the fair ones."

"But no one can match you, Prema."

"How do you know the difference?"

The sharpness of her voice made his muscles tense, and he stopped caressing her.

"I don't," he answered. "But why are you sniping at each and every word of mine?"

Prema caught his hand, but he jerked it.

"Is it my fault that Madhu is younger, taller and fairer than you?"

"No."

"There were so many girls on the beach who were much prettier and younger than you. What can I do about it?"

"You can admire them from a distance but do not have a fling with them. If ever you do, you will lose me for I'll not forgive you."

Kranti rose, lighted a cigarette and sat down on an easy chair facing her.

"You are a cop and I understand the working of your mind," she said looking at him with piercing eyes. "If ever you force yourself on anyone against her wish, I'll drag you to a court of law."

"Spoken like the daughter of a Supreme Court Judge!" Kranti applauded. "Bravo!!"

Next day, after dinner, Madhulika and Prema went for a stroll on the beach. The receding sea was unusually violent. When Prema looked up and saw the blood red moon tossed on the cloudy skies, she shivered a little.

"Are you okay?" Madhulika asked.

"No, I am not." Prema replied and told her about a story of Jean Tommer in which the sighting of the blood red moon brought devastation and death. "Intuitively, I am scared of the future."

"But why?"

"Something warns me of approaching disaster."

Prema was tense, and sad.

"But why the sudden interest in Vinay and Madhu after the Puri trip?" Prema asked.
"Come on, I have always respected Vinay for his intellect and academic achievements. After all, he is a world-famous physicist."
Adjusting his pillow, he clarified that after the Puri trip, Madhu was easier and more natural in her behaviour. "Earlier we had never interacted much with her, and she also behaved a little snooty as she is teaching at Miranda House."
It was true that Madhu had never shown any warmth whenever she called upon them. Often, Vaishali commented after their departure that 'the duty visit for the month is over.' But now sometimes, she was bubbly, cheerful, and vocal. Vaishali hoped that Madhulika's happiness would translate into something more tangible — an addition to the family.
"Don't you think that Vinay is slightly on the dull side?" Prema asked.
"Maybe, you are right." Kranti felt that Vinay was obsessed with physics almost as if it were his first love. He was so reticent that it was not easy to converse with him. Switching off the table lamp, Kranti said, "All his life, he has been trying to prove that he is better than papa in all walks of life - academics, status, money."

(5)

Vaishali ran the house in a domineering manner and tolerated no interference from anyone. Compromising on even trivial issues was not a part of her nature. Sheila was perturbed at the thought of spending the next few months at Vaishali's place and shared her fears with Vivek.

Though Vaishali enacted the role of a model prospective mother-in-law, everyone dreaded the fireworks at Sheila's prolonged stay. Overprotective of his fiancée at the critical hour when she needed him, Vivek felt helpless. Once a day, at the least, he had to personally plead with his mother to be more flexible. Within a week, the situation reached a breaking point, and Sheila was in tears.

She called her mother, now settled in Los Angeles after her second marriage, and told her predicament. Her mother invited her to LA for six months. Vaishali was relieved when Sheila flew to the US in less than a fortnight. Sullen, Vivek went back to Lehriya straight from the airport.

(6)

Communication between Vinay and Madhulika almost ceased as he considered Madhulika's meeting with Jean without his approval as an act of defiance bordering on misbehaviour. He felt that Jean's antagonistic relationship with him had touched the rock bottom when Madhulika threw the peppered lemonade in her eyes. He feared Jean's personal vendetta though nothing significant happened. Madhulika avoided him completely by taking more interest in the extra - curricular activities at college.

Vinay's file relating to his promotion as Deputy Scientific Advisor did not return from the PMO (Prime Minister's Office). It was rumoured that the PM was under pressure from Governor of Andhra Pradesh to select his nephew for the same post. The Principal Secretary to the PM informed Deepak that the proposal was shelved for the present. Deepak was aware that the Governor's term was to expire in five months, and the proposal would be revived only thereafter.

On reading a news item about the forth coming All India Science Congress at Kolkata, Madhulika asked Vinay whether he was going to attend it; he told her that he had already declined the invitation.

Last year he had given the Keynote Address at the Congress Session as the leading scientist in the country. Glowing tributes were paid to him for his rich contribution to science, and he was awarded the newly constituted President's award. Madhulika's face had lit up with joy and pride as she applauded along with hundreds.

"Your absence may be conspicuous," she added after a thought, "and now you need to be extra careful."

"Thanks for your advice," he answered coldly. "But I care a damn."

"I am thinking only of your good."

"I know." But there was no change in his tone.

"Were you able to speak to Kranti?"

"No."

"Have you changed your mind?"

"Stop pestering me, Madhu." He bellowed at her. "Don't you have anything better to do?"

Angrily, she rose, and went to her room.

"He is cracking," she muttered.

About a fortnight later, Vinay decided to play tennis in the evening, and Madhulika went for a drive. Before going home, she decided to have a round of the campus. She liked the quietude settling down as the evening lights were switched on in the campus. Suddenly, it dawned on her that so many secrets were buried under this quiescence. If her husband's secret ever came to light, it would cause major explosions in the institute. On seeing her husband playing under flood- lights, she stopped the car, and switched off the headlights.

Vinay was losing all the points though he had been the champion at Cornell for four years. His taut frame, attractive profile, and easy flowing movements were a treat to watch. Observing him minutely, she understood that he was unable to concentrate. It occurred to her that he was a hypocrite, a phoney. Was that the reason she had got bored with him in less than four years? But he was a handsome thief.

She returned home, had coffee, and was lost in her thoughts. Any other girl would have been happy to marry such a man. He had done so much for her and her family. Without batting an eyelid, he blew all his savings on the marriages of her two sisters. But for him, she would never have got a doctorate. Her father had died as a primary school teacher, whereas his father had retired as a Cabinet Secretary, and now was Chairman UPSC! If she had been a little more understanding, perhaps he might not have pined for Stella?

"But a thief who stole his lover's research work and became world famous!"

Madhu said aloud and shook her head in disgust. "It's not easy to be magnanimous."

Slowly, a feeling of abomination against her husband spread through her body.

Because of her poor background, Madhulika was meticulous about her accounts; in contrast, Vinay was grossly negligent. On going through her bank passbook, she was surprised to see a withdrawal of Rs4000/, which she was certain she had not made. Disconcerted, she decided to report it to the manager in the morning, when Vinay entered looking unusually cheerful.

"You seem to be quite happy; did you beat Gupta?"
"No, I lost both the sets, but I enjoyed them."
"But you were not concentrating?"
Looking quizzically at his wife, he laughed easily, and answered, "No, I was missing my shots by inches. Were you watching me on the TV?"
She explained, and added, "Two years back you were superb."
"Age and lack of practice," he said ruefully.

Vinay was about to go for a shower when she mentioned about the withdrawal of Rs 4000/-.
"Oh, I withdrew Rs 4000/- from the bank last week and the bank have wrongfully deducted from your account."
She explained that a blank check from her check book was missing.
Vinay sniggered. "It appears I have used your check book and the bank cleared it without proper verification."
Both had accounts in the bank within the campus, and Vinay's account preceded hers.
"You mean you have defrauded me of Rs4000/," she said coldly. "In the US, you could have been jailed for it."
"Perhaps," he replied glowering at her, "you are right. You can file a complaint. If you are lucky, you may succeed."

Instead of a hot shower, Vinay had a cold one, and sneezed on emerging from bathroom. Wrapping himself in a semi-woollen gown, he prepared a large mug of coffee, and retired to his bedroom.
Madhulika was busy in the kitchen. At dinner time, she banged on the door of his room. "Do you want dinner or not?"
"Gupta treated me to hamburger and chicken patties; I don't feel like taking anything." He lied but didn't open

the door.
"But I didn't take any patties and burger?" She retorted.
"Go ahead and have a lavish dinner."
Madhulika could not eat anything. She realized that she was also unable to handle the pressure and was getting bitchy. Introspecting for a long time, she resolved that she needed a break for a few weeks from her husband. Whenever they fought, they slept in different rooms.

□□□

IV

Peep Into Another Secret

Amit and Kavita Bhardwaj threw a lavish party in honour of Kavita's brother on his first visit to India with his new second bride. Prema in silvery black sari and a flimsy blouse, and Kranti in black trousers, and a tight-fitting red T- shirt made a handsome and youthful couple. Exuding vitality, Kranti, and Prema stole the limelight in a group of two dozen guests. At his third peg, Kranti was enjoying himself as he regaled the group with his feats of heroism. When he had started indulging in such rhetoric about four or five years back, it was about real factual incidents; gradually fictitious incidents were added, and imaginary characters introduced till the narrative attained the status of a thriller. Pamela, the new American bride had her eyes popping out when she exclaimed, "How could you have done it single handedly?" Kranti placed his solid hand on her almost bare back and went into minute details, and she cackled with a boisterous laugh. Amit winked at his wife, and she rescued her sister-in-law from Kranti with a little jostle, and said, "You are at it again."

"You are spoiling my evening." He laughed.

"Do you know what I have lined up for you?" Kavita had a twinkle in her eyes. In fact, she enjoyed a mild flirtation with Kranti though never admitted to it. "You are going to love it."

An imperceptible gesture of her hand and the DJ took over. The couples moved to the centre of the hall in search of their partners.

Nothing escaped Prema's sharp eye; nonetheless, she let Kranti have his fun. She was having a great time with Kavita's brother, a sociologist, who was of a serious disposition. He was eloquent on his favourite subject of marriage break- ups in metros and listened with rapt attention to what she had to say on the subject, with specific reference to Nari Rakshan Kendra, an NGO, that she had started a few years ago.

Kranti and Prema outshone the others in dancing. Exhausted, others left, but the debonair Chopra couple continued to dominate the floor with their lyrical movements. When the music stopped, the couple got a long, standing ovation. An overwhelmed Prema whispered into his ears, "Today, I am so happy that I can forgive you for any misdemeanour."

"Really?"

"Yup!" she said mimicking Sheila, and both broke into uninhibited laughter.

Prema's sartorial elegance and figure had bewitched Kavita's brother, who was extravagant in bestowing rich praise on her stating that she was the most beautiful woman amongst the guests. Under his mesmerizing words, her heart fluttered, and she could notice it flitting away from her like the data transferring from the pen- drive to the laptop. She smiled at him covetously giving her tacit willingness to any advances from him. Graciously, therefore she had ignored her husband's sensual touch on Pamela's fair back.

With basketfuls of jasmine flowers located in inconspicuous corners, Kavita's spacious lounge had a luxuriant jasmine fragrance creating a mysterious atmosphere of excitement and sensuality. Everyone was hit by it and wanted to share the feeling of joy with others. Anything was an excuse to convert the restful smile into laughter. They were all grown up adults struggling against the advances of middle age and were fully aware that this was a temporary moment of happiness, and wanted to hold on to it, for the next morning it would not be the same. The new day might unravel hidden secrets, and perhaps harsher, uglier realities. Some of them were on their fourth peg and could pretend not to be sane; the women smelling of sherry or red wine didn't mind a peck on the cheek or a brush on the bare waist or back.

Someone had to remind Kavita that it was past 11.30, and it was rather late for dinner, though for many it was of little consequence. Once the dinner was announced, the guests realized they were hungry, and attacked the scrumptious food ferociously. In less than half an hour, the guests were through with their dinner, and were at their coffee when suddenly, power failed, and it was pitch- dark. Someone opened the main door and pulled the curtains. The guests stretched their arms, groped for nearest seats in the faint light of the full moon filtering through the door and windows, and settled down there till the hostess was able to make some arrangements. Some of the guests were critical of Kavita for not getting the inverter repaired.

"Where is Julian?" Amit called aloud to his wife.

"She is sleeping upstairs in her room," Kavita answered.

Amit went up the flight of stairs, brusquely knocked at her door, and instructed her to get the candles.

Attired in a short, black slip with long noodle straps, Julian came down slowly, step by step, with a big lighted candle, and three packets of candles in other hand. With her pinkish bare arms and legs, the flushed face, and loose hair, she had an electrifying effect on the guests. Everyone rose. Amazed, they stared at her as if she was an apparition from the other world. Unmindful of her skimpy dress and the glowing radiance on her youthful face, she lighted three candles. More than fifty eyes were riveted on the beautiful angel who had suddenly appeared out of the darkness to give them light. Not withstanding the aura of innocence surrounding her, there was an unmistakable raw sexuality exuded by her presence, which aroused the concupiscence of all men, with no exception, and even affected many women.

Kranti gazed at her as if she was a shadow out of his past that he had seen seven or eight years back at Nongpoh. To make sure, he cleared the way, and reached the other end of the long table. In an instant, his face turned death pale, and he felt the earth give way under him. He caught the table for support. Everyone was so bewitched by the girl that no one noticed the metamorphic changes taking place in Kranti. Julian's slow breathing, the slight cleavage, the rise and fall of her heavy breasts, the twinge of pain in her fingers as the molten wax touched her finger, the little flutter of the eyelashes: nothing was missed by the guests. But she was ignorant of her impact on them.

Completing her assigned task, she was about to go back when she turned, and stared with awe at Kranti. Fear and panic gripped her. Pointing her finger at him, she shrieked aloud in the semi-lit hall, "The devil!", "The devil!!" She turned, threw her arms in the air, and wildly ran up the flight of stairs. She slipped, rolled down, hastily recovered herself, and dashed up the stairs again as if she was running for her life, and finally banged the door shut.

The guests were stunned. No one moved or whispered a word. They all looked at the one whom the girl had called `the devil!' The declaration of the girl was affirmed by the mute stares of the guests. Without giving any benefit of doubt to Kranti - standing grave and ashen in red T- shirt - he was proclaimed Satan. They all waited for him to act or do something. Prema caught his arm and led him through the exit door.

(2)

Born at Nongpoh, the headquarters of Ri Bhoi district in Meghalaya, (at about 48Km from Guwahati) Julian was brought up by her grandfather, a caretaker in the PWD guest house located less than 100 yards from the expressway. She had no memories of her parents. According to her grandpa, they had died in a car accident though she had heard rumours that her mother had run away with her Naga paramour, and her father had committed suicide. Ravishingly pretty, devoutly religious, she was the soul of Nongpoh. Half the young men of the town were looking forward to marrying Julian when she came of age. Michael, the old man, had the ambition of educating her so that she could become a mathematics teacher like her father; however, his resources were limited. He took a heavy loan from Joe, a building contractor, who wanted to marry Julian. In the small township, Joe made sure that everyone knew that he was investing money on his future bride. But Michael scoffed at him that he would not allow such a marriage alliance. "Look at her and look at you. She is going to be a lady and you are a ruffian."

When Julian finished schooling, Joe approached Michael and again sought her hand in marriage. "Go away," Michael said treating Joe as if he were a pest. "She is still a kid and not even eligible for marriage." Michael informed that he was sending her to Shillong for college education. "Marry her to me or return my loan," Joe said.

Michael was insistent that the debt of Rs 30-40000 would be paid by Julian once she became a schoolteacher.

Michael ignored Joe, took further loans from other money lenders hostile to Joe, and sent Julian to Shillong at about 50 Km for college education.

A year later, Joe lost patience and requested Michael to solemnise the marriage. Michael bluntly refused. The argument between the two escalated, and Joe grew belligerent. "If you don't marry her to me, I will rape her and turn her into a prostitute." He threatened. "Christmas is the deadline."

A worried Michael wrote a long letter to Julian and spoke to her on the phone. "Never come back to Nongpoh again - not even on my death," he told her.

On Christmas, she received a phone call from her close friend that her grandpa was on deathbed. She dashed back and reached grandpa's house late in the night. Rain and thunderstorm lashed the town. The house, at the back of the guest house, was empty as his grandpa had gone to the town to celebrate Christmas. Instead, Joe's men were waiting for her behind a tree.

There were seven of them, and all tipsy. No one listened to her mercy appeals. Her screams were buried in the din of the explosions of Christmas crackers, and the rumble of clouds. She pleaded that she was willing to marry Joe. He laughed, and said, "It's too late now, darling."

They dragged her to the main hall of the guest house that was closed for major repairs. It was used as a sleeping room for the labour force (who had taken off because of Christmas) and contained about a dozen cots. The room was dark and chilling cold. Since there was a power breakdown in that part of the town, someone lighted a small candle making the room look ghastly. When the shadows of men fell on the wall, they appeared monstrous. They stripped her and tied her to the bed. She heard their vulgar talks, and it scared her.

"Pretty girl!"

"It's going to be a real party."

"Thank you, Joe for such a Christmas present."

"But I'll be the first," Joe said.

"Of course!"

When Joe moved towards her, she shrieked, cried, and prayed to her Lord to help her.

Her prayer was answered. A young man appeared from the main door, almost like a chivalrous knight. Instead of the shiny armour, he was dressed in black trousers, a red T- shirt, and a cream-coloured coat.

"Stop, otherwise I'll kill you." He took out a pistol, and

again threatened them with dire consequences. The goons ran away.

The young man glanced at her for the first time, and feeling the cold, lighted logs of wood in the fireplace. Julian expected her saviour to untie her hands and legs. Instead, he pushed the cot near the fire, massaged her legs and body. When the flames leapt from the wood, it was a great relief to her. "Please untie me," she said. The small candle was extinguished by now. Without answering her, he struggled with knots, and could not undo all of them. All of a sudden, he stopped. In the light of the burning wood, he looked grimly at her for a long time. He had never seen such a pink complexioned, youthful nude girl from such close quarters. In a dilemma, he was unable to decide his further course of action. Without a word, he removed his clothes, parted her legs, and entered forcibly. Stunned, she had forgotten to even scream.

Joe and his men returned with the intention of fulfilling their mission. The stranger saw the locals, and contemptuously fired at them. Out of the three shots, one hit Joe and the second one his close aide. The hoodlums again disappeared. Unhurriedly, the stranger wore his clothes, and left.

No one had heard Julian's screams, but everyone heard the bullet shots. The crowd moved towards the guest house and caught Joe and his men. The town folk misunderstood that Julian had been raped by Joe, and his men, and thrashed them brutally. No one listened to their protests that they had not raped her. Michael wanted to lodge a police complaint; Julian refused.

Julian's girlish smile and laughter froze. Her face turned hard like granite. She had nothing against the

Lord; after all he had sent his knight. But instead of rescuing her, the knight had betrayed and raped her. How could he do it? A representative of God! A protector had turned violator of her dignity. Julian wanted to take revenge, but she had not seen his face in the poor light and could not recognize him even in broad day light. Her attempt to find out the particulars of cars and Jeeps at the checkpoint failed as the post was deserted due to Christmas celebrations, and the storm.

Julian went back to Shillong. Four months later, she was kidnapped by Joe and his men, gang raped for a week, and sold to the highest bidder in the red- light area of Kolkata.

She had heard rumours that both the legs of Joe were dysfunctional; he was a cripple and could move around with only crutches. She felt relieved that God had punished him. But the stranger had got away scot- free.

Because of her beauty, and the high price paid for her, she was under surveillance 24x7. About six years later, one evening when her security was slightly lax, she escaped from the brothel, and raced away in a taxi to the station. Madam Katrina's (the owner of the brothel) men hovered all over the station. In the first AC of the Rajdhani Express, Julian saw the formidable Jean Simpson, and fell on her knees, and told her story. Moved by her beauty and sad tale, Jean Simpson called the ticket collector, and told him that Julian was her friend, and purchased her ticket. Later, she had told Amit to take her under his wing and give her protection.

Amit had hesitated to take on such an onerous responsibility as her past was mired in prostitution. However, he didn't want to annoy Jean Simpson. He was banking on her help to get a fellowship at Johns Hopkins School of Medicine, Baltimore, Maryland, one of the premier schools of medicine in the US. Appreciating his reluctance, Jean smiled and said, "Take care of Julian, and I'll get you the fellowship at Hopkins." The bait of a quid pro quo worked.

Initially, Kavita had resisted. Once Amit explained about the fellowship, she readily agreed as she was also desperately searching for a servant; Julian was prepared to do any kind of job.

One day, Kavita was puzzled with a maths problem of her eleven-year-old daughter, Julian helped her out. Kavita appreciated Julian's potential and promoted her to a governess giving her more money and status. "I want to be a schoolteacher," she told her mistress. Kavita encouraged her and allowed her to join BA (Pass Course) in the nearby Evening College.

Julian had not forgotten the rape by her knight. Neither had she forgotten the gang rape and her years in prostitution. Unfortunately, she could not recognize her first rapist. But on the night of the party, the surroundings were as unearthly as at Nongpoh. The party hall lit with only three candles and dozens of guests staring at her with their overblown ghastly shadows produced an eerie atmosphere. And there stood the same man in red T-shirt and black trousers.

When she was raped by the stranger, she was numbed by the sheer shock of it. Since that fateful night, she had gone over the incident many a time and had hated him. With years, he had turned into an ogre, and eventually into the Devil incarnate. His dress and the strange supernatural atmosphere had helped her recognize him instantly. All the simmering anger of the past burst out in her wild scream. It was a spontaneous reaction; she had no control over it.

(3)

Once they were out of the party room, Prema abruptly left her husband's arm jolting him. Her face was stern, and often during the drive back home, she looked angrily at him without uttering a word. Kranti was agitated, she could see, and therefore, she controlled her sharp tongue till they were secure in the privacy of the bedroom. Ensuring that her children were safely tucked away in their room, she returned, and found Kranti had changed, and was about to sleep.

Acidly, she said, "This calls for an explanation."

Kranti feigned sleep and yawned.

"Are you listening to me?"

"Yes, I am."

"Why did the girl shriek on seeing you?"

"How do I know? Why don't you ask her?" He retorted.

"I will, but I want to hear your version."

She realized that he was subdued; he was not the usual aggressive self given to loud intemperate bursts. He was tense, the veins on his forehead and throat were throbbing, but her immediate concern was to ascertain the truth. Slowly, he moved out of bed, pulled out a cigarette from a pack of 555, and lighted it. His hands were steady, though the overall demeanour was ruffled. He sat down on the sofa taking his favourite corner seat, and placed his solid, powerful legs on the centre table.

"I'll tell you everything truthfully, but don't get hyper."

"Why should I? It's not I, but you who have to do the explaining."

He ignored her rebuff, and said, "I don't think I know her, but I can't deny that whenever I have gone to Amit's, I had a feeling that her face is familiar. Remember the days when you were carrying Namita, and I had to go to Shillong in connection with arrest of the dreaded dacoit Billa who had robbed a bank."

Prema nodded, and he told his story.

Billa was in the habit of shocking the police. Invariably, he indulged in the most bizarre and daring dacoities that could not be dreamed by others. In broad daylight, he looted Rs 50 lakhs from a bank located just opposite the police station in Paharganj. One woman and three school children of the nearby school were killed in the crossfire. Billa escaped with money despite a massive manhunt. Kranti as the ACP of the area was under intense pressure. To make matters worse, it turned out that the woman and one of the children killed were the wife and son of the local MLA. `Inefficiency of the police' made the headlines in the newspapers. To protect him from the wrath of the media and legislators, Kranti had to proceed on leave, and later was posted at headquarters.

Eight months later, he received a message from Shillong that a gangster hailing from Delhi was arrested supplying arms to Nagas. The local police were unable to contain the turbulent criminal, and desired that he should be taken to Delhi. From the telephone conversation with his counterpart, Kranti intuitively felt that the person apprehended was Billa. It was a long shot, but worth taking a chance. Next day, he flew to Guwahati. The flight was badly delayed, and the plane landed after nine in the night.

Because of the severe cold, rough weather and festive

season of Christmas, the local police had not made any arrangements for transporting him to Shillong that night. "I am sorry, but I must be in Shillong tonight. Prisons are generally broken on such stormy nights," Kranti told SP Biswas, the local Supt. Police who was apologetic that he could not work out the logistics.

"Look at the storm. And it is Christmas tonight."

"I have a job to do. I'll not rest till I sight my man. If you can arrange for a driver, I'll be grateful."

"It's a sleepy town." Biswas drawled. "No one would obey me tonight. Tomorrow, I'll personally escort you to Shillong. We can leave early, say sevenish."

Irritated, Kranti asked, "Can I get a vehicle?"

"Oh, sure," Biswas said sheepishly. "But you are not familiar with this part of the country. It can be quite dangerous; you are taking too much of a risk."

"I'm known for that."

Snubbed, Biswas felt insulted.

"It's your life," he said.

Kranti drove off on the unfamiliar roads where hostile attacks by rebels on government vehicles were a common occurrence, though he had taken the precaution of taking a private car. The weather grew worse. Kranti was at his best in such hostile conditions. Humming a tune, he crossed the checkpoint, and was a little surprised that no one was on duty. He made a mental note of briefing Biswas on the subject. After about two or three hours, while taking a blind turn he heard piercing shrieks of a woman. He pulled over, explored the place, and found that the piercing screams were emanating from the ground floor of a PWD guest house. He rushed inside and saw half a dozen men surrounding a naked girl.

Perhaps, the girl was semi -conscious; he was not sure whether she had been raped or not.

He warned the men to run away. One of them, who appeared to be their leader, continued to assault the girl, and Kranti had to open fire. The leader was hit on the leg, and all of them ran away. He lighted the fire, untied the girl, massaged her arms and legs infusing some life into the cold limbs, and was about to help her to dress up when he heard loud noise outside. He realized that the gun shots had alerted the locals, and they had rushed to ascertain the reason for the shoot out. Suddenly, it dawned on him that without a uniform, the circumstantial evidence of a naked girl in such lonely surroundings could go against him. He could be declared a criminal for assaulting the girl. No one was going to believe that he had saved the girl from the rapists, and he would be beaten up or even lynched before he could convince them of his bona fides. Kranti beat a hasty retreat and drove away.

He reached the jail and was shocked at the feverish activity on the campus. Billa had bribed the guard on duty, and with help of other accomplices, shot down the deputy jailer and escaped. "I feared it," he muttered, and blamed himself (for wasting time in helping the girl) when he learnt that the escape had taken place only an hour before his arrival. Taking charge of the operations, he was able to arrest Billa in the next 48 hours after a daring shoot out. A bullet had injured his arm. For his valour and commitment, he was awarded the Police medal.

"I believe she is the same girl." Kranti concluded.

"I wish you had told me about it," Prema said. "But it does not explain why she screamed and called you a devil."

"Either my presence reminded her of that horrible night, or she considers I am one of men who raped her."

Prema assured him that she would clarify the position to the girl.

"What is the need to explain? Let her think whatever she wants."

"Come on, Kranti! More than two dozen guests of Kavita's consider you a devil. I must tell them the truth that you actually saved and protected her."

"I don't know whether I was able to save her or not. Maybe, I had reached late and all of them might have had her." He looked gravely at her. "And it is possible that she may be thinking that I am also one of them."

"How can you be one of them?"

"Perceptions of a girl in such a condition can be very unstable."

"You have saved and protected her, why should you have such negative thoughts? I'll talk to the girl and explain."

Kranti was emphatic that she should not pursue it with Julian though Prema was insistent that she would do it — after all it was a question of her husband's honour. Kranti's attitude did not fit in with his aggressive nature; it irritated her till the early hours of morning, and she could not sleep.

Prema had lost her mother on the threshold of adolescence; it was her father with whom she shared the pains of growing up. In his spare time, he was a naturalist, a photographer who explored the wild. Religiously, he took a month off every year to pursue his passion. Some of his articles and photographs on the mating habits of the big cats had made it to the National Geographic. Before marriage, she often accompanied him on his adventures.

When she was married for a couple of years, he had, in a philosophical mood, once confided to her that in nature, sex and creativity were always accompanied by violence. "The hallmark of refinement of culture evolved by man is that in a man- woman relationship, love should replace violence in sex. That's the only thing that distinguishes a man from an animal," he had said. It made a deep impression on her. Invariably, she judged her husband by those norms. Kranti was so tender and considerate while copulating that once she had whispered, "You get ten out of ten."

How could such a man be a devil for an unknown woman?

Kranti was in a much worse state. He had turned his head towards the wall and closed his eyes.

Kranti and Julian were both shocked at recognising each other at the party. However, Kranti was able to identify her first. Julian was the centre of attention of the entire group as she had lighted the candles, whereas Kranti was hidden in the outlying shadows. If he had not made the mistake of breaking through the group and standing in the forefront, she would not have even noticed him. Once she saw him, she was seized by terror. When she had pointed her finger and called him a devil, his feet had grown numb and were rooted to the ground. How could she be at Amit's place? He was bewildered.

Was she an agent of Kali, the destroyer? He wondered and was frightened of the wrath of the Goddess. He realized he was perspiring even with the air conditioner on. The fear haunted him throughout the night.

(4)

Next morning, before leaving for office, Kavita asked Julian, "Why did you scream on seeing Kranti?"

"Ma'am, I am sorry for my behaviour."
"That's not a reply to my question." Kavita was annoyed. "You have been here for more than a year, and you have seen him a number of times, but you never reacted in such a way."
Not getting any response, Kavita shouted at her, "I want the truth."
Julian's lips quivered.
"Amit and Kranti are very good childhood friends, but this is one side of Kranti of which we both are ignorant."
"Ma'am, you both are very fond of him and if I tell the truth, you will not believe me."
"You are right, but if Kranti has wronged you, I should know."
Julian told her entire story.
"But Kranti was never posted to north-east," Kavita muttered.
"I don't know, ma'am, but when I saw his taut face and intense expression in the candlelight, the conditions were almost identical as on that night at Nongpoh. And he was wearing the same red T shirt and black trousers. He looked as devilish as on that night at Nongpoh."
To Kavita, Kranti had not looked devilish the previous night; on the contrary, he had appeared dashing and handsome. But the girl had no reason to tell a lie.
"I know you don't believe me," Julian said.
"Amit has known him since school days, and I know him for the last thirteen years. Kranti may sometimes flirt with fair women, but I can't imagine him forcing himself on anyone." Kavita said more to herself than the maid. "At Nongpoh, there was no light, and it was dark. Perhaps, you were semi- conscious. Could it be that you

were mistaken, and it was Joe or one of his men instead of Kranti?"

"No, I am not mistaken. And I was not semi-conscious."

Julian looked at the disturbed face of her mistress, and added, "If you think my presence is going to disrupt your relationship with Mr. Chopra, I will leave. Now, I know a few people, and will be able to find another job."

Kavita hastened to assure her that she didn't want her to quit. She was grim. She had implicitly trusted Kranti, and four of them had played cards on some weekends in her bedroom. How could she have faith in a rapist?

"Ma'am, you are unnecessarily worried about me. Supposing, Mr. Chopra had not arrived, then I would have been raped by Joe and his men at that very time instead of four months later. And then how many men had me in those six years at the brothel? Does it really matter, who was the first or the second? The only thing that has upset me is that Mr. Chopra is a police officer and is supposed to protect women in trouble and not rape them." Julian had tears in her eyes. "Ma'am, I am sorry for my overreaction in the party."

"I am upset, there is no doubt about it," Kavita said. "And I am more worried about Prema. If she gets wind of it, she is going to divorce him and wreck her home. Promise me that you will not tell her."

"Ma'am, I promise. I would not like to break up a happy home."

On hearing Julian's story from Kavita, Amit was enraged. "How can she talk like this about my childhood friend? I don't believe her story, it's all bull shit."

Kavita tried to argue from Julian's viewpoint, and Amit shouted, "Tell her to change her opinion about my friend

otherwise I'll throw her out of the house."
"Is it because the truth is so chilling that you can't stand it?"
"How can you believe a prostitute and not believe Kranti? We are almost like brothers. No, even more than brothers! I can depend on him much more than Prakash. And you are aware of the number of times he has come to our rescue."
"No woman will tell a lie in such matters."
Infuriated at such a preposterous suggestion, he said, "My honest opinion is that she would have tried to seduce Kranti rather than the other way round."
"You men!"
"Look at her background - her mother ran away with her lover, the father committed suicide - and look at Kranti's antecedents. His father, a retired Cabinet Secretary and now Chairman, UPSC, and brother a world-famous scientist! How can you compare Kranti and Julian?"
"But in this case, I am with Julian."
"You, who would swear by Kranti earlier," Amit said, and laughed. "One incident has shaken the foundation of your friendship."
"Yes, it has. Violation of the dignity of a woman is not a laughing matter. Don't break the relationship but turn a little lukewarm; he will understand."
When Amit continued to argue, Kavita was annoyed. "I want to discourage his entry in my house. You should appreciate that Radhika is eleven, turning twelve. She is not a babe now."
"Kavita!"
"Don't raise your voice. You too have some duty as a father."

"You are getting insane. I have told you a few times that half the girls in our class in school were crazy about him. He didn't need to hunt them."

"You should also remember that there is a difference between a student and a man in his mid - thirties."

For an instant he was subdued and then asked, "There was no power and it was dark. How could she have recognised Kranti?"

"She is certain that it was Kranti."

Both the husband and wife continued to argue and had an unpleasant night.

V

Crisis Deepens

Burdened with the thought that her husband was a criminal, Madhulika had sleepless nights. She lay awake staring at the ceiling wondering how she could have fallen in love with such a man. His very proximity disturbed her equipoise. She had to remind herself repeatedly that he was her husband, and like a good wife, she should be standing by his side. But it was not easy. Despite her best intentions, she found herself indulging in some argument with him in the evening even over a non- issue like the weather as it gave her an alibi to escape to another room. Whenever forced to share the bed, she moved so close to the wall that she could smell the new paint.

An ominous ring in the early hours of the morning jolted Vinay and Madhulika from their sleep; after a bitter quarrel they had slept in separate rooms at night and met at the door. It was past six in the morning, and it was still dark because of the grey clouds hovering in the sky.

"Who could it be?" Madhulika asked.

Vaguely, he shook his head, and opened the door.

Both were dazed to see Deepak, Kranti, and Vaishali. Unannounced visit of the in-laws at such an odd hour meant trouble.

"Papa, is something wrong?" Madhulika asked.

Deepak nodded and inquired if she had seen the morning paper.

"No, we just got up."

Deepak handed a copy of the newspaper to Madhulika. (Deepak and Vaishali knew that Vinay did not switch on the news channel on TV.)

'Prof. Vinay Chopra, world renowned physicist, charged with stealing the work of his beloved' the dark lettered headlines splashed. There was a big write up with photographs of Vinay, Stella and Jean Simpson.

Vinay and Madhulika froze.

Madhulika was about to intervene with 'It is true papa,' when she decided to let Vinay handle the situation. Both scanned the paper hurriedly.

Jean Simpson was one of the invitees at the All India Science Congress at Kolkata; she had managed the invitation through US ambassador. Just before the address by the Vice President of India, the chief guest, she had sought permission to say a few words, and charged Vinay with stealing Stella's research work. Jean was so convincing that some of the scientists believed her. However, patriotic fervour took over, and many leading scientists challenged her to produce evidence. The situation could have taken an ugly turn but for the intervention of the Vice President who snubbed Jean Simpson for using the Science Congress forum for settling personal scores. "This is not the proper place for settling personal disputes. We have laws, rules and well-established procedures in our country. For getting justice, legal agencies should be moved," he said. The US ambassador was also annoyed at being exploited by Jean Simpson.

"It appears that both of you were prepared for it," Deepak said.

Vinay told him how Jean had met and threatened him.

Vaishali looked at the discomposed face of her eldest son, felt something was amiss, and asked, "But why should she do so?"

Lucidly, Vinay told them the story without any mention about stealing the research work. "I had sent Jean the original thesis. If I had such plans, I would not have sent her the thesis."

Kranti thought over the matter deeply, and said, "Right."

"Jean's argument could be that you just forgot about it." Deepak remarked.

"Beta, is there something you are hiding?" Vaishali asked.

"Nothing ma,"

"Then you have nothing to worry about; we will face it." Vaishali placed her arm affectionately around his neck. "Our house had the reputation of facing many storms." She looked meaningfully at her husband. "In my youth, I used to say that we Chopras have the knack for being where the storm is."

Though the chips were down, they all smiled cheerfully to shrug off the descending gloom.

Vaishali added a word of caution. "But your papa was always upright, honest and well intentioned. The worst of politicians could not harm him. You are his son. No harm will come to you if you have maintained the same standards of integrity."

"Of course, ma," Kranti said with sheer confidence in the family pride. "How could it be otherwise?"

At the breakfast table, Kranti looked at his brother and said, "If any help is required to fix this Jean woman, it is my area."

"Actually, we were thinking of it," Madhulika said out of turn, and Vinay stared at her.

"No," Deepak said sternly. "I don't trust a cop's reaction in such matters. We will sue that woman for defamation."

Vinay fidgeted uneasily, Madhulika shook her head.

"We will consult Rangaswami." Deepak announced.

P P Rangaswami was the former Additional Solicitor General of India, who had taken up private practice again.

"I'll think about it," Vinay said.

"Think!" Deepak was irritated. "It's a question of family honour. We must react fast."

"Sleep over it for a day." Vaishali advised. She had not missed the exchange of furtive glances between the couple.

Deepak and Kranti didn't agree.

"Mama is right." Madhulika interrupted.

Deepak declared that he would arrange a meeting the very next day.

"Let Vinay decide," Vaishali said concluding the discussion.

On the return journey, Vaishali confided her fears. "Vinay is not straight forward, there is something he is hiding."

Kranti nodded his head vigorously. "Perhaps, I may have

to use some of my unconventional methods."

Wary of the cop's attitude, Deepak put down his foot. "No. If you slip up, Vinay had it. Jean is not a shady character of the kind you deal with; she is a world-famous oncologist."

He pondered over Vinay's prospects of being the Deputy Scientific Adviser. A little aspersion could ruin his chances, and this was downright cheating. "Vinay has to come out clean without any blemish otherwise his future is ruined."

"I am worried." Vaishali was grim.

"Oh, come on ma! He is your son. You don't have to worry."

"Your ma trusts no one. She didn't even spare me." Deepak smiled wryly.

"You – papa?" Kranti slowed down the car. "I don't believe it."

Deepak nodded.

Kranti, who had attended a Management Development Program in the National Academy of Administration, Mussoorie the previous year, said, "Do you know that in the Academy, whenever they had to give an example of a bureaucrat of high integrity they talked of papa. 'No one can be more honest than Deepak Chopra' was the general feeling. And you doubted him, ma."

"Yes, beta," Vaishali answered sheepishly. "My misfortune."

Unable to accept the irrationality, Kranti shook his head with disgust. "How can anyone be so unreasonable?"

"My womanly intuition was wrong, and I am very happy that I was wrong," Vaishali added.

"But you were very cruel to papa."

"Yes, I was," she replied softly. "But I paid a very heavy price for it."

"If Prema were to do such a thing, I would never forgive her." Kranti spoke passionately. "I would have thrown her out of the house."

"Kranti! Careful!!" Deepak placed his hand on his shoulder. Kranti expertly avoided a two-wheeler coming from the wrong side and swore at him. Apologising to his mother, he asked, "Do you think Vinay is hiding something?"

"I am sure."

(2)

Last week Madhulika and Vinay had shifted to the new house earmarked for the Dean, Faculty of Sciences, and Madhulika intended to unpack and arrange the house over the weekend. She was also contemplating to buying some additional furniture as the new bungalow was more spacious compared to the old accommodation. It had an unusually large drawing and dining room, four bedrooms— one on the ground floor and three on the first floor— a study, a common room and a servant quarter. But after the in-laws' visit, she was upset by the new development engineered by Jean Simpson.

"This house is jinxed," she muttered, and looked worriedly at her husband.

The day the allotment letter of the house was received, it had brought trouble in the shape of Jean Simpson.

"What do we do now?" she asked.

"I don't know." Vinay shuddered and sank on the sofa. "Everything is lost, Madhu."

"Vinay, we will fight it. Together."

Vinay looked through the windowpane and observed some people with cameras moving towards the main gate. Madhulika caught the anxiety in Vinay's eyes and followed the gaze. "It's the reporters," she whispered. "Run up stairs - I'll handle them."

Vinay didn't need to be told a second time. With long rapid strides, he escaped to the first floor, and hid himself.

On glancing outside, she noticed that the number of reporters had swelled. Sprucing herself, she tightened the belt of the soft blue gown marked with prominent splashes of water. By the time the bell rang, she was ready to receive them and went across to the door, and flung it open with a large scowl.

"What's it?" she asked hoarsely.

A hush descended on the murmuring group of two dozen reporters, mostly male, as they felt guilty for invading the privacy of the mistress of the house engaged in her daily chores.

"Could we talk to Prof. Vinay Chopra?" A youngish looking female reporter asked.

"He is not at home," Madhulika answered.

"Where is he, ma'am?"

"He had a meeting with the VC, Delhi University?"

"I am sure it was cancelled, ma'am."

"But Vinay left early."

"Oh!"

The woman's remark hung in the air. There was an uneasy shuffling of feet. Some believed Madhulika, a larger number didn't, but they were clueless how to get past the lady. The formidable way she had placed her hands on both sides of the door guarding it, dissuaded those who might have considered making a forced entry in the house. Madhulika could hear the hushed voices, "She is lying," rise above "Maybe, she is speaking the truth," Her churning brain visualized that they could waylay her husband anywhere in the campus, and then perhaps she might not be there to help him out. Home was a familiar turf, and it would be easier for Vinay and her to handle them. But they needed time to plan their strategy. She saw the mounting anger in some of them as they retraced their steps towards the vans. She beckoned the woman who had spoken to her.

"You could try in the evening, say fivish."

The woman smiled and thanked her. It established Madhulika's credibility. They all waved to her as the vans passed her house.

To her horror, Madhulika found Vinay trembling inside the large cabinet.

"It's all right Vinay," she said. "They have gone and will be back in the evening at five."

The whole afternoon was spent in developing a strategy acceptable to Vinay.

Instead of five in the evening, they trooped in at about six when it was twilight; the drizzle had just started and ushered in a slight chill. The number of journalists had swelled to almost three dozen including a few foreigners, and Madhulika playing an eager, warm hostess ran out of chairs, and stools. "It's all right ma'am," a young man said rescuing her from embarrassment. "We are used to standing." Madhulika opened the bottles of drinks and offered hot coffee to those who had refused alcohol.

When all of them were comfortably settled, Vinay walked in gracefully from the study without betraying any signs of having suffered an emotional upheaval in the last 2-3 hours. Faced with an overconfident world-famous physicist who was an authority in his field, the reporters were awed by his depth of knowledge. He told them the whole story so convincingly that there was no room for any doubt. When they questioned his relationship with Stella, he did not deviate from his "no comments" stand. One of the two American reporters was scathing. "If you were in America, you would have been behind the bars by now."

Despite the provocation, Vinay was sang-froid — something he had borrowed temporarily from his father — and hinted in reply to another journalist that he might sue Jean Simpson in a court of law for defamation.

The drizzle turned into torrents. Madhulika served them hot potato rolls, and small samosas. The scripted act was professionally so well executed by Vinay that in less than an hour, the journalists left the house thanking Madhulika for being a thoughtful hostess in such inclement weather. The only exception was the duo of American lady journalists who continued to frown till they were picked up by their chauffeur driven car.

Madhulika heaved a sigh of relief and was rather pleased with the press conference. But Vinay collapsed after a scintillating performance.

"Vinay," she screamed. "What happened?"

"I can't take it anymore," he muttered. "I have been lying for the last so many years that I just can't carry on with this burden anymore."

"But you have no choice, you have to play on."

"How long?"

"Till the storm is over."

But the thought that she was defending a criminal disturbed her.

Deepak Chopra was also not spared by reporters both at office, and home. Like a seasoned war veteran, he faced them with a stoic smile, and only said, "No comments, please." Vaishali was more offensive and told the security man to call the police if the reporters turned up again.

(3)

Lanky and fair, P P Rangaswami, rose and hugged Vinay affectionately when he called upon him at his residence. With a broad grin, he said, "It appears Deepak has forced you to see me." Rangaswami had a soft spot for Vinay as his only daughter had a crush on him when Vinay was in college though Vinay was unaware of it.

Deepak had wanted to accompany Vinay, Vaishali put her foot down pointing out that he should respect the confidentiality between the counsel and his client.

P P Rangaswami owed a lot to Deepak Chopra. As a rare friendly gesture, Deepak had helped Rangaswami to become the Additional Solicitor General of India by putting in a word to the PM, whereas the then Law Minister was interested in someone from his own constituency.

"Tell me what I can do for you." Rangaswami smiled affably. "I have one request. You may hide many things from your wife, father or even mother, but don't hide anything from your counsel. It may not only harm you, but it can also ruin you."

Sipping the hot cup of coffee, Vinay took a long time to consider this advice. He finished the coffee slowly, placed the empty cup on the side-table, and looked at his counsel.

"Yes, Vinay."

Vinay hid nothing.

"I am glad you had the courage to speak the truth for I am sure you have not told your secret to your parents."

"How could I? They will not be able to take it."

"Let me give a thought to your problem." Rangaswami was unusually gentle. "But do you know what Deepak would recommend?"

Vinay looked blankly at him.

"He would advise you to go to the press and admit everything."

"But uncle, how can I?"

"I know you can't. Deepak has tons of moral courage. He is like a solid mountain."

"But mountains also explode when there are volcanic eruptions."

Appreciating that Vinay had not liked the comparison, he added, "I have nothing for or against the mountains. We are all made different. What is good for Deepak may be poison for you?"

Vinay nodded.

"Give me three or four days. I'll call you or drive down to your place."

Again, he asked, "Does Madhu know?"

"Yes."

"That's good. Carrying such a heavy burden on one's conscience can be dangerous."

Deeply worried about her husband's appointment with the counsel, Madhulika paced up and down in the lounge. When she saw Vinay's car, she unbolted the door, ran up to him, and inquired what Rangaswami had told him. He gave her the broad picture.

"Did you tell him everything?"

Throwing the coat on the chair, he said angrily, "Yes, everything including my love affair with both the sisters."

"Cool down, Vinay." She pleaded.

"How will I face everyone?" His tone was contrite.

"We will do it together."

I I T was closed for a four- day Diwali break, and the couple had taken another three days off and made reservations at a hotel in Goa for a week. After the scandal made the headlines in the dailies, Vinay cancelled the bookings. Putting up a brave face before the neighbours, colleagues and friends who visited them for exchanging Diwali greetings was not easy. The atmosphere had grown so vicious that the couple felt that an escape to any remote place on the planet would have been better.

Diwali festivities were muted both at the Akbar Road bungalow and the couples' new residence on campus. However, candles had to be lit as in the past to avoid malicious gossip and maintain the façade of continuity and normalcy in life. While lighting the candles at the back of the house, Vinay muttered, "Why do we have to do it?" His hand quivered, and he threw away the candle. "It has to be done," Madhulika said sombrely, and lighted the rest of the candles, fully aware that all the lights of Delhi would not be able to dispel the darkness from his life.

(4)

In the last few days, Madhulika had undergone a radical transformation; her sole objective was to protect her husband. She cosseted him to such an extent that Vinay became wholly dependent on her for all his needs. Nestling close to him, she asked, "The Kranti angle, did you explore it?"

He explained that he had met him yesterday in his office. Vinay and Kranti had discussed the option of bringing up a trumped charge of smuggling narcotics against Jean or roping her in as a secondary offender. On learning the details, Madhulika grimaced, and shook her head. "It will not do. Jean is a world-famous oncologist and knows the ambassador personally."

Vinay shifted uneasily.

Madhulika was quiet for a long time, and then asked, "What else was discussed?"

"The permanent solution," he whispered.

"Oh!"

She looked thoughtfully at her husband wondering to what extent he could go to protect himself.

"But it has a snag. Any accident to her now would throw doubts on me. If we had done something before the Science Congress, the risk would have been the least."

He asked her to fix a large drink. She was aware he was overdoing it, but she obeyed without comment.

Young couples faced with a new crisis in life often go through the same issues repeatedly (in search for a solution) making sure that every angle is considered. A small ray of hope from an unknown corner lights up their sad faces. When Madhulika again mentioned about ascertaining the sanity of the Chinese professor and having a conference at Beijing, Vinay said in exasperation, "Do you really think that any of the things we have discussed is really workable?"

She shook her head. The lurking tears in the corner of his eyes moved her. "Vinay," she murmured, "it will pass."

"It is ironic that Stella had spoken the same words about 10-11 years back. And the dark clouds passed momentarily, but today I am in the thick of a storm. From here, where do I go? Jail or death."

"Please don't talk like this, Vinay."

Whispering words of love, she lulled him to sleep. Madhulika realized late in the night as he snored next to her, that her mother-in-law was right when she had confided in her that Vinay was the weakest of all her children. Kanupriya had emerged more matured after the crisis in her life and Vivek was planning to get married without any resources of his own; he was entirely dependent on Vaishali and government funding. He did not consider his penniless existence as a hindrance in his forthcoming marriage. And of course, Kranti was a symbol of confidence and pride.

Next day in the afternoon, Madhulika forced Vinay to accompany her to the Hanuman Temple adjacent to Rivoli in C P. There were very few devotees at that hour, even the temple pujari was absent. Both were not religious, still, they folded their hands, and prayed. "I have sinned," he said slowly. "Forgive me god."

Madhulika was louder. "We have sinned, forgive us Lord. Be merciful, be merciful."

(5)

At dinner, when Prema told Vivek of Vinay's expose` by Jean Simpson, his spontaneous reaction was that he expected something of this kind. "Vinay has a phenomenal memory. All his life he has been mugging up his notes; how can he discover the Vinay particle?"

"But he was rated as the genius of the decade at Cornell," Prema said doubting Vivek.

"Genius, my foot!" Vivek laughed.

Unable to stand Vivek's laughter and sarcasm, Vaishali glared at him. Abruptly, the laughter ceased.

"Who gives you the right to run down your elder brother?" she said. Vivek did not respond to his mother and looked uneasily at the plate.

"Especially, when he is down," Vaishali added. "Of all my children, he was the best in academics. You barely managed a first class in Honours whereas he topped in the university."

Deepak tried to pacify her.

"Let me finish," she said. "This is the hour when he needs us, and we all should support him. Am I clear? And no snide comments otherwise I'll spare no one."

The veiled threat did not escape Vivek; she could stop his monthly stipend.

Later, when Vivek showed surprise at mama's overreaction, Prema said, "Ma is always like this. The only difference is that she is defending Vinay for the first time, generally she is doing it for you."

"Me!" Vivek was surprised. "Holy Saints! I can't believe it."

She nodded and smiled.

(6)

Immediately after Diwali, Vinay was reluctant to take classes, and wanted to proceed on long leave.

"No, Vinay, no," Madhulika said. She told him to lead a normal life as if nothing unusual had happened. If he went on leave, it would give an opportunity to his enemies to wag their tongues.

Convinced, Vinay took the classes, smiled at his colleagues, and talked of the weather, the movies, and politics. He put up a brave front before reporters of The Hindustan Times and Times of India with 'no comments.' He feared being summoned by the Director, who was away to the US. However, in the evening Vinay broke down. "How long will I continue with this pretence?"

"Till we last," she said.

Vinay could not get any sleep for three-four days despite a heavy dose of sleeping pills.

Unannounced, one afternoon, Rangaswami called on Vinay. Madhulika was alone at home.

"How is he taking it?" He inquired.

"He is not well."

He shook his head with empathy. "I am not surprised for basically Vinay is a decent human being."

Vinay entered cheerfully and stopped short on seeing the counsel. His smile disappeared, and he mumbled, "Hello, uncle."

Handing over a folder to his wife, Vinay looked tentatively at his papa's friend, and said, "Yes, uncle."

Madhulika left the room saying she would get some coffee.

Rangaswami apologized for the delay, looked at the elegantly dressed professor, and added, "I have given lot of thought to this but considering the delicate situation, I have not consulted anyone. A defamation lawsuit is not prudent when you are on a weak wicket. It can backfire. Some very clever clients have done it in the past and got away. But they were unknown in comparison to you. The Vinay particle has given you the status of a celebrity.

Your stakes are very high. My advice, therefore, is to ignore barking dogs and bitches. Jealous men have not spared even Shakespeare and doubted that Marlowe or someone else had written his plays. But Shakespeare is still at the top in literature. So are you in your field. Treat Jean's outburst as a small perturbation in your long life as a scientist. Suing for defamation in a court of law is too risky. It will force the US Government to back Jean

Simpson. If it turns into a dispute between the two nations about the rights to the Vinay particle, you will be doomed. The Americans will dig out everything through FBI. And the FBI is not like our CBI; it is ruthlessly efficient. Then no one will be able to protect you."

Madhulika brought coffee and snacks and left though Rangaswami was keen that she should be present. He felt a little uncomfortable in Vinay's company. He appreciated the coffee, and carefully took half of a creamy biscuit.

"Consider Jean Simpson's denunciation at the Science Congress as the hysterics of a frustrated woman who had lost both her sisters in a car accident, and her sibling love coloured her better judgement."

Rangaswami patted him on his shoulder, and added, "I know it is not easy to sit quietly and accept all the denunciations being hurled by Jean. The urge to react is very strong. But lie low and act as if nothing has happened."

Rangaswami talked to him for another fifteen minutes, and then left thanking the hostess for an excellent cup of coffee.

Vinay briefed Madhulika about the discussion.

"The old man is solid. We should follow his advice." She voiced her opinion. Vinay agreed whole heartedly, and said, "Today, I was relieved that all the faculty members backed me to the hilt. 'This woman should be taught a lesson' was the consensus."

Aware that the faculty members didn't know the truth, she kept quiet.

Kranti called at night, and Vinay told him that Rangaswami was against filing the defamation suit.

"The old man is too cautious and with age is turning

nutty. Consult a younger counsel; I'll introduce you to someone."
"No, no, Kranti. His advice is sound. And papa trusts him implicitly."
"Papa is also past his prime, he is no longer young."
"I'll think about it," Vinay answered. It was pointless to argue with him. "But don't consult anyone," he added sternly.
It dampened Kranti's enthusiasm; he didn't persist, though.

(7)

Madhulika pulled out all the stops to control the situation, but Vinay continued to withdraw into his own shell, and grew unbearably reticent. Except for the use of monosyllables, he refused to talk to her, and depended heavily on body language. Slowly, his basic needs of hunger, thirst and even love were drying up. Helplessly, she watched him slipping into a slough down. Earlier, she could not forget that he was a criminal who had planned the theft and deserved what he was getting for cheating his lover, but now she felt otherwise. The slow disintegration of the façade (he had been projecting over the last 8 -9 years) was pathetic, and she was aware of the agony and the tribulations he was undergoing. It had moved her, and aroused empathy in her. Over the last few weeks, she also realized that her future was interwoven with his. If he went down, so would she. Right or wrong, she had to rebuild his psyche, and restore his confidence.

After the press conference, stories and news items kept on appearing in the print media periodically making the couple nervous when they opened the paper in the morning. Fortunately, the electronic media was not so active in those days. The journalists did not spare Deepak, Kranti and Vivek and reported on their activities making them miserable. Jean Simpson missed no opportunity to give interviews to the press wherever she was invited. A crusader for her sister, she went all over India defaming Vinay and his family members.

Whenever Madhulika approached small groups of women in the I I T campus, she felt that conversation abruptly ceased or turned into hushed whispers. It was the same unpleasant feeling of unease she had experienced at Ithaca. At parties or gatherings or even when she was amongst a smaller group, she got the vibes of being unwelcome. Subtly, the topic was changed, or they praised Vinay when it was not called for, and she had to smile at them stupidly. At Ithaca she had the feeling that she had usurped the place of Stella who was one of them, and therefore they didn't approve of Madhulika's presence by Vinay's side. Now in retrospect, she felt that maybe many of them suspected Vinay's credentials, and believed he was incapable of such a breakthrough in physics. Now, the same situation was replicated on the I I T campus.

Sleeping in separate bedrooms was initiated by Madhulika whenever she got disgusted with him. Now, immediately after dinner he hastened to his room, and locked it isolating her from his world for the night. 'I am getting a taste of my own medicine,' she reflected.

Madhulika introspected that the change in him was triggered by the appearance of Jean Simpson in their lives, but the climacteric was something of recent origin that she could not identify. Till the press conference, he had managed quite well; something had cropped up after

Diwali break that had jolted him and sent him into a hole of depression. She had to find out the reason.

In the evening she visited the library to make inquiries with some student of Vinay known to her. Just outside the library, she spotted Nikhil, a second-year student of electrical engineering who had escorted her on the fresher's party. She waved vigorously, and he ran up to her saying, "Good evening, ma'am."

"I have not seen you for weeks, Nikhil. And how is your mom?"

Nikhil's mother taught History at Lady Sri Ram College. He talked of his mother at length, and Madhulika inquired unobtrusively if anything untoward had happened in Vinay's class recently. The boy's smile disappeared, and he clammed up.

"Something did happen," she said, and fondled his hair. "It's important to me."

The boy shifted from one foot to the other and avoided eye contact.

"Please, Nikhil."

Slowly, the boy narrated the details. About two-three weeks back when Vinay, in his usual cheerful manner had asked whether they had any doubts in 'Thermodynamics', Jaganathan, a brilliant student had said, "Thermodynamics is all right, sir, but there are doubts in other areas."

"Ask me, I'll clarify to the extent I can."

"You are the only one who can, sir."

It was not the first time that the students had reposed their faith in his abilities and Vinay, with his usual cocksureness, encouraged him. "Yes, Jaganathan."

"There are lot of stories circulating in the corridors

of science block about your research. We want a clarification."
There was a death like silence.
"Instead of asking others, I thought it best to approach you directly. I hope you don't mind, sir."
"On the contrary," Vinay said, and had walked over to him with a rich smile on his face. "I am glad you asked me."
With supreme confidence, he explained the facts which he had rehearsed more than a dozen times in the recent past.
"But why is Jean Simpson asking for your blood?"
Suddenly, Vinay was bombarded by a volley of questions. Earlier, he was dealing with sober adults, now he felt he was thrown amongst a pack of wolves. Brilliant teenagers, full of certitude, and indulging in one-upmanship questioned him straight from the shoulder. Vinay found his hold over the situation slipping.
"Physics is full of marvellous discoveries. Even we have produced Bose, Raman and Chandershekhar. But no one has questioned their bona fides." Satish Malohtra, the topper of Joint I I T Entrance Examination and known to be a quiet, sober student was full of fire. "Such a thing has happened only in your case, sir." He looked directly into his eyes. "But why?"
His hands turning a little clammy, Vinay defended himself with aplomb pointing out that there was never a dearth of doubting Thomas's in the world. "Some have doubted even Shakespeare."
"But not after only 7-8 years," said a boy whom Vinay had noticed for the first time.
About to counter, Vinay saw a young girl raise her hand,

and without waiting for his permission, said, "Very little is known of Shakespeare, sir, but we know so much about you."

It occurred to him that she was the one whom he had seen in Nirula's after meeting Jean Simpson at Taj Mansingh.

"Shakespeare is dead and gone more than four hundred years ago but you are living amongst us."

"It is my bad luck." Vinay smiled bravely.

"It is our misfortune," Malohtra said.

"And a calamity for this prestigious Institute!" added Shalini, the most vociferous student of the class giving it the final punch.

The whole class burst into a fit of laughter, and Vinay watched them helplessly.

At the beginning of the session in July, Vinay had ridiculed a boy by telling him of Disraeli's cryptic comment on Gladstone highlighting the difference between misfortune and calamity, and Shalini had paid it back on behalf of the class.

Abruptly, Vinay left the classroom.

"Thanks, Nikhil." Madhulika shook the hand of the boy affectionately. "You have been a big help."

Walking back home, she realized it was serious. She was so lost in her thoughts that she had crossed her home, reached the boundary wall of the campus, and could see the mad rush of vehicles at the peak hour on Aurbindo Marg. It was not surprising that Vinay, known to be an excellent teacher, had reacted adversely after such an incident. His fears of reaching the dead end of life were proving true.

(8)

On return from college, Madhulika saw Sabina, and

stopped the car. Sabina and her husband, Prof. S.R. Azad, the Head of Chemical Engineering Department had been away to the US for three months. Madhulika warmly embraced her and felt slightly cheerful. Exhausted from fighting storm after storm in her daily life, she tried to seek solace and joy in the most mundane things of life.

"My dear, I have been hearing terrible rumours about your husband," Sabina said. "I hope they are wrong."

Madhulika dismissed them with a smile, and briefly explained the background.

"But men can be very cruel especially those who are jealous," she said.

Madhulika asked her to clarify.

"Last Tuesday, Prof. Misra of the Physics Department retired. During his farewell address he made some derogatory remarks about Vinay."

Madhulika frowned. "What did he say?"

"Misra pointed out that the world was changing too fast for him, and men of his generation could not adjust in such an alien environment. Earlier, the faculty of our prestigious institute had luminaries of which any university in the world could have been proud of. Now, its chairs of Professors and Deans were occupied by cheats and thugs. He said, 'I am glad I am retiring. I wish all the thieves, the best of luck.' The gathering clapped and Vinay left the party."

"But how do you know?"

"My husband was also invited."

Madhulika could not face the woman and wanted to escape.

"I am sorry for Vinay. Hostility against him is increasing. I heard a rumour that once the Director comes back, the faculty members are going to present a memorandum to him to have a thorough inquiry conducted so that the fair name of the institute is not tarnished. Some want inquiry conducted by CBI."

"I'm glad you told me."

"You need all the courage, dear."

Madhulika nodded and thanked her friend. She was certain that the whole institute was talking only of the Vinay scandal.

Vinay admitted to the two incidents told by Sabina and Nikhil. Madhulika was furious with him for not confiding in her, though later she appreciated that sharing one's humiliation with one's spouse time and again was not easy.

"I know I have to continue suffering till I die," he said solemnly. "But it may not be too long."

Madhulika had heard that sex therapy was the best in such extreme cases, and she lay nude beside her husband. However, Vinay was past the stage of reacting.

"Vinay," she whispered endearingly, "God will forgive us."

"I don't know."

It came to her as a shock that in the hour of crisis, Vinay felt alone. He had no interest in anything; her existence didn't count.

The next few days were hard on her. Despite her protestation, Vinay refused to take any class. He locked himself in the room, and behaved like a recluse, as if heading towards slow death. Without raising another finger, Jean Simpson was going to achieve her ambition of annihilating her enemy.

"I'll not allow this," Madhulika said to herself aloud in her room. "I'll fight the gods if I have to."

It was not love, but a commitment to her home, her family, a commitment to fight Jean Simpson. She needed her husband. Vinay had to survive this crisis: he had to live.

Withdrawing all her savings, and taking some advance from her provident fund, Madhulika purchased a piano.

"How do you like it?" she asked.

"Like what?"

She pointed towards the piano.

"It is nice. Have you started taking classes in music?"

"No, I got it for you."

"But I don't know anything about music."

"Music was your first love."

"No, I dislike music," he said.

Madhulika was in tears. She realized that she could not handle Vinay and needed help.

Madhulika consulted Dr. A. Varmani, one of the well-known psychiatrists in the capital, and briefed him about her husband's condition. She wanted to know why he had stopped interacting with her. Dr Varmani was sympathetic, but blunt. "Is he innocent?"

She hesitated.

"Whatever you tell me is strictly confidential and will not be leaked to the press or anybody."

It was not her secret but his, and admission of guilt to anyone could jeopardize her husband's interests. He could be jailed. She refused to answer.

"If you will be as tight lipped as the patient, how will he recover?"

"To the best of my knowledge, he is innocent."

"You are wasting my time and yours. Your face is too transparent for even a novice," he said looking at his watch. "I have other patients waiting. I squeezed you between two appointments knowing about Prof. Vinay Chopra."

"You know him?" Madhulika was surprised.

"Who doesn't? I am in this business for the last many years."

Madhulika had tears in her eyes.

"As and when you change your mind, call me. I'll give you all my time." He looked at her, and added, "Have courage. If you'll break down who will look after your husband?"

She drove straight to Dholpur House, her father-in-law's office.

Entering his room, she said, "Papa." Deepak was chairing an internal meeting. One look at his daughter-in-law's puffy eyes and he cancelled the meeting.

"Is Vinay in bad shape?" Deepak asked. She nodded, and told him that she had consulted Dr. Varmani, the psychiatrist.

"You two have been hiding many things from me."

"Yes, it is true. But I can't take it anymore."

Madhulika blurted out everything and broke down.

"My son — a crook! A fraud!! A thief!!!" He shook his head in desperation. "I can't believe it."

He felt the world spin around him. "He richly deserves where he is. Stealing the research work of his beloved! The bastard!!"

Minutes on, he looked tenderly at his daughter - in – law's swollen eyes and felt sorry for her. He rose and fetched a glass of water. Even now, he refused to accept the truth, and stared stupidly at her. The glow of autocracy, and the charisma that Madhulika had always admired in her father-in-law had faded, and he appeared as weak as her husband.

"It's true papa. Your son is a thief."

"The bastard," he said aloud as if declaring to the world that he had disowned him. "Throw him into a mental asylum. That's what he deserves."

Memories from the past flooded him. He remembered him as an innocent teenager when he had wanted to join fine arts or even humanities, and how he had pushed him into physics. At each stage he had been indirectly responsible. But he had not told him to go and steal the work of his lover.

"Papa, he is my husband. I have to protect him and save him."

"You must Madhu. But after he is okay, he should make a press statement and admit all."

"He will never admit it. Before that he will commit suicide."

"Let him," he said. "The bloody rascal!"

"Have you gone crazy?" she shrieked at him.

"Yes, I have gone mad," he said slowly. "I have been proud and arrogant about my integrity and this bastard - who I thought would do much better than me – has let me down."

He remembered how he had suffered in life and faced the wrath of chief ministers, union cabinet ministers and sometimes even the Prime Minister, but had never compromised with his beliefs, and the interests of the country. His commitment to his principles had helped him to stand up against corrupt politicians always on the prowl for making a monetary kill. To be straight and upright was the only way he knew. But his son had chosen the path of deceit. Where had he gone wrong?

Coffee arrived, and they sipped it slowly lost in their confused thoughts. Suddenly, it occurred to him that it must have been the genes of his father. He had been a notorious crook who in his later life renounced the world and turned into a sanyasi. Once he diagnosed the problem, his tense body relaxed, and it restored the colour on his face.

But his dream of Vinay becoming the Deputy Scientific Advisor in his late thirties was shattered. Now, it was a question of protecting him.

He looked at the young woman fighting a lonely battle to save his wretched son. Gently, he patted her arm, and said, "But you can't handle him alone. You must move to our place."

Gratefully, Madhulika accepted the offer. She also realized that the old man would need the approval of Vaishali who ran the house with an iron hand and brooked no intervention from anyone. Inviting the son's family was a major decision; she had to give him sufficient time to sort it out with his wife. She went to the washroom to refresh herself.

Deepak called Vaishali and told her that Vinay was in a bad condition and needed to move to Akbar Road. Vaishali agreed; she also invited Madhulika personally.

Deepak contacted Kranti and directed him to come fast as it was an emergency.

Madhulika looked at her father-in-law, and said, "You have to promise me that you will not tell mama, or anyone about Vinay's secret."

"I promise."

Before dusk, Kranti escorted Vinay and his wife to Deepak's house. Vaishali was at the gate to receive them.

□□□

VI

Safe Haven

Surrounded by the entire family, Vaishali gave a warm reception to her eldest son and his wife embracing each one of them but showered her care and attention on Vinay only. Vivek recalled that she had been almost formal with Sheila when she had gone to the house from the hospital in almost identical situation; it hurt him though he was aware that he was being unfair to her: how could he compare a son to a prospective daughter-in-law?

Though the house was vast and had sprawling lawns with scores of trees including some fruit trees, a kitchen garden, and open spaces, the covered area was limited. Major adjustments had to be made to spare the best room for the new arrivals. Earlier, Deepak and Vaishali had two rooms to themselves with a connecting door. The pretext given was that Deepak read late in the night, and it disturbed Vaishali. The fact, hidden from the family, was that the senior couple never shared the same bed. In the new arrangement, they were forced to manage with just one room.

Sleeping on the same bed after a hiatus of many years was not easy for Deepak and Vaishali. Troubled by the brahamcharya vow he had taken many years back at the most catastrophic phase of his life, Deepak invariably slept at the extreme end of the bed lest her touch aroused him, and he was forced to have sex with her. One night, blabbering in his dream, he toppled on the ground in his sleep, and sprained his hand slightly. Vaishali laughed merrily in the dead of the night adding to his discomfiture. Applying the gel, she assured him that she had no intention of making any overtures to seduce him till he was prepared. She went a step further and offered to sleep on the small sofa in the room. "After all, what is this sofa for —" she laughed — "to take care of only such emergencies in life!" She made a face, and added, "So relax Deep, your head is not on the guillotine."
She grew so adamant about sleeping on the sofa that poor Deepak had almost to beg her to change her decision.

Her own emotional response to the new situation was the opposite of his, though she was successfully able to camouflage her feelings. Every night, she hoped that he would take her hand in his or embrace or kiss her. With his presence, even the air in the room had turned aphrodisiac. But alas, nothing happened. Sometimes, the very nostalgia of love making in bygone years rekindled the emotions and turned her on. Legally, morally, she had a right on him, but she did not want to impose herself on him against his wishes. After Deepak's vow, she had a little pride left in her—and whatever little she had — she wanted to preserve it and didn't want to let it sink below a certain benchmark she had set for herself. As he slept by her side, she wondered at the complexities of human nature and the associated inhibitions developed over the millenniums that had prevented her from touching him.

(2)

Vaishali told Madhulika that based on facts narrated by her she didn't expect her son to break down. "Is there something that you are hiding?"

"What ever I know, I have told you." She lied.

Confused, Vaishali looked at the drained face of her daughter –in- law and felt sympathy towards her though she was not fond of her. She was sure that Madhulika was protecting him. But had he really cheated as the media made out? She wondered and refused to believe it.

Madhulika waited for her mother-in-law to leave the lounge, and then joined Deepak on the sofa, and discussed what Varmani had told her.

"Varmani is right. You should disclose all the facts to him."

"Even if it means taking the risk of sending him to jail?"

"You have to choose between a nervous wreck and a mentally healthy cheat. I would prefer the second. Incidentally, according to law, admission of a crime by a client before a professional is not a piece of evidence."

Deepak advised her to act fast, and she nodded.

The news of Vinay Chopra's shifting from I I T campus was reported in all the leading dailies. There was a big write up in a leading daily regarding his mental health. Doubts were expressed whether he would ever be able to go back to work.

After Vinay had moved in with his parents, he had proceeded on long leave. He enjoyed reading the newspaper in the lawn while soaking in the early sunlight with a mug of hot coffee; at IIT such a privilege was available only on the weekend. Vainly, he searched for the paper that day all over the house. Vaishali had read the paper, noticed something adverse against Vinay, and had hidden it in her room. With a prominent scowl, he inquired about the newspaper from Vaishali, and she denied having set her eyes on it. Angrily, he barged into her room, and recovered it from one of the drawers. "Here it is," he shouted at her. "And stop protecting me from the world."

"I am not protecting you from anyone but your own self."

"Nothing is going to happen to me. I'll die when I have to," he said, and sat down in the lawn.

Madhulika had watched the entire exchange and was slightly pleased that Vinay had at least reacted after many weeks. She felt happy with her decision to shift him in the joint family.

Unfortunately, it was a one-time exception, and he slipped into his old state of being immune to his surroundings.

(3)

Dr Varmani read the write ups on Vinay Chopra, his siblings, and parents with interest. The stories were exaggerated, distorted and sometimes utterly false. Coupled with the saucy interviews of Jean Simpson who made it a point to emphasise that Vinay stole the research work of his own lover whom he was planning to marry, it caught the imagination of the entire country. Readers of the print media were excited, and looked forward to such stories, and media churned out more of them to satisfy their vicarious pleasure. Vinay was the hot topic of discussion in all intellectual gatherings, academic and scientific groups, and bureaucratic circles, and the most oft - used phrase was "What's the latest?"

Within five years of private practice, Varmani had earned a high reputation as a professional. One of the significant reasons was that he was extremely careful in selecting his clients. They had to be known people if not the crème de la crème of the society. From that angle, Vinay fitted the bill. If he could cure Vinay and help him to face the crisis, he would be known nationally. When Madhulika did not seek a second appointment, he grew anxious. It was then that he realized that the face of Vivek Chopra, whose photograph had also appeared along with other family members of Vinay, was familiar. A few phone calls, and he was able to arrange an appointment with him at India International Centre (IIC).

Sipping coffee in the lounge of IIC Annexe on the third floor, Varmani waited for Vivek. Many years back, as the captain of the St. Stephen's cricket team, Varmani was a worried man. His college had been routed by Hindu College in the cricket final for two years in a row. It was his last year in the college; he wanted to salvage the pride of his college and his own. Desperately, he wanted to win, but nature was against him. They had had a close shave in the semi final against KM College. Though they won the match, their three top order batsmen sustained injuries during fielding, and were ruled out for the final. Vivek Chopra, an unknown first year student was picked up because of the non-availability of any other batsman. It was a Hobson's choice for the selectors, no one expected much from him.

At the end of 2nd innings, Hindu college had piled a lead of 320 runs, and St. Stephen's were down to 112 for 5 on the 4th day after lunch when Vivek took the crease. The havoc was caused by Hindu College spinners. Boos and catcalls from Hindu supporters dominated the university cricket ground; the match was almost written off. Once, Vivek understood the turn of the spinners, he thrashed them all over the pitch with his drives and hooks. He amassed 20 runs from one over shocking every one including his captain. On the last day of the match, the fans of both the colleges were charged, but he was stolidly cool when he lifted the ball for a six bringing victory for his alma mater. Vivek was unbeaten with 135 runs on the board. The Stephenians went crazy and lifted him on their shoulders and had a victory lap of the kind that was never witnessed before or after that day. Such was the frenzy that despite the deep-rooted rivalry of over half a century, even Hindu fans cheered the new hero.

Varmani took some time to recognize Vivek as he casually strolled inside the hall.

"It's been years," Varmani said.

Vivek smiled at the short, obese man with curly hair. Varmani didn't waste any time, and told him about Madhulika's visit, and her refusal to divulge the truth.

"I didn't realize that Vinay is in such a bad shape." Vivek admitted.

"My interest in your brother is only professional. According to your sister-in-law, Vinay is cracking up and needs help otherwise she fears that he will be in a mental hospital. Now, I can take up the case only if she gives me the correct details."

"What do you want me to do?"

"To pressurise her to tell me the truth; I assure you, it is in the best interest of your brother."

“That’s for my sister-in-law to decide.”
“But you are also involved; after all he is also your brother.”
Vivek wondered why the doctor was volunteering his services; even the NGOs took up only those cases that brought them some limelight.
“All right, consider whatever I am doing is for old times sake.”
“You don’t owe me anything,” Vivek said.
“You helped me to win the finals.”
“I didn’t do it for you but for my college.”
“I genuinely want to help. Why should I take the trouble of finding out your number and call you here.”
Varmani had a point. Despite his midget size, everything about him - right from the bulging tummy to bursting cheeks - was big. Strangely, his smile intimidated Vivek. He felt as if Varmani was waiting to pounce upon the world and grab whatever he wanted. Vivek didn’t like him and tolerated him for his brother’s sake.
The waiter brought black coffee and left. There were no pots of milk or sugar.
“How do you know that I take black coffee?”
“Remember when you were in the first year, you had helped out a drug addict one late evening.”
Years back when Vivek had emerged from a friend’s room in the hostel, Varmani had met him in the corridor, and asked for help. Varmani’s roommate, a drug addict, had collapsed because of an overdose. Surreptitiously, under the cover of darkness, they removed the patient to the hospital, their hearts beating wildly lest they were spotted by the warden or his cronies. At stake were the patient’s life, and their own future. If caught, it could lead to their rustication, and possibly tarnish the image of the

college. Both had spent the night at the hospital with the patient. When Varmani had asked him for coffee, he had told him that he took only black coffee.

"Too much of past," Vivek mumbled incoherently. Aloud, he added, that he would talk to his sister-in-law.

He turned his motorbike towards Miranda House and caught Madhulika just as she was coming out of a class. Taken aback, she asked, "What is it, Vivek?"

Vivek told her about his meeting with Varmani. It perturbed her.

"Does Vinay really need the cure as Varmani says?"

"Yes," she said.

"Why?" he asked coldly. "Did he do all that Jean Simpson has been telling the world?"

Without looking at him, she lied. "I don't know, but Vinay needs a psychiatrist."

Her face was tense and worn out. Mixed emotions hit him; a wave of empathy surged for her, and indignation erupted against his brother.

"Some how, I feared it," he muttered. Unsure how much to air his thoughts, he kept his trap shut. In the past, his interaction with her had been minimal. It surprised him that though Vinay had been married for about four years, he knew so little about his sister- in- -law. Tentatively, he asked, "Can we sit somewhere, and talk?"

"Why not?" she answered and led the way to the café.

Unlike the cafés in boys or co-ed colleges, it was strikingly neat, and prominently advertised a well-known cola brand. Madhulika brought coffee, and they sipped quietly.

"If you don't want to confide in me, it is okay by me but please tell everything to the doctor. Don't hide anything from him; it can be dangerous for Vinay. And please don't delay it."

Madhulika vacillated.

"I'll personally escort both of you and wait in the waiting hall."

Not getting any response, he added, "Trust me, Madhu, I am your brother-in-law and will do what is best for you."

She looked directly into his eyes. The honest expression of affection, and sympathy was more convincing than his words. Amazingly, it was the same expression that had endeared her to her father-in-law. Tears welled up in her eyes, and she nodded. When they finished coffee, she said, "Fix up an appointment. And thank you."

Vivek kept his promise, and escorted Vinay and Madhulika to Dr. Varmani. She told all, and hid nothing: Vinay's relations with Stella, Steffi, the theft of the research work, Vinay's relationship with her, their differences, sex life, life before and after the Science Congress at Kolkata, the meetings with Jean Simpson, the incidents in the institute, and Vinay's relationship with his parents and siblings.

"His condition has deteriorated during the last few weeks. Initially he took it in his stride but after the two incidents in the institute he has clammed up. Except saying 'yes' and 'no' he hardly talks. Nothing seems to register with him — TV, newspaper, or any conversation. Not even music though I spent thousands on the piano. There is no sign of anger, laughter, or joy. If I give him food, he gulps it down, if I don't, he does not ask."

"Do you sleep in the same room?"

She explained the position. "Now we are sleeping together on the same bed. But it makes no difference to him whether I am with or without clothes."

Later, he had a session with Vinay.

Vinay did not have an arranged marriage. On a visit to India, Vinay had met Madhulika in a seminar and had fallen for her. Deepak and Vaishali had pointed to her zero status, but Vinay was adamant. The senior couple were not as warm to her as to Prema; Kanupriya, and Prema did not fail to show their condescending attitude. Madhulika had reacted with equal if not more snobbery and kept the female members at a distance. Kranti was the only one who was pleasant, affectionate, and often, good humouredly chivalrous. Now, Madhulika felt grateful to the family, and made her best endeavour to bridge the gap. The senior couple had responded, but Kanupriya and Prema continued to be indifferent.

The entire household showered their affection and attention on Vinay, and still there was no change in his condition. The air in the house grew so protective of Vinay that no one discussed their personal or official problems before Vinay and his wife.

Unaware of the secret and refusing to believe the media reports, Vaishali was baffled. From the details given by Madhulika, how could her son get mentally deranged? She was sure that Madhulika was telling lies. She recalled Vinay's worried expression in his teens when he had confided in her that he didn't like physics. Had he really cheated? Wanting to share her doubts with her husband, she was about to reach up to him when it occurred to her that for the last so many days, she had found him under strain, and decided to let him sleep peacefully.

(4)

Someone lost 1000-1500 rupees in the Miranda House

staff room, and the news spread like wildfire. Such an outrageous act had never occurred in the college's history and the faculty members were terribly agitated over it.

As Madhulika had arrived slightly late, she had gone straight to the only class she had that day. When she entered the staffroom, everyone stared at her though she was ignorant about the incident.

"Here comes the lady who is the talk of the town!" The high-profile Head of the English Department made a sarcastic comment.

"Only she can tell," said a younger member of the History Department.

"Oh, Madhu knows all the tricks of the trade."

"Ask her."

"No, you do."

Ugly, nasty remarks flew from different corners of the room.

Initially, Madhulika was amused, later she frowned, and when it dawned on her that they were insinuating something wicked, she became red with anger.

"What is the matter?" She shouted at them. "I can't stand such contemptuous stares."

"Do you know that Latika lost more than 1000 rupees from her purse in the staff room today?" asked Savita, a woman saner than most.

"I don't know," Madhulika replied.

"Naturally, you wouldn't, for it was my purse." Latika spoke for the first time.

"Stop acting bitchy." Madhulika snubbed her.

"No one but you could have the opportunity." Vanpreet, a snooty woman, voiced authoritatively.

"We were all here in the morning except you, and I had

the money in the purse," Latika said.
"So?" Madhulika inquired arrogantly.
"It is only she and no one else." Latika persisted.
"It is a family of thieves and robbers," someone said aloud. All of them knew about the Vinay scandal.
"Shut up, you bitch!" Madhulika screamed at the top of her voice.
"Let us see her purse." Everyone spoke in unison.
Amongst piercing shrieks, and melee, Madhulika's purse was forcibly snatched, and its contents spilled on the table. To the surprise of everyone, there were just ninety odd rupees, and some change.
A first-year student of BSc (General) entered and replaced all the contents.
"Listen, you madams!" She raised her voice so loud that it echoed in the common room. The Head of the English Department recognised Ratika, the ace debater of the college.
"I was with Madhulika ma'am right from the time she alighted from her car till now, and I attended her class. She didn't even collect the register from the staffroom and took the attendance on this sheet of paper. I'd come to give it to ma'am."
She showed the sheet to everyone.
"You have all wronged her," she said. "And all of you should be ashamed of such a beastly act."
Ratika had tears in her eyes.
"I don't know about others, but I am ashamed of being in this college."
Slowly, she left the room. In an instant, everyone dispersed from the room except Madhulika.

Disgraced by her colleagues, Madhulika raced

away from the college campus. She felt that the entire ambience of the college was monstrous, out to threaten her very existence. Narrowly escaping an accident with a DTC bus, she pulled up on the side of the road, thought for a while, and then diverted the car towards the Kamla Nagar coffee house. She needed to cool her bursting nerves. She sat for a long time and had a cold coffee. No wonder, Vinay, disparaged by society, was unable to cope. Her heartbeat went up when it crossed her mind that whatever had happened in the college was because of him. In the last three years, no one had ever dared to doubt her integrity. His sins had passed on to her, and she was labelled a thief for no fault of hers. Papa was right that his place was in the mental asylum. But she needed to be strong; she could not indulge in the luxury of being on the casualty list.

(5)

When Prof. A.N. Sinha, Director I I T, returned from the US, Deepak Chopra phoned him and sought an appointment. A little surprised, Prof. Sinha said, "No, no, I'll come over instead whenever you are free."

Moved by his gesture, Deepak invited him the very next day in the forenoon.

Prof. Sinha was at Dholpur House on the dot; he had heard that Chopra was fussy about punctuality.

"I have come all the way to take orders from you." Prof. Sinha laughed. With an amiable demeanour, and baldness trimmed to perfection, Sinha was all smiles as he shook Deepak's hand.

"You are embarrassing me, I have a favour to ask," Deepak said.

Of course, Sinha knew. "Ask me anything."

He felt pompous that Deepak's room was ordinary in comparison to his own splendiferous room.

"I have been hearing of some rumours floating in the science block that the faculty members want some inquiry to be conducted against Vinay. You are aware about his poor health."

"There is no question of any inquiry being conducted at the behest of I I T. But if any inquiry is ordered by the Government, I cannot stop it." Sinha made his stand clear.

Deepak thanked him. "Vinay is in a bad shape and needs to be protected."

Sinha nodded understandingly. "We are all with him." Sipping coffee, he added, "The demand for an inquiry is rubbish. These are tantrums of those who have not succeeded in life and are downright jealous of Vinay. I am sure this furore will subside soon."

He looked empathetically at Deepak.

"However, there is one issue raised by Vinay's enemies which is discomforting," Sinha whispered, craning his neck a little closer to Deepak. The latter did not approve of Sinha's hush-hush manner; he also feared there was a catch. Life was not simple.

"What is it?" he asked.

"Recently, an article has been published in an astrophysics journal which contradicts the existence of the Vinay particle."

"That can happen in case of any scientific discovery especially in field of astrophysics."

"I concede but sometimes the cumulative effect of small, insignificant things is difficult to contain."

"But you can handle the I I T front."

"No problem, but I am retiring in the next few months."

"For a person like you, getting an extension would not be difficult."

"I hope not." Sinha smiled affably.

He had to help the bastard, Deepak thought. Sinha was known to be a great manipulator. But he was not a cheat like his son.

Sinha talked of the weather, the growing corruption, lowering of the standard of research, and in the same breath, invited him for dinner whenever he had time, making Deepak feel sheepish as it had not even occurred to him to ask Sinha for lunch. When will he learn to be worldly wise? If Vaishali got wind of it, she was sure to reprimand him.

(6)

Rattled after the meeting with Sinha, Deepak wondered how to protect his son without tarnishing his image. He had another cup of coffee, pondered over the situation, and sent for Supriya, the officiating Secretary of the Commission. (The Secretary was mostly on leave as she was suffering from breast cancer.)

Supriya was the trouble-shooter for all his complex problems in the office, and personal life. When he took over as the Chairman of the Commission, all other members had resented his appointment: it was against the earlier precedence of the senior most member automatically becoming the Chairman. Deepak's hubristic attitude hurt the pride and sensitivity of other members, and they were up in arms against him. Supriya had turned out to be his glamorous shield and protected him against their combined opposition. Knowing the weakness of men, she relied more on her beauty than brains, and used her charm as a soothing balm to their bruised egos. She requested them to give him time to settle. Gradually, over the months, they had started appreciating Deepak's brilliance, integrity, and leadership qualities. Once, when the former Home Minister unfairly snubbed one of the members in a conference, Deepak had defended him to the hilt, and threatened to put in his papers. Thereafter, there were no murmurs of protest.

With her unflinching loyalty towards her boss, she did not mind taking up cudgels with any member now, and if the situation demanded, even bullied him. Under her protective mesmerizing umbrella, Deepak felt that the office was more of a haven than his home, where Vaishali did not mind trampling on his emotions.

Fascinated by the fragrance surrounding her, he looked forward to meeting her, the first thing in the morning. Her presence was like a joyful piano note; it gave a new meaning to his life and filled it with ripples of excitement. From her dress and its colour, he attempted to assay her mood, and was mildly surprised that sometime his assessment was correct.

Supriya basked in the glory of his love, and the vast power she wielded in the office. And looked prettier. Whenever the two sat on the sofa side by side and talked softly of books, movies, economy, politics and life, they both felt that it was the climax of happiness.

A light knock, and Supriya walked in with a broad smile ushering all the joys of the world into his room. In a plain maroon silk sari, she looked beautiful. Noticing the scowl on his face, she said, "Cheer up, sir, and take a peep outside your window. The chrysanthemums are in

bloom, and you have not even noticed."
He acquiesced to her suggestion, rose, and looked through the window. "You are so right," he said, and smiled realizing that he was losing sensitivity. Vinay had derailed his life.
"Is it Vinay? Is there no improvement?"
"None. He has stopped reacting. Sometimes his looks are vacant, almost that of a frightened child. He has been going to Dr. Varmani for last few weeks but there is no perceptible change though the doctor is confident that his patient will improve."
"Is Vinay scared of police?"
"Possibly."
"Is it really that bad?"
"It is quite bad," he answered sadly.
"You mean — he cheated."
Unwilling to tell a lie to someone who was so close to his heart, and neither prepared to break his promise to his daughter-in-law, Deepak was quiet.
"You don't have to commit if you have given a promise to someone."
Perhaps, no one understood his thought process better than her. He confided in her that Sinha had promised to help, but with a rider that he wanted extension. Reluctantly, he also added that he did not approve of Sinha.
"You must watch your step. He is known to be greedy; one favour will not satisfy him."
One of her cousins was the Head of the Department of Electrical Engineering at I I T, and she was aware of many stories about the Director.
"I would not like to go into the sordid details of what

he did to become the Director of the Institute, but he is rotten to the core."

He wanted to ask her if he was a cheat like his son but changed his mind on seeing her charged.

"If you do a good turn to him and it is traced to you, you may forget about Governorship or even a Padma Vibushan."

Confused, he looked at her, left his chair and sat down on the sofa.

"Why do you want to protect one who is a cheat, a thief?" Her voice was no longer gentle. "Just because he happens to be your eldest son!"

"Do I not have some duty as a father?"

"Yes, certainly. But how can you help a criminal? According to the newspapers, Stella was his first love and he planned to marry her and even then, he stole her research work! Come on sir, how can you be on his side?"

"I'm not on his side; nonetheless, he is my son."

"We all have to pay a price for our actions. Let him go to jail."

"Don't ever talk like this before Vaishali, she will never forgive you."

"You do whatever you have to as an individual, but sir — for god's sake do not compromise with your role as Chairman, UPSC."

The PA entered, obtained his signatures on an urgent file, and withdrew.

Ignoring the slight interruption, Supriya continued. "Sir, help him with money, care, but do not interfere with the law."

"Please calm down, Supri. I have done nothing which

will interfere with the rule of law."

"Then why must you do anything for Sinha whom you can't stand."

Deepak had no answer.

"There is one and only one person in the bureaucracy by whom I can swear. And it is you. And I am not the only one; there are many others of my generation. You are our hope. If you too compromise, whom will I look up to, Deep?"

He looked sharply at her; it was the first time she had addressed him by his name.

"You have a noble pedigree; don't stain it for a lousy son."

Deepak laughed.

Puzzled, she inquired the reason for his laughter, and he promised to tell her one day.

(7)

Vivek's suggestion of a picnic at Nehru Park was not appreciated by the family. When he hinted to his mother that it will have a good impact on Vinay, Vaishali ensured that everyone joined. Vivek collected his old cricket kit and entrusted it to Vinay who had been a cricket buff at school. He fiddled with the bat for sometime and agreed to go to the park and play.

Except for the blooming white chrysanthemums on the Ashok Hotel side, there were no flowers in the park. However, the bright, sunny day had made the Sunday revellers come out in hordes with their families; and Kranti and Vivek had a problem locating a suitable place.

Vinay opened the innings with his father and sent the ball all over the ground for fours and sixes. Excited, he managed to take a wicket also.

But once the game was over, he again retired into his

own world as listless as before. Everyone played cards except Vinay. Vivek took him for a stroll, and the two brothers had a round of the park. Out of the blue, Vinay asked, "Why did you plan the picnic?"

"Look at the hundreds of people around you. Doesn't it amaze you that so many people are happy at the same time? If I were a painter, I would have painted this scene."

"But I am not happy."

"Why are you not happy like others?"

Vivek looked at the stressed face of his elder brother and felt sorry for him. Without answering, Vinay walked ahead, and Vivek had to try to catch up.

"Running away will not help. You must face it."

A little irritated, Vinay stopped.

Known for his bluntness in the family, Vivek added, "And a little honesty will help."

For an instance, Vinay's face reddened, and he wanted to retort, and then changed his mind. Vivek missed nothing. To pacify him, he said, "Maybe, you are not lucky."

Without responding, Vinay returned to the place where others were assembled. Deepak looked at his two sons minutely. Vinay had aged considerably during the last few months, and Vivek without any tangible responsibility in his life, even his fiancée was away to the US, looked almost boyish.

(8)

At night, Deepak thought of Vinay, and remembered that Supriya had mentioned about his noble pedigree. The past troubled him. The ringing of the phone startled him, and he picked up the receiver with apprehension. A gentle voice from Rishikesh informed him that his father had passed away peacefully 2-3 hours ago, and the

cremation had been fixed for the next day. "Would it be possible for you or any other family member to attend the cremation?"
"I'll come," Deepak answered.
"Actually, Babaji didn't want any family member to be informed but I have on my own, gone against his wishes."
Deepak obtained the address, and again assured that he would reach there by afternoon.

Along with Kranti and Vivek, Deepak left for Rishikesh at dawn. None of the ladies accompanied them.

Vivek had visited the ashram about three –four years back, and he guided the driver. Deepak was astonished to see about five or six hundred devotees inside the ashram, and a long queue outside; men and women were waiting in severe cold of January for his father's last darshan. On their arrival, the locals moved towards the cremation ground with Ram Narian's body. Deepak and his sons were bewildered to see a crowd of two or three thousand waiting for them. The chant of "Ram nam sat hai" reverberated in the cosmos. In less than an hour, the ceremonies were over, and Deepak lit the pyre.

No one cried. Deepak noticed that the eyes of a few women were red. He felt like an outsider, who at the spur of the moment had been asked to attend the funeral of a stranger, whereas the men and women who formed a part of the gathering, perhaps, knew him more intimately. Ironically, he was the only progeny of the dead man. Though born of his loins, he had hated him for over five decades, and had been totally indifferent to his very existence for the last two decades. But thousands were present on his last rites. Deepak wondered whether any one of them knew the kind of man he was in his past?

A thoroughly corrupt railway official, who had made millions and blew them all on his women in Lucknow. A debauchee! Or even if they knew, had they forgiven him? Would he be able to forgive the devilish man he had dreaded since his childhood? Without exception, they all prayed for his soul, and told one another, "He was a param atma". They talked of his gentle deeds, caring nature, and his love for humanity of which Deepak was ignorant. Many of his father's followers belonged to the very upper crest of society. An elderly, suave gentleman walked over to Deepak, and told him that he had a great regard for his father. "He was truly a spiritual man," he said, and left. His face was familiar; perhaps he had seen him on TV though he could not place him. Another youngish looking intellectual said, "I wish I had known him longer."

Deepak and his sons spent the afternoon in the ashram. They learnt that the ashram was spread over twenty acres and the donations from Ram Narian's devotees from all walks of life ran into hundreds of millions every year.

Confounded by the new avatar of his father, Deepak and his sons were at a loss for words on the return journey. Despite his hatred for the man, his eyes were wet when the car entered the gate of his bungalow late at night.

At the Chautha ceremony, hundreds of his followers had come in buses from Rishikesh; Deepak's widespread lawns were brimming with a sea of humanity. A passer-by asked Deepak's driver, "Was he a 'mahan' atma?" and the latter nodded his head.

VII

Knock From The Past

As a child, Deepak's impression of his father was that of a ferocious monster with frightening moustaches and red cheeks; his fits of rage made him piss. Over the years, the opinion turned into a cardinal belief, and did not undergo any change throughout his life till his father donned saffron robes. Even then, Deepak felt that his father would strip off the mask of sanyasi and reappear as the ogre he had known him to be. In his childhood and youth, Deepak did not have the nerve to look straight into his father's eyes. Once when his father was ill, Deepak— then in his forties — had looked into those light blue eyes and was shocked to see them clear and transparent like the waters of a lake.

With a frame of 6ft and 4 in, and broad shoulders, Ram Narian, the assistant stationmaster, Faizabad, was a terror in the district. His deeds of valour were legendary: how with bare hands, he had faced a leopard or how he had fought ten dacoits single - handed and thrashed them. His image was so fearsome that a servant filling water had fallen inside the well when hollered at by Ram Narian. Stories were in circulation that the founder of the family was a Pathan tribal leader who had fled from Afghanistan with his men and established a zamindari near Dera Bassi. He married Hindu girls and enlarged his fiefdom. One of the descendants did not have any child for many years and eventually had a son after getting the blessings of a Hindu pandit and converted to Hinduism though others believed that he had adopted a Hindu boy. The family riches swelled with years, but Ram Narian and his father squandered all the ancestral wealth on women, wine and gambling. Under mysterious circumstances, Ram Narian left Dera Bassi, and took up a job in the railways in Uttar Pradesh. By passing a series of examinations, and pleasing the English sahibs, he climbed the ladder of hierarchy much faster than others and retired as Assistant General Manager. Except for the emotion of fear and hatred, there was not a single pleasant memory of his father engraved in Deepak's conscious mind.

Once when he was about seven years old, he visited Kanpur with his parents. At a crossing, the tonga in which they were travelling was made to stop. An Englishman driven in a decorative chariot with caparisoned white horses was to pass en- route, and all traffic was halted to provide a clear passage to him. Deepak had a glimpse of the proud Englishman with a touch of royalty in his demeanour. The bright January sun made the world appear resplendent. Unable to contain his curiosity, he asked his mother about the man.

"Beta, he is the Commissioner," she told him.

Deeply impressed by the entourage, and the flurry of activity associated with the Englishman, Deepak said to his mother, “I would like to be a Commissioner.”

His father laughed heartily. “Don’t talk like a joker?”

Deepak insisted, irritating his father.

“Shut up!” His father slapped him.

The boy did not cry; he was determined.

(2)

On Sundays and holidays, his father visited Lucknow. His mother explained that his father, then an assistant station master, Faizabad, had to go on official duty as the big bosses at Lucknow had more faith in him than the station master. His father went up in Deepak’s esteem. In the month of February, an Englishman was expected to visit the office for inspection, but did not turn up, and his father could not go to Lucknow. Ram Narian was livid and cursed the Englishman.

At night, his father barged into the room where Deepak was sleeping with his mother.

“Vidya, Vidya,” Ram Narian whispered to his wife.

“What is it?” She rose. “You are disturbing Deepak.”

“To hell with him,” he said. “I need you.”

But she spurned him. (Once she learnt that he visited the prostitutes, she had not allowed him to touch her.) “Go back to your room and sleep.”

“No, you have to come.”

Anxious that her son should not awake, she obeyed.

In less than ten-fifteen minutes, Deepak heard noise from his father’s room. Apprehensive that his father might be beating his mother, he rushed, and peeped inside the room. Without a sari, and her blouse ripped at two-three places, his mother looked pathetic, and indecent. His

father was trying to push her around.
"Go to your women in Lucknow but spare me." She begged. It had no effect on Ram Narian; it was as if he was possessed by the devil.
"Don't touch me," she screamed. "You will go to hell."
"I am your lawful husband; how can you deny me what is my due?"
"Go to your whores. You are a leper, and I will treat you like one."
Unable to control his sexual desire, Ram Narian hit her hard, and she fainted.
"Bhapaji!" Deepak shouted. His voice cracked in the night. "How dare you beat my ma?"
From somewhere he caught hold of an iron rod and hit his father on the head. Dazed by the blows, Ram Narian crashed down.
"You scoundrel, I knew that you will be my ruin," Ram Narian muttered groaning with pain.

Ram Narian was in hospital for over a week, and gradually recovered his strength. Strangely, he treated Deepak with more respect, and did not hit him again.

About a fortnight later, when Deepak got up early in the morning, fortuitously, he saw his mother praying to tulsi. With her wet hair clinging to the white dhoti, she appeared to be a goddess to him. He stood next to her and folded his hands. After the prayer, she placed her arm around his neck, and smoothed his dishevelled hair.
"Ma, you are looking like a goddess, today."
Vidya smiled at her son.
"But you looked filthy that night."
She froze. Looking into his eyes, she said, "Forget that incident. It was a bad dream. Your bhapaji was drunk and

he did not know what he was doing."
"Does he do similar things to women in Lucknow?"
Nonplussed, she was at a loss for words. She continued caressing his cheeks, and then slowly added, "When you grow up, you'll understand these things."
Deepak made no comment, and stopped sleeping with her stating that he was grown up now.

On Janamashatmi, he went to the temple with his mother. Wading through a river of jostling humanity, their bones crushed, clothes crumpled, and soaked in perspiration, they had darshan of Lord Krishna, and his consort Radha. Deepak was a little disappointed on seeing the dark, uncouth, and fat face of Vishnu's avatar.
"Why do we worship god?" he asked his mother.
"So that god blesses and protects us."
"But ma, why didn't god protect you that night?"
Flabbergasted, Vidya looked at her son with grave concern. Patting him on the shoulder, she told there was no simple explanation in case of God as he was too complex to comprehend.
"Maybe, I too was at fault," she added after a thought.

For the first time, it occurred to him that his mother was not perfect, and God did not protect human beings all the time. His faith in his mother, and God was shaken.

As stationmaster Bhadoi, Varanasi, and Kanpur, Ram Narian earned tons of money through unlawful practices, and passed on a sizeable portion of it to the white sahibs. The money he squeezed from the traders for booking cargo on priority basis, was termed 'handling allowance' by him. But Vidya did not use this money at home. Ram Narian blew all these illegal earnings every Sunday in Lucknow and returned dead drunk without any money in his pocket.

(3)

Along with his mother, Deepak visited Allahabad, and was excited at the confluence of Ganga and Yamuna. He wanted to continue bathing at the Sangam; his mother dragged him away for Gandhiji's darshan. His father refused to escort them.

"That semi-nude faqir is a fraud and a crank. No one can drive away these Englishmen from India? They are here to stay," he said.

Reluctant to go, Deepak sided with his father.

"There are thousands of faqirs like him, what is so special about him?" Ram Narian asked Vidya.

"He is a living god," she answered.

"He is a hypocrite. He was unable to do anything in South Africa. What can he do here?"

Refusing to indulge in any argument with her husband, she caught her son's hand, and left.

A mammoth crowd listened to Pandit Nehru on the banks of the Sangam; he electrified the audience with his speech, and enthusiasm. When the skinny Gandhiji rose, a deafening applause greeted him. He spoke in stuttering Hindi, and to Deepak's surprise, the multitude listened to him in rapt attention. Deepak could not understand most of it and expressed his feelings to his mother; she snubbed him to keep quiet.

After Gandhiji's address, the mother and son waited in the long serpentine queue for Gandhiji's darshan. Unable to stand the blistering May sun, Deepak wanted to get away, and take rest under a neem tree. Vidya overruled him and forced him to stand by her side. By the time they reached the podium, it was almost evening, and the last rays of the setting sun lighted up the stage. Deepak wondered why so many thousands had waited to have the blessings of such a weak, bony man. Gandhiji looked at mother and son and smiled. He placed his hand on Deepak's head, and asked Vidya, "What have you brought for the country?"

His innocent, toothless smile charmed Deepak.

Vidya removed the necklace, earrings, and placed them at his feet.

"This is all I have," she said.

Gandhiji grinned. "Will you not spare the bracelets?"

"The necklace and earrings were given by my parents. The bracelets belong to my in- laws."

Gandhiji understood and blessed both.

Though Gandhiji had uttered only two sentences, they had such a reverberating quality of sincerity that he remembered them all his life. Later, Deepak told his mother, "I like Gandhiji, I like the way he smiles."

All through the return journey, Deepak kept on contemplating, and then said to his mother, "I liked Gandhiji more than the Commissioner. Ma, I want to be like Gandhiji."

Vidya turned sad. "I am not going to lose you to the country, I need you more. No, Deep, you will be a Commissioner. Work hard."

Deepak had liked Gandhiji's persona, and he persisted.

"Your bhapaji has already made our lives very messy. I want a cloak of status and respectability. Promise me that you will be a Commissioner."

Deepak was hardly eight years old; he could not fully grasp the meaning of her words. However, he could make out that she didn't want him to be like Gandhiji.

He nodded.

But the only meeting with Gandhiji had an ever-lasting impression on him. Gandhiji's humility and childlike innocence often flashed across his mind in his later life. He had spoken just a few words, and yet they had the resonance of verisimilitude. For Deepak — like many lakhs of Indians — the father of the nation was more of a quintessential saint searching for truth than a statesman.

Along with millions, Deepak had cried on Gandhiji's death. In his adolescence, and youth he read most of his works, which had a profound effect on his life.

(4)

In the 1950s, Jaunpur was a small place. The only high school in the district had not turned out a single first class in matriculation for last 11-12 years and the principal was banking upon Deepak bringing the laurels. However, the whole school including the principal were flummoxed on seeing Deepak's name at top of the merit list: they could not appreciate what it stood for. The apprehension was that perhaps he had flunked. Ram Narian, the stationmaster, had a wireless message sent to Lucknow. On the third day, it dawned on the Jaunpurites that Deepak had topped in the UP board!

Vidya was jubilant. Ram Narian was perplexed and stared hard at his son. "I took so many years to pass and managed a third class," he said. He wanted his son to take the railway guard's examination; his wife had different plans. With all her gold and savings, she sent him one night to her first cousin stationed at Allahabad. Ram Narian hit the ceiling, and despite his threats to kill her, she refused to divulge Deepak's whereabouts.

The sophisticated Allahabadis scorned the Jaunpur

lad for his poor breeding and manners, though they were forced to respect him for his sharp intellect. The vice - principal of the college encouraged him to visit his place as his daughter Niru needed his help. Deepak liked Niru's company, but had a crush on pretty Shilpa, her best friend. When Deepak broke the university records in Intermediate and BA, Ram Narian accepted that his son was born for higher things in life. He did not disappoint his parents in post-graduation also and topped in the university.

With years, Deepak's adolescent infatuation for Shilpa flowered into love. When Deepak desired to marry Shilpa after post graduation, she disclosed that her father was the Commissioner, and would not allow her to marry into a station master's family. Confident of his looks, and ability, he went to Shilpa's residence, and sought an audience with her father.

Commissioner Anand dismissed him in a minute. "Go and be somebody before you have the cheek to ask for my daughter's hand."

Deepak took the IAS examination, bagged the first position, and went back to Anand.

"Sorry, but I cannot allow my daughter to marry you. Marriage is a relationship between two equal families."

Though apologetic, Anand did not waver from his stand.

At Vidya's instance, Ram Narian begged Anand to reconsider his decision for the sake of his only son. Spurned by an adamant Anand, Ram Narian was infuriated. "If I were in his place, I would have kidnapped your daughter."

"Dare it!" Anand bellowed.

Ignoring his outburst, Ram Narian said, "I would have

done it, but my son would not approve of it. And maybe, your daughter is not worth it. I am told she is suffering from T.B."

Ram Narian remembered the lovelorn face of his son and wanted to smash Anand's head. However, he knew it would make matters too difficult for him to handle as his adversary was a very senior officer. Aloud, he said, "In a way it is better for posterity. I want my daughter-in-law to give us many sons and Shilpa is too sickly."

(5)

Vaishali, a student of MA (Political Science) at Allahabad University, often visited her younger cousin at Ewing Christian College where Deepak taught while preparing for the IAS. Once she saw Deepak in a function sitting alone, lost in his own world. His tall handsome profile, and the air of vulnerability around him touched a chord in her. Whenever she crossed his path, her heart fluttered. Unable to resist the young lecturer, she frankly told everything to her father, a reputed physicist and the Head of the Physics Department in the university. Appreciating her candidness, he called Deepak to his chamber, and proposed a marriage alliance for his daughter. Deepak had not fully recovered from the humiliating experience with Anand; it was too early to think of a new relationship after being in love for 3-4 years with Shilpa. He politely declined the offer without even meeting with Vaishali.

Sanjay Bhasin, Vaishali's maternal uncle and a building contractor, took the responsibility of fixing the match. He threw an exclusive party in a five-star hotel, invited Ram Narian, and gave him all the attention. Sipping Scotch whisky, Ram Narian asked, "What do you want from me?"

Sanjay told the truth.
"Is your niece healthy and beautiful?"
Sanjay nodded, and added that she was also bright, and intelligent.
Ram Narian told him to change the strategy. "Focus on my wife instead of me."

It was made to appear serendipitous when Mrs. Bhasin and Vaishali met Vidya in a temple and befriended her. There were three incidental meetings in the next one week, and on the fourth arranged meeting, Mrs. Bhasin proposed the marriage alliance. Vidya liked Vaishali and forced Deepak to agree. "Every thing changes in life Deep. Even your bhapaji is a different man now. Everything passes, and so will your sorrow and longing for Shilpa."
Reluctantly, Deepak gave his assent without bothering to see the girl. As Deepak had to join the foundation course at Mussoorie, the marriage was solemnised in early July.

Vidya had briefed her daughter-in-law about Shilpa, and Deepak's fondness for the skinny girl. The marriage was to be consummated in the stolid, gloomy bungalow allotted to Ram Narian by railways at Varanasi. The bare sprawling bedroom, huge open doors and windows with thin curtains fluttering in the late evening breeze made Vaishali uneasy as there was no privacy. The noise emanating from the adjacent room occupied by Ram Narian added to Vaishali's discomfiture, and irascibility. Observing that Deepak was unusually reticent, she asked him directly, "Are you still thinking of Shilpa?"
Dazed by the mention of Shilpa's name on the wedding night, he was speechless.
"Did you kiss her?" She inquired.
The second salvo staggered him, and he took some time

to recover. Deepak was upfront and told that on a rainy day his lips had accidentally brushed Shilpa's when she sat on his bike.

"Place her on a pedestal and worship her," she said sarcastically. "But the present and future belong to me."

"Knowing everything about Shilpa, why did you marry me?"

Vaishali told him everything: her attraction for him, how she had persuaded her father to talk to him, and the role of her maternal uncle, and his wife.

"You are a manipulator!" He snarled at her and walked out of the room.

Vaishali went back to Allahabad to complete her post graduation. Vidya was indulgent towards pretty Vaishali and her intellectual father but was extremely critical of the wily Bhasins for duping her. She wondered whether Deepak would ever forgive his wife, and kept her fingers crossed.

Ram Narian was confused as to why his son was not aroused by his wife's beauty. "I am at this age," he said to Vidya.

"You are a beast," she replied though in her heart of hearts she was equally worried.

Vidya and Vaishali struck an instant rapport with each other when she turned up during the autumn break. All secrets of the family were shared, even the minutest detail of Deepak's childhood and Ram Narian's vices were discussed and dissected. Vaishali made it a point to spend all her vacations with her mother-in-law though she disliked her father-in-law.

During the Christmas holidays, she met her husband. He ignored her completely as if she did not exist; Vidya's attempt at rapprochement between the two failed. Ram Narian also pitched in and sent the daughter-in-law twice to his son on some errand. It didn't work. Deepak continued to be hostile and indifferent towards Vaishali.

Unexpectedly, black clouds raced across the bright afternoon sky. It turned pitch dark. There was thunder and lightning in the sky, and with it came rain in thick drops. Vaishali dashed up the terrace, removed the washed clothes from the clothes- line, and brought them inside the room where Deepak was glancing through a magazine under the table lamp. Soaked to the skin, she threw the clothes on a chair, and squeezed the water from her wet sari. With her fair, shapely calves exposed, and the deep cleavage of the blouse showing off the curves of her pink breasts, Vaishali was perhaps not that ignorant of her seductive act. Even at a tender age, women know how to lead men up the garden path of desire. Famished of the touch of a woman since puberty, Deepak could not take his eyes off his wife. He rose, and abruptly kissed her. With sheets of rain pouring outside, a gentle breeze swept into the room drenching the bed on which they made love. When she sneezed twice after copulation, he ran, and closed the door.

One look at her daughter-in-law, and Vidya knew that the marriage had been consummated. A week later, Deepak realized that he had missed so much in life by his stupid decision.

The birth of Vinay was a great event in the life of his parents, and grandparents. Holding the grandchild in his hands, Ram Narian said, "Vinay will atone for my sins. God has forgiven me."

"How can your grandson atone for your sins?" Vidya

looked gravely at him. "You have to do your own penance and seek your own redemption."

Her words were devoid of bitterness, yet they perturbed him. He nodded and closed his eyes.

Vaishali's love, warmth, and tenderness smoothed all the kinks of Deepak's past. After every two-three years, he added another child to the family. "I want to have a horde of them," he said to Vaishali. "I know what loneliness can do to a child."

By now, memories of Shilpa had faded away.

(6)

Immediately after Vivek's birth, Deepak moved to Varanasi. Often, Vaishali was suspicious about concessions given by businessmen and traders to bureaucrats, and politicians. Some of the shopkeepers dealing in silk saris camouflaged bribery under discounts by giving rebates to the tune of 70-80%, which made Vaishali comment in a ladies group, "The shopkeeper should give it free, why have such a farce?"

She was fully aware that the bureaucrats sometime made payments of goods purchased after a year, and some of them conveniently forgot altogether on the pretext of pressure of work; the businessmen accepted it with a smile or a chuckle.

Bhadoi was famous for its carpet industry. Kanhiya Carpets were known to give a concession of 20% to bureaucrats, but a word was sent that they would be too willing to give a rebate of even 40% to the Collector sahib.

Deepak was enamoured of carpets; he knew that Shilpa had carpets all over in the house including the bathroom. Deepak decided to have one for his drawing room.

Deepak and Vaishali saw many carpets, and fell for one that had a Kashmiri design, and was beyond their reach. Sheepishly, the husband and wife looked at each other.

"It is a befitting carpet for the Collector sahib," the owner of the factory said, and lavished rich praise on their selection.

"We don't have the money, we will buy it some other time," Vaishali said, and rose decisively.

Glib words rolled out from the owner reducing the value of money to insignificance and embarrassing the couple. But Vaishali insisted that they would buy it next time.

"Money is no problem.'Paisa aa jaiga', madam." The owner persisted and indicated that it was the last piece.

The couple knew there was not sufficient money in the bank also. Vaishali did not vacillate from her stand, but Deepak was smitten by the glamorous carpet. Incidentally, the design, and texture of the carpet was like the one he had seen in Shilpa's lounge.

Reading the expression on Deepak's face, the owner told the salesman, "Pack up this for the Collector sahib."

Vaishali had heard the story of dozens of carpets in Shilpa's house, and she could appreciate her husband's dilemma. To save the situation, she removed her bracelets, and handed them over to the owner telling him to adjust it.

Vaishali's gesture rendered the owner speechless, and Deepak felt humiliated.

"Please," Vaishali said, and gave the pair of bracelets to the salesman.

All through the return journey, Deepak simmered in wrath. Once home, he blasted her. "Jewellery gives honour and status to the family. How could you give away your bracelets? You have insulted the honour of the family."

In a way, the pair of bracelets was a family heirloom passed on by mothers-in-law to daughters-in-law for the last many generations. Vidya had not given it to even Gandhiji and saved it for her daughter-in-law.

"Honour, my foot?" Vaishali sneered. "Whose honour are we talking of? A lowly stationmaster, and his harem of Lucknauvi prostitutes?"

"Shut up!" he shouted and left the room.

At night, he explained to her that these were small favours accepted in bureaucracy, and he would have paid the shopkeeper after sometime.

"But I don't approve of it," she said arrogantly. "I am the daughter of a vice-chancellor, and not a corrupt stationmaster."

He felt like hitting her, but controlled himself, and slept in the drawing room.

Aware of the corrupt practices and the debauched lifestyle of her father-in-law from Vidya, Vaishali felt Deepak had imbibed many vices from his father through his genes. Deepak's emotional insecurities in his childhood added to the credence of her convictions. Behind the façade of his integrity, she feared, Deepak had all the ingredients to slip into dishonest practices under slightest pressure.

Vidya endorsed her daughter-in-law's action. Though it annoyed Deepak, at the back of his mind he knew Vaishali was right. The bickering between the couple sapped away the joy of the new purchase.

On Diwali, Vaishali refused the packets of sweets, and gifts from everyone except the close relatives, and friends. Initially, it made Deepak uneasy, gradually he got used to it. Vidya was vociferous in supporting her daughter-in-law: she too had taken a similar stand with her husband.

"I hate to sit in a government vehicle," Vaishali told Deepak one night, and pestered him to buy a car for her. Till an old Fiat was purchased, she did not allow him to touch her.

"Now, I am all yours," she said after the purchase, and nestled close to Deepak.

In a tender mood, one night, he asked her, "Promise that you will stand by me through thick and thin."

"I shall, my dearest." She assured him.

On a December night while she lay in his arms, he confided to her that sometimes he felt sorry for his father who had to seek warmth, and comfort in other women's arms. "Maybe, ma was unfair to him," he said.

"So, behave with me," she replied, and laughed. He didn't like her comment but did not react.

(6)

At Deepak's unexpected transfer to Lucknow as Secretary (Urban Land), Vaishali was happy for she had some pleasant childhood memories of the place. Deepak was also excited to be a part of the State Government Headquarters, the seat of power, instead of being in operations for the last many years.

A prime piece of land had been earmarked for St Bishop's school five-six years back. Unfortunately, the school ran into a fund crunch, and could not make the payment, and asked for more time. This was the third extension sought by the school. Though many politicians and business houses had an eye on that land, the most formidable of them was Mahesh, son of R S Dubey, Minister (Urban Land). He pressurised Deepak to cancel the allotment and give it to him at a slightly higher rate. Ignoring the message, Deepak allowed the school another six months to make the payment.

RS Dubey threatened Deepak. Fully aware that Dubey was a cousin of the Chief Minister's wife, Deepak countered that he could have him shifted but the land would not be allotted to his son. The Minister went through the file and read a long note of Deepak's justifying the reasons for not cancelling the land allotted to the school. Deepak had also pointed out that if the school authorities were not able to make the payment, the land should be auctioned.

Infuriated, the Minister complained to the Chief Minister (CM).

Next day, the CM called Deepak, discussed a few files, and asked him if he had any interest in St. Bishop School.

"None except that they deserve it."

"Supposing, I were to make a personal request. Mahesh is my wife's darling, and she has given her promise."

Deepak regretted he could not change his note.

"You are the CM. You can overrule me, sir."

CM smiled and did not pursue it further.

The school authorities made the payment a week after the last day of the extension and wanted a covering sanction from the government condoning the delay. The reason cited for the delay was stoning of the school bus en route by rioters involved in Shia- Sunni riots. A dozen children were grievously injured and had to be admitted in the hospital. Deepak recommended condonation of the delay, and marked the file to his boss for approval as everyone was aware of the Minister's interest in the land. His boss approved the proposal, and the land was transferred to the school authorities. A week later, Deepak's boss sent the file to the Minister for information.

The Minister hit the roof, and called for explanations from Deepak, and his boss. Both were shifted. Deepak was transferred as District Magistrate at Lucknow, and his boss moved to Centre as Additional Secretary. Eyebrows were raised at Deepak's getting the coveted post, but the CM and the Minister both felt that it was easier to fix him in a field posting.

It was a period of rebuilding the nation; Deepak put his heart and soul in his work. His name became synonymous with development, reform and efficiency.

There was an innocuous news item in a local paper that no DM had the guts to do anything about a large sized pond in the newly developed area of Mahanagar. The same day, Deepak saw the pond that was a source of nuisance to thousands of inhabitants. The stink of the stagnant water was so revolting that it was difficult to stand there for more than a few minutes. He empathized with the residents, and felt a little ashamed that he had done nothing as DM. After going through the relevant file, Deepak discussed with his officers, and engineers. Two attempts had been made about nine or ten years back to dry up the pond, and level the land but without success. The Chief Engineer clarified that in the past, technical knowledge and skills were wanting now it could be accomplished if the work was awarded to a reputable contractor. On being assured that technically and financially the project was viable, tenders were floated within the country.

Four tenders were received, and after completing all the associated formalities, Deepak sanctioned the project in favour of M/s Ganesh instead of M/s RK Misra, the lowest tenderer, as M/s Ganesh had better expertise, more experience, and a high credibility in the country. He recorded a long note why he had decided in favour of M/s Ganesh in comparison to M/s RK Misra. There were a few dissenting voices in the Secretariat, but no one doubted Deepak's integrity based on his clean track record, and high standards of propriety maintained by him.

Incidentally, Dubey happened to be the MLA of that area, and he was opposed to the project as he wanted the funds to be utilized for building a new block of the local hospital. The Mahanagar residents were apprehensive that Dubey's supporters would obstruct the project. On hearing about it, Deepak got the foundation stone laid by the CM checkmating his adversary.

The work started with great fanfare. Later, Deepak could not monitor the project closely, and there were slippages. Only 70% of the work was completed in the scheduled time. The contractor wanted more funds, and more time, and the residents were embittered when they learnt the truth. Deepak penalised the contractor heavily for not adhering to the time schedule. The contractor connived with Dubey and went to the press stating that work could not be completed as Deepak had demanded exorbitant cuts. Dubey demanded Deepak's transfer, and an impartial inquiry. He also wanted a probe as to why the work had not been awarded to the lowest tenderer. The news papers were full of the scandal.

Vaishali was away to Gorakhpur where her father had

settled after retirement. She dashed back on reading the papers; Deepak was at the station to receive her.
"How could you do this Deep?" she asked him as he helped her with the children.
Visibly hurt, he shouted at her, "You too, Vaishali?"
"Are we enacting Shakespeare?" She questioned.
He didn't miss the sarcasm in her voice.
"No, we are playing it with our lives," he bawled.
A budding journalist on the prowl overheard it. 'Julius Caesar Revisited' was splashed on the first page of the local newspaper with a big story detailing the background of the case. Questions were raised as to why the project was taken up when attempts in the past had failed, not once, but twice.
"My god! I didn't mean it." Vaishali was shocked on seeing the daily.
"Try explaining it to the press, and people of the town."
Deepak was upset because the story also hinted that even the DM's wife had doubts about the integrity of her husband.
"My career is going to get ruined — and all because of you." He spoke angrily. "It would have been better if you had stayed put at Gorakhpur."
"How can you blame me? You and you alone are responsible for it." She retaliated.
"Don't you trust me?"
"That isn't important. Your government doesn't trust you. Thousands of people of the town do not believe you!"
Deepak protested that his bosses were with him.
"Read the last page, the CM has ordered a CID inquiry."
Flabbergasted, he read the news. There was a photograph of CM inaugurating a hospital at Varanasi.

"The swine," he howled. "They have all ganged up against me."

Vaguely, she shook her head, and said, "I don't know."

Deepak was told to proceed on long leave till the completion of inquiry. Vaishali grew more difficult and sniped at him for no reason. Often, he caught her staring hard at him. On being questioned, she said, "I am trying to figure out why you didn't award the project to M/s Misra, the lowest tenderer."

Deepak explained the facts.

"Why isn't anyone convinced? Are you hiding some thing?"

"No, I am not."

Fortunately, Vidya arrived next day. Noticing the increased tension between the couple, she packed the bags of Vaishali and children, and took them to Varanasi as schools were closed for the summer vacation. Deepak was left alone to fend for himself.

Deepak desired the inquiry to be conducted through the CBI instead of Supt. (CID) as he did not trust him. Dubey declared in his speeches that the CM was soft on Deepak; any other officer in similar circumstances would have been placed under suspension.

Aware of his son's high integrity, Ram Narian was puzzled. All his life, he had made millions, and still was never caught, and his own son was so stupid that he got his fingers burnt without taking a dime.

"I don't understand it, oh, lord!" Ram Narian muttered to himself in the dead of the night. Was God punishing Deepak for his sins?

Ram Narian bribed the CM's PA, and had a meeting arranged with CM.

"I am Ram Narian, Deepak Chopra's father," he said introducing himself. "I am told that you are annoyed with my son because he obstructed your nephew from getting a piece of prime land. I'll give you a bigger piece of land if you promise to protect my son."

"You interest me," the CM said, and smiled. "Now, I understand from where Deepak draws his strength."

"You are mistaken. Deepak doesn't know that I am here and would not approve of it."

"Ram Narian, your face is familiar. Were you in S.D. College, Lahore?"

Ram Narian nodded.

"But you were Ravi Narian then."

"You have a remarkable memory. But Ravi or Ram, I am the same Narian."

"An impostor!"

The CM smiled, and Narian smiled back unashamedly.

"We will take care of your son, Narian. But I want it in hard cash."

"I have only one condition that my son should not know of the deal."

The CM was confused but agreed.

Deepak was in the same complex and had a glimpse of his father entering the CM's room. Categorically, he refused his help. "Bhapaji, I lose or win on my merits. I request you not to intervene."

"Think of your wife and children, think of your future. Remember your ma's dream of seeing you as a Commissioner."

"I have left everything on god, so should ma."

Ram Narian was disappointed, and he called off the deal.

Deepak visited Delhi, and met the Director CBI,

officers in the Home Ministry, Secretary (DOP&T), and the Minister of State (DOP&T). The latter was an old enemy of the CM, and was aware of his wily tricks nonetheless, he gave no assurance to Deepak.

Supt. (CID) completed inquiries within a month and exonerated Deepak of the bribe charge but found procedural irregularities.

On return from Delhi, Deepak was served a charge sheet for minor penalty by the Government and told to join as DM Ballia. However, he continued to be on medical leave, and joined his family at Varanasi.

Issuance of the charge sheet added to the simmering bitterness between the couple. Many a time, he tried to explain why he had been served a charge sheet; she refused to listen. Three -four times he had tried to catch her hand and attempted to appease her. But she rebuffed him. "Don't try to touch me till the charge sheet is quashed," she screamed at him.

Vidya and Vaishali were having a heated argument on Deepak's integrity. Vidya reprimanded her daughter-in-law for her unseemly behaviour especially at a time when he needed her support. "It is mean on your part that you are cold to him and sleep in another room. Why don't you understand that he needs you?"

"You also didn't allow bhapaji to sleep in the same room." Vaishali reacted furiously.

"My reasons were different. Bhapaji was a womaniser, a drunkard and a thoroughly corrupt rascal."

"I don't blame Deepak, I blame his genes," Vaishali replied loud, and clear.

Deepak overheard the conversation and flared up. "Woman, what nonsense are you talking?"

"Exactly what I said!" Vaishali retaliated at the top of her voice.

Deepak sat alone in the late evening contemplating why he and Vaishali did not miss any opportunity to attack each other like a warring couple. Last week he had seen a movie that was mostly shot in the snowy landscape of Switzerland, and he had thoroughly enjoyed it. Maybe the two of them needed to escape to Manali or Srinagar, where it was snowing, and rediscover their lost love. Wanting to call a truce, Deepak went to Vaishali's room. She was at the window watching the twilight slip into darkness. He tiptoed and hugged her from the back. With a jerk she freed herself from his embrace, and shrieked, "How dare you touch me when you are still dirty and tainted?"

Stunned, Deepak could not believe that the woman he loved could have such contempt for him. One who had borne him four adorable children? Why couldn't she understand that the charge sheet was issued only because he had gone against the CM's wishes? Neither had she the sensitivity to appreciate that he could never take a bribe from anyone?

He was sure that she loved him in her own way. But love alone was not enough in life. Each one of us had a different idea of love and its varied manifestations. Love was like snow; pure white, soft and capable of being moulded into any shape and size. Happiness arising out of love, lent sheen of exuberance to the ambience, and made everything look beautiful. But once snow turned into ice, it was hard, slippery and treacherous. Had their love lost its fragrance and effervescence with years? His body language of affection had no impact on her, he reflected. She had turned stiff like the ice. Love needed to be nurtured by caring and being responsive to others' feelings otherwise it withered away.

"Why are you standing like a statue?" she said. "Please go!"

He withdrew, and she closed the door.

Humiliated and crestfallen, he struggled to his room. For a long time, he mulled over his relationship with his whimsical wife. How could she get away with such arrogance? Finally, he resolved to never touch her again.

Late in the night, he told his mother that he wanted to throw Vaishali out of his life. Stupefied, Vidya admonished him. "What will happen to your children? How will she survive? Have you thought of it?"

She gave him a long sermon that conflicts often occurred in marriage and told him to be patient. "I will talk to her." She assured.

Next day, Deepak was trying to have a siesta, and Vidya and Vaishali were discussing the pond-case heatedly in the adjacent room.

"He is a chip of the old block." Vaishali sneered.

"What are you comparing?" Vidya said angrily at her daughter-in-law. "His father was the devil incarnate; Deepak is a saint in comparison."

"Saints don't make love 2-3 times a day without bothering to know whether the other person likes it or not." Vaishali giggled; she remembered the times before the pond case had cropped up.

Given to eves dropping since childhood, Deepak had not missed anything. Bewildered by his wife's utterances in the presence of his mother whom he almost worshipped, he entered the room, and looked strangely at his wife.

How could she dare to talk such nonsense? Unlike his father, he had never forced himself on his wife. Already insulted by her the previous evening, his body shaking with anger, he yelled at her, "You will have no such complaint in future." His face was dark and contorted.

Glowering at her, he banged the door and left.

He shunned her the whole day; his countenance was grim. Skipping the dinner, he wandered on the banks of Ganga lost in vague thoughts about life. For a week, he went to the ghat every evening and watched the setting sun. Ashamed by the wife's humiliation and ridicule, he could not face his mother and avoided her. Deepak ignored Vaishali completely; she retaliated with arrogant disdain refusing to even look towards him.

One evening at sunset when the sky glowed in crimson and gold, he solemnly said to his wife in his mother's presence, "Today, I take the vow that I will have no sexual relationship with you."

His face was grave as if he was reciting a prayer.

"Theatrics!" Vaishali laughed. "It will not last a week."

But the week changed to a month astonishing her. Irritated, she said, "How long will we stay here at the mercy of bhapaji?"

Vaishali wanted him to join at Ballia without waiting for the CBI inquiry. Deepak refused.

"Supposing the CBI also finds you guilty of procedural irregularities."

Nonplussed, he muttered, "It's possible."

"So, why not join?"

Relentless in her mission, Vaishali drove him crazy. One day, he packed his bag, and left Varanasi for a couple of weeks.

(8)

Deepak passed on a message to his batch mate P. Shetty, Deputy Commissioner, Dakshina Kannada at Mangalore, and boarded the train. Shetty had arranged a small independent cottage for him right on the beach.

He lay on the beach for hours soaking in the sun, sand and sea. The waves rolled over him and receded carrying the sand along, creating little hollows, accentuating the uncertainty in his life. Gradually, he liked the languorous intimacy of his body with the sand below, and to his surprise discovered sensuality in the slippage of the sand as if it had a teasing effect. The repetitive process had a rhythm: it sucked away his ingrained sorrow, and tensions, and he liked it. Within a few days, he grew cognizant of the heartbeat of the sea. He could distinguish its wild cry of exhilaration and its moan in the eerie nights. The morning hour was the quietest; he had all the sea to himself. He learnt how to converse with the sea and talked of his inner thoughts he had not shared with any man or woman. In the afternoon, he walked along the beach collecting little shells for Kanupriya. Vaishali would have been amazed if she learnt that he even hummed a tune. Before the sun went down into the bed of the mighty ocean, it looked helpless, vulnerable almost like a small babe.

At night, the sea roared like an injured lion, and it made him uneasy. For the first one week, he was so scared that he could not sleep. With the passage of time, he felt that maybe the sea cried because it was lonely: for miles and miles there was no one around. And strangely, he felt a surge of empathy for it. He too, was all alone in this world. He felt distanced from his wife, children and even his mother. One night after walking for a while, he stretched himself on the sand and looked up at the dark sky brimming with millions and millions of stars. Suddenly, he felt that he was the only human being in the cosmos abandoned by everyone. Gripped by a wave of loneliness, he felt so desolate and lost that he had tears in his eyes.

But as the days turned into weeks, he started liking the loneliness surrounding him. He shunned company; the sea was his only companion.

The locals invaded his privacy in the evening. They arrived in groups or pairs, shouted, laughed, played games creating a hullabaloo, disturbing the quiet and harmony of the surroundings. They dispersed late after dusk leaving the leftovers strewn on the beach, reminiscent of their visit. The morning tide swept them away into the sea.

During his lazy schedule, there was not a single day when he did not think of his wife's blatant, crude behaviour in front of his mother. He had given all his love to her, bared his inner thoughts, and yet she did not trust him. Amongst the IAS fraternity, he was considered one of the most honest officers in U.P cadre, and she had the cheek to doubt his integrity just because she had a better lineage than him. Was there something wrong in his conduct and actions that deserved such repugnance from his life partner? In his ruminations, he did not even spare his mother for confiding everything of his and his father's past to Vaishali. Where was the need to be so outspoken? All his suffering was because of it.

Deepak kept himself occupied with cooking, reading, and introspecting about his life, his relationship with his father, mother, wife and children. He was not sure whether he had done the right thing by taking the vow under the influence of Gandhiji's teachings, and wondered if he would be able to honour it all his life like Gandhiji.

Deepak had not made any effort to interact with anyone including his batchmate. Strangely, he struck an instant rapport with Sunderam, a retired bureaucrat in his eighties who often came for an evening walk with a Labrador. The old man talked, and Deepak listened. He had hidden his identity by passing himself off as a schoolteacher though the old man did not believe him. "We men are so funny," Sunderam told Deepak with a smile flickering over his lips. "At home, I don't talk at all and here I am blabbering away for the last two hours over a cup of tea which I never take."

Often, Sunderam dropped in at his place, and had tea with him. One day, a raging storm forced him to spend the night in Deepak's cottage. Sunderam talked of his past and the interminable loneliness in his life.

Two days later, on going through the local paper, Deepak read a news item on the first page that P. Sunderam, ICS, retired Chief Secretary of Karnataka, had died of a massive heart attack. Deepak recognized him from his photograph. Sunderam was survived by his wife Laxshmi amma, the State Home Minister, and three daughters, but at the last hour there was no one by his side.

Sunderam's death upset Deepak, and he recalled all the moments he had spent in his company.

About two weeks later, he heard the familiar bark of the Labrador. The dog, escorted by a young girl of nineteen or twenty, licked his feet, and hovered around him.

"You must be Deepak uncle — ajja talked to me about you."

Vaguely, he looked at her beauty, and youth.

"I am Supriya, his granddaughter." She offered her hand. "Ajja was all praise for you."

"Were you by his side when he died?"

"No, I had gone out of town for a few days. There was no one with him."

"He died a sad, lonely man."

"You are right, he was a lonely man. He never talked of it to any one though I had guessed it. But how do you know?"

"He told me."

She shook her head in disbelief. "Ajja talking to strangers is unheard of. He was a pukka sahib of the old order. Very rigid, very proper. His talking of his loneliness to a total stranger comes as a rude shock to me."

"Sometimes one can talk of one's inner feelings to a stranger, which one would not like to share with even one's wife."

"Can it happen?"

A quaint expression of surprise, and curiosity made her eyes pop out. Deepak could not help smiling.

"What do you do, Supriya?"

"I am doing MA in History."

Her eyes riveted on him, she asked, "And what do you do, uncle?" With a little twinkle in her eyes, she added, "And please don't tell me that you are a chef at Ashoka!" She laughed. "For ajja would never talk to chefs."

"What do I look like?"

"You look like a Secretary in the State government."

She was so close, he thought.
"That's not my opinion but ajja's. Was he right?"
"No, I am a schoolteacher at Mayo's, Ajmer." He lied.
"You are too bureaucratic for a schoolteacher. To me, you appear to be a younger version of ajja."
But Deepak refused to budge from his stand of being a schoolteacher.
He invited her for a cup of coffee, and she readily accepted. For the next two hours she kept on chatting, and he listened to her appreciating her long fair legs in a short white skirt, her long tresses, and the laughter of youth in her eyes. He kept on thinking about her the whole night.

Next day, she turned up in the evening when the sun was about to sink into the sea. She waved from a long distance, ran towards him, and stopped just in front of him, her heart pounding. The heightened excitement, and anticipation turned her cheeks red; it mingled with the twilight of the setting sun mesmerizing him as she offered her hands to him.
"Hello, Supriya," he said, holding both her hands.
Gazing at the sunset, she murmured, "Isn't it beautiful?"
He nodded.
"Let's walk." He suggested taking long steps as the waves swept at his feet.
"Look at the sand close to the waves," she said. "No, no, move a little further."
Deepak looked at the receding waves. Under the light of the setting sun, the monazite sands below turned luminescent.
Moved by the sheer beauty of the scene, he whispered, "It's fascinating."
She pressed his hands.

Perturbed by her unbridled emotions, she declined his offer of coffee, turned, and disappeared into the approaching darkness. Wrapped in his vague thoughts, he remained standing there for a long time.

A day later, he boarded the train for Lucknow.

(9)

"There he is!" Vaishali yelled at Deepak on opening the door. "And I have gone over half the country on phone trying to track him down!!" Her face was red with rage.

Vidya tried to mollify her, and explained that the Superintendent, CBI was at Lucknow for the last one week, and was about to go back in the evening. Deepak contacted him on the phone, and rushed to the Circuit House where he was staying.

For a cop, M. Srivastava was too suave, and a thorough gentleman. He had fully exonerated him of all the charges. It came as a surprise to Deepak that the CM had three pieces of land in Mahanagar in his family's name, and the news item was also engineered by him in the local paper. "Dubey considers you his bitter enemy. The CM and Dubey's interests may be at variance occasionally, but all said and done, they are very close. It would be prudent to move to Delhi or you may consider changing your cadre." Deepak's first deputation to Delhi in the Prime Minister's Office had been disastrous. He felt he was doing well, but one day he was shunted back to Lucknow by the Principal Secretary to the PM. He had been made a scapegoat when a small embarrassment at international level was caused to the PM.

Vidya was overjoyed on hearing that charges against Deepak were quashed, but Vaishali was more guarded, and kept her fingers crossed till the findings of the report were known formally. She was also cut up with him for disappearing for more than three months.

"Do you still doubt me?" Deepak looked angrily at his wife; his knuckles were at the bursting point as he clasped the dining chair hard.

Vaishali did not respond and left the room.

When a copy of the CBI report was received in the office, and he was absolved of all the charges, Vaishali ran up to him, embraced and kissed Deepak right in front of her mother-in-law.

Ram Narain had returned from pilgrimage only a week back, and he was in tears on hearing the good news. He told his son, "I have never asked anything from god except vindication of your honour."

"Had you gone to Amarnath yatra only for this?" Vidya asked.

"Yes," he said.

At night, Vaishali was flirtatious and created an atmosphere of romance. Coyly, she entered Deepak's room, and despaired on seeing him asleep. She didn't give up, and said softly, "Deep, let us go out on the terrace, the sky is full of dark clouds."

Irritated, he scowled at her. "It is the first time in many months that I am having a sound sleep. Why are you disturbing me?"

Tap, tap, and tap. Huge drops fell on the window.

She pleaded again, and he refused curtly.

"I want to make love," she whispered.

"Why?"

"Because you are clean again!"

"A report of a lousy Superintendent makes me clean."

"Yes, the Government has exonerated you and you are

my darling again."
"Why did you doubt me?"
"Anyone who knows your father as well as I do, will doubt his progeny."
"The day you start respecting me then come to me." He spoke harshly, pushed her out of the room, and bolted the door.

Deepak was summoned to the CM's residence. On reaching there, he found the CM was surrounded by his party members. The atmosphere was charged with feverish activity as the list of candidates for the forth coming state elections was to be announced. He was offered a chair next to the CM. "Congratulations, son. The Central Government has cleared you of the charges and your image and reputation are as high as ever."
Deepak was floored by his gesture. Congratulations were showered on him by the CM's supporters. "On this day I would like to announce your promotion as Commissioner, Bareilly. You are one of the youngest to get this promotion."
The promotion was on ad hoc basis; Deepak's eyes grew misty.
"Look at his luck. A few weeks back, I thought he would lose his job and now he is at the top of the world," the Finance Minister said. "But sir, how could you make such a mistake in the case of such a brilliant officer?"
"The fault is mine," CM said caressing his multi layered paunch. Known for his ruthless, autocratic attitude, the admission of his own failure astonished the gathering. He smiled indulgently at the dazed coterie, and added, "Unfortunately, I knew his father in my college days.

He was the most dangerous gangster of his times, and the whole of Lahore feared him. A debauch surrounded by loose women, he was the personification of evil. He was so brilliant that he took four years to pass Inter and could not clear BA in even six years. By some quirk of destiny, he decided to change himself. He killed Ram Narain, an intelligent clerk in the railways, and stole his identity. Later, he retired as a senior officer in the railways. Knowing him so well, I didn't expect his son to be so righteous. But I have erred in my judgement, and I am sorry."

Deepak turned pale.

"You are telling a lie!" He shouted.

"Go and ask your father." CM exploded in full fury.

Unable to withstand the public humiliation, Deepak rushed home, and inquired of his father. Ram Narain told him the truth.

On an emergent visit to the village, Ravi Narain had been shocked to see his father jailed for bankruptcy. Ravi Narain decided to run away before he too was thrown in prison. He ran into the new postman who handed him three letters meant for one Ram Narain. One of them was an appointment letter for the post of a railway clerk in U.P. Ravi Narain's brain worked rapidly, and by the time he reached home, he had crystallized his plan. In the dead of the night, he boarded a goods train with his wife. Changing a couple of trains, they reached Lucknow. Vidya's entire jewellery was sold to bribe the officials of the Recruitment Board to change the records. After completing his mission at Lucknow, he joined at Rai Barielly.

Deepak was relieved that he was not the son of a killer.

(10)

As Commissioner Bareilly, Deepak's hands were always full; there was so much to be done. He had not forgotten the advice of Superintendent CBI and was trying for a central deputation in some prestigious Ministry.

After the vow, Deepak missed feminine company that provides softness, smiles and laughter in life. He became glum and cynical, while Vaishali tried to focus on the children. After Deepak returned from office, the air was charged with anxiety and uneasiness. Both avoided each other; Deepak escaped to his room immediately after dinner. To minimise the tension, he returned late from office and was served dinner by the servant; all other members retired for sleep including Vaishali. Within weeks, he realized that he was turning into a stranger to his own family; the weekends were an ordeal, and he returned to his old lifestyle.

One night, Vaishali barged into his room. He scowled and turned his gaze from the book to her.

"I have come to apologise for my mistake, Deep."

On seeing no reaction on her husband's face, she said, "Now, I am sure that I was in the wrong. I am ashamed of doubting you."

"You let me down when I needed you the most."

"I apologize for that, Deep."

She wept.

A slight disturbance at the door diverted Vaishali's attention; she dashed outside and saw her eldest teenage son walking away awkwardly through the long corridor towards his room.

On returning, she went up to Deepak and again apologised.

Unmoved by her tears, he said, "We will continue to live as husband and wife discharging our duties and responsibilities."

"Can't we be together?"

"We are together, but I cannot revoke my vow."

"Sometimes, I need the warmth of a man."

Coldly, he replied, "You can divorce me, and marry someone else."

"Who is going to marry me in my late thirties?"

"That's your problem, Vaishali."

The husband and wife maintained the false pretence of being a normal couple in the presence of their children and others, but actually they had two rooms with a connecting door. The other room was called Deepak's study where he studied and slept in the night. Because of the profound impact of Gandhiji on his life, the vow had become an imaginary umbilical cord with the father of the nation, and he did not want to sever that link. Ironically, Deepak' vow was a reaction to Vaishali's insult and ridicule; it had little to do with Gandhiji's brahamcharya vow meant for purifying the body and soul. Under the spell of Gandhiji's views on celibacy, thousands of young men of that generation had ruined their marital lives. Though of a later generation, Deepak was so much influenced by Gandhiji that he considered his writings as the gospel. Vaishali accepted what he had ordained for her as her penance. Partly because of the social taboos, and partly because of Vidya's influence and the children, the marriage did not snap.

As months rolled into a year, he started interacting with her. Though he refused to have sex with her, they had their pleasant moments.

The DM Bareilly phoned Deepak and sent two IAS probationers in the afternoon for briefing. One of them was B K Singh, who hailed from Allahabad, and the second one was Supriya Rao from Karnataka. He was surprised to see her after about three years.

“Sir, I have seen you some where,” Supriya said.

“You must have seen my cousin who resembles me and is a schoolteacher at Mayo School.”

Doubtfully, she nodded.

BK Singh’s mother was on deathbed, and he managed a transfer to Allahabad. Supriya felt bored in the company of the promoted DM, and on some pretext or the other, spent some part of the day with Deepak. He invited her to his home and introduced her to his wife and children. Later, Vaishali commented that the girl was a good influence on him. “You are becoming more human.”

“Am a I cold blooded tyrant?”

“No, but you are totally indifferent to the existence of your wife and children.”

Deepak stared angrily at her before closing the door.

While touring the region, Supriya invariably accompanied Deepak. When the locals aired their grievances about shortage of water, Deepak and Supriya decided to see the nearby rivulet at about two km. In the blistering sun, they walked down the distance as the car could not negotiate the rough terrain. Supriya slowed down allowing the villagers to go ahead, and then surprised him. “You really don’t have any cousin who is your look alike.”

Deepak apologised that he had lied to her about his identity and told her the circumstances under which he had fled from Varanasi.

"In fact, I didn't believe you the first time when you concocted the story. Because you are so much like ajja, and I adored him."

He looked forward to her company, and she missed no opportunity to be with him. On rare occasions, when she turned coquettish, it electrified her long tresses that shook with sheer excitement. Moved, he wanted to caress her hair, but it was not in his nature to indulge in such liberties. She was enamoured of his good looks, and his slightly arrogant smile, which she might have detested in someone else.

One day, on return from office, he was pensive.

"So, what did Supri tell you today?" Vaishali asked. It occurred to him that he had been blabbering too much about her.

"She didn't come to office today."

"No wonder you are so serious."

He never talked of Supriya again.

Supriya's stint brought a whiff of fresh air in his life. When the assignment was over, she shook hands with him, and said, "I'll always remember you, sir."

"So will I," he answered.

Sipping tea in the evening, Vaishali said to her husband, "So Supriya's training is over."

"Are you keeping a watch over my office activities?"

"No," she replied offensively. "It's written all over you."

(11)

Five years later, while on deputation to Delhi, Deepak was transferred to the Finance Ministry. He was about to leave his room to call upon the Finance Secretary, when there was a knock and Supriya entered. Excited on seeing him, she moved quickly, collided with the small glass

table, lost her balance and might have tripped if Deepak had not caught her.
"I am so glad to see you," she said almost hugging him. In the prime of her youth, she looked ravishing.
"We do seem to be running into each other," he said guiding her to the sofa, and making her comfortable.
"It's in the stars," she replied.
"Married?"
She nodded. "To Kappu. He is in business. Very bright and makes lots of money. He has given me a beautiful son."
"And how is madam?" she asked.
"As usual." His voice lacked in enthusiasm. Supriya inquired about the children, and he zealously explained in detail. Treating her to a cup of tea, he invited her to his place.
"Of course, I'll come," she said warmly, and added that she would not monopolize him on the very first day as he had to meet so many seniors.

Unannounced, Supriya with her husband and son, called upon the Chopras at the weekend startling Vaishali. Introducing Kappu to Vaishali, Supriya added, "He can spin money from yarn."
"As simple as that!" Vaishali laughed.
Kappu had wit, ease, and elegance, and Vaishali enjoyed his company. Belonging to a family of textile mill owners, he had about a dozen mills in Mumbai, and Ahmedabad, and was setting up a mill at Bhilwara.
"Shouldn't you be in Bhilwara?" Vaishali inquired.
"Delhi is more central, it helps me to keep an eye on my pretty wife," he said with a glint in his eyes.
When they left, Vaishali told Deepak that the couple

reminded her of the happy times they had shared in their youth.

All at once, she said, “Can’t you forgive me? Even the gods forgive one mistake.”

“But I am human. You didn’t give me even a benefit of doubt.”

Near the dining table, she went down on her knees. “I apologize once again.”

Touched, he picked her up, took her to his room, and said, “I cannot break the vow. Excepting sex, we will be like old times.”

“What is in a vow? Is it more important than life?”

“Honestly, I don’t know,” he said a little perplexed. “But I would like to keep it.”

“If you are so adamant, keep it. But should you feel the need of going to others,” she murmured, “remember me.”

She felt a little degraded with her confession, but she had wounded the pride of a man who had the lineage of hailing from a tribe of the north -western provinces: she had to go to a great length to assuage his pride.

“You should appreciate that whatever I did was because of my beliefs — good or bad.”

“I do,” he said, “ but you don’t.”

He explained to her the relationship of his parents, and how he had attacked his father one night. “I felt I was being equally unfair to you.”

“But I have always enjoyed it,” she said.

“Why did you ridicule me in front of ma?”

“I have treated your ma like a friend. I am very free with her. But I am sorry for insulting and ridiculing you.”

“Vaishali, help me to keep my vow.”

“Okay” she said and did not persist again. “But don’t

break down under it."

"I will not," he said.

"Sometimes, I'm worried. Supriya is at the peak of her youth, and I am forty."

"And I am more than 15-20 years her senior. You see the grey in my hair. Come on, I'm an old man now."

"You look more handsome to both of us and —" she looked at him — "she has an electrifying effect on you."

"I didn't realize it," he muttered, a little confused.

Supriya's visits decreased at home and increased in the office. When Deepak commented on it, she said, "Maintaining contact with you is good for my image."

Gradually, it dawned on Deepak that Vaishali was right: he was getting fond of Supriya, and she was in love with him. One day, he tried to be indifferent to her, and she immediately reacted. "Don't worry, sir, I'm not having an affair with you." She looked full at him with her dark, liquid eyes, and added, "And no one is talking about us. Your honour is not at stake."

"But yours can be."

"I am too small a fry to be noticed. And I can take care of myself."

But the exchange had an immediate impact on her visits. She did not see him for months. It was then that he realized how much he adored and missed her. He was enamoured of her long fluttering hair, her impish smile when she made fun of someone and the accompanying gestures with her long tapering fingers, the way she modulated her voice like the resonance of music, the blush on her cheeks (which now he realized was the colour of love) and her impeccable dress sense. It came as a surprise to him that he liked everything about her. Even in the thick of official activity, her presence lighted up his existence and gave it a meaning. Everyday, he expected her gentle knock at the door, and was disappointed in the evening when she did not show up. However, he did not have the courage to ask anyone about her whereabouts. At home, he was extra careful in presence of his wife, and invariably projected his best.

One day, when he had just opened his lunch box, Supriya knocked, and entered with her lunch pack. Impulsively, he rose, and with rapid strides came up to the door, and held her hands. She threw her arms around him and embraced him. With tears in her eyes, she asked, "You missed me!"

He nodded and kissed her hand.

"Where were you for the last seven months and three days? Were you unwell?"

"I am glad you noticed." She smiled wiping her tears. "Actually, I was blessed with a daughter."

He congratulated her.

"Ironically, she has your sharp features."

Her laughter filled the room; it discomfited Deepak.

"The way you talk makes —"

"Makes others feel that we are having a torrid affair."

Deepak did not approve of such silly conversation.

"Kappu does not think so. He is quite confident of me and himself."

Suddenly, she turned sad.

"You are the only person whose company I enjoy, even more than Kappu's. Honest."

Though he was aware of her love for him, the open expression of the deep feelings was something he feared. Unbridled emotions could destroy the lives of many.

She told him that she had joined a fortnight back but could not muster the courage to enter his room.
"At least twice everyday, my feet of their own accord move towards your room — I cannot help it — but I didn't knock at your door. Today, I could not control myself."
She gave him the halwa she had prepared after taking the assistance of her north Indian colleagues, and he relished it.
A call from his boss disconcerted them, and he dashed away clumsily.

For the next five months, she didn't visit him though she met him in some formal meeting or waved to him whenever they ran into each other in the North Block corridors. One evening, after office hours, when he was working on an important report for the Finance Minister, she walked in demurely, and without a word embraced him, and planted a deep kiss on his lips.
"Goodbye, sir. My tenure is over, and I am going back to my parent cadre."
She shook hands with him, and literally ran away from his room.

Every night he remembered her, the way he had seen her running towards him at Mangalore beach, her face refulgent in the light of the setting sun. And every night his lips burnt with her kiss. Sometimes, he wondered whether his love for her had anything to do with revoking the vow.

VIII

Storm In A Teacup

Memories of the past bombarded Deepak at night, not in tidal waves, but in scores of discrete packets like photons. Unlike them, they were of different sizes and intensity. They did not rain down as consecutive events in time; instead, were pronounced by their randomness creating confusion and chaos. When he rose on Sunday morning, his eyes were a little puffy, and he felt drowsy. Vaishali handed him the morning mug of tea, and inquired if he was buried in the past.

He nodded. Though he had no affection for his father, so much of Deepak's past was associated with him. A little disturbance made him raise his head, and he saw a harassed Madhulika. Vaishali knew that the two were exchanging notes about Vinay and withdrew. Madhulika wanted some advice, and the two discussed for a long time.

The absence of Vivek's fiancée enabled him to visit his parents more often, and he made it a point to interact with each member of the family. Now, he talked at length with Vinay about his project. Madhulika had started appreciating Vivek more after he had escorted her and Vinay to Dr. Varmani.

Over breakfast, Madhulika looked at the male members of the household and realized that Deepak, Vinay and Vivek had the same tall bearing and sophisticated manners. Kranti was different. More handsome and virile than others, he was a little rough and overbearing in his demeanour. She pinned it on the nature of his job. In his spare time, he captained the Delhi Police football team, a top team of the State.

Perturbed about Vinay's future, Vaishali asked her husband at night, "Did you meet the Director I I T?"

"Yes, he came over to my office last week. He is willing to help but in return, wants my help in getting extension."

"We all want it. Don't you? Do what you can."

He explained that Sinha was a shifty character, and he was apprehensive about the consequences.

"But we have no choice; we have to help Vinay," she told him emphatically. She thought for a while, and asked, "Is Sinha really rotten?"

"To the core. Supriya thinks so."

She did not like Supriya's reference; he realized he should not have quoted her.

"Supriya's judgement in such matters is sound though I do not approve of her in other areas."

He was in no mood to defend Supriya and kick up a row.

"Could you be hurt, even remotely?"

"If I put in a word, it would be too obvious."

"But he may get extension even otherwise."

"Possibly," he answered slowly, and explained that if

Jean Simpson was successful in converting it into a controversial issue between two countries, it would turn murky.

Almost in a whisper, she said, "You too feel that Vinay has cheated."

He did not affirm, neither denied it. His eyes turned dim.

"Could he be jailed?"

"I don't know, I really don't know."

"Where have we gone wrong?" She mumbled.

"Sometimes, I wish I had taken the vow even before Vinay was conceived."

She lost her temper. "And denied me even those few years of happiness?"

Later, she told him how she had seen Vinay — then in his teens — eavesdropping at their door whenever they quarrelled. "Do you think it could have affected him?"

"Yes. Emotional security lends lot of strength during weak moments. It is likely that when Vinay was frustrated, he took the easy option."

"Could it be your father's genes?"

He did not respond.

Vaishali fired from her broadsides. "Your father stole someone's identity; Vinay stole the thesis of his lover who was already dead. In a way, Vinay's crime is insignificant in comparison to bhapaji." Perhaps, she could not have put up a better defence than this for her son.

"I don't know," he muttered, and turned his head on the other side.

Next morning, Vaishali kept on staring at Vinay wondering how he could be a criminal. Madhulika noticed, and in the evening told Deepak, "You have let me down papa; you told mama."

"I didn't tell her, but she has guessed it."

Sympathetically, he looked at her, and added, "There has been so much of discussion in the media that my general feeling is that everyone knows though no one will admit."

"If it is so bad, then it will be difficult to protect him."

"Fortunately, there is no proof except the Chinese professor."

"Papa, can we find out how sane he is?"

Shekhar Srivastava, his batch mate, was the ambassador at Beijing. He assured her that he would think about it.

Deepak's assessment of the situation was precise: everyone suspected that Vinay was a thief and had stolen the research work of his lover. But no one even hinted about it in the couple's presence. Among outsiders, they all rose to circle the wagon and defend the honour of family. Melancholia had settled down on the Akbar Road bungalow and stifled the life of its inhabitants, and even affected the tree line and swathes of green. Kanupriya and Prema's laughter was subdued; when the children made merry or created a pandemonium as children are given to, it upset Vaishali. To a stranger, it appeared as if the house was in mourning. Earlier, if someone's conduct in public life was slightly below the high standards laid down by Deepak, it was frowned upon during discussion over dinner or lunch. Usually, Vivek was at the receiving end for his non- conformist attitude and lifestyle. Now, no one mentioned such matters even obliquely: they were reduced into insignificance in comparison to the conduct of a criminal. At the dining table, it seemed everyone was playing a part given to them and were glad when the act was over and they were back in their rooms, where they could be their natural selves. Vivek was the only one who dared to say his own lines and was often snubbed by his mother.

(2)

Till the last week of December, the Delhites were disappointed at not getting the feel of winter. The joy of breaking the groundnut pods, listening to their crackling sound and munching them or relishing the hot somasas and pakoras or savouring the divine 'jalebis' and tempting halwa was missing. To top it all, the woollens remained in the confines of the cupboards and those purchased in the season's end sale the previous year, were not flaunted before friends and relatives.

When one night, the biting cold winds from the north suddenly hit the capital, the Delhites were taken by surprise. In the next 24 hours, dark clouds covered the skies bringing rain and squall, and the capital shivered. The sunlight could not pierce through the dark clouds for a week, and a thick mist pervaded the atmosphere of the kind that Delhi was not familiar with. The maximum temperature during the day plummeted to 5-6 degrees Centigrade making it colder than Shimla and London.

Sleeping at the two ends of the bed under a quilt was not comfortable for the senior couple in such extreme weather. Often, Vaishali tossed in the night, introducing perturbations in the warm layers of air and creating pockets for cold air to slip in. It disturbed Deepak's sleep, and he mumbled something incoherently. To get some warmth, Vaishali had considered breaking her self-imposed inhibition and nestling close to him, but at the last moment changed her decision. Instead, the next day she bought a new oil heater, and Deepak felt grateful to her.

Two days later, Deepak was totally exhausted after dinner though the bedroom was warm and comfortable. For a man of such high integrity, a mentally sick criminal in his house was a liability, and he felt terribly ashamed of himself. Living with a criminal son would have its side effects. Perhaps Supriya was right, a little false move, and he could forget about another assignment. For the second time in his life — the first time was when he had run away from his home to Mangalore — he had no control over the situation. It irritated him, and he felt helpless. Now, he didn't have the luxury of a separate room where he could have the freedom of being on his own; he was forced to be cheerful in her presence, and it added to his stress levels. Surrounded by complexities, he felt a niggling headache, and he stretched himself on the opposite side of the bed, his eyes closed.

A soft touch, almost like a caress, made him open his eyes. Applying Amritaunjan balm on his forehead, Vaishali said, "Are you feeling better, Deep?" Her voice was husky. To his astonishment, he realized that the headache had vanished, and the room was filled with luxuriant warmth reminiscent of the past. He didn't open his eyes and stretched his arm above his head touching her temples and played around with the buttons of her dress. Slowly, she helped him remove her nightie, and they snuggled themselves under the quilt. His touch aroused her instantly, and when he did enter her, it was almost as if he was making love to a virgin.

Half an hour later, she switched on the table lamp and squeezed herself into the crook of his arm. Their bodies filled with love, numbness stole over them; it felt strange and exceedingly pleasant.

"It was sheer bliss. I have never felt such intense pleasure in my life," she said.

He kissed her lightly and she responded. "We have wasted away so many years," she said. "Are you worried about your vow?"

He was quiet.

"Something which is so beautiful should not be denied to us because of a vow."

Anxious that he should not develop any guilt complex, she argued that he had not gone through any sacred rituals.

"No, it isn't that. It is the surprise, suddenness, and intensity of happiness that has shaken me."

"We should have the capacity to absorb intense joys also," she said more to herself than him.

"Yes," he said, sending waves of sensual enjoyment through her again.

An hour or so later, Vaishali felt the chill sweep across her body, and it made her shiver. She rose, took out another blanket from the cupboard, and threw it over the quilt. Before slipping beside her husband, she felt the rain pelting down and peeped through the window. A hailstorm had hit Delhi, and under the garden floodlights she noticed that the entire lawn was covered with hail. For a woman who was always tense over her husband and children, an unusual feeling of peace and harmony swept over her. She felt rich and full as she had never felt before; and surprisingly forgiving towards the world. She wondered whether it had anything to do with the sexual experience that had shaken her earlier. Wanting to share these mixed emotions with Deepak, she moved towards him, and was unsure whether it would be wise to disturb

him?
Her gentle movements had already woken him. "What is it Vaishali?" he asked. She caught his hand and showed him the lawn. Moved, he embraced her, and said, "Do you want to pick up some of them?" he asked. Many years back when he had gone with her to New York, she had insisted to touch the snow and walk on it.
"No, we are no longer young. One of us is sure to catch pneumonia." She laughed.
Rationality and laughter evaporated the emotions that had purified her soul. And she no longer felt like sharing her inner thoughts with him.

When they went back to the bed, they could not sleep, and Deepak expressed a desire to have coffee. Apprehensive of being caught red handed in this nocturnal activity by the younger women in the house, she made sure that there was no one in the lounge, and hurriedly dashed to the kitchen on her toes. About to switch on the light, she saw a woman in a white coat picking up the white pellets and touching them to her cheeks. From her height and gait, she could make out that it was Madhulika. She waited for Madhulika to return to her bedroom, and then prepared coffee.
When Vaishali informed him about Madhulika, Deepak confided that Madhulika was on the edge. Vaishali appreciated her concern for Vinay. "She has changed," Vaishali said. "Now she is more considerate and loving. Even her hardness is softening, and she is looking more beautiful. Earlier, I was afraid that they were drifting away from each other. But now she does not allow any criticism of Vinay from anyone. Not even me."
"I had a funny feeling once," she added. "Intuitively, I

realized that she was inching closer to Kranti. He has a liking for the fair ones, and I was afraid that this mutual fondness may not take an unpleasant turn especially when she is not satisfied with Vinay."

"You women read too much meaning into the moods and expressions of individuals." He frowned and switched off the light.

(3)

As he chaired a routine meeting, Deepak reminisced about the previous night's intense passionate interaction with his wife. Devoid of her love, he had missed out a lot over last two decades, he reflected.

Meeting over, he returned to his room and was amazed to see his batchmate, D. Prasad, Chairman, Monopoly Commission. Short and obese, Prasad had a cheerful disposition, but could be scathing, if provoked. Deepak invited him for lunch to which he willingly agreed. They talked of the past and the great times they had in various ministries, and how they had circumvented the demands of their political bosses. Finally, Prasad handed him a letter.

Prasad briefed him that some of their enemies had been digging into their past and had unearthed that the Panch Sheel land on which he and Deepak had constructed their bungalows, was sold at one third of the market price. On a complaint, some inquiries were initiated by the Government, but he was successful in thwarting them. Now, some activists had approached the High Court; he was keeping a watch on the proceedings. Of late, things were going against them.

Deepak was taken aback that there was something dubious in the deal.

"The land was actually meant for a hospital: that is why the price was so low." Prasad explained. "Kurrani as the Secretary, Urban Land and Development, manipulated and converted the usage to residential and made his brother-in-law Asnani, the Secretary of the Cooperative."

As the top bureaucrat of the country, Deepak had no time for his personal problems. Whenever Vaishali pestered for a house or a piece of land, he dismissed it with a smile. Vaishali was wild with him one day. "Remember, you have to retire one day. Where will we live? Have you thought of it?"

"You have three sons."

"I don't trust anyone."

That upset him. She gave him a month to decide.

His Joint Secretary, AP Tewari was a resourceful bureaucrat of UP cadre. When Deepak unburdened his problem before Tewari, he promised to do something.

The day he was to fly to Paris with the PM for a conference, one Rajiv Gupta, Joint Secretary from the Ministry of Urban Land and Development had turned up in his office.

"Sir, Tewari told me that you are looking for a plot."

His eyes glued to a report, Deepak had nodded.

"It is a three hundred square metre corner plot and is fairly cheap."

Deepak was about to call his PA to fill the form when Rajiv Gupta told him that he had already got it filled.

"Good," he had said crisply though much later in the flight it had occurred to him that it was a little unusual. He had signed at the places he was told to. A couple of weeks later, he was told to pay the first instalment. When he tossed the papers to her, Vaishali blushed a little with excitement.

"At least now I will have a roof above me," she had said.

Bureaucracy can act fast if they have some vested interest. In six months, Deepak was allotted the land. In another two years, he completed the construction of the house.

"The only fortunate aspect is that those who cleared the files are not direct beneficiaries — only their sons and daughters are!" Prasad laughed.

"That smacks of mala fide." Deepak winced.

"Kurrani helped his son-in-law and brother-in-law's daughters get the land. He roped in a few Cabinet Ministers, Governors, five Secretaries, a few Lt. Generals, two Admirals, an Air Marshal and finally the Cabinet Secretary."

"But I didn't know," Deepak said.

"Neither did I, till three years back." Prasad clarified.

"It smells rotten."

"In retrospect, he should have even invited a few Judges of Supreme and High Courts!" Prasad sneered.

Deepak was in a foul temper; he didn't like the sarcasm.

"The image of all of us would be tarnished. I should have been careful," Deepak said. "I am already having a rough time because of Vinay."

"I heard about it; I am sorry."

"What do you want me to do?" Deepak asked.

"Your credibility is high, and you are the only one who has access to all the ministries and even the judiciary. One word from you can help."

"Prasad, be specific."

"Justice Gupta is known to you. One call from you can help."

"Do you think I will do it? And knowing Gupta, do you

think he will listen?"
"We had considered both the angles, but we have no choice."
"It can rebound. It could be worse."
"Possibly, but we will take a chance."
"At my expense — no, thank you."
"Give it a thought. You are equally involved."
"You have come on behalf of Kurranis and Asnanis."
"I represent all — including you."
"I'll suffer it." Deepak was calm and self assured.
"How much can you suffer?" Prasad mocked him. "Vinay's ignominy, Kanupriya's divorce, and Vivek is without a job for years. And now your reputation will be tainted."
"You are well briefed, but these are my problems."
"Mull over it for a week, I'll call you after 7-8 days." Wearing a smile, Prasad rose. "And lunch was excellent – thanks."

Next week, when Prasad phoned, Deepak refused to take the call.

(3)

Thick fog had settled over Delhi, disrupting flights, train schedules and creating traffic snarls and chaos. The Delhites who had the option of staying put at home were surrounded by sad and gloomy thoughts. In a reflective mood, Vaishali confided in her husband at night that what Vinay had done, perhaps, had little to do with his genes. "We all have a streak of this kind. It is basically a question of circumstances and opportunities."
Deepak asked her to explain.
"I was in school, perhaps in 5th or 6th class. We were given dictation test. There were two of us on a bench, Suchi and

me. I was the topper of my class, but Suchi was better than me in English. There was one word `psychology' — I still remember it — I had got it right, but Suchi wrote it without a `p' and I, believing in her, cancelled my word, and copied her. The teacher ridiculed both of us."

"You were lucky that you got caught the very first time."

"Yes, but it didn't end with it," she said.

In BA (final), the history paper shocked her. She knew only three questions and had to attempt five. After half time, she grew nervous, and looked around. The student just behind her was slightly acquainted with her. He understood her predicament, and asked for an extra sheet, and gave the main one to her. She took about 10-12 minutes to rapidly glance through it. As she finished and kept the neighbour's answer book below hers, one of the young invigilators, a research scholar from physics department, stopped and looked down at her.

She panicked.

"Is everything okay, Vaishali?"

"Yes sir," she muttered.

She considered it to be the worst moment of her life. The invigilator had seen the neighbour's sheet protruding from her answer book, and he shook his head with disgust, and disappeared. Vaishali returned the answer book of the neighbour.

About 15-20 minutes later, the Superintendent Examination, a ferocious looking baldy, had a round and snatched Vaishali's paper. He compared it with other student's paper. She had only taken the points but had used her own language and style that was much better than his. The Superintendent was foxed and kept on scratching his head. The student who had helped her said,

"You are wasting our time, sir." Others also protested. Even Vaishali had the courage to say, "Sir, you can check whatever you want to, but please do it later."

After scrutinizing all the pages later, he said, "You are a very clever girl. I can't fix you under copying."

"It was very close," the neighbour whispered after the Superintendent left.

The incident was the talk of the campus. Superintendent Misra was a bitter enemy of her father, and everyone believed he had done it to embarrass him. In the evening, she was summoned by her father.

"I want to know the truth," he asked. She was quiet for a long time, and it infuriated him.

"The whole campus does not believe Misra, but I know him too well. Though he hates me, there are many things he will not stoop to, and this is one of them."

When she did not respond, he caught both her hands at the back and looked fiercely into her eyes. Finally, she broke down, and admitted.

"Why?" He thundered.

"I was confused, frustrated. The fear that I would flunk made me accept my neighbour's offer."

He slapped her hard, real hard.

"Get lost," he shouted.

He didn't touch food for two days; she begged for forgiveness. He relented on the third day when the doctor was called.

She was second in the university, and that boy got a third class.

"That changed you," Deepak said.

"For weeks, I was in turmoil. If I had been caught, my father might have resigned," Vaishali said. Thereafter, she

decided not to be weak again.
She looked into his eyes. "Deep, it could be my genes too."
"Does it make any difference whether Vinay has mine or yours or my father's genes? Vinay is Vinay and he is our son."
"During the initial years of our differences, Vinay was the only one who comforted me and wiped away my tears like a grown up."
Fondling his hair, she added, "Help him within the law. I don't want you to compromise with your dignity or principles."
"I'll do what I can." He assured her.

But sleep eluded Deepak. When he was nine or ten years old, one day, on his return journey from school, he saw `imratis' (a sweet) being prepared by the 'halwai' and was fascinated by it. Ma was a miser and considered purchase of `imrati' a wasteful expenditure. His request for `imrati' was invariably turned down as sweets were bought only on festive occasions. Whenever ma sent him for some shopping, he made it a point to pocket some money, and bought `imrati' while returning from school. Ma had so much faith in him that she never doubted him. Every time he cheated; he felt a little guilty. Since he never got caught, it emboldened him. On a cold December day, he bought two 'imratis', and ran into the nearby field. The 'imratis' tasted divine. But later, pangs of guilt tortured him, and he was filled with so much remorse for betraying his mother's trust that he never ate 'imrati' again.

(4)

One day, on the return journey from college, Madhulika turned the car towards Varmani's clinic, and barged in without an appointment. He was astonished to see her alone. She felt a little frustrated that even after one and a half months there was no tangible improvement in her husband's condition.

"These things take time," he said. He had no scheduled appointment and spent sometime asking about her relationship with her husband. He advised her to engage him in some physical activity he liked. "It helps," he said.

Since she did not have any class next day, Madhulika told her husband to teach her how to play tennis.

"Why not?" Vinay spoke spiritedly, surprising her.

"But where?" She inquired.

"I I T grounds?"

"No, Gymkhana."

"That's still better," he replied, thoughtfully.

In mini white shorts, and a loose sleeveless matching top, Madhulika looked extremely seductive as she ran across the court on that sunny noon. It had a magical effect on Vinay for she noticed an emotion in his eyes. Though Madhulika belonged to a conservative, lower middle class, the one-year exposure in the US had liberated her, and she had started wearing bold dresses.

Vinay taught her how to hold the racket, serve, and use her backhand. "Two hours a day and within 3-4 months you will be my mixed doubles partner."

Unfortunately, his enthusiasm evaporated when they reached home, disappointing her. He went to the bedroom and closed the door.

Excited, Madhulika told everyone how Vinay had taught her tennis. Without changing her clothes, she sat down in the lawn to catch the late afternoon sun. She realized that she should not expect miracles in one session; she had to do it for many weeks before expecting a change in Vinay.

Kranti returned early from office, learnt about Vinay and Madhulika's visit to the gymkhana, and walked over to say a 'hello' to her. Flipping the pages of Star Dust, her right leg over the left, she was carelessly sitting on a reclining chair with a cold drink and liking the warm feel of the setting sun on her body. Cross legged, he sat down on the grass just opposite her, and said, "Hello!"

His close presence disturbed her. The youthful almost boyish looks, the rippling muscles visible in his half- sleeve uniform shirt, the pink cheerful face: Kranti's persona exuded raw masculinity and mesmerized her. The Puri scene flashed before her.

"So, good news," he said, and grinned at her. Though shorter and a shade darker than other men in the family, he was more attractive. Looking full into his eyes, she smiled back at him, and said, "I'll get a chair for you."

As she rose, he caught both her legs with his strong hands, and pinned her back on the chair. His hands on her thighs, he continued to enchant her.

"Oh, please sit down. I prefer squatting on the rough ground. After all, I am an earthy cop, and not an intellectual."

"Please, Kranti." She pleaded and pretended to remove his hands from her thighs. His head was too close to hers, and his exuding sexuality made her heart bounce.

A sweet sensation suffused through her body, and strangely, she felt wetness between her legs that she had seldom experienced before.

Suddenly, her womanly intuition made her feel that somebody was watching them. She looked up and saw

Prema, her eyes popping out, and glowering at them from the terrace, where she often strolled to have a view of the setting sun or mull over a complex problem.

Ignoring her plea, he asked, “Did you learn anything at Gymkhana?”

Her honour at stake, she instantly shrilled at him, “Yes, not to wear such a dress at home.”

Forcefully, she pushed away his hands, and ran away to her room.

Kranti was petrified. He didn’t expect his sister-in-law to react in such a manner. He was under the impression that Madhulika was fond of him, and he could get away with such a flirtatious act. “When will I understand women?” he muttered to himself and swore. About to enter his bedroom, he was stopped by Vaishali.

“Kranti!”

“Yes, ma.” His heartbeat went up.

“Come and sit down here; I want to talk to you.”

She took a seat in the drawing room and gestured him to sit next to her. Flustered, he obeyed.

“You are a grown-up man and married for more than eleven years. You have also fathered two children. But when will you act responsibly?”

“What have I done, ma?” He tried to be smart.

In a moment, he realized that ma’s bedroom window faced the spot where he and Madhulika were sitting. He was in trouble.

“I saw the way you were misbehaving with Madhu.”

“I was only telling her not to get up.”

“Is that the way?”

“She is not a stranger but my sister-in-law.”

“Yes, she is,” Vaishali exploded. “And what did she say?”

"I don't know why she behaved in that way. I had a feeling she would not mind."

"Are you aware what she is undergoing?" She hissed. "Is this the way we plan to help her?"

He hung his head in shame.

"I personally invited her to stay with me without realizing that there are goondas in my house."

His body tensed, but he did not react.

"You have insulted Madhu and all the women of this household."

"I didn't mean to insult her in any way. I am sorry."

"Go, and say it to Madhu."

"I am not going to apologize to Madhu, she is younger to me."

"How would you react if someone had done it to Prema?"

"Let us leave it at that, ma." Kranti rose, a little irritated.

At that very moment Madhulika emerged from her room after changing the dress.

"Let it go, mummy. I don't want to create a scene."

Her sudden appearance unnerved him, and he pleaded. "You know, I didn't mean it. I'm sorry."

Graciously, Madhulika walked up to him, offered her hand, and told him that he was forgiven. Tenderly, he took her hand, and thanked her.

But Kranti felt humiliated in the presence of the two women. To assuage his hurt ego, he went alone to Amit's home for dinner. When Julian made her appearance in the kitchen to assist her mistress, Kranti felt uncomfortable, and left in a huff.

(5)

"Come, come, my chivalrous husband!" Prema welcomed Kranti when he returned home. "Did you enjoy yourself in the company of Kavita and that north- eastern girl?" She continued to rattle off while watching the TV. He understood that Kavita must have briefed Prema on the phone. Without a word, he changed into his night dress.

"Did Madhu say something?" He spoke for the first time.

"No."

A load off his chest, Kranti stretched himself on the bed. Very slowly, Prema switched off the TV, and sat down on her side of the bed.

"But I saw and heard everything from the terrace." She threw a bombshell at him. "I also overheard the affectionate conversation between mother and son."

Her face hardened.

"I warned you earlier also, Kranti," she said with fire in her eyes. "A display of vulgarity or outraging the modesty of a woman, I'll not tolerate. And you are doing it to your sister-in-law especially when she is down."

"It was so sudden and impulsive that my hands went over her bare legs."

"And you liked them so much that you ignored her protests."

"I am sorry."

"If she had not protested vehemently, you might have had her right there in the garden."

"That's exactly what I felt," he said to himself. Aloud, he objected. "You have gone out of your mind, Prema."

"You should have married a fair coloured woman, and not a dark one like me."

Kranti made no comment.

"On seeing a fair girl why do you get turned on? Be it a servant, your sister-in-law or anyone else."

"But beyond mild flirtation, I've never had sex with any

woman except you. I don't know why you and Kavita are out to spoil my image."

"Now, I'm certain that you had had Julian, otherwise she would not have called you a devil. Like a street dog, you don't allow any opportunity to slip."

"Oh, shut up!"

"You are a pig and a filthy dog!" she screamed at him.

Scared of drawing the attention of others in the late night, he said, "I apologise, Prema. Please!" He begged.

Unmoved by his appeals, she scolded him for the next half an hour.

"I don't know why I tolerate such a rascal like you."

"Because you love me," he said wiping away her tears. "And I adore you."

When she did not protest to his kiss, he kissed her all over. She responded and they made love.

"Despite all your weaknesses, unfortunately, I love you," she said. "But your flirtations are hurting me. Really."

"I'll not repeat it." He promised.

"One day, if you cross the limit, I will file a case against you in the court of law."

"For what?" He laughed. "Outraging the modesty of my wife!"

"No, for molesting your sister-in-law or any other woman." She was dead serious.

"I would like to see your performance in the court one day; I am told you are turning into a reputed counsel."

In the second year of Prema's marriage when they stayed at C-I flats near Khan Market, one of their part- time maids was thrown out of the house by her husband at the instance of his parents. Without shelter and with the additional responsibility of a three - year - old daughter, the woman was at breaking point. Prema had given her a servant quarter and dragged her husband to a court of law. After two years of harassment in the courts, the husband apologized, and agreed to take her back. Prema realized the need of an institution for fighting such cases. After a lot of contemplation, five years back, Prema founded Kanooni Nari Rakshan Kendra (Legal Protection Centre for Women), an NGO, that rendered legal assistance to destitute women. After a few months, the prefix 'Kanooni' was dropped, and now it was simply termed as NRK. Often, she appeared in the court on behalf of her clients.

"Just pray that I should not drag you to a court of law," she said gravely. "It would be very sad and unfortunate for you."

When Deepak heard about Kranti's indecent behaviour, it distressed him. "They are all rotten. It is a matter of degree only," he said to Vaishali.

(6)

Madhulika opened a novel as Vinay slept peacefully under sedatives. But her heart was not in the book. Lovingly, she played around with Vinay's hair. Over the last few weeks, he had aged considerably. The thought of Kranti disconcerted her, and she stopped fondling her husband's hair. She needed to bridle her emotions and keep herself at a distance from Kranti. Deep down in her heart she was aware that arousal of such feelings was not the right thing: it was inappropriate. Not at a time when her husband was in such a shattered mental state. But she had no control over the responses of her own body that had reacted to Kranti's amorous touch. At Puri, the contact of his leg over hers was abrupt, and her body did not have the time to feel anything. They were all numbed by the suddenness and incongruity of the situation. For the sake of her reputation, it was necessary that no one should get a whiff of her fondness for Kranti. She felt that she might have saved the situation by concocting some explanation to Prema; unfortunately, Vaishali's intervention had turned the situation messy.

Madhulika's dress sense was discussed by the ladies of the house, and they decided unanimously that she had the right to wear what she wanted. Overtly critical of Kranti's transgression, Kanupriya, a feminist, raised the issue at dinner. Vaishali tactfully changed the topic, and later forbade her to discuss it in presence of men. Though Kranti had been of immense help to Kanupriya when she was physically assaulted by her husband, she missed no opportunity to pass a scathing comment whenever she ran into Kranti. Often, Prema and Kanupriya discussed the episode in their cosy chat, and once Prema told her sister-in-law and friend, "One of these days your brother is going to get into serious trouble."

Deepak was not considered for the Padma Vibhushan that year. He blamed it on Vinay, and Trevedi confirmed it. At the 'At Home' thrown by the President on Republic Day, the Home Minister assured Deepak that he would get the award next year.

IX

Meeting With An Old Friend

"I am taking out Madhu for dinner," Deepak told Vaishali.

"Why?"

"I'll tell you about it on return."

"A Madhu sympathy wave is sweeping across my home. First, it was Kranti getting more affectionate than required. Now it's your turn."

"Come on, I am not going to do anything stupid." He laughed, and she smiled, and glanced at her daughter-in-law who had just entered the drawing room. In a soft green crepe sari, a sleeveless blouse, and a shawl thrown carelessly on her shoulders, Madhulika looked bewitchingly beautiful.

"Ready?" he asked giving her an appreciative glance.

She nodded.

In the cheerful ambience of Eau De Monsoon, Le Meridian, Deepak introduced his daughter-in-law to Shekhar Srivastava, India's ambassador to China.

"My pleasure." He rose, and gently shook her hand. "Deepak, you have a knack of selecting pretty spouses for your children."

Deepak smiled affably.

Shekhar Srivastava was stocky with prominent sideburns, and a respectable paunch. He had a presence, Madhulika thought.

"Shekhar and I were together at the Academy and belong to U.P cadre."

"How has life treated you?" Deepak asked. They were meeting after almost three years.

"Not bad," he said, and smiled wryly. "I have another year in China. I am constructing a house at GK which will be ready in 4-5 months. My son has set up a factory in Bhiwadi, Rajasthan. I want to retire from active life and settle down."

"Men like you don't retire; you are sure to join politics."

"No, no," he said, and laughed, "unless —."

"Unless you are forced by the High Command!"

They laughed like old buddies.

Over dinner, Deepak discussed his son's problem, parting with the minimum information.

"I heard about it. The story was covered by BBC, and all the western media. Even in China. At that time, it never occurred to me that Vinay, the famous Vinay, is your son."

"I want you to meet Prof. Tse Tung and find out whether he is sane or not," Deepak said.

"We want to find out whether he is as sharp as he was earlier." Madhulika explained going into details, though hiding the core truth. She had overruled Deepak's suggestion of being candid.

"How would it help Vinay?" Srivastava asked point blank.

Deepak struggled nervously with the chicken.

"He is the only one who can establish about contributions made by Vinay and Stella." Madhulika clarified.

Condescendingly, he looked at Madhulika. "You are underestimating Jean Simpson. The letter of the Chinese professor was published in some American papers along with the whole story. And I know everything about the cheating of your husband."

"Oh," she muttered. Her bluff was called, and she could not face the ambassador.

Deepak apologized for underrating his friend and told all he knew. Madhulika supplemented where necessary, and again said, "We want to find out if the Chinese professor can distinguish between the work done by Vinay and Stella."

Without responding to her, Shekhar concentrated on the food, and said, "I've relished such excellent food after months."

Restless, Madhulika looked from her father-in-law to the ambassador and could not understand the reason for the latter's indifference. Deepak watched her sympathetically.

"You are playing the diplomat and not a friend," Deepak said.

Abruptly, Shekhar turned aggressive. "You have not treated me like a batch mate – hiding the real facts and trying to dupe me. You felt that like the Chinese professor, I have also turned dumb and imbecile."

"Sorry uncle, it's entirely my fault." Madhulika had tears in her eyes. "I forced papa on such a strategy."

"Save your tears for a more appropriate occasion, young lady." Srivastava was sarcastic. "First," he said flashing his angry eyes on her, "I don't like the thought of anyone pulling wool over my eyes."

"I said, I am sorry," Madhulika answered.

"Don't interrupt me." He snubbed her again. "Second, the China scenario is not like India or the US. Every step of the foreigners is watched. Remember that the professor was imprisoned for the high treason of engineering a coup. Though his daughter-in-law holds a high position in the party, she has achieved this by playing many dirty games. She is a suspect in at least two political murders and people do not have a good opinion of her. The professor is highly respected but under surveillance. Any attempt to approach him will be too risky. I'll not recommend it to anyone."

Srivastava had another sip of the coffee.

"Third, I don't want to do anything with a family of cheats and thieves."

"No one has said that to me and got away," Deepak said softly, so softly that even Madhulika could not hear it, but his tone was menacing.

Srivastava realized that he had gone too far but it was too late to withdraw.

"I am scared." Srivastava smiled arrogantly. "I am trembling all over."

"You are within your rights not to do a favour, but you have no business to insult me and my daughter-in-law."

"Despite your best efforts, your son will be in Tihar, one day."

"Shut up!" Madhulika hissed.

"No, Madhulika. No." Deepak gently placed his hand on her shoulder. "Control yourself."

He looked at his batchmate with all the contempt he deserved, and said, "I have never harmed a soul in my life on account of my personal reasons, but I'll bloody well teach you a lesson."

"I'll look forward to it." Srivastava was cocksure and in complete command of the situation. "And thanks for an excellent dinner. Good night."

"The bastard!" Madhulika said after Srivastava left.

After a long time, Deepak muttered, "I have never had it so bad in my life even when I was down in the dumps." His eyes were blurred.

"I am sorry, papa."

"It has nothing to do with you, it is because of Vinay. I am ashamed of him."

"I was about to repeat what I did with Jean Simpson, but you stopped me."

"Srivastava is not Jean Simpson; it is good that you controlled yourself."

On the return journey, he suddenly asked, "What were you mixing in the coffee?"

"Common salt and pepper. That was for the bastard's eyes."

Deepak smiled.

"I wish I had ignored your advice, I would have felt better," she said.

She gently pressed his hand. She knew that a decent gentleman had been badly mauled, and his pride wounded. And all this because of her husband!

A bond developed between the two. Earlier, he had always looked down on her zero status, and she had felt that he was a snob.

"If Vinay pulls through, it would be only because of you," he said.

"No, it would be because of help from all of you. I couldn't have managed him alone. That's why I moved to your place."

Madhulika was accepted by Deepak and Vaishali now, but Prema and Kanupriya continued to be lukewarm to her. Her attempts at befriending even the kids of Prema, and Kanupriya had misfired. Prema's unusual warmth at Puri was a one-time exception; at Akbar Road, she just tolerated her. After Kranti's flirtation with Madhulika, Prema had distanced herself from her. Knowing the weakness of her husband, the presence of a fair complexioned sister-in-law in the house was a constant threat to her. Unable to dismiss the thought that in some tacit way Madhulika had encouraged him, some animosity had crept in their relationship. As Kanupriya and Prema were close to each other, it was easy for Prema to influence Kanupriya.

(2)

In the early hour of the morning, when Deepak and Vaishali were at their first cup of tea in the lawn, Madhulika walked across, and said a 'hello' to them.

While scanning the newspaper, suddenly, Vaishali removed her spectacles, and looked at both. "So, yesterday you treated Shekhar to a dinner at Meridian."

"Were you chasing us?" Deepak grinned.

"No, a photographer was," she said, and handed over the paper to her husband.

Deepak and Madhulika were appalled to see an overblown photograph of the trio with a prominent caption, 'Is the Chairman, UPSC trying to pressurise our ambassador in China?'

A ten-line report described the background of the case. The story was not damaging as it stated facts, but the photograph with its caption was damning.

Shattered, Deepak collapsed.

"Deep!"

"Papa!"

"Are you okay, Deep?" Vaishali caught his hand.

"Yes, I am fine," he said slowly. "For an instant, I just blacked out."

Madhulika massaged his hands, and Vaishali his feet. "It's nothing, it will pass," Vaishali said. "You have seen much worse in life when you were all alone. Now you have so many of us - me, Prema, Madhu and all your children."

"I have never felt so low in my life; maybe I am getting old. I should watch my step."

"It is my battle, papa," Madhulika said. "I'll handle it."

"You are too raw and young— it is a war of veterans."

"Your papa is right," Vaishali said. "We all have to pitch in."

At Vaishali's insistence, Madhulika narrated the incident of the previous evening.

"Shekhar has stabbed us in the back," Vaishali said angrily.

Deepak nodded.

Two hours later, Deepak told Vaishali that he was taking off. When he went to bathroom, Vaishali whispered to Madhulika, "He was never like this. Always strong to the extent of even being arrogant when he was in a soup surrounded by his enemies."

"Were papa and Srivastava great friends?" Madhulika asked.

"Friends! No, they were like brothers as both didn't have any sibling. For four years at Lucknow, we were together in the same complex as a close-knit family. Our houses faced each other, and on Sundays and holidays, starting from breakfast right up to the after- dinner coffee, we were together. Deepak abhorred so much of intimacy and termed it 'devilish'. But Shekhar, Veena and I basked in its fervour and exuberance." Vaishali went on explaining the strong bonding that they had.

"I'm not surprised that papa is shocked," Madhulika said.

The past flashed across Vaishali while she was in the kitchen supervising the arrangements for the breakfast. "Veena is all right, but there is something crooked in Shekhar's thinking, attitude and breeding." Deepak had a supercilious air. "Keep him at a distance, I don't like the way he looks at you." Vaishali liked the couple and ignored Deepak's comments. Deepak and Vaishali's relationship was at its lowest; he was forced to gel in the company of Shekhar and Veena.

Committed and ingenious, Deepak's credibility was rated high in bureaucratic circles. In any crisis in the State or in a difficult or sensitive mission, he was picked up to spearhead it. His opinion and views were listened to with great respect. In contrast, Shekhar was a part of the coterie of the Chief Minister or the most powerful minister and did all his dirty work. It suddenly occurred to Vaishali that maybe Shekhar was jealous of Deepak because he missed no opportunity to ridicule or slight Shekhar. She had observed some unguarded expressions of Shekhar, which lent credence to her belief. In those days, she had not given a second thought to it because they trusted Shekhar. The jealousy and hatred against Deepak had built up over the decades and had now burst. She was beating the eggs, and suddenly her hand stopped functioning, and she stared stupidly at the eggs. "That's it," she muttered. "There could be no other logical reasoning." Baffled, Prema and Madhulika stared at their mother-in-law.

Deepak was unconvinced by Vaishali's theory of jealousy because competition and associated jealousy were deeply entrenched in bureaucracy. It was a vendetta: it was a deeper feeling of resentment that Shekhar had nurtured over the years, and it had exploded now.

Deepak dug into the past. He had forgotten the actual context, but he remembered that once Shekhar Srivastava had tried to avoid a meeting at Lucknow with a Union Minister of State and instead rushed to Delhi to meet his family and boarded an express train from Lucknow. In a bizarre incident, Shekhar was forcibly pulled out of the train at Kanpur, brought to Lucknow, and the meeting was held at night. Deepak had accompanied the Union Minister from Delhi. To make up, Shekhar had to abandon all pretence of dignity and literally prostrated before the Minister. Shekhar had held Deepak responsible for his fall from grace.

(3)

Deepak tried the Home Secretary several times, and finally caught him when he was about to leave for the airport.

"You saw the morning paper, Trevedi."

"It's very unfortunate."

"Get it checked up through your boys."

"I'll handle it. But your image has taken a beating. You must do something about it."

They conferred for fifteen minutes. Deepak lost his composure after the discussion.

As soon as Kranti reached the office, he was summoned by Krandhikar. An hour later when he reported at Head

Quarters, Krandhikar tossed the newspaper, and asked, "What is this? I didn't expect this from your father. I was slightly associated with him many years back when he was the Home Secretary; I had nothing but admiration for him. He was like the pole star guiding thousands around him. I don't like this new image of him."

Kranti could not stand the contempt in his voice. Because of the unusual importance associated with the newspaper that morning, it had not left Vaishali's room, and Kranti could not browse through it. Dazed at seeing the photograph and the caption, he muttered, "Its sheer nonsense."

"To me, it makes sense." Krandhikar retorted.

"It doesn't!" Kranti thundered. Where family pride was concerned, he didn't bother even about his boss. "Shekhar Srivastava and my papa are batchmates and great friends. Someone is out to malign us."

Kranti narrated how close the two families were. "It was like one family."

Krandhikar assured him that he would get it checked through someone. "But you will not inquire into it." He warned and entrusted it to Sudha Verma though it was not in her jurisdiction.

Whenever Vinay was unable to lay his hands on the paper, he suspected there was some news item about him, and ma would have hidden it. Papa's not going to the office without a valid reason also struck him as unusual. He sneaked into ma's room, retrieved the paper, and sat down in the lawn next to Prema.

"Oh, my god!" he muttered on seeing the photograph. "Papa must have been badly hurt."

"Yes, that's why he didn't go to the office," Prema answered.

"So, papa is the Number 2 on the casualty list. I have stained the image of the family— it will have its repercussions. A few casualties are expected. Some price must be paid."

Prema didn't appreciate the logic of his argument and frowned.

"There is only one way to avoid it — to discard the criminal. Throw me out of the house." He raised his downcast head and looked at her. "I have given lot of thought to it for the last two weeks; it is the only solution."

"You are talking nonsense," she said.

But the remark registered.

Maybe, there was some truth in his statement. Kranti often hinted that Vinay's presence was creating its own problems in the house. Who would be the next casualty? she wondered.

(4)

With a little effort, Sudha made the bony photographer spill the beans. She was shocked to learn that Shekhar Srivastava had engaged him for ten thousand rupees.

Three hours later when Sudha told the entire story to the Commissioner in Kranti's presence, he said, "Sorry, Kranti, the stars are against your family." He placed his massive hand on Kranti's shoulder. "In the world of today, no one stands with losers. But I and Sudha will always be by your side."

"Thank you, sir, thank you." Kranti caught his Chief's hand affectionately.

"Be brave, and upright," Krandhikar said, and dismissed them.

Later, Kranti thanked Sudha for her support.

"Even if the whole world is against you, I will be on your side, sir," she said.

(5)

Madhulika escorted her husband to the Gymkhana, played tennis, and swam in the pool with him. Sipping coffee in the restaurant later, she grew a little emotional. "We should always be like this — playing, swimming, and laughing together."

Looking affectionately at her and adjusting her long curl that had slipped out of its position, Vinay said, "Madhu, you have been an excellent wife to me for the last few months, which I did not deserve. But for your love and care, I would have been in a mental asylum. Like all good things in life, it has to come to an end."

"But why? We have understood each other only now."

"I could be jailed."

"How? There is no evidence."

"How long will I carry this burden?"

She assured him that both will face it together.

"No, it is my crime. I'll pay the price."

"Whether you like it or not, we all are in it. You are a part of the family; we all share the kudos and ignominy together."

"My presence in the house is casting aspersions on others. I understand the working of bureaucrats' mind."

"It will pass. And if others can't take it, we will rent a house and shift there. After all, Delhi is a big place."

He looked at her sad face embroiled in tension, and said, "Would you promise me something?"

"No," she said fiercely. "No, I'll not promise anything."

Prema had divulged the conversation she had with Vinay to Madhulika, and she knew where he was leading her. Signalling the waiter for the bill, she rose abruptly, and said, "Let us go."

□□□

X

Confession

In a state of confusion, Kranti reached home and briefed his father.

"When we were young, we had the impression that Srivastava uncle was your bosom friend. Why did he stab you in the back?" Kranti asked.

"Honestly, I don't know." Deepak confessed.

Vaishali blamed it on Veena's death. "Shekhar has changed. But how could he be so vicious? He seems to hate us. Is there something wrong with us?"

Most of the time, Vaishali was stressed over family matters, however, she was able to camouflage it under her charming smile. But today, her poise was shattered; she was ferocious and would have murdered Srivastava if he had crossed her path.

"He planned it," she muttered, "and succeeded."

Kranti looked at the disorientated face of his father, and said, "Now I understand. It means Vinay really cheated. He stole the work of Stella. And you knew it all along."

"We will talk about it after dinner," Deepak said as if postponing an unpleasant meeting.
A few minutes later, Madhulika knocked, and entered Deepak's room. "You wanted to see me, papa."
Deepak told her about Kranti's findings. "It is high time that everyone knows the facts."
Noiselessly, Vinay walked in. "I agree. Keeping everyone under suspense is unfair. I propose to tell my story after dinner."

After dinner, everyone including Vivek (who was visiting Delhi to attend a meeting in the ministry) huddled in the drawing room. Vinay rose as if to deliver a lecture. They listened to Vinay's story attentively as if it was a piece of fiction.
"That's my story or confession, if you like." Vinay concluded. "And I am prepared to pay the price."
Vivek was the first to react. "What do you have in mind?"
"Admission of cheating on an affidavit in a court or to police. I am mentally prepared to go to jail for seven years."
"Nonsense. Without any evidence how can you be sent to jail for seven years?" Madhulika spoke intensely.
"You are out of your mind. Why do you want to admit it in a court or before the police? Let Jean go to police if she wants to," Vaishali said.
Deepak advised that a press conference would be the best choice.
Everyone opposed it except Vivek.
"Your father stole the identity of someone, but he didn't admit it before the law. It was much worse than what Vinay has done," Vaishali said, and added with a sneer, "though he became a sadhu later."

"He suffered." Vivek voiced. He knew his grandfather more intimately than any other family member. "But he had the inner strength to withstand the suffering. Any other person might have shattered under stress or gone mad."

"Personal prejudices apart, let us see what is best for bhaiya fully appreciating that Vinay is Vinay and not Dadu." Kanupriya tried to steer the conversation back to the main issue, but crosstalk dominated for the next few minutes.

"There is another option," Vinay said. "To resign."

Everyone was hushed into silence.

"And then do what?" Vaishali asked.

"Business?" Prema suggested.

No one took her seriously for there was no surplus money for a business venture.

"It could be a school job." Madhulika proposed.

"My son and a schoolteacher?" Vaishali grimaced.

"I think it's an excellent idea," Vivek said, and placed his hand on Vinay's shoulder.

"A schoolteacher?" Kranti made a face as if the thought was repugnant to him.

"It is much more honourable than being a Deputy Commissioner, Police." Vivek retorted.

The women talked politely whereas the men were more aggressive, and passionate.

Vinay rose, clapped his hands calling them to attention. "It has really become a rowdy class."

Everyone laughed; they needed it.

"You may discuss my future at leisure, I have time. At least I think so for Jean Simpson does not appear to be in a hurry," Vinay said. "But keep it in mind that I want

to live."
Each one looked sadly at him.
"Nine or ten years back, I was frustrated and dejected. I opted for a soft option. At that point of time, I didn't realise that I would be such a world-famous physicist. Neither had I bargained for such a fall. But now, I will not be able to take a second fall. One was enough."
Catching his wife's arm, he rose.

(2)

The eyes of all the family members were transfixed at the door as Vinay leaning slightly on his wife, opened the door, exited, and then gently closed it. The air was dense with sympathetic murmurs for the fallen angel. The brightest child of the Chopra household was now in such a state of low esteem and humiliation. They all disliked him for the treachery, but considering his repentance — their hearts went out to him. For the first time, Vaishali realised that the family was united, and stood by him, though each one had a different suggestion for handling the crisis. When Deepak was in the doldrums, he was alone; ironically, she was the one who had fired the salvos at him. Unlike his son, Deepak was always righteous. Suddenly, she felt very proud of her husband.

A few minutes later, there was shuffling of feet, and the noise of pushing chairs. Deepak told them to remain seated for some more time. It was already past 11 pm, everyone was sleepy. Vivek was in a hurry to leave for Meerut. "Papa, we will think about this, and get back later."
"It is not that. Will you sit down?" Deepak snapped at Vivek; he didn't approve of his insubordinate son.
"Trevedi told me that there is a possibility that I may be

offered a governorship after my term expires in UPSC, and possibly a Padma Vibushan next year."

He was congratulated by all his kin.

"He hinted something else in that connection."

Everyone looked at him with anxiety. Deepak was nervous; he didn't know how to break such news to his own children. Life was less complicated in office, and as Cabinet Secretary, he could handle the most delicate issues even relating to the security of the country with aplomb.

"Come on papa," Vivek said growing restless. "I'll miss my last train."

Kranti assured him that he would arrange to get him dropped.

Uneasily, Deepak continued, "Vinay's involvement in a case, which borders on cheating, is bad publicity. Trevedi was saying —"

Kranti nodded, he also felt the same way.

All at once, Vivek understood, and broke into laughter. Everyone stared at him in disbelief.

"Trevedi wants you to disown Vinay, isn't it, papa? Issue a press release that you have nothing to do with him and throw him out of the house."

"Not exactly, but something to that effect."

"But where will he go?" Vaishali was deeply worried.

"Vinay can stay with me but what will happen to Madhulika?" Vivek said.

"That's why Vinay had hinted about leaving the house," Prema muttered to herself. Kranti glanced at her with annoyance.

"Would it matter if you forget about the governorship or a Padma Vibhushan?" Vivek mocked at his father.

Deepak disliked that arrogant smile of his son, that he knew, was his own gift to his progeny.

Vaishali was utterly confused; she didn't know whether to support her husband or Vinay.

"Stop it, Vivek. How can you behave like this to your papa?" she said.

"They are all entitled to misbehave whenever they choose to," Deepak said trying to calm his wife. "Yes, it would matter."

Disgusted, Vivek shook his head. "How? Is it name, fame or glory?"

"Our first duty is to our son, Deep."

"It's much more. It is more important than our duty to our son, Vaishali. He is in his late thirties and should handle his affairs himself."

The family was aghast; no one had heard Deepak speak the language of an egotist.

"I have debts to the tune of 4-5 lakhs. If I don't get an assignment, our survival will be difficult. We will not be able to maintain this lifestyle."

It stunned them.

"I've never said it earlier but today, driven to wall, I will make things clear." Deepak turned his eyes on his youngest son. "You are thirty-one going to be thirty-two. You are also planning to raise a family. Till date, you have not earned much. And you have the cheek to insult me as if I am a mean, petty father who is so selfish that he is only worried about himself – his fame and glory. If Vaishali were not giving you a monthly allowance, you would have been begging on the roads!"

Deepak realized he had to do it to put his recalcitrant son in his proper place.

"And you Kranti?" Deepak turned his head towards his second son. "Since your marriage you have not contributed any thing to the household expenditure. I am not sure, but maybe you will be willing to pay off the loan against the house, provided the house is given to you. You have the money — about 12-13 lakhs — but you want to do it on your terms."

Vaishali squeezed his arm. "Deep, please Deep, we can talk of it later." She didn't want him to get so worked up.

Ignoring her, he continued, "It's so surprising that the man we consider as a thief — is the only one who has a large heart. He has blown all his savings on his in - laws. If I had given a hint, he would have probably paid off the entire loan."

He took a glass of water offered by Kanupriya, and again looked at Vivek. "Now, do you understand why I am trying for another assignment?"

"I am sorry, papa," Vivek said.

"In a way, all four of us are dependent on papa," Kanupriya said making situation clear. No one was contributing to running of the house. "We should all pitch in."

Vivek and Prema nodded.

"I am also sorry that I was so petty in talking about things which I do not want to talk about. You forced me."

He rose, patted Vivek on the shoulder, and turned towards his room.

"But papa, please do consider that second shock might be Vinay's last," Vivek said apologetically, and left the room.

Shaken, Vaishali ran, and opened the door of her room for Deepak.

"Deepak was never like this," she murmured to herself as she changed her clothes. Later, nestling by his side, she

said, “You should have told me.”
“I had a feeling, I would be able to handle it, but Vivek made me lose my cool.”
“He is still irresponsible — he does not know what he is blabbering. But what he said about Vinay is true.”
“Let all of them go to hell,” he said furiously. “Talk of something pleasant. And let nature take its own course.”
“Love me,” she whispered.

Prema and Kranti kept on arguing about money matters till the early hours of the morning. Whatever Deepak had pointed out in the family gathering was factually true. Prema had been gifted Rs 5 lakhs by her father that had increased to 8-9 lakhs. Since they did not contribute to the household expenditure, Kranti’s savings were also about 3-4 lakhs. But Kranti did not want to part with money and kept it for the future of the children.
“The old man wants the money — let us give it to him gracefully?” Prema said.
“Why should we give all the money? Let all the four children share the burden,” he said. “Money always comes in handy. Keep it.”
He turned his head away from her wanting to catch some sleep. Prema felt mean that they had been sponging on the old couple. If Kranti as the son of the family did not volunteer, why should she spoil her sleep over it? But the thought disturbed her throughout the night.

Vaishali was transformed after the change in her equation with Deepak. The bliss of love coloured her face and body. Often, she laughed, even at inappropriate moments, raising the eyebrows of the younger women though men, involved in their routine and office stresses (or lacking in sensitivity), didn’t notice. She moved with alacrity, her step had a bounce, and her wit was more accentuated. Aware of Vinay's tribulations, she had to make an extra effort to suppress her cheerfulness, but invariably it spilled over at dinner time helping everyone to face the prevailing storm.

Worried about her husband, Vaishali could not sleep. At dawn, she slipped out of the bed, wrapped herself in woollens and stepped out in the lawn. Cold wind hit her, but she liked the feel of it. Dew covered the lawn, the bushes, ferns, and the red roses. Except for the chirping of some birds at the other end of the garden, it was unusually quiet. On an impulse, she removed her chappals and stepped on the dew. Her feet trampled the dew below, leaving an imprint. As she walked on the grass, she realised that the gardener had been careless as the grass had not been cut for last 2-3 weeks.

Strolling for about half an hour, she brought a tea tray and had it all alone. She looked at the chaos her feet had made on the sheet of dew and was amused at the disharmony her presence had created in nature. When the first rays of the sun splayed on the top of the blades of grass, they glistened like a sea of micro lights. Excited like a child, Vaishali wanted to rush inside and share it with Deepak. She rose, and all of a sudden changed her mind.

After a little while, the dew melted. She wondered whether she would leave an indelible impression on the lives of her children, or would she be forgotten immediately after her death like her steps on dew? Will the stigma on Vinay also fade away or haunt his progeny, if any?

(3)

Two weeks back, Sheila had returned from the US looking

fresh and plump. To mitigate her bitterness, Vaishali had made it a point to receive her at the airport. Ignoring her gracious gesture, Sheila decided to drive away to Lehriya village straight from the airport almost snubbing her prospective mother- in-law. For her son's sake, Vaishali pocketed the insult though Prema could not contain her temper and frowned at Sheila. "Not a wise thing to do," she told Vivek. Excited to be alone with his fiancée, he had endorsed Sheila's decision.

Despite his father's vitriol, Vivek was not unusually disconcerted when he reached home. He noticed Sheila at the balcony and waved at her.

"So, your brother again obliged you," she said. Her tone was offensive.

"Of course, but you don't seem to like him. Why?"

"As a cop, he is useful but some how he intimidates me."

"Strange, he was very popular with the girls in college. Women have invariably adored him. Out of all of us, he is the only one who is virile and exudes masculinity."

"It depends on what one is looking for?"

"And what are you looking for, Sheila?"

"Vivek, Vivek and only Vivek." She kissed him.

Smitten by flattery, he hugged her, and asked, "And there is no trace of Vivek in Kranti."

"Strangely, I find lots of traces of you in Vinay and your father."

"Holy saints!" he said using his favourite expression. "I don't like both. Vinay is a phoney and now an established crook. And I can't stand my father since childhood. And you see me in him."

"Yep, I do."

"You are nuts, and I do not relish this thought."

"Because you cannot face the truth."

"No, I can, but I can't stand what is absurd."

"Okay, listen to me, my prospective husband. According to the existing established norms of the society, you are a failed version of your papa."

Dazed, he stared at her as if he had been knocked out by her.

"But I don't consider myself as a failure," he said roughly, and disentangled himself from her long, thin arms.

"Neither do I?" She smiled sweetly, and possessively again threw her arms around him. "That's why I am here."

Uneasily, he looked at her wondering whether she was pulling a fast one.

"Dinner is ready."

He informed her that he had had his dinner with ma.

"Fully knowing that I would be waiting for you. At least, you could have sent a message."

A PCO was installed at a grocery shop about a furlong away, and the owner often sent a boy to relay the message.

"There was some problem in the lines." He lied. "In future, you need not wait for me."

Unconsciously, his voice had cracked, and become hoarse. Intuitively, she knew that he was lying.

"Do not raise your voice. It is not my fault if for more than a decade you have been carrying wrong notions about yourself."

Without retaliating, he left the room. It was their first major quarrel after they decided to stay under one roof. Unable to stand the resentment, she invaded his room, apologized for hurting his ego, and made up by having sex with him.

She fixed drinks, and inquired about Vinay's progress,

and he told her all that had happened.

Thoughtfully, she said, "You should not be throwing an invitation to your brother. How will we manage in these two rooms?" She shook her head disapprovingly. "We will lose all our privacy."

"Come on, we will manage, if we have to." He spoke spiritedly.

"Have you thought of the impact Vinay's presence will have on your project? Your high moral standards will suffer, and your credibility will go down. With Vinay in our house, people will stop believing in you."

"But Vinay is not as bad as you think."

"He is a cheat — no, a thief who stole his lover's work. How can you be forgiving towards such a cold-blooded criminal?" She continued to rattle.

"Sheila, please listen. Vinay has suffered, he has repented."

"Vinay should be in a jail or in a mental asylum otherwise he will be a bad influence on others."

"How can you talk like this as if he is a monster? He is a decent gentleman. He did all this in one weak moment."

"Gentleman – that bloody f**** thief!" she shrieked shrilly in the early hours of dawn. "He is a criminal and cannot stay here."

Her extreme intolerance upset him for generally she was a pleasant, sensible, and a witty woman. How could she behave in such a way? Where was her compassion and kindness for humanity that had endeared the locals to her?

"We will talk about it tomorrow." He tried to postpone the crisis; it was a technique practised by his father.

"No, let us decide it right now," she again screamed. "You have to choose between me and Vinay."

The vodka she had been consuming since evening, had added to the instability of her temper. With superhuman effort, he didn't react, and instead said softly, "I am not a dunce to fight on behalf of my brother at this hour. Of course, I choose you." Without giving further opportunity to her to indulge in a reprisal, he picked her up, and very slowly lowered her onto the bed. Mumbling sweet endearments, he made love to her again, and caressed her on the temple for a long time, something he knew she liked, till sleep stole over her.

He rose, went to the balcony, and saw the pinkish red orb of the sun about to emerge. Unable to control any longer, he burst into tears, and muttered to himself, "And imagine — I wanted to change this world with her help!"

(4)

After Deepak, and Shekhar Srivastava's picture appeared in the print media, Deepak proceeded on leave, and it upset Supriya. Unable to reach him on the cell, she called upon him in the evening with a large bouquet of roses for Vaishali. She welcomed her with a rich smile, and lightly hugged her. Deepak was pleased to see her.

When Vaishali went inside to arrange for tea, Supriya asked softly, "It's the photograph, isn't it?"

He nodded.

"I am sorry, sir. It's getting more complicated. How many weeks will you be on leave?"

"At least one or two. I don't know how I'll face the other members?"

"It is not your doing but Vinay's," she said, and craning her neck a little closer to him, added, "Let Madhu and Vinay stay in some other place, and you can wash your hands off him saying you have nothing to do with such a son who has criminal tendencies. After all, he is not a kid; he is going to be forty and should manage his own affairs."

"I have some duties as a father. You'll understand it when your children grow up, though Trevedi also advised me on similar lines."

"Because he is fond of you. He wants to make sure that you get the governorship and Padma Vibhushan next year."

"But everyone here is advocating Vinay's cause. My telling him to leave will shatter him."

When Supriya saw Vaishali bringing the tea -trolley, she changed the topic.

The phone rang, and Vaishali rushed back. She handed over the cordless to her husband saying that the Director I I T was on the line.

"I am told that you are not well," Prof Sinha said.

Deepak informed him that he was better.

"Everything is fine at the I I T front except that some people are acting funny. But nothing to worry, the situation is under control."

Deepak thanked him.

"Incidentally, Chopra sahib, my son's father-in-law is trying for the Directorship of CRRI (Central Road Research Institute). The interview is tomorrow. His name is Sudhir — Sudhir Bhatnagar. TK Shourie will be in the chair. I am told that he knows you personally."

"I'm on long leave."

Sinha laughed, and hinted obtrusively that it was for the general good of everyone. "However, I will leave it to you."

Deepak told both the women about the favour sought

by Sinha. At Kurukshetra University, a couple of years back, Sudhir Bhatnagar had swindled many lakhs.

Supriya advised Deepak to watch his step as the photograph had already done a lot of damage. "You have lost the Padma Vibhushan once; you should not lose it again next year."

"And Vinay?" Vaishali looked in dismay at her husband.

"I don't know." Deepak was confused.

"Ma'am may not approve of me, but sir, your wavering disturbs me."

"I too am interested in the welfare of your boss, Supri," Vaishali said, desperately trying to control her rising temper. "But I am also worried about my son."

Deepak and Supriya were quiet and looked uncertainly at each other.

"Look at the world around us. There is rampant corruption, nepotism, and favouritism." Vaishali said using her husband's jargon. "It is a world of opportunists, and self seekers, not idealists. The norms and standards of the three of us look almost ludicrous. I don't want my son to be sacrificed for such a world."

"But he is guilty," Deepak said.

"Let the law takes its own course. If they find him guilty, let them hang my son. But why go out of the way to sacrifice him."

"But I am not advocating it," Deepak told.

"This business of resigning, taking up a school job and press conference. What else is this?"

"Resigning and school job was Vinay's idea, not mine. Press conference was mine but —"

Aware that she had hurt Vaishali's visceral feelings, Supriya receded from her aggressive stance. "Madam has a point, let things take their own course." She looked at Deepak. "But Sinha?"

"Either way it is dicey and can backfire. But keep in mind Vinay's future." Vaishali made her point.

"It is too risky, ma'am."

"I understand Supri, let us not do anything." Her voice was hostile, and she looked angrily at her watch.

Hurriedly, Supriya was on her feet.

"Bye ma'am, bye sir!"

After Supriya's abrupt departure, Vaishali looked crossly at her husband. "How is it that both of you speak the same language."

"After all, we are in the same office."

"She is the Secretary of the Commission and not your PS." Vaishali snubbed him.

"You are unnecessarily losing your cool. You were also rude to the poor girl."

"I don't approve of anyone advocating idealism at the expense of my son. Neither do I appreciate any woman showing more concern for your welfare than your wife."

"Then show it!"

"What?"

The little mischief in his eyes made her look quizzically at him. Appreciating the incongruity of her comment, she laughed, walked up to him and kissed him.

"Bad news, sir," Supriya told Deepak on the phone the next afternoon. "Sudhir Bhatnagar was insulted and humiliated in the interview."

One of the selectors was known to her, and she had obtained information from him.

Bhatnagar had made a snide comment about plagiarism in research and hinted obliquely at Vinay. Shourie lambasted him and made a reference to the swindling of twenty lakhs by him when he was at Kurukeshtra. Bhatnagar protested that he had been exonerated in the inquiry, but Shourie said that they all knew who got the money. At the end of the interview, Bhatnagar was on verge of tears.

“Sir, Sinha will be furious,” Supriya added.

“Yes,” he said.

“Even if you had put in a word, it would have made no difference, and you might have earned a bad name.”

When she got no response, she again asked, “Are you still there, sir?”

“Yes, I am wondering what Sinha will do. How much will he harm Vinay?”

“Sir, I don’t think he will do anything till he is certain of his extension.”

But Deepak was not sure.

XI

Julian's Entry

Since the day Jean Simpson denounced Vinay in the All India Science Congress at Kolkata, and the subsequent shifting of Madhulika and Vinay to Deepak's place, Kranti and Prema had felt marginalized. They found that papa and ma were all the time obsessed about Vinay's physical and mental health, and its aftermath on Madhulika. At breakfast or dinner, the conversation revolved around the latest news on Vinay, and how to minimize the damage to Vinay's future. How the scandal affected others' image, reputation and lives was of least concern. After Vinay's confession when the issue had cropped up, Kranti had also wanted to endorse Deepak's viewpoint that the scandal was tarnishing his image; however, he was unable to intervene. He had located an unpopular guest house and was about to suggest to his parents that Vinay and Madhulika could stay there for six or seven months, but after Deepak's reaction on money matters, he lost the nerve. There was such a powerful tidal wave of empathy for Vinay and specially Madhulika that everyone appeared to be drowned in it including Kranti's children. Prema and Kranti's relationship was also slightly fractured after Julian labelled him a devil at the party, and his flirtation with Madhulika.

On learning that his son Kunal had flunked in maths in class v, Kranti was angry and severely criticised Prema for ignoring him at the expense of NRK. Of late, its activities had expanded considerably, and Prema had little time to spare for the children.

"Find out a good tutor for him instead of blaming me." She retorted. One argument led to the other, and the trivial issue blew up out of proportion; Vaishali had to intervene and restore order. But finding a good tutor was not easy.

Vaishali developed trouble in her legs, a belated consequence of her accident last year, and the orthopaedic surgeon suggested traction at home for a couple of days. It impaired her mobility, and adversely affected the running of the house. Desertion of both the servants turned the situation into a nightmare.

When Prema confided the problem of domestic help to Kavita, she told her that she was leaving for the US next fortnight. Amit had bagged a two- year fellowship at the Johns Hopkins School of Medicine, Baltimore, Maryland and she too had managed a fellowship in the school for social work in the university. Prema congratulated her and was critical of her for not informing earlier.

"I am surprised why Kranti has not told you as he knew about it more than two months ago."

Though confused, Prema defended that he might have forgotten due to the pressure of work. Vaishali overheard the two friends' conversation and mentioned to Prema that she should ask for Kavita's maid Julian, known to be a willing worker, and good at maths. Disconnecting the phone, Prema voiced her fears aloud. "You are not aware that Julian is a very fair and pretty woman."

"So what?"

"You know your son."

"Don't talk nonsense. Julian is a servant."

"If you insist, I'll talk to Kranti."

Kranti was enraged when Prema suggested it in the evening.

"What are you trying to prove?" Kranti asked.

"That you are a faithful husband, and your wife trusts you implicitly."

"I don't give a damn. But Julian will not come in this house," he said furiously.

Prema was also opposed to Julian's presence at home, but somehow, Kranti's overreaction made her retaliate.

"What if I bring her?" She challenged.

"I'll give you hell!" He threatened.

Over dinner, she gave the gist of her husband's reaction to Vaishali's proposal.

"Why can't Julian be a servant in this house?" Vaishali questioned her son.

"I don't want it." Kranti was emphatic.

"Your views have to be rational." Vaishali persisted.

"If I have a say in this house, Julian will not come here."

"Decisions of this nature should be left to the women of the house." Deepak and Vinay advised Kranti.

"And the wise men will look after the matters of the state!" Kanupriya had a dig at them. Her remark diffused the tension before the family broke up for the night.

Under a barrage of questions from his wife, Kranti felt helpless; he did not know how to weather this new kind of storm in the shape of Julian. Frustrated, he charged at Prema, and caught her arm roughly. She winced in pain.

"Julian will not enter this house." He yelled.

"Sort it out with your ma."

"It's your doing."

"You scoundrel – go and ask your mom."

He twisted her arm again; this time the pain shot through her shoulder, and she screamed.

"This? For a servant? Now, I'll not only make sure that Julian comes here, but will get to the bottom of it."

She looked at him with fire in her eyes.

(2)

Determined to find out why Kranti vehemently opposed the idea of Julian working as a servant at their place, Prema drove to Kavita's office in the morning when she had hardly settled. Her unannounced arrival surprised Kavita.

"What are you going to do about Julian?" Prema asked.

"She is likely to get a job in an embassy."

"We all want that she should come to our place and get the same salary and status that she enjoys at your place."

"Have you taken Kranti's assent?"

"No, but I want to find out the reason for his refusal."

"Why are you trying to dig out unpleasant things?"

"Being the wife, I am directly involved," she said. "And do you know, because of this he assaulted me last night?"

Kavita was grave and confused.

"Tell me what you know," Prema asked.

"It's not my secret."

"Is it Kranti and Julian's secret?"

"Yes."

"Then I'll talk to Julian."

In the next forty-five minutes, Prema reached Kavita's residence, and rang the bell.

"Come ma'am, I was expecting you. Madam phoned me."

Julian was grim.

Prema made the offer to her for working at her place. Julian refused on the ground that hers was a large family, and she would not be able to handle the pressure of work.

"Is that the only reason?"

"Yes, ma'am."

"Why did you scream on the night of the party?"

"I remembered something out of my past."

"Connected with my husband?"

Julian refused to answer.

"What did my husband do to you?"

Julian was tense, her lips quivered, but she remained quiet.

"Made a pass at you?"

She shook her head.

"Kiss or molest you."

Again, the woman shook her head.

Out of the blue, Prema asked, "Did he rape you?"

"Yes!"

The woman cried and sobbed.

Shocked, Prema's fingers trembled. As the President of NRK, it was not easy to get information from the rape victims; Prema had to be slow and patient before she was able to draw out the bits and pieces of the facts and get a total picture before lodging the formal police complaint. But in this case, the victim was willing to part with all the details, and the criminal was her husband whom she had known for the last eleven years and more.

"Are you sure it was Mr. Chopra? You could be wrong; it may be somebody else."

"I am sure."

"Could you give me all the facts of the case, the way it happened?"

"What difference does it make?"

"To me it matters." Prema insisted.

Julian told her tormenting tale, and added, "I was the most sought-after prostitute of Kolkata who was groomed to look after the VVIPs. The only difference is that your husband was the first one, and my hands and feet were tied."

"I am sorry," Prema muttered.

"You have seen my husband a few times earlier, but you were not able to recognize him?" Prema asked.

"It was dark when I saw him at Nongpoh; I could not recognize him distinctly. At the party, he was wearing the same type of clothes and the atmosphere was similar. I had no difficulty in recognizing him from his body language."

Prema was confused.

"But it is true that if your husband had not come, I would have been raped by six or seven of them the same night instead of four months later."

The thought that she had been sleeping with a man who had raped an innocent, helpless girl in her teens troubled Prema. Bewildered, and unable to accept Julian's story, she said, "My husband belongs to one of the illustrious families of Delhi. He had the best of education, had many girl friends in school and college. I wonder how he could rape you?"

"If you are indicating that I was a party to the rape or I seduced him — no, you are mistaken."

Prema looked deep into Julian's eyes trying to fathom any element of falsehood.

"Yes, I was nude - my hands and feet were tied, and I was helpless. To that extent I was responsible."

"If what you say is right, such a man deserves to be punished. Would you like to be avenged?"

Julian was in for a surprise. "Your husband is a senior officer in police. I was a famous call girl of Kolkata. The complaint will not be even registered in a police station. And why would you do such a thing ma'am?"

Tenderly, she looked at the woman, and said, "My father retired as a Supreme Court Judge. Often, he told me that in our society, everyone fears the mighty and powerful, and they are above the law. Whereas the weak and the poor are trampled by everyone - there is no one to protect them. 'Look after them, Prema.' he has told me repeatedly. I have started a voluntary organization, which looks after very poor women wronged by society. I take up their cases and help them get justice."

"Are you aware that you will ruin your family and your life?"

"I know what I am doing."

"You are doing it for a lowly maid who was once a whore."

"You are a human being first - a whore or not a whore. If my husband has raped an innocent girl, he must be punished."

In disbelief, Julian looked at Prema. "Can there be such a thing as justice for a woman like me?"

Ashamed of answering Julian, Prema asked her, "Do I expect you the day after Kavita flies to the US?"

"Yes, ma'am."
"And it is not going to be easy for both of us."
"I know it, ma'am."

(3)

Julian's entry in the Chopra house was received with curiosity and warmth by everyone except Kranti who proceeded to Chandigarh for a day. The men - Deepak, Vinay and Vivek - were bowled over by her youth, beauty and charm; the women were taken in by her professionalism, and her willingness to do all the odd jobs.

"She does not give the impression of being a maid," Vivek said. "With a servant like her, the standard of our house has gone up a few notches."

Above all, Julian also promised to teach maths to Kunal solving Prema's problem of finding a tutor for her son.

In a sleeveless pink check shirt, and a long matching skirt, Julian was cleaning the paintings in the lounge when Kranti returned cheerfully from Chandigarh. On spotting her, he was flustered, and marched up to her.

"Why are you in my house?" he shouted.

Julian refused to reply and continued her work.

"Answer me?" he thundered at her.

"Prema madam has hired me."

"I want you to get out."

"I'll go if she orders."

"You are not afraid of me?" He snarled at her. He moved forward, caught the front portion of her shirt, and brought her forcibly closer to him.

"Do you know that I can rough you up?" He looked fiercely at her. "Beware of me, and don't ever cross my path."

Drained of blood, Julian became numb.

"So, you are afraid of me." He hissed.

Suddenly, he shoved her back. Unprepared, she lost control, and would have stumbled if she had not caught the sofa. He was pleased with the result and smiled at her.

Slowly, she rose, and with all the venom bottled up for years, she spat right into his face.

Kranti raised his arm to strike her when his eyes met his mother's through the window; she was strolling in the lawn with help of a walking stick.

He froze, his hand in the air.

Vaishali had a knack of catching her son in the most embarrassing situations.

"Are you all right, Julian?"

"Yes, ma'am."

"I am coming," Vaishali said, and slowly walked in. Meanwhile, Kranti had fled. Vaishali told the maid to sit down next to her. She noticed a scratch near her bosom, and a button on the shirt had become loose.

"Do you know Kranti?" Vaishali asked her.

Julian did not answer.

Prema entered the room, and said, "Why don't you tell madam everything?"

Julian broke down. Prema had to pitch in and told the entire sordid tale.

Stunned, Vaishali muttered, "My son and a rapist!"

Unable to accept such a preposterous thought, she mumbled, "This woman is a liar."

But after a little while, Vaishali shook her head in disgust, and said, "But no, from what I saw and heard, she can't be wrong."

Her face became dark as if she had seen a ghost.

Surrounded by chaotic thoughts, she rose to go to her room, and told her daughter-in-law, "Protect her from Kranti."

"I will, mummy."

"I'll go and sleep for some time." Disoriented, she clumsily made way to her room.

Kranti had slipped away and gone to office for sometime. He returned late and did not join the rest of the family for dinner on the plea that he had taken some snacks with a friend.

Shaken after the incident, Julian felt that she had made a mistake in taking up the new assignment. Despite the assurances of her new mistress and the sympathy shown by other women, she seriously considered quitting. Her tormentor was a famous cop in Delhi Police and the son of a reputed bureaucrat. It was almost like a wishful thinking for her and her mistress to get her first rapist punished. Who would register a police case against him? Julian tossed in the bed and could not sleep.

Late in the night, her helplessness was replaced by anger, and she decided to make her rapist pay for raping her. How dare he rape her when it was his duty to protect women in trouble?

Kranti kept on switching the channels till Prema arrived after settling the kids in their room. When the door was closed, he told her, "So, you brought the bitch home."

"That's no way to talk about a decent maid."

"Decent my foot," Kranti said, and smiled. He had got her past unearthed. "She was the highest paid prostitute of Kolkata and was in great demand. And she knew how to please her customers."

Suddenly, Prema did not like her husband. She wondered how she had spent the last eleven years and more with such a boorish man.

"She says that you raped her."

"No, I didn't, though now I wish I had. She must be delicious in bed."

"Perhaps, you are not aware of the nonsense you are talking before your wife. Anyhow, I believe Julian."

"That's your problem, Prema. You are being carried away by Julian's dramatics. And you want to deliver justice where no injustice has been done."

"It can become your problem if a case is registered against you."

"Who will register the case against me?" Kranti laughed. "You?"

"Yes, I or Julian."

"A prostitute filing a rape charge against the top cop of Delhi?" Kranti sneered. "It will be a funny situation."

With fire simmering in her eyes, Prema said, "I have loved you for the last so many years. Look into my eyes and say that you didn't rape Julian."

"What nonsense is this?" Kranti pushed her aside and rose from his seat.

"I know you did it," she said angrily. "Go and apologize to Julian. If she forgives, I'll not pursue the case in a court of law."

"Apologize to a maid who was a prostitute for six or seven years. No, thank you."

"But when you raped her, she was not a prostitute but an innocent college girl."

Confused, he was speechless.

"In another eight - nine years, it could happen to our

Namita."

"You are getting psychotic. For god's sake don't lose your sanity."

"A sincere apology at this stage will save us a lot of bother of court visits," she said. "I am dead serious, and I repeat: apologize to Julian."

"For what?"

Irritated, she almost shouted at him. "For raping her."

"I didn't do it."

"Okay, what is your story?"

"I have already told you and I'll repeat it."

This time he made it look more plausible, and she was almost convinced because she honestly wanted to believe that he hadn't done it. An imperceptible smirk on his lips undid everything.

"I used to believe you earlier; not now."

"Because of one woman, Julian," he said, and went up to her. "I love you Prema, and I have never done anything stupid."

"You have made passes at the fair ones including Madhu."

She told him to apologize to Julian several times, but he refused.

She rose and went to the sofa.

Quickly, he was up on his feet, and with a cocksureness developed over the years, lifted her in his powerful arms. His touch sent ripples of excitement in her body. Remembering what he had done to Julian, she said gently, "Stop it Kranti!"

Ignoring her protest, he brought her on the bed, and tried to kiss her.

"Don't touch me Kranti," she said.

For an instant, he fumbled with her nightie, and she

shrieked in the dead of the night, "Don't you dare touch me — you scoundrel?"
Her scream resounded in the night.
Kanupriya, whose room was just adjacent to Prema's, leapt up from her bed, dashed, and knocked.
"Are you alright, bhabi?"
"I am okay, thank you, Kanu."
But she didn't open the door. Vaishali, Madhulika and Vinay met Kanupriya in the lounge, and they looked uncertainly at one another.
"Go to sleep," Vaishali said thoughtfully. "She'll be alright."
Apprehensive, all of them went back to their bedrooms.
"You have woken up everyone. What do you want to prove? That I am an animal," Kranti said.
"You are worse."
Scared that her emotions would get the better of her, Prema settled down on the sofa, and refused to share the bed with him.

In the morning when Kranti got up, Prema had already left the room. He noticed his mother going through the morning paper alone with a cup of tea on the table; he walked over to the her.
"I hope there are no headlines about me, ma." He smiled at her fully confident of the effect it had on her.
It was mistimed.
"Not yet," she replied coldly. Handing over the paper to him, she added, "I am ashamed of you."

(4)

"Do you believe Julian?" Kanupriya asked her mother next day. "Isn't Prema bhabi dramatizing the whole thing?"
"I would not have believed it, if I was not a witness to

Kranti's meeting with Julian." Vaishali gave the details.
"But why did he do it?"
"I'll tell you." Prema entered from the side of kitchen. "Easy meat; pink and fair. And helpless with her hands, and feet tied with a rope to the cot."
"It sounds bizarre." Kanupriya remarked.
"Rape of a virgin is much worse. Your brother should be in jail for seven years."
Vaishali dwelt on Kranti's younger days, and how friendly he was with the girls. "That such a man — my son — could stoop to such a level to rape a helpless woman. I can't believe it."
"We all have our weak moments." Kanupriya defended her brother, though she was a known feminist.
"He has too many. Look at what he tried with Madhu." Prema explained.
"But Madhu's dress was provocative." Vaishali chipped in. "And earlier, in our house, no one was used to such exhibitionism."
Prema was critical that such excuses were given by men who assaulted women.
Cornered, Vaishali said, "We have a problem at hand. What do we do about Julian?"
"The crime has been committed by Kranti, and not by Julian. She is a victim and needs to be protected." Prema clarified. She thought for a while and emphasised that throwing out Julian would be a double whammy for the poor girl.
Kanupriya was puzzled. "How can you throw out Kranti? He is one of us."
"He is a maniac and should not be allowed to roam about freely. He should be in Tihar jail."

"You are going crazy." Both Vaishali and Kanupriya spoke in unison.

"That's the law of the land, mummy."

Kanupriya inquired what she proposed to do.

"File a complaint against him with the police."

"You will do it against your own husband?"

"Yes, I will do it to any rapist. The weak must be protected. And remember, Kranti is a protector of law. His crime is even more heinous." Prema was categorical.

"It sounds fine in the Gita or in the scriptures, but it does not work in real life." Kanupriya tried to dissuade her sister-in-law.

"What do you think my organization stands for? We take up only such cases. It is purely incidental that the rapist is my husband and your brother."

"But you will ruin your family, your children and your own life." Vaishali appealed to her.

"You are going to do it for a whore whom you hardly know." Kanupriya added.

"Kanu, I am going to do it for the dignity of a woman," Prema answered.

"What will you tell your children? That their father is a rapist? Will it not affect their mental health and their future?" Kanupriya asked.

"If the law went into these details, no criminal will ever be punished."

"Is it absolutely necessary?" Vaishali asked.

"Yes, it is. Your son refuses to apologize," Prema said.

"'Bhabi, you want him to apologize to a servant who was once a prostitute?" Kanupriya said.

"I have requested him several times, but he refuses to listen. I am left with no option."

Kanupriya looked at her mother. "Maybe, you could persuade him."

"Kranti is too proud to admit his mistake. Neither has he the moral strength. Apologizing to Julian is out of question. And you have to appreciate that apologizing will tantamount to an admission of guilt." Vaishali explained.

Vaishali attempted another strategy. "Prema, if I request you—."

"No, mummy. No. I apologize, but nothing will make me change my stand."

"This house is heading for a calamity. We will be all confused whether to be with you or with Kranti. Loyalties will be divided. Have you taken all this into account?" Vaishali asked.

"I know what I am doing."

"Good." Vaishali conceded. "The family will go through it for a principle."

Her `good' meant that she didn't like the situation. She mulled over something, and added, "I hope you are aware that such things are not easy to prove. First, the victim was a notorious harlot. Second, Kranti is a competent cop, and thirdly, the rape took place about seven or eight years back."

"I concede that mummy. But my organization is quite used to such cases."

The telephone ring disturbed them, and Prema went to attend the call.

"Has bhabi gone mad?"

"Prema has a point. She is fighting for the dignity of a woman. And you have to appreciate her background."

Prema returned. An unpleasant silence hung in the air.

"So, the die is cast." Kanupriya looked sternly at her

sister-in-law. Suddenly, something occurred to her. "Is it possible that bhaiya has not taken your threat seriously?"

"Often, wives have little influence on their husbands. You also can try at your level."

"It's useless. Kranti will never apologize to a servant and a former prostitute," Vaishali said.

Vaishali went back to her room. Kanupriya looked offensively at Prema and left.

"Enemies all around," Prema muttered. "How will I manage?"

Walking in the garden at twilight when the sun had slipped away in the horizon, Kanupriya whispered to her mother, "I wish I had as much courage as bhabi when Arjun (her husband) sexually assaulted and beat me repeatedly."

Considering the poor health of her eldest son, Vaishali made sure that he and Madhulika did not get a whiff of the new scandal. Madhulika suspected that some secret relating to Julian was being discussed in the house in whispers, but she did not have any idea that it was linked to Kranti.

(5)

Finding Deepak a little relaxed next evening, Vaishali told him of the Kranti scandal, and what Prema proposed to do. She was a little surprised that Deepak had not reacted as aggressively as she had expected. "After Vinay's cheating, I am prepared for the worst from my other sons. When Julian joined our house, I expected something of this kind was at the back of it," he said.

Vaishali was extremely critical of Prema for proposing to file an FIR against her own husband. "I've never heard of such a breach of matrimonial vows. Don't you think that

she is crossing all limits?"
Deepak reminded Vaishali of her behaviour with him and his father when she was young.
"I've not forgotten how you used to mistreat the old man because of his dubious past," he said. "Neither have I forgotten how you misbehaved with me so that I was forced to leave the house for a couple of months?"
"But I never filed a complaint against bhapaji."
"You had no proof!" He retorted.
The senior couple discussed Prema's background for a long time and the consequences if Prema decided to file the FIR. Finally, both agreed that Prema had as much right in the house as Kranti and decided not to intervene or take sides.

When Vaishali again blamed it on the old man's genes, Deepak was infuriated. He was about to say something nasty when he noticed his youngest son walking towards them.
"Here comes the most worthless of all our sons," Deepak said under his breath.
As a broad-based principle, Vivek avoided his father. However, after learning that Kranti had raped Julian in the past, he was agitated. "Papa, how could Kranti do it?"
"Why don't you ask him?" Deepak countered.
Tentatively, he looked from one parent to the other. "It is such a delicate matter; how can I ask him such a thing?"
"You are in your early thirties; you are not a babe." Deepak vented all his frustration on him.
Tacitly, Vaishali diverted their attention by asking, "How can men behave like animals?" She looked at her son, and asked, "What would you do if you were in Kranti's situation?"

"I am sure, I'll not rape her," he said with embarrassment.

"Vivek and Kranti are two very different individuals," Deepak said cautioning Vaishali. "Right through his childhood and youth, Kranti was enamoured of the fair girls, but somehow, he was so smitten with Prema at that time that he entirely forgot what was deep in his subconscious: his fondness for fair complexioned women. We also were stupid and got carried away by her father's position, and failed to remind him what was good for him."

Deepak looked at his wife, and continued, "Kranti's flirtations are only a consequence of it whether with Madhu or someone else."

"But a rape?" Vivek said.

"He got the opportunity on a platter and did not let it slip. A lonely PWD guest house on a stormy night, and a nude girl lying on a cot, with her hands and feet tied. He never expected to see the same girl at Amit's and now at this place. Imagine where Nongpoh is? Over 2000 kilometres away!"

"Are you trying to defend your son? If so, do it in front of Prema."

"I am not defending my son. If the rape is proved, he has to suffer the consequences of his action – dismissal or jail or both - there is no excuse for raping a helpless, innocent girl. I am only trying to analyse the working of his mind." Deepak turned his attention on Vivek. "It is easy to be judgemental on others. If in your actual life you ever face such a situation, you can't be sure of what would transpire? However, you are fortunate that you don't have Kranti's weakness."

Vivek felt a little discomfort, and Vaishali asked, "What

would you do, Deep?"

"Honestly, I don't know," Deepak said. "Men have reacted in different ways. The passions of some men have been all consuming. They have waged wars against other nations merely on hearing about the beauty of a woman in that land. The sexual drives of some men are so powerful that they can blow up the world. To what extent men can go to achieve their needs of passion vary depending on the individual, culture, its ethos, the times, and the laws of the land."

Suddenly, he turned his eyes sharply at his wife. "But I am sure bhapaji would have never done it though you don't miss any opportunity to run him down even after his death. He could not harm anyone — not even a lamb or a dog. He was more like Prema — go out of the way to help the weak and the downtrodden. And never like Kranti. It is unfortunate that my mother turned me so much against him that I refused to imbibe or appreciate some of the qualities in him, which neither I nor any of my sons ever had."

"Except pleasing the loose women, he had no other quality," Vaishali replied.

He looked at his son, and said, "Your ma like your grandma is prejudiced against him. He had a horde of qualities: his courage, bravery — what we appreciate in Kranti; his generosity and lack of greed for money. It is true that he made a lot of money illegally but bhapaji blew everything on his women and the poor of Lucknow. Despite everything, his eyes had a certain innocence, which none of us has."

Vinay and Madhulika walked in; they had to confide something in Deepak and took him inside the house for some discussion.

After hearing his papa, Vivek was a little awed. "Ma, I was so wrong. I considered papa to be a phoney and a hypocrite, but he is so different."

"I don't know who has been feeding you on such wrong notions. He has been always like this."

Vivek was quiet as if jolted by a new revelation. Suddenly, it occurred to him that maybe what Sheila had told him about his father was right. He looked at his mother for a long time, and said, "Whether you believe in it or not, whatever he said about bhapaji is right."

"I don't know," she mumbled, and went to the kitchen. Everything in life seemed out of place, and all because of one prostitute who was working in her house as a maid.

Kanupriya was perplexed. How could her own brother known for exemplary heroism, rape a helpless woman? Though she was extremely critical of him in Prema's absence, she pleaded with her not to file the case in a court of law and be forgiving.

(6)

It was a bright and cheerful Sunday morning, but Deepak and Vaishali, languishing in wicker chairs were sad and worried over Kranti's future; they wondered how one of their own flesh and blood could stoop so low.

"Where have we gone wrong Deep?" Vaishali was frustrated.

"I don't know," he answered. "But we have never ignored them, especially you."

All their joys and happiness centred on their children. The two had never gone on a holiday by themselves. Lost in their respective pasts, they were quiet.

Kranti arrived on his mo-bike after a football game in the

morning. Soaked in sweat, his youthful face was flushed, and he looked macho and handsome. Gracefully, he alighted, waved at his parents with a broad smile, and was about to enter the house when Deepak beckoned him.

Throwing the helmet on an empty chair, and removing his jersey, he crossed his legs and sat down on another chair. His rippling muscles accentuated in shorts and T shirt: he was a symbol of masculine beauty.

"I want to talk to you about Julian," Deepak said.

Kranti frowned; Vaishali too was worried.

"How do you know her?"

Assuredly, Kranti told his version. However, neither of the parents was convinced.

"But she says she was raped by you," Deepak said.

"She is a liar," Kranti was emphatic. "The unfortunate aspect is that she has been able to fool Prema with her sob story. It was not I but Joe and his men who gang raped her. You know that Prema is given to dramatics, and she has taken up her cause."

"I have not seen Prema indulging in theatrics. She is a sensible woman." Deepak was categorical.

Kranti did not like the discussion going against him.

"But papa, I don't know why they have joined hands?"

"But why would Julian tell a lie?"

"Maybe, after the gang rape she lost her balance of mind and got confused and considered me also as one of them."

"But she was gang raped after four months," Deepak said.

"Yes, that is what she is telling everyone. But she is wrong in her conclusions and is mixing up the time factor."

Deepak looked at his son for a long time, and said, "Your version is that you did not rape her."

"I did not."

"You are sure."

"Yes, papa."

Kranti left abruptly.

The elderly couple looked at each other with dismay.

The men of the house were shocked that their maid had been a notorious prostitute of Kolkata. Ashamed that one of their own blood had raped her, they avoided eye contact with her, and were extra polite.

Vaishali's father had a heart attack, and Deepak and Vaishali rushed to Gorakhpur the same night.

XII
Lodging The FIR

In February, when the sun sizzled in the afternoons, the Delhites felt that summer was not far away. Vinay and Madhulika were facing shortage of storage space. When it was an off day for Madhulika, Vinay said excitedly to her, "Let us go and dump our wollens." Dwarka, the servant, helped them load the pieces in Kranti's Omni. He wanted to go with them to I I T, but Vinay overruled him explaining they would get local help. Madhulika didn't intercede; she felt that he had something up his sleeve.

The gateman at the entrance of I I T saluted them, and Vinay's spirits soared. "Somehow I like this place; let us have a round of the campus," he said appreciating its familiar tall building, open spaces, and its gardens bursting with riotous flowers. After her nasty experience in Miranda House, Madhulika was suspicious of the ambience associated with academia; one never knew how much hatred was shrouded under its rich green trees, and spacious lawns. Intuitively, she had not liked the idea; however, she did not want to dampen her husband's enthusiasm as he was rarely cheerful. He reminisced about the day the Director had told him of his appointment as Dean of Sciences. "On that day I had a strong urge of being the Director of the Institute some day," he said negotiating a bend. "And imagine where I am?"

"Varmani assured me that it will pass." She placed her hand on his shoulder.

"Possibly, but it will never be the same again," he said, turning the Omni towards his house.

On reaching the bungalow, they were shocked to see the front portion painted in black paint, and the words 'This is the house of a thief — BEWARE!' were scribbled in bold white. 'Thief' 'Cheat' were splashed all over the house. 'GO AWAY' was scrawled on the side door. The windowpanes were broken as if some goons had tried to ransack the place.

Both froze and clasped each other's hand.

"Bastards!" he hissed. His hands trembled when he tried to open the lock; she had to assist him. Both carried the brief cases inside the house. Shards of glass were scattered in some rooms where the curtains had been pushed back by the rowdy elements.

"They tried to burn the place," Vinay shouted showing her half-burnt pieces of paper, and cloth. "But why Madhu?"

She stood by his side tightly grasping his arm.

"Do I deserve all this?" he said and sank down on the sofa breathing heavily and she sat on the carpet, her hands on his knees. "This is how they feel about me?"

He had tears in his eyes.

"No," Madhulika said forcefully. "It is the handiwork of

a few goondas at the instance of those who hate you for being the Dean."

A little later, she added, "Vinay, let us beat a retreat. I don't like the smell of the place."

"Do you know why I brought you here?" He looked at her affectionately. "I thought we will make love here. I don't like the bedroom at papa's."

She threw her arms around him, and whispered, "Oh, my darling."

She was up on her feet, and said, "Why not?"

"I want to go away to a remote place where the stigma of thief will not haunt me." He caught her hand tenderly. "And then I'll love you."

Wanting to help him fulfil this small wish of his, she entreated him to go up to the first floor.

But he refused.

Suddenly, the slogans of `chor', 'murdabad', ` Vinay – hai hai' reverberated in the air.

Terrified, both dashed outside the house. A group of twenty or twenty-five – a queer assortment of different categories of nonteaching staff, and research scholars of the institute, with banners and placards, marched towards them shouting slogans with all their lung power.

"Let us get away." Madhulika suggested. But Vinay was rooted to the ground. "It is the end of me," he muttered, and leaned against the wall for support.

"Hurry, Vinay."

Vinay wanted to talk to them, whereas she was worried about their safety. She scooted inside, got the lock, and was about to fasten it on the door of the house when some of the youngsters in the crowd understood her intentions, and surrounded the van.

"Down with the cheat!" ranted the crowd.

Another group of twelve or thirteen trooped down from the other side; they were a rougher lot and carried hockey sticks.

With all her force, Madhulika caught Vinay's arm, and forcibly pushed him inside the house, and bolted the door.

The crowd shouted, "Go away; leave the campus."

"I will go and talk to them," Vinay said, "I am sure they will listen to me."

"No," she shrieked. "They will beat you up."

Ignoring her pleas when he tried to move towards the door, she caught his legs with both her hands, and didn't allow him to go to the door.

Some of the hoodlums threw bricks and stones at the windows, others tried to break the door down. Madhulika called Kranti but could not reach him. Then she tried Sudha, ACP, on her mobile, and told her to come fast as their lives were in danger. Sudha had just emerged from a meeting with the Special Commissioner at the headquarters. She assured Madhu that she would be there in twenty minutes.

Madhulika dialled 100 and realized that the phone lines were snapped by one of the hoodlums. Their cells were unable to catch the network now.

The hammering at the door increased and Madhulika trembled realizing that the door might give way. For the first time, Vinay appreciated the danger. Together, they pushed the heaviest sofa against the door, and threw themselves against it.

"Don't worry, the door will not breakdown for another 10-15 minutes," he said surveying the state of the hinges, and its material. After the initial reaction, Vinay was more sober now. "You have a round of the house, and see the condition of the side- door, I'll take care of this door," he added.

She obeyed and found some of the ruffians trying to loosen a metal bar of the window at the back. Heating up a big kitchen knife on the gas, she shoved it on the face of one of the intruders. Screaming in pain, he cursed her, and retreated. Unfortunately, another replaced him.

Shouting, hooting, and abusive language filled the atmosphere. Fortuitously, the immediate neighbours had called the police otherwise the situation might have taken an ugly turn for the couple. The police siren startled the hooligans; they tried to run away but some of them were nabbed by the police. Five minutes later, Sudha arrived with a Jeep load of cops, and rounded up those who had attempted to flee.

"Thank god!" Madhulika muttered on seeing Sudha.

Dr. Sinha arrived in his white Mercedes and was quite agitated on seeing the condition of the house. He was apologetic to Vinay for the misbehaviour of the hooligans. Addressing Sudha, he told her to teach a lesson to the mischief-makers who had threatened Vinay and his wife's lives. "Please make sure that such things don't happen again at my institute," he said.

"If Kranti Chopra, my boss was here, he would have broken the bones of a few by now. He happens to be Vinay's younger brother."

"Oh, I didn't know." Sinha said.

Sinha wanted Sudha, Vinay and Madhulika to take a cup of tea at his place, which was turned down by Vinay.

"I have a request to make," Sinha said to ACP. "You can

let the research scholars go."
"Why?"
"The research scholars are young and innocent - they have been incited by someone and got carried away."
"Tell me who? I am interested in meeting that man."
"How would I know?" Sinha answered.
"How can you plead for them when such a barbaric act has taken place in your campus? Are the research scholars not adults? They know what they are doing."
Sinha was quiet for a while, and then told the truth. "Actually, one of the research scholars is my nephew. I am interested in him only. At least, he can be allowed to go."
Sudha refused.
"Before you take a final decision, please talk to Chopra Sahib - Chairman, UPSC."
"My boss is Mr. Krandhikar, the Police Commissioner, and not Chopra Sahib."
"It will be in best interests of Vinay." Sinha persisted.
When Sudha was again told by Sinha to cross check with Deepak Chopra, it puzzled her. But Vinay told her to follow the rules.
Sudha escorted them to the main gate of the campus.

When they exited the campus, Vinay murmured, "It's the last of I I T." Madhulika wanted to assuage his feelings, but refrained as it would have sounded hollow.

Vivek had got a message from Sudha about the unfortunate incident that had occurred at I I T campus, and he met them in the porch. Both Vinay and Madhulika were shaken after the traumatic experience. Madhulika was at the wheel, and comparatively more composed than her husband. Leading the couple into the house, Vivek prepared sundaes of Chocó- fudge ice cream in coca- cola and offered them. “We need to chill,” he said lightly trying to cheer up the couple.

Occasionally, Vinay’s hand quivered; to hide it, he placed the glass of cold drink on the table and locked the fingers of both hands. Vivek could feel the pain and suffering that the couple was undergoing. Papa, ma, and he were also suffering because of Vinay. But Vinay had suffered the most, and without support from Madhulika, he might have been in an asylum. However, he was not sure whether Sheila would back him to the hilt if he were in the doldrums like Vinay.

Like his grandfather, Vinay was keen to redeem his guilt. What more could he do? Vivek wondered. But Kranti refused to apologize for his crime, and Vivek was sure that Prema would not let him get away.

(2)

When Deepak got a notice from the private bank, it disturbed him. He had taken loan from the bank for construction of the house and had defaulted on payment of the instalment for the sixth consecutive month. The last paragraph stating that ‘If this continues for another two months, strict steps will be taken to make the recoveries,’ was worrying. Deepak met the manager of the bank; he was courteous, apologetic, but quoted the rules.

Agitated, Vaishali raised the issue after dinner. Though the children knew about the debts, they were not aware that the situation was so bad that instalments were not being paid regularly. Prema agreed that some solution had to be found out, the situation could not be allowed to drag. Not receiving any response from Kranti, Vaishali asked him directly, “What do you say?”

“Give me some time, I’ll discuss with Vinay and Vivek.”

Vinay and Madhulika had gone out for dinner, and Vivek was at Lehriya.

"Don't worry. At the worst, I'll sell the house and take a flat across the Yamuna in East Delhi or move to Noida." Deepak explained.

"No, papa, it does not behove a retired Cabinet Secretary to stay in a flat across the Yamuna," Kanupriya said.

"All the children have a share, should they not contribute?" Kranti looked at his mother.

"Supposing after us, you get the house. Will you pay off the loan?" Vaishali asked Kranti directly. It had never been discussed so candidly before.

"In that case, I'll do something," Kranti replied.

"Thank you, son." Deepak smiled, and rose, dismissing the meeting.

"You are a fool!" Prema scolded her husband once they were alone in the lounge. "Can't you control your avariciousness? Don't you see that your ma has exposed you?"

"I am a straight- forward cop. I don't want to be misunderstood. I want to play it straight."

"Greedy for money, greedy for flesh," Prema muttered.

"Prema?"

"The old man needs help. Why not give it gracefully instead of tying him in knots?"

"You need not get emotional because of him."

"Are we not living under the same roof?"

"So are others."

Suddenly, something struck her. She looked at him minutely, and asked, "Did you really untie the knots from the rope with which Julian was tied?"

"Of course, I did!" he said looking at her with narrow

eyes wondering what she was up to. “You think - I am lying.”
“You are not as simple and straight forward as you are making it out to be.”
“Prema, you are going crazy! I am your Kranti!!”
“I don’t know why I am getting a feeling that you are a very complex cop and maybe a devious one.”
“What are you saying Prema?”
It occurred to her that this was not the Kranti she had known for the last so many years and grew suspicious of his bona fides. When he tried to take her in his arms, she rejected him.
“The bastard?” Deepak muttered in the privacy of his bedroom. “You have produced worthless sons, Vaishali.”
“I am sorry, Deep,” Vaishali said. “For a person who has never cared much for money, it must have hurt you.”
He was quiet.
She opened the side door, caught his hand, and moved towards the garden. “Look at the starry night, Deep.”
Deepak gazed at the sky. In the moonless night, the stars twinkled brightly.
“It occurred to me that in about a year’s time, we will not be staying in this house, and I grew a little sentimental”, she said.
He placed his arm around her waist, and slowly the couple had a round of the garden.
“I was wondering how many families have stayed in this house and have been happy.”
“Have you been happy?” Deepak asked.
“Immensely happy. I have got you back. I feel grateful to God for it.”
“Despite Vinay and Kranti —?”

"Yes. Your love has helped me to face the crisis of my sons. Any other woman in such circumstances would have been shattered. Our new bonding has helped me to rationalize that each one of us has to suffer one's karma."

"Perhaps,"

They sat down on the wicker chairs, and Deepak placed his legs on another chair. Hand in hand, they sat for a long time. The light was still on in Kranti's room.

"I believe the two of them are still quarrelling," Vaishali said. "Sometimes, I am more worried about Kranti than Vinay."

"So am I."

Then he told her about Prasad's visit and impulsively, she admonished him for being careless. Appreciating that the reprimand was untimely, she accepted that they would manage in a flat somewhere.

Many years later, the High Court gave a verdict against the cooperative society. It ordered heavy penalties against the members and directed that market rent for the land should be charged. Unable to pay the exorbitant amount, Deepak sold the bungalow and bought a flat in Gurgaon.

(3)

Director, AK Sinha was nonplussed on reading Vinay's resignation. The son of the Chairman, UPSC, and such a spineless man! He had expected him to fight it out, but Vinay had surrendered almost like a coward. None of his sons would ever act so stupidly. Dr. Sinha was worried about his nephew languishing in jail for the last three days as his bail had been rejected by the magistrate. He wondered how he would face his elder brother.

He phoned Deepak Chopra again and could not reach

him. In the last two days, Sinha had tried him a dozen times.

Sinha refused to accept the resignation and forwarded it to the Chairman of the Board of Governors giving the factual details and recommended a top-level enquiry preferably by a retired High Court or Supreme Court Judge. Prof. Sudhakar, Chairman of the Board of Governors, knew Deepak Chopra well. He rejected Sinha's proposal and accepted the resignation. Sinha was not the kind of man to give up so easily. He convened an emergency meeting of the Board on the plea of acute shortage of funds, and before the discussion of the items on the agenda, surreptitiously introduced the resignation of Vinay Chopra for discussion.

Sudhakar felt humiliated. He was red in the face, and lambasted Sinha for reopening a subject on which he had already taken the decision. "You are out to insult me. For this, I can have you removed from your present post."

"Technicalities apart, the matter is of grave importance and needs a second look." Prof. Srinivasan, another member said.

Sudhakar threatened to walk out of the meeting. Another member supported Srinivasan.

"But there is no evidence." Keshwani, DG, CSIR said.

"Prime facie there is no case." Kulbhushan, a former Director, I I T pointed out.

"Why not have an inquiry conducted?" PS Sharma, the IAS officer from Delhi Government argued.

"Let the government decide on that," Keshwani answered. "Why are you gunning for Vinay Chopra?"

"But we are the Government." Sinha laughed.

"You are the Director of I I T, and not the Government."

Sudhakar chastised him.

With every argument, the unpleasantness increased, and the Board meeting was reduced to a fish market.

"Considering the broader interest of this institute of national and even international importance, I have accepted Vinay's resignation otherwise the image of the institute will be tarnished." Sudhakar clarified.

Srinivasan and others opposed to Vinay gradually mellowed down except Sinha who wanted Vinay's blood.

"I think Sinha has some personal agenda," Keshwani said.

Cornered, Sinha realised that he was fighting a lonely battle, and moved to the first item on the agenda.

"Thank god!" Deepak murmured when Sudhakar gave him all the details.

"I have a request to make," Sudhakar added.

Deepak's heart missed a beat. Sudhakar gave the details of a post for which his son was to take the interview. "The interview is next week, and he is depending on you."

Earlier, no one asked him such favours, and even if someone dared, he would bluntly say a categorical `no'. After Vinay's scandal had come in public light, such demands had increased, and he lacked the courage to turn them down. Vinay had tainted his image, and his pride had suffered. Now, Deepak wanted favours from others, no wonder they demanded their pound of flesh. Even if not that, at least a gentlemanly mutual reciprocity was expected. Fortunately, Kranti's case was still under wraps.

"Deepak, are you still there?"

"Yes, I am."

"If you have any reservation, you can be frank with me. What are you thinking?"

"Do you really want me to be frank?"
"Of course."
"There is not much of a difference between you and that bastard Sinha."
Fuming, Deepak banged down the phone.
He was still agitated when he told Vaishali the details. "Vultures all around, and no one to trust."
Vaishali looked worriedly at her husband. "Deep," she said, and caught his arm.
The phone rang again.
Vaishali handed the phone to him saying, "Here is someone you can trust."
He raised his eyebrows.
"Supri, who else?"
Supriya informed him that the Foreign Secretary was desperately trying to reach him. "Sir, please talk to him, it is urgent."
Deepak called Arun Dastur and learnt that the US ambassador had filed a formal complaint to the Foreign Minister regarding stealing of Stella's research work by Vinay and there was pressure to order a high-level inquiry against Vinay. Dastur explained that it was no longer an internal matter as the Americans were an affected party. It was difficult to reject a demand from the US when the Government was trying to improve relations with them. No decision had been taken but it could go against Vinay.
"What have you recommended?" Deepak asked.
"A CBI inquiry. But it may go to the Foreign Minister or even the PM for approval."
"Thank you for warning me."
"I am sorry, sir - I really am."
"I understand and appreciate it."

Slowly, Deepak put the phone down. This was serious. A CBI inquiry could be devastating for Vinay's mental health.

When Deepak told Vaishali about it, she said, "One does not know who is with us or against us?"

"You can't blame Arun; he is doing his duty. If I were in his position, I might have done the same."

"Isn't the net result the same?"

"I don't know." In sheer disgust, he banged his hands on the table.

"A CBI inquiry can kill him," she said.

"You have to make him strong, Vaishali."

"You too need to be strong, Deep."

Sadly, he nodded.

(4)

In the evening, Deepak was at his favourite second cup of tea in the garden when the leggy Madhulika walked down towards him in white shorts, and a white top looking stunningly fresh and cheerful. She said a "hello", sat down on the wicker chair crossing her fair legs, and creating an atmosphere of glowing femininity. She had returned from the Gymkhana after playing tennis with her husband.

"Thank you, papa," she said. "I am told Vinay's resignation has been accepted."

She pulled the chair closer to Deepak's and informed him that Vinay and she had decided to settle in Darjeeling where Vinay had been offered a teaching assignment in a school. She was trying for a lectureship in a college, if she failed, she would not mind a school job. Deepak listened without a comment.

"You don't approve of the school job."

"On the contrary, I endorse it though you will be ruining your future."

"There is no choice." She smiled.

"There is a little problem," he said, explained the discussion he had had with Dastur, and added, "I'll try to stall the inquiry, but the kind of man I am, I have very few friends, and of late they have all become very demanding."

Her fingers clenched; her jaw became resolute.

"Don't worry, papa, we will face it. But you should not compromise your dignity because of Vinay."

"Thank you," he said.

The young woman's face glowed in the light of the setting sun.

"In this crisis, you have emerged as a very strong and a brave woman," he said. Not knowing whether it was the right thing to say to his own daughter-in-law, he added unsurely, "And more beautiful."

She blushed and looked still more attractive. She rose and walked away.

He saw her long legs, slim arms, the fluttering hair, and somehow felt sorry for her. Suddenly, he felt anger at his son, and muttered, "The bastard!"

(5)

The last quarrel between Vivek and Sheila turned out to be a major conflict; it affected their relationship in two ways: one of trust, and the second of love. Though they made up their differences, the scars did not heal, and showed up whenever their relationship was under strain. The spontaneity of emotions when their hands touched, or their bodies grazed each other disappeared. Their glances lacked in warmth, and the eyes forgot to light up when they met after a gap of a few hours. Over the weeks, Sheila's dislike of Vaishali had turned into hatred, and she could not stand her for even a short time. His inability to break away from his joint family and be wholly a part of her world — the world they had created together — hurt her the most. It was like a wound that refused to heal. However, they went through the motion of sleeping on the same bed, and satisfied their sexual hunger as often as before, but their hearts no longer fluttered.

Lack of possessiveness was the one thing Vivek admired in their relationship, but now if he spent a single night at his parents, Sheila created a ruckus, and refused to talk to him for many days. Trying to control the damage on a day-to-day basis, they entirely forgot to fix a date for their wedding. Sheila remembered it when there was a marriage in the village, and they were invited to bless the couple. Both felt their relationship had hit rock bottom, and it was pointless to legalize the informal arrangement.

Sheila's father called her to inform that her mom was to undergo surgery for breast cancer, and inquired if it would be possible for her to spend a couple of weeks with her mom.

"Of course," she answered.

The frenetic activity of rushing to the bank in Delhi, purchasing the ticket and completing the barest essential shopping over the next two days brought them together. Before her departure, they had a round of the rooms to ensure that she had taken whatever she needed. To his dismay, he noticed that she had almost packed everything except the discarded clothes.

"I – I hope you are coming back."

She nodded. She was tense, unsure, and he saw the tears in her eyes.

"Of course, you are coming back," he said taking her in his arms. "The project — the village — the children will miss you."

Intuitively, he realized it was their last meeting. Both had invested all that they had in their relationship for the last four years. Without her help, Lehriya village would not have been the same. She knew more women and children in the village — she could rattle off the names of many of them — and the locals admired her for her beauty, compassion and commitment to the task they had taken up. Without her, he was nothing.

"Will you miss me?" she asked.

"All the time," he muttered.

She tossed the purse on the chair and kissed him. Undressing, they made love.

At the airport, they had tears in their eyes.

Both were uncertain of the future.

(6)

Prema could indulge in arguments or rhetoric with her mother-in-law or sister-in-law on a principle; however, to discuss issues with the same intensity with the men of the house was tantamount to a grave misdemeanour. While discussing with women on gender issues she was carried away by her emotions and paternal breeding, but to even contemplate to file a rape complaint against her husband was sacrilege. The arrogance in Kranti's conduct and his stubbornness in refusing to apologize had forced her to consider filing the FIR in a police station.

Before Kavita's departure to the US, the two friends had a heart-to-heart talk on the subject. Prema had told

her that she might seek justice for Julian in a court.
"You love Kranti. How can you drag him to a court of law?" Kavita had asked.
"For justice to the downtrodden I can go to any lengths, it's in my blood," Prema said. "And I am doing it for the dignity of a woman."
Unconvinced, Kavita had advised her not to ruin her life by filing the FIR.

The momentary infatuation with Kavita's brother being a one-time exception, there was no one in Prema's life. Barring the few hours, she devoted to NRK, Prema's life revolved around Kranti, his children and his parents. He was her whole life. To step beyond that threshold by breaking those bonds for an infamous prostitute was not easy for her. It was an act of transgression. Kranti's refusal to apologise was forcing her to take the plunge.

Last year when Kranti was in Hyderabad for a few days, he had served her father with such utter devotion that her own brother had felt ashamed of himself. Because of the sudden disappearance of the male nurse and non-availability of another, his father lay in his shit throughout the day, but his brother didn't have the courtesy or the heart to do the dirty job. On return from the training program in the evening, Kranti had taken control of the situation. "You are a hero material," she had whispered to him in the night, her body and soul filled with his love.

Sandwiched between her two children now, she tossed the whole night. A flood of swirling emotions hit her. The house would be divided, and there could be a remote possibility — if Vaishali was swayed by her maternal instinct — that she might be told to leave the house. Then, it could become difficult for her to survive.

Going back to her father might not be easy; the first resistance would come from her brother. Her life would be ravaged by storms, and all that for a woman who had been a notorious prostitute. But she had been raped by her husband and had a right to justice. And, unlike Vinay, Kranti did not exhibit any remorse. Torn by the dilemma, she could not sleep through the night.

In the morning, when Prema saw the sad profile of Julian as she handed her the morning cup of tea, she was convinced that her rapist must be dealt with severely under the law.

About a week back, Kranti had gone to Hyderabad for an in-service course.

At about 10 am, a cop from the office handed over a small packet addressed to Kunal. It turned out to be a CD and was played in the presence of the family members. The video showed Kranti going up the rostrum and receiving a certificate from the President who had visited the Police Academy at Hyderabad. Though all the members smiled, the swagger in Kranti's gait twisted Prema's heart. There was not even a trace of repentance on the face of the incorrigible man. To be conceited after such a dastardly act of rape was unpardonable. Suddenly, she felt like crushing this pride, this haughtiness. At that moment, she finally resolved to punish him.

Now, there was no going back.

(7)

Prema dressed up early and dashed to her husband's office. Sudha was mildly surprised to see the boss' wife in the office when he was at Hyderabad.

"Hi, Sudha!"

Sudha gave her a warm welcome that was in sharp

contrast to Kranti's scowl.

"There should be more cops like you, pleasant and cheerful. You seem to change the image of police."

Sudha was fully aware to what Prema was alluding to. "Yes, sir is always tense, as if he is out to achieve something."

"To be better than others." Prema corrected her and smiled.

"Yes, that too." Sudha conceded. "But who can know him better than you ma'am."

"Kranti gave me an assignment," Prema said boisterously. "I am sure you have many more."

"Dozens of them!" Sudha laughed easily.

She explained that Kranti wanted his old file of TA bills, about eight years old.

Sudha grimaced. "Not easy, but fortunately we never weed out old records. I will try."

She picked up the internal phone and ordered someone.

"Your Nari Rakashan Kendra is making the headlines and keeps some of us on our toes."

Prema had her coffee as they discussed more about the activities of NRK. About 40-45 minutes later, a dozen files were brought in. Unable to control her excitement, she went through them. Finally, Prema selected one file.

"Can I give it to you after two days?"

"Of course. No problem."

Sudha confided that her boss was quite upset these days and did not miss any opportunity to get away from Delhi. "He is sniping at everyone including the Chief. I hope everything is okay at home."

"No, it is not. It's almost war." Prema controlled her rising emotions and managed to smile. "But it is a part of marital life."

Prema rose and thanked her.

"Bye. Anything you want, please give a ring. The whole office is at your command."

"I will, if need arises."

Two days later, Prema told Vaishali that she was flying to Guwahati next day with Julian. All arrangements were made with Sudha's help.

"Prema, let the unpleasant secrets lie buried in the past. Sometimes, their resurfacing is accompanied by catastrophes."

"I am sorry, mummy."

"Go ahead, but I will not wish you luck."

"I don't expect it," Prema said. "But please do not be angry with me."

Vaishali relented; her tone changed. "No, I'm not. We all have to live by our own convictions."

"Yes, mummy."

The entire household was upset by Prema and Julian's departure to Guwahati.

(8)

Julian's reappearance at Nongpoh after an interval of eight years astonished the locals. Her reputation as a prostitute had reached them; they had felt terribly let down by her as they expected her to become a respectable schoolteacher. The news of her return was electrifying. Half the town came to see her in the guest house; all the men and especially the women were extremely sympathetic towards her. Julian learnt that the locals had socially ostracised Joe and his friends who had gang raped her. Joe had managed to stay at Nongpoh because of his business connections, but all his friends were forced to leave the town and were settled in Shillong.

Joe returned from Dr H Gordon Roberts Hospital at Shillong where he had gone for a routine check up of both the legs. Since he was unable to move easily, Prema and Julian walked down to his home along with the locals. One leg of Joe was fractured as a result of the bullet injury and the second one was severely damaged due to a fall in the bathroom. Joe, who had ruled the underworld in that region, was now a cripple. With great difficulty, he could hop around using crutches. Seeing the miserable plight of her former rapist responsible for destroying her life, Julian was mollified. The hatred and bitterness she had nurtured over the years melted, and she felt avenged.

Prema and Julian spent a long time with him. He squarely blamed the stranger for everything.

"I saw with my own eyes that he tied Julian's hands and feet and raped her."

Julian objected that he was telling lies. Ignoring her, Prema asked him, "What were you doing there?"

"I came to help her on hearing her screams but was shot at by the stranger."

Voices of dissension rose; the locals blamed him and his friends for raping Julian. Everyone knew about the kidnap and the gang rape. "He is the man who has ruined our Julian. There was no stranger; he has cooked up the story."

However, most of them were not willing to give any evidence and wanted to keep away from police.

Prema showed many photographs, and Joe was immediately able to recognize Kranti.

"Will you be a witness against this stranger in a court of law?" Prema asked Joe.

"Of course, I will. My entire life has been ruined by him.

I want that swine to be punished even if I have to go to hell."

"You may," Prema answered.

Nonplussed, Joe asked Prema, "On whose side are you, ma'am?"

"I am with Julian. All those who have wronged her will be punished."

Prema spent a week at Nongpoh collecting evidence, proofs, and recording statements of witnesses.

"I don't mind if I am punished, but I want that stranger behind the bars." Joe assured her.

Francis, the emerging gangster wanted Joe to be hanged for the gang rape and promised all help to Prema.

On the return journey, Prema and Julian spent two days in Shillong and talked to Joe's friends and recorded their statements.

In the third week of March, the Secretary of Nari Rakshan Kendra filed an FIR against Kranti Chopra (Deputy Commissioner, Delhi Police) and Joe and five others for Julian's rape, outraging her modesty and assault on her on the night of 25th December 1992 and the night of 25th April 1993.

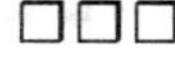

XIII

Complexities

Unexpected snowfall and avalanches hit Shimla. As an aftermath, the Delhi sky was swept by tidal waves of dark clouds, and the temperature plummeted. It rained in torrents as if the demons had escaped from hell and perched themselves on the treetops at Deepak's bungalow at Akbar Road.

Kranti arrived late at night from Kolkata and rang the bell. Julian, who was still busy in the kitchen, opened the door and was a little surprised to see him as he was expected the next day. On sighting her, he flew into a rage. The bitch was responsible for all the trouble in his life. Hurriedly, she turned to go; he caught her by the shoulder-length hair and pulled her towards him. Without raising an alarm, Julian pushed him back with all her strength. Kranti reacted fast and caught her waist. A little scuffle ensued. Amazed at the energy of the small woman, Kranti liked the feel of her body against his during the struggle. With her hands on his chin, she

tried to push away his mouth when suddenly the light was switched on, and Kanupriya caught them unawares.
"Bhaiya?" Her voice was muffled as she did not want to awaken the house.
"Why does she cross my path purposely?" Kranti spoke harshly.
"Julian, go to your room." Kanupriya commanded. She then turned towards her brother. "What are you trying to prove?"
"I am not trying to prove anything. But my whole-body revolts whenever I see her," he said, "and look at the audacity of the woman that she continues to stay in our house."
"You can do nothing about it," Kanupriya answered. "And don't disturb others otherwise you are the one who is going to be embarrassed, and not Julian."
Sheepishly, he dragged himself to his room. Fortunately for him, Prema was not there, and the children welcomed him with open arms.

The second assault on Julian did not upset her as much as the first one for she was mentally prepared for such unexpected contingencies. But it hardened her, and she swore to teach Kranti a lesson.

Discomforted by the thought that both her sons whom she adored had turned out to be criminals, Vaishali could not sleep after Kranti's arrival and the subsequent struggle with Julian. Today, she was unusually disturbed by Kranti's behaviour. His hatred of Julian gave a new dimension to the problem. Was her presence in the house an indicator of a time bomb that could blow up everything? Possibly, she may have to throw Julian out of the house. But she knew it was not easy to go against Prema who was fighting for the downtrodden and the dignity of women. And how could the Chopra household — considering its past track record— take an unprincipled stand?

Vaishali felt restless.

Just before dawn, she rose, slipped into the gown, and tip toed out of the room so as not to disturb her husband. The lawn was full of puddles; she avoided the garden, and instead strolled leisurely on the dimly lighted pathway. The air was moist and cool. It was so still that she could feel the warmth of her breath. Total silence had descended on the house that she had not experienced before. Even if a feather were to drop, she would have heard its fall. Strangely, she liked the quiet, and felt very close to understanding the meaning of life. Out of nowhere, a waft of breeze rustled past the trees, and the leaves shed the water stored by them, giving a drizzle effect. Her hair turned damp. She looked at the dark trees, the fuzzy lights and realized to her surprise that the burning sensation near her heart had disappeared. And suddenly, she felt light.

Later, she prepared a pot of tea for herself, and sat down under the neem tree lost in her reflections. When the sun bounced out of the clouds, the gate man brought a bundle of newspapers. Reluctantly, she opened one of them, and browsed the headlines. She frowned on going through a news item at the bottom.

Kranti observed his ma sitting alone; he opened the side door of the bedroom to go to her but changed his mind. Instead, he waved to her, and strolled away on the opposite side. She beckoned him, and prepared a cup of tea for him that was meant for his father. "It is so pleasant here," he commented. She did not respond. When he had taken tea, she handed him the newspaper, and said coldly, "Today, your name is flashed on the first page though it has not made the headlines yet."

The look on her face disconcerted him. He withdrew his outstretched hand, and she threw the paper on the wicker table. As she rose, the main gate opened, and a taxi entered the driveway, and stopped in the patio. Prema stepped out, smiled at her mother-in-law, and paid the driver.

It occurred to Kranti that his mother, a light sleeper, would have woken up when he rang the bell in the night, and might have heard or witnessed his brief tussle with Julian. Kranti read the small news item at the bottom of the first page. It related to the FIR against him in connection with the rape of a woman. He knew it was sufficient to send shock waves in the Delhi Police.

"I feared it," he mumbled.

Sudha was the first one to react and called her boss.

"It is all bull shit," he howled. "Be in the office at 8.30. We have lot of work to do."

"Yes, sir."

On going inside the room, he caught his wife in the process of unpacking, and demanded to know where she had gone.

"I went to see papa."

Showing the news item, he shouted at her, "What is this?"

"I had told you to apologize to Julian. Even Kanu had begged you, but you refused to listen."

"I have done nothing wrong to that woman. She is making a monkey out of you, and you are a stupid fool to believe in her."

"If this is your stand, I don't want to talk to you."

"You are going to ruin the family."

"I am doing my duty."

He reminded her that her duty was to stand by him instead of filing an FIR against him.

"I will not stand by the side of a criminal whether he happens to be my father, husband or son. I am on the side of the law."

The arguments took an ugly turn and Kranti shouted and abused her.

"That woman will not remain in this house. I am going to throw her out. You can also follow her," he yelled at her.

Vaishali was passing near the room and overheard the expletives hurled by her son. How could he behave in such a way with his wife after raping an innocent girl? Vaishali felt revolted. A feeling of disgust spread through her, and her face was distorted. Suddenly, she entered the room and said, "You are right, son. We have to decide who stays and who goes?" Vaishali's sudden appearance in the room dazed him.

"Come back from the office — you have a lot of work to do to save your skin — then we will take a view on this." Vaishali left as abruptly as she had entered.

(2)

When Deepak reached office, Supriya inquired whether he had seen the newspaper.

"No, I was busy with the report we are sending to HRD (Human Resource and Development)."

She showed him the innocuous news item at the bottom of the first page. He winced a little, and added, "I expected it. Prema was working hard on it."

"That means Kranti did it." Her face was grim trying to

assess the future repercussions.

"He is innocent till proven guilty."

His overcautiousness put her off, and she turned the pages of a file she had brought for discussion.

"Honestly Supri, I am too ashamed to talk about it. First it was Vinay, and now Kranti. And this appears much worse."

"I am sorry."

"Sometimes, I find it easier to discuss these things with you than with Vaishali. She gets too hyper."

He told her everything he knew about the heinous crime.

"The unfortunate fact is that Julian, the victim, is staying with us. It's Prema's strategy to torment Kranti."

"But your daughter-in-law has lot of spine."

"Of course," he said with pride. "But all my sons are worthless. Only my daughters-in-law and Kanu are decent human beings."

"And Vivek?"

"He is okay as a human being. He is principled but can be stubborn on a trivial issue. He has his fads." He looked at her, and added, "Ironically, he dislikes me."

Supriya looked pensively at her boss. Life was full of contradictions; how could anyone dislike Deepak?

"Today, we don't have much pressure of work and you are depressed. Why not tell me your life story."

Casually, he glanced at the day's timetable, and told his PA to postpone the 11am internal meeting to the next day.

"Yes, you are right. I am quite perturbed. Today, I'll confide in you about my noble pedigree you had hinted at once." He smiled, ordered coffee, and relaxed himself on the sofa.

Sipping coffee, he told her everything except his relationship with his wife. For the two hours that he narrated his long, sad tale of childhood, adolescence, youth and his later life, she listened more attentively to each word he uttered than to the discussion in any meeting he had chaired.

"You go up in my esteem, sir," she said, when he had finished. His melancholia had touched her heart. She wanted to go up to him, and hug him, but knowing his attitudes, she continued to remain glued to her seat.

His face turned grave. "You have known me for years Supri. Why did Vinay and Kranti do what they did? I mean —."

Behind those sombre eyes he had bravely hidden his tears.

"I understand Deep. These are exaggerated human weaknesses, and no one can do anything about it."

"Do you think I could have done what Kranti did?"

"I can't imagine you hurting a fly."

"Could you imagine Kranti doing it?"

"I can't imagine Kranti also doing it though he may not mind pulling down his colleagues to score a few brownie points in his career."

"Then why?" Deepak's voice choked.

She rose, sat down beside him, and caught both his hands.

"How can you blame yourself for Vinay's cheating, Kranti raping a helpless woman, or Vivek not doing anything or even Kanu's divorce? They are not babes but grown-up adults and have to suffer the consequences of their actions."

The warmth that exuded from her mellowed his self

persecution for a while. Later, he disentangled her hands, paced up and down the room, and then all at once sat down on the sofa.

She didn't know how to handle him. Suddenly, she said, "Sometimes, I wish you had a streak of Kranti in you. You are cold like a freezer!"

"What do you mean?" He looked angrily at her.

"Sorry." She smiled impishly.

(3)

Sudha would have dismissed the FIR news item with a pinch of salt if NRK was not founded by Prema. As the President of the Kendra, Prema was extremely meticulous, and thoroughly professional. The Kendra picked a few cases in a year, worked hard on them, and invariably succeeded in court. The only instance where they had failed was when the complainant withdrew the complaint in the middle of a trial under pressure from the family.

"But how could Kranti do it?" She was perplexed. She had known him for about four years, and he had never betrayed any sign of emotion. "I don't believe in emotions while on duty," he had told her once, and by and large he had adhered to it even though she had a soft spot for him. Three years back she had her divorce, and a divorcee was vulnerable in the Delhi Police and treated as easy game. But Kranti making a pass at her was unthinkable. He had supported her in many ways against her in-laws, and she was greatly indebted to him for those small favours. They had rubbed shoulders during skirmishes with gangsters or the men of the underworld, but he had never taken advantage of her. Neither was he protective of her. He was uniformly rude in his conduct with all the juniors.

But the FIR lodged by his own wife, who adored him? Sudha was confused.

The buzzer disturbed her thought process.

"Come in," Kranti yelled.

When she entered his room, she was a little surprised to see that within the last three -four weeks his bright face had withered as if he had undergone a lot of turmoil in his life. Despite the hideous crime for which he had been charged by NRK, she felt sorry for him. She pulled a chair and sat down; she could see that he was scribbling something on a white sheet.

"Who is the SHO who has dared to register such a FIR?"

"Tapan Sinha, SHO Subzi Mandi. It is within the jurisdiction of NRK."

"Have you spoken to him?"

"No," she replied looking straight into his eyes. "He allowed the Secretary of NRK to write the FIR and within an hour reported sick and produced a medical certificate."

"Send some one to his house."

"He has disappeared and has yet to reach his village. But 90% chances are that he has gone to some other place."

"Oh!"

"But according to the grapevine he was pressurised by the Joint Commissioner at the instance of the Special Commissioner. Possibly, he too was also under some pressure. Maybe, Director CBI or IB."

"We have to find out whom?"

"Has ma'am pulled some strings?" she asked.

He looked up at her with some respect, and muttered more to himself than her, "Of course, her father."

He understood that Prema had gone to Hyderabad to ensure that her father used adequate influence to register the case.

Spontaneously, Sudha answered, "It is becoming a family affair," and regretted it.

"You are right in your conclusions. The family quarrel is being dragged into a court."

"Is ma'am cut up about something?"

"I'll tell you later. Join me for lunch."

Krandhikar was away on leave, and the Special Commissioner Kulwant Singh was in charge. Kranti called upon him; he did not like the burly sardar.

"Sir, I'm told that you have forced Tapan Sinha to register an FIR against me."

"He was simply told to do his job."

"I would have suspended him if he were not doing his job properly."

Kulwant Singh felt uneasy.

"Has someone put pressure on you?"

Cornered, Kulwant Singh hit back. "I don't like a DCP talking to me like this."

"An FIR has been filed against me in Delhi. Are you aware of the consequences?"

"No one is above law."

"I will be the laughingstock of the Delhi Police force. Who is going to obey my orders?"

"That's your problem."

"If I don't get results, it's going to be yours too."

"No one talks to Kulwant Singh like this."

"You have pushed me to the wall. If the Chief were here, it would not have happened."

"Despite his misplaced fondness for you, even he would have succumbed to pressure." Kulwant Singh raised his voice. "Do you know who called me up? Director IB."

Hanumant Singh as the Director, Intelligence Bureau, was the senior most police officer in the country, and was highly respected by the entire police fraternity.

"Oh!" Kranti exclaimed. He sat back, his anger melted. Now, he was able to tie the loose links. Hanumant Singh belonged to the UP cadre, and Prema's father was the Chief Justice, Allahabad High Court before his promotion as Supreme Court, Judge.

"Did you do what the FIR says?"

"No." Kranti retorted and left the room.

He realized that his days in Delhi Police were numbered. With the stigma of a rape FIR slapped on him, he could not face his juniors. Urgent official matters kept him occupied, and he entirely forgot to invite Sudha for lunch. At about 7pm, he remembered her, and called. When she arrived, he told her to close the door, and sit down.

For an instant, she hesitated, but obeyed.

"Are you worried about your reputation?"

"No. But there are two reasons. First, the office is closed, and it will make the tongues wag in the morning. Second, as a rule you always keep the door open; any unusual conduct now will be conspicuous."

"Is there a third reason also?"

"There is none."

The firmness in her voice made him breathe easily.

"How long have you known me?"

"Four years and two months."

"Do you think I could have done what the FIR says?"

Confidently, she said, "No."

"In this entire world, I have one ally."

"But your parents, brothers, sisters-in-law and sister — are they all with ma'am?"

"I don't know why, but it appears to me that all the ladies of the house are with Prema. Even ma."

"Then it's very serious." Sudha had a great regard for Vaishali.

She looked at his forlorn face, and asked, "Would you mind if I have all the details of the case?"

"Of course," he said, and told her everything the way he had narrated it to his parents. Since it was his fourth time, he made it still more convincing than the last time.

"There does not appear to be much of a case," she said. "No credible witness and the victim, a notorious prostitute of Kolkata. All the ladies of the house going against you, is not good for you. But why is ma'am so stubborn?"

"She wants to play a heroic drama in which she can proclaim to the entire world that in her pursuit of justice, she does not spare even her husband. Or it is possible that Julian has been able to fool Prema with her sob story."

"All the women of the house going against you, weakens your case. But hopefully, when the crunch comes during the trial, they may not depose against you. And please, do try to have Julian thrown out of the house. Her presence is tilting the scales against you."

"I don't know what will happen?" he muttered.

She told him how Prema had taken the copies of the TA bills. He was a little upset.

"Sorry, sir."

"It is all right, you didn't know the background, and Prema is efficient."

He rose, and said, "I am depending on you Sudha."

"I will always be with you - right or wrong."

He looked up sharply at her to see whether she disbelieved him. But there was not even a flicker of doubt on her face.

"At this stage —" she looked directly into his eyes — "would it not be better to go on deputation?"
"I was also thinking on those lines," he murmured.

After Sudha left the room, he sat for a long time clearing the pending files till it was almost dinner time. He was reluctant to go home and face the family members. Sudha was right that he was getting isolated in the house. How was it that he was unable to garner the sympathy of any member of the family though each one of them was indebted to him in one way or the other? Because they all felt that he had done it.

At lunch when the discussion centred on the FIR, Madhulika and Vinay learnt about Kranti's scandal for the first time and were stunned on learning the truth. Vaishali narrated the squalid incident avoiding the details.
Vinay said, "How could he —?"
Madhulika tightened her grip over her husband's arm warning him that he was stepping out of line: he was no less a criminal. Abruptly, he stopped, and looked down at his plate. Vivek was itching to retaliate when Vaishali placed her arm gently on his hand saying, "How is the dal? I told the recipe to Julian."
"Dal is okay ma, but —". He stopped eating and stared at Vinay.
Though Vinay had obeyed his wife as a natural reflex, he felt humiliated at his younger brother's body language. The atmosphere was tense, someone was sure to explode. Madhulika took the initiative and dragged her husband to the safety of their room.

The very thought that she was touched by a rapist on

her thighs made Madhulika feel like a whore. The core of her being experienced a feeling of creepiness as if she was defiled by Kranti; ironically, when he had touched her a pleasant feeling of excitement had pervaded her body. Unable to stand the emotion of disgust now, she had a shower and washed her legs with soap and Dettol and rubbed it hard with a sponge. "They are all rascals," she muttered to herself.

Vinay had cut short his comment without appreciating the situation as he was acutely dependent on his wife. Only within the confines of his bedroom it dawned on him that he was no less a criminal and that the punishment for both the offences was of the same order. Vivek was right, how could he have the cheek to criticise Kranti?

The unravelling of the new family secret stupefied the couple, and suddenly they stopped talking to each other. Vinay's own guilt complex made him clam up, whereas Madhulika was worried how her husband would react if he learnt of Kranti's attempt at flirtation with her?

Kranti's entry in the house was met with blank stares as if he were an intruder. He went straight to his bedroom (Prema had shifted to Kanu's room), kept his briefcase, and returned to the drawing room. It was empty. He was about to light a cigarette when Vaishali entered. As if pre-planned, the entire family trooped in from their respective rooms.

Conspiratorially, Deepak asked Madhulika if it was something special.

"Yes, it is very serious." Madhulika responded grimly.

Vaishali clapped her hands drawing the attention of everyone. "Kranti wants to throw out Prema and Julian from the house. We have to take a decision on it."

Kranti was appalled.

"I didn't mean it, ma," Kranti said. "I had just lost my cool."

"Are you sure?" Vaishali asked.

"Yes, ma."

"So, it is decided that no one will quit the house, and will discharges the duties and responsibilities taken over by him or her." Vaishali concluded.

"Yes, mummy," Prema answered.

The meeting broke up.

Deepak smiled at Vaishali. "I wish we were able to take such quick decisions in the government."

Later, Deepak volunteered to intervene between Kranti and Prema, Vaishali overruled him.

"The charge of rape has upset all the women. Let Kranti convince everyone of his innocence and come out clean. All on his own."

"Is it so bad?"

"Yes, it is."

Whenever alone, the thought of going against her own son troubled Vaishali. One evening, Vaishali, Prema and Kanupriya had a long discussion on the subject. The previous occupant of the bungalow had a large joint family, and he had given the servant quarter to a nephew and his family. Two rooms were constructed at the other end of the bungalow for the servant. Now, Julian was asked to shift there. It was more of a face-saving for Kranti as Julian went there only to sleep at night. There was a tacit understanding between Julian and her mistresses that when she worked late or there was an emergency, she spent the night in her old room. Later, even when the family was able to get another servant, Julian continued to work in the house.

(4)

Sheila's sudden departure had a dramatic effect on Vivek: he grew disinterested in the project, lost the ease and familiarity with Lehriya, and felt more comfortable in the noisy ménage at the Akbar Road bungalow. Large scale transfers in the bureaucracy at various levels in the district upset him as he could not relate to the new team and wanted to run away from the village.

Once while travelling in the train to Jaipur, he ran into the Rajasthan Minister of Community Projects and Development. On learning about the work he had done at Lehriya, the Minister showed keen interest in his project. Within a week, the young, dynamic Minister visited Lehriya alone, and was amazed that one man's enthusiasm could change not only the village, but thousands of lives in the district. He invited Vivek for discussion to Jaipur. Entrusting the Lehriya project to his second in command, Vivek worked out a plan for replicating the Lehriya model with significant changes to suit the local needs of Eastern Rajasthan. The news was blown up in the national papers as the project was inaugurated by the Chief Minister.

Apprehensively, when Vaishali opened the newspaper, she was pleasantly surprised to see her youngest son's smiling photograph on the seventh page staring at her. Thrilled on going through the 700 - word story on Vivek, she ran up to Deepak, and showed Vivek's photograph with the Chief Minister and the write up.

"My god! What great news!!" He was ebullient, his face wreathed in smiles.

"To me, he looks a younger version of you. It reminds me of our days in UP."

"But I never made it to the national papers at such a young age," he said.

Surrounded by gloom, any good news cheers up the spirits, and this coming from the worthless son, and that too prominently displayed, was nothing short of a miracle for the family. The older couple was almost ecstatic. Vinay heard of it from Madhulika, and grinned. "At last!" he muttered. Kranti was more passionate in showing his exuberance and lavished rich praise on him. "It was overdue," he said aloud to Kanupriya. "We needed something of this kind at this stage." He phoned Vivek, and everyone congratulated him.

Happiness arising out of a family member's proclaimed success can be heady; it forced a temporary ceasefire between Prema and Kranti.

Vivek's arrival was greeted in the house with great fanfare, almost like the return of a victorious hero whose legions had conquered half the world. He was more vocal and dominated the dining table discussion. Vaishali felt that the old happy times were back with the difference that now Vivek had donned the mantle of his father in garnering glory.

When Vivek learned of the FIR against Kranti, he was shocked. "But you love Kranti? How could you drag your own love to a court?"

"I love that rascal brother of yours." Prema had tears in her eyes. "But for a principle, I'll go against him."

"But I would not drive my own love to a court for the sake of a prostitute."

"You are entitled to your views," she said, thought for

an instant and added, “Helplessness of a young, pretty woman can arouse the baser instincts of men.”

“Then why blame him? He is not a saint.”

“To morrow, he will do it to Sheila, Madhu, Kanu and maybe his own daughter Namita. He is not a gangster but a defender of law, an officer in the police force. And belonging to such an honourable family!”

The disdain in her tone upset both Kanupriya and Vivek. Both glowered at her and rose from their seats to leave the room. Kanupriya and Vivek were the two persons she adored in the house, and she needed them in this hour of crisis. She tried to make amends and caught Vivek’s arm. “You would never act in such a manner to a helpless woman.”

Her touch toned down his hostility. “Honestly, I don’t know, we all have different needs.”

Kanupriya went to attend the ringing phone.

“Am I wrong? Do you think I am going crazy?” Prema asked.

“No. If you feel wronged you must do what you have done.”

“It is not a question of my being wronged but that poor girl Julian.”

“Kranti will never apologize but I can do so on his behalf.”

“No, that will not do,” Prema said firmly.

(5)

The low-down on Julian’s rape by Kranti revolted Madhulika and now she feared him. He was the same man who often smiled at her, was exemplary in courtesies to the point of being gallant; it embarrassed her at times and made her blush. But now she felt that he was devious, and his manners seemed a camouflage for hidden sinister designs. When alone in her room, she made sure to bolt the door. Over lunch or dinner, she was cold to him and did not even glance in his direction. Initially, there was no change in his behaviour, but within a week his smiles disappeared, and his expressions were almost wooden.

Though Madhulika supported Prema, she was not sure that her action of dragging her husband to the court was appropriate. When Vinay asked, "Do you think Kranti really raped Julian?" Madhulika was confused and reluctant to offer an opinion.

Vinay persisted.

"I don't know," she said. "But I believe in Prema more than Kranti. However, it is also possible that Prema is overreacting."

"Did Kranti make a pass at you?"

Flabbergasted by the suddenness of the question, she turned speechless. Who could have told him? she wondered. All at once, she realized that loitering behind the trees he must have watched the whole scene personally, something, that she didn't want him to know. Honestly, she told the details, worried all the time how it would affect him.

"His reaction was spontaneous, and not premeditated. Maybe, I too overreacted."

He recalled the Puri episode and was critical of over familiarity. "In your case, we were also to blame, but Julian was a total stranger," he said. "And since school and college days Kranti is known to be a flirt where fair girls are concerned. Somehow, I believe in Julian and Prema more than my own brother."

"So do I." Madhulika responded hurriedly.

(6)

In search of a suitable deputation, Kranti was engaged in feverish activity. With little help from his father, his deputation application was accepted, and he moved to the Border Security Force (BSF) at Delhi. Krandhikar was promoted, and shifted as DG, CRPF, and Kulwant Singh took over as Police Commissioner on promotion. He sent four teams to the north-east and got the inquiry against Kranti completed on priority basis and had the charge sheet filed in a court of law. The case was taken up for hearing by Additional Session Judge, Ms Ekta Aggarwal, a known feminist. The media turned active and highlighted the main features of the case. As the case involved a top cop, Ms Aggarwal had mentioned informally in a function relating to gender issue that she would have the case finalized in five-six months.

XIV

Mixed Bag

In the last ten months, Deepak's government bungalow at Akbar Road had seen many shades of fluctuating fortunes. It had witnessed the unfolding of Vinay's hidden secret that had shaken the tranquillity of the house and disturbed the equipoise of the scientific community in the country. Luckily, the crisis was contained though the danger of a CBI inquiry still loomed over the family. The tumbling out of Kranti's secret was another bombshell for the household, and its shards had landed straight with the police, and later in the court, which had been adroitly averted in Vinay's case.

But worse was to come.

Before the trial began, the judge called the senior prosecutor and the defence counsel into her room and told them to cooperate in getting the case finalised early as it involved a top cop and had generated a lot of misgivings in society. Both assured her of their support.

At the first hearing of the case that had been put on

the fast track, the senior prosecutor moved an application for issue of a non-bailable warrant for Kranti Chopra's arrest. It was rejected by the judge. Another application was then moved for his suspension as he could influence the court proceedings. The judge postponed the decision to the next hearing.

However, the media lapped it, and the news was splashed on the first page of many leading dailies. The journalists surrounded Kranti, and Deepak at their offices and home. When they found that Prema, the President of NRK, happened to be Kranti's wife, and she stayed at Kranti's house along with the victim, it made the news saucy. Some of the journalists traced the Vinay scandal and linked it to the same house astounding the readers. A few were more enterprising and traced the family tree going back a hundred years; stories of which even Deepak was unaware. Most of it was malicious gossip. Ram Narain and Deepak's stories were highly exaggerated, and distorted. Vaishali and Deepak read the garbled stories helplessly and did not react. "This is what I feared in the last year of my career," he told his wife. Prema felt deeply hurt but had no control over what had been engineered by the publicity wings of various women's organizations. Though of a tough hide, Prema was not prepared for such an onslaught by the fourth estate.

"Papa, you should a make a statement to the press giving facts," Prema told Deepak.

"What should I tell them?" He stared angrily at her. "Do I tell them that I am going to disown Kranti?"

Humiliating a babu who was once the topmost bureaucrat of the country, turned out to be media's delight, and it offered a lot of vicarious pleasure to the readers. Some journalists were found loitering 24x7 near Deepak's house.

Many women's organizations collected at Jantar Mantar, carried out long rallies, and processions through the city, and finally converged at Akbar Road in thousands. When they started shouting slogans against each member of the family, Prema went out, and begged them to stop. They ignored her pleas and continued to shout till the police had to be called. Some groups from the north-east also assembled and clamoured against Kranti and Deepak.

Prema lost the sympathy of all the family members and was completely isolated. "And all this for a whore?" She wondered whether she had overreacted.

"The Chopra house is full of scandals," was the gossip floating in the corridors of power in the North, and South blocks. The air at I I C, Habitat Centre and Gymkhana was charged with the Kranti scandal. Vinay's case was on a slightly different footing as it involved scientific research, and many babus could not appreciate the nuances of scientific discovery, and the distinction between the contributions of Stella and Vinay. The flavour of patriotism also had not allowed the scandal to blow up. But in Kranti's case it was downright brutal rape — more earthy, and horrid. It made the man in the street smirk. Middle- and upper-class men and women sniggered and broke into rip roaring laughter at the mention of the FIR filed at the instance of an infamous prostitute. Within a few days, when their imaginary pleasures were satiated, they realized that a rape was a rape whether that of a whore or a woman of the north-east. The half-suppressed laughter was replaced by anger and hatred against the

Chopra family. Some of the celebrities and bureaucrats felt ashamed that they had wined and dined with the Chopras.

When the situation continued to deteriorate, Deepak decided to pull the plug on this brazen invasion of his privacy, and met the Principal Secretary to the PM. As he had worked with Deepak when he was the Cabinet Secretary, P. Das Gupta was courteous, and went out of the way to make him comfortable. "I'll see what I can do, sir," he said, but promised nothing. A harassed Deepak returned home frustrated. Two days later, the journalists disappeared, and the processions melted.

(2)

On the occasion of the visit of the US Under Secretary of State for Political Affairs, the Foreign Secretary personally sent the dinner invitation to Deepak.

"Ms Elizabeth Hopkins," Deepak muttered. "The name seems familiar." But he had forgotten when and where he had met her. If Arun Dastur had sent it, he must have a purpose.

Amongst an exclusive gathering of about three dozen guests at The Ashok, Deepak knew only the Foreign Secretary. Escorted by the US ambassador, when the Under Secretary of State for Political Affairs arrived, Dastur introduced them to Deepak. The ambassador was rather curt to him; it appeared that he knew the entire background about him, and Vinay. But Elizabeth Hopkins was warm and friendly, and it boosted Deepak's spirits.

"You were awfully nice to me when I came to India about thirty years ago," she said. "I was in my early twenties then, and rather stupid."

The arrival of the Minister of State, for Foreign Affairs, diverted the attention of the guests, and Deepak was brushed aside by other bureaucrats. As the Chairman of the Commission, Deepak was not involved in the thick of political activity. He helped himself to a drink and strolled casually towards a window.

"Hey!"

Deepak turned and found Ms Hopkins smiling at him.

"I don't think you remember me," she said.

"Honestly, no."

"I was madly in love with Vijay Rathore, ADC to the President, and you had helped me twice when I was in a real spot."

Deepak was a Deputy Secretary in the Prime Minister's Office for a few months when Mrs Indira Gandhi was the PM. Elizabeth had arrived an hour before the Secretary of State's meeting with the President and was with the ADC all the time. A few seconds before the arrival of the Secretary of State, Deepak had found them in a very intimate position, and alerted them just in time. "These Americans," he had muttered. Again, at a reception given by the Prime Minister, he had quietly pointed out to Elizabeth to adjust her dress before she entered the banquet hall. Throughout the visit, he had been helpful in getting them together clandestinely.

"Now, I remember," Deepak replied.

"Now, I am more responsible." She had a twinkle in her eyes.

The Minister of State, for Foreign Affairs, walked towards them.

"Give me a few minutes more," she said looking towards the Minister, and catching Deepak's arm walked away a little farther from the others.

"Isn't there something you would like to talk about your son Vinay?"

Taken aback, Deepak muttered, "Oh, yes, yes."

"I have been well briefed by your friend, the Foreign Secretary."

"Thank you," Deepak said. "When can we meet?"

"Day after: 6 pm, at the Embassy."

Thanking her, Deepak had another drink. Arun Dastur waved to him when he was about to leave.

Ms Hopkins was warm though formal when he called on her at the appointed time. Without wasting any time, she asked directly, "What do you want me to do?"

"Your ambassador has lodged a formal complaint against Vinay; I want that to be withdrawn.

"Is Vinay innocent?"

"No," he said, and explained how Stella had discovered the particle, and Vinay had tested it with many galaxy clusters. "Rightfully, it should have been called Stella -Vinay particle. It was an act of a frustrated young man at breaking point. But now Stella is no more, and nothing can bring her back."

The ambassador knocked, and was about to enter, but on seeing Deepak said a "sorry," and turned to go back. Ms Hopkins asked him to sit down, and told him, "Mr. Chopra is a friend of mine as I am of yours."

He took the farthest seat from Deepak. She summed up what had transpired between them, and asked, "Is he speaking the truth. What do our experts say?"

John Whitefield went to his room, returned with a file and said, "Mr. Chopra's assessment is right, but it's an act of cheating and forgery. Vinay should go to jail. He can

choose whether he prefers an American or an Indian jail."
"Dear me, is there a need to be so sarcastic?" Ms Hopkins rose from her chair and placed her arm on the ambassador's shoulder. "We all have some skeletons in our cupboard. Some are very old and monstrous. I have mine, and so have you, John?"
Drained of colour, John turned white.
"Mr. Chopra, I would need a written confession from Vinay of his misdeeds by tomorrow. It will remain in my personal custody and would never be used against him."
Deepak was satisfied with this arrangement.
"And you, John?"
He nodded.
"Don't look so sullen, John. It's necessary in the broader interests of cooperation, and goodwill between the two major democracies of the world."
She recorded a long note in her own bold handwriting.
"I want the complaint to be withdrawn by tomorrow."
She smiled at John, and he left the room.
Deepak thanked her, and she hugged him lightly.
Next day, Vinay handed the confession to her personally, and thanked her.
"I am doing it for your father," she said coldly. "If I had my way, you would be in some barbaric prison of Africa from where you would never come back alive."

(3)

At last, it was celebration time at Deepak's home. The air was imbued with rejoicing. Vinay could not believe his good fortune; the clouds of gloom disappeared, and he basked in the luxury of his exoneration. The three amaltashs (also called golden rain) near the gate were in their prime glory shooting out golden streams of happiness and the two gulmohars at the other end had already burst into full bloom a few weeks earlier. A jubilant Madhulika infected everyone with irrepressible joy. The family had a grand party in the lawns and all of them danced, and later toasted to Vinay and Madhulika's future. For once, Vaishali was made to break her taboo, and raise her champagne glass.

But it was not unblemished joy for the family; the shadow of Kranti's trial lingered in the backdrop. The family members were indulgent towards Kranti, but he preferred to seek refuge in the dark corners. Under stress, Prema too was listless.

After dessert, Deepak announced that he was due to demit office by the end of February and had to give up the government accommodation and shift to his bungalow. It quietened the entire bustle and made his children, and their spouses contemplate on their future. Deepak wanted to give nine - ten months notice to his sons to make alternate arrangements.

The Panchsheel house had only three bedrooms; in all probability Kanupriya's future was cast with her parents. Vinay and Madhulika's plans to settle in Darjeeling had still not materialized though the couple had visited the hill station twice. Prema was in a conundrum; her future was linked to the court case. If Kranti was convicted, she had no future with him. Would she be forced to file an application for divorce? What would happen to the children? Since her marriage, she had always lived with her in-laws and moved with them from one government bungalow to another. Now, where would she go? Everything was nebulous. Kranti reflected that it was high time that he should apply for a government residence, but he was not sure how things would pan out depending on the results of the trial, and the stance taken by Prema. To Vivek, it made little difference. His needs were limited, and he could stretch himself for the night even on a divan in the lounge. He preferred it to his temporary abode in Banswara.

"I may be allowed to retain the house for two to four months more," Deepak added giving a breather to his children and their families. "But I'm not sure."

(4)

PS Nair, Director General, BSF, summoned Kranti. The short, dark Keralite with sparkling eyes asked him the details of the rape case. When Kranti had finished, he looked quizzically at him and asked, "Is it true that your wife is the President of Nari Rakshan Kendra as the media makes it out to be?"

"Yes, sir."

Vainly, Kranti tried to explain Prema's background, and her dramatics at heroism.

"You are talking crap." Nair was furious. "I have never known a woman drag her husband to court unless it is a genuine case."

"But sir, based on facts there is hardly any case against me. There is no credible witness, and the woman was a notorious whore. The police and the prosecutor are a stupid bunch and are lacking in grey matter."

"The police and the prosecutor are not exactly the fools that you are making them out to be. I am a cop and so are you."

"They are all ganging up against me."

"You mean the Police Commissioner, your colleagues and your wife?"

One argument led to the next. Nair shouted at him. "What do you take me for? I also have a job to do. I'll place you under suspension as soon as I take the approval of the Government."

"But sir, my image and reputation will be tarnished?"

Nair had liked the dash in the young man that he had found wanting in many other officers, but he refused to help him.

"If the court exonerates you, you will be back with us."

Crestfallen, Kranti returned to his room.

Trevedi, the Home Secretary, was apathetic to him, and dismissed him in less than a minute saying that no one was above the law. The Home Minister's PA refused to give him any time stating that the Minister was busy in a meeting with a delegation from Tamil Nadu. Kranti informed Deepak about the reaction of the Home Secretary and his (Kranti's) inability to meet with the Home Minister.

With so much of ignominy heaped on him by the media, Deepak could not muster the courage to meet the Home Minister or the Home Secretary. However, he tried to reach them on the phone. The Minister's PA refused to connect him, and Trevedi's PA disconnected the line. When he caught him at his residence, Trevedi was cold, as if Deepak belonged to a family of criminals.

In the next hearing, the judge again rejected the application for Kranti's suspension as he was no longer working in Delhi Police.

But within three days, he was placed under suspension by the Central Government. It shocked the family members and bewildered others.

"Congrats!" Kranti tossed the suspension letter to Prema. His red eyes were full of hatred.

"It is the beginning of the end." She retorted bravely.

"It will not be my end only — you and the children will also perish."

"I am prepared for the worst." She shook her long tresses in defiance.

But her brain refused to relax even at night. Half asleep, she suddenly rose muttering something. Her sister-in-law switched on the light. "What's it, bhabi?"

"Kranti has no money. How will he get a good lawyer?"

Most of their savings were in Prema's account.

Kanupriya switched off the light. "Go back to sleep, you have a busy schedule with the Public Prosecutor tomorrow."

A few days later, when Kranti was about to go out, Vaishali told him that Prema had transferred most of the money to his account.

"I don't need her money."

The roughness in his tone hurt Vaishali.

"It's not mine but yours. I would not give you anything of mine," Prema said.

He muttered "Thanks," and turned towards the door when Prema said aloud, "And change that pretty lawyer of yours. She is thoroughly useless, and stupid unless —."

Kranti scowled at her and left.

"Is Nidhi Talwar really stupid?" Kanupriya asked.

Prema nodded. "Dumb, snooty and beautiful!"

"But why are you bothered, bhabi?"

Without answering, Prema sat down for breakfast, her face taut and grim. She could not swallow anything. Kanupriya saw the tears lurking in the corners of her eyes. Applying the butter on her half-burnt toasts and crushing them in her fingers, Kanupriya said, "The war has just begun, and you have started cracking up."

"Not me." Prema retaliated with effrontery.

"You have no choice now. You have initiated the circus of making a mockery of our respect and dignity. We are all small players and suffering our roles. But the director-cum- producer cannot afford to break down midway."

"Have you considered," Kanupriya added, "if you succeed in sending your husband to seven years of imprisonment, how it would affect your marital status?"

"Yes, Kanu. It is possible that Kranti and I would part ways and lead independent lives. I may go back to my father and start my own practice in Hyderabad." The clarity in her thinking was not matched by her tone as her throat was choked with emotion. "The question of custody —"

Prema could not go on and stopped abruptly. She pulled a tissue from the tissue- box, cleared her nose, and had a sip of tea that had already gone tepid. Vaishali, who was sitting next to her, placed her arm affectionately on her shoulder. She was fully aware that it was a temporary phase in Prema's attitude, and it had no bearing on her resolve to punish Kranti.

"Is it worthwhile to pursue the court case?" Kanupriya asked hoping it was the right moment to strike.

"Yes, Kanu," she said determinedly. "It's too late to withdraw."

"You are impossible."

Controlling her emotions, Prema finished her breakfast, and raising her head high went back to her room.

"Never make the mistake of throwing down the gauntlet

to her. Such sensitive moments, which in other individuals are weak moments, in her case they are cathartic. It helps her to harden her stand."

"Sorry, ma. You know her better."

"I know, because I too, am like her."

Kanupriya stared at her mother in surprise.

(5)

The news of Kranti's suspension was electrifying in the Delhi Police. A decorated and highly respected officer known for bringing laurels for the Delhi Police, a favourite with political and bureaucratic bosses, Kranti's downfall shocked most. And it was engineered not by a court order, but by the same Government that had glorified him earlier. Worse, he was suspended primarily on a whore's statement. But there was not even a ripple in the BSF because no one knew him there.

Immediately after suspension, Kranti was a changed man. He had suspended a few cops in his career of over thirteen years; now he realized the psychological effect it could have on an individual. Before his suspension, he was cocksure that nothing would ever happen to him. The Police Commissioner, Home Secretary and even the Home Minister had nothing but praise for him. Ironically, the Home Secretary was a good friend of his father's. Despite all this, no one gave a second thought to his future.

Kranti's case was discussed by the Home Minister with the Minister of State, and the Home Secretary at great length. There was a growing feeling amongst the public that men in power and those under their protection, or the sons of politicians or top bureaucrats got away even with murder by using influence. Unfortunately for

Kranti, he was not only in a position of authority, but also happened to be the son of a top bureaucrat. The pressure from the media and women's organizations had forced the Government to send a clear message. The PMO had also been sounded because Deepak Chopra could even approach the PM, if need arose.

Sitting alone in the bar of I I C, Kranti was engulfed in self pity. Excoriated and humiliated by his seniors, his future was dark like the asphalt. No one gave a sign of recognition to him by raising his hand or even by the flicker of an eyebrow. The pink complexion had turned sallow, and his movements were slow and slightly awkward. He had developed a slight paunch, whereas a few weeks back he had sported the body of a fitness trainer. He realized that he had made a mistake in marrying the olive-coloured Prema. Why did he marry a dark woman? Was it the warmth and candid look in her eyes that had moved him or was it the harmony in the coupling of their bodies during the brief premarital courting that had paved the way for marriage? But he could not have changed his decision after agreeing to the marriage, especially when she happened to be the daughter of a Chief Justice. Prema was right that the semi-nude fair women turned him insane, and he was unable to control his basic urges. Though he loved and adored Prema, he had little control when opportunity knocked at his door. He should have married a fair one and not Prema, he reflected, swallowing the last bit of whisky in one gulp. But she was the mother of his children, and he loved her, and he was certain that she loved him even more.

After his aimless wanderings in the city in anonymity without his uniform and official vehicle, when he reached home in the evening, his feet were slightly unsteady because of over drinking. Prema opened the door turning him nervous. He wanted to project the image of a tough cop, but his unsteady steps were a poor reflection of his psyche. Incoherently, he apologized and stretched his slouched posture to its full height, walked to his room and gently, very gently, closed the door.

Straight away he went to the bathroom, had a shower, and changed his clothes. But it did not mellow the anguish, and he caught his head in both hands. "Oh god, where have I landed myself?" he said aloud. His plaintive cry of pain would have moved even a stranger.

"In hell!" Julian screamed at him. At instance of her mistress, she had brought tea and biscuits.

"Get out," he shouted at her, his eyes flashing fire.

"This fire will burn you alive," she hissed, and left the room.

Julian went back to Prema to faithfully report what Kranti was undergoing; she was surprised to see that her mistress too was torn within and was crying. "Ma'am, please?"

Julian pondered for a long time, and said, "Ma'am, I am watching you for the last few weeks, you can't take it anymore. I am going to withdraw the case."

Prema rose, threw some water on her eyes, wiped them with her dupatta, and said, "Yes, it is true that I am a little low for the last few days, but my convictions do not waver."

"Is it worth it?"

"It is worth all the trouble on this earth."

The firmness in Prema's demeanour made the woman nod with respect. "Then it is okay, ma'am."

Alone in his room at night, Kranti was in a state of depression. Why did he rape Julian? When he had threatened to fire at the goons and they had run away, he had moved towards the victim with the genuine intention of untying her and helping her. Unfastening the knots was not easy, and he had to go down on his knees. While undoing the knots, he had watched her minutely. He had never seen such a beautiful, pink complexioned nude girl from such close quarters except in 'Playboy' or 'Men Only' magazines. Interacting with pretty girls in school and college or even flirting with them was quite another thing. Here the nude girl was on the bed — her hands and feet tied — helpless and vulnerable. Almost like a dream or fantasy. Driven by his concupiscence, he forgot everything: his duty, morality and love for Prema. Obsessed by her youth and beauty, he satisfied his desire. When the girl did not shriek, he felt that she too had enjoyed the experience. At times, he wondered if the girl's feet and hands were not tied or had she screamed, or even protested mildly would he have had the courage to rape her?

According to rules, suspension only debars the government servant from holding any post so that he is unable to influence the process of inquiry though he is treated as on duty and gets a reasonable allowance. However, in real terms, it has far reaching implication. Suspension is like putting a government seal on his character and integrity: he is disgraced. Shunned by the society, his equation with his family can get fractured.

Kranti was not suspended because of misappropriation of money or selling secrets to enemy nations affecting the security of the country or an act of indiscipline. But rape. No crime is more heinous than rape in the Indian Penal Code. There can be a moral justification for even murder; there is none for rape. It pronounced him a devil.

His honour, his pride was crushed.

The FIR had set the tone of his crime. But it was never taken seriously. No one had believed it would be established in the court of law, and some of the legal experts felt that it would be dismissed in the very first hearing. The Central Government's affirmation of the crime by suspending him, suddenly made everyone realize that he had actually done the crime; it was a question of time that it would be proved in the court.

An emotion of revulsion was associated with him now. He symbolized the lowest levels of depravity to which human nature could stoop: the worst of shameless, unpardonable crimes. Many felt that any punishment less than death would not meet the ends of justice.

His spontaneous reaction was to flee. Kranti could not look into the eyes of the family members and felt ashamed when he ran into them or crossed their path. He had tears in his eyes when he overheard Namita asking Kanupriya,"Bua, what is suspension? Is it a gold or silver medal?" He refused to take food with the family members and preferred the safety of his room.

Kranti had been the darling of the family. Exceedingly helpful and useful, he was dependable like a rock. Each member of the family owed a lot to him. Deepak and Vaishali's hopes of a comfortable future rested on him. Vinay had been away to the US for eleven or twelve years, and even after his return, their relationship with him and his wife was formal. Though affectionate, Vivek was a liability. He had a streak of quirkiness and was unreliable. Kranti was steady, ambitious, and a decorated officer who did them proud. And he had always been a part of the family, even after his marriage.

Deepak had mentally accepted that if the charge was proved, his son deserved the punishment. Aware of the slow and tardy way in which the courts functioned, he was certain that it could take 15-20 years before the case was finalized, and he would be dead and gone by then. When the case was put on the fast track, it jolted him. Kranti's suspension had stunned him. Why did the Government have to make an example of his son? How would he face other members of the Commission? He had to abandon the dream of getting Padma Vibhushan and the Governorship.

With the passage of time, and interaction with lawyers, Kranti slowly turned optimistic. "There is hardly any case," Nidhi Talwar had assured him. The more he talked to legal luminaries, the more confident he grew. At the worst, it was a weak case, he was told, and it would be blown away by any competent lawyer. The dark puffy eye bags disappeared, and the colour on his face returned slowly like the sunlight replacing the shadows on earth when the sun emerges out of the dark clouds. In less than two months, he bounced back to his hubristic pride.

(6)

Finally, Vinay got the letter from Darjeeling and the couple was happy to escape the strained environment of the house. In a way, Vaishali was happy with the news for the sake of her eldest son. She knew that Madhulika's sincere attempts to gel with the family were thwarted by Prema and Kanupriya. Consciously, they isolated her in their tittle-tattle and did not allow their children to be friendly to her. Deepak was the only one who missed the pretty daughter-in-law at the dining table or in the garden. Strangely, no one missed Vinay; it was as if the family had one criminal less.

Jean Simpson smiled smugly when she learnt that Vinay Chopra had resigned from the IIT, Delhi, and had taken up a school appointment in a remote part of the country. She did not visit India again.

(7)

The Chopras looked forward to the monsoon season. That year, the monsoon arrived early. After a scorching spell of heat wave when the first rain drops hit Delhi, the senior couple rushed out to greet them. They revelled in it as if all their shame and ignominy would be washed away by the sheets of rain. Kanupriya smiled at them but refused to join. Deepak and Vaishali soaked themselves in the rain for a long time and felt buoyant.

"It was great," Vaishali said to her daughter, "as if my soul has been purified."

Vaishali's sudden illness and the doctors' diagnosis that it was pneumonia alarmed the family members. Last year, when she had a collision with a car, everyone had accepted it as accidents can happen to anyone, but an attack of pneumonia in August? How could a healthy and active woman like Vaishali who went for evening walks everyday have such an illness? She spent three anxious nights at Moolchand hospital, and on returning home was under a nurse's care for four days. "It's getting very expensive," she muttered to her husband, and virtually threw the nurse out of the house though she was debilitated after the attack.

Vivek was travelling in the tribal region of Banswara in Rajasthan when he heard the news. He rushed back to Delhi. Hugging her, he said, "You must fall sick after briefing me, ma. For a veteran like you, it is hardly the way to behave." He laughed trying to cheer up her low spirits. His arrival was a great relief to others as he took over the sick member's care.

Vaishali's medium-sized bedroom had two big windows facing the main garden, and a window each on the other two sides that helped her to keep a watch over the activities of all the members of the house. Vivek was amazed at the changes that had taken place in her room in the last few months. The old shabby brick-coloured curtains were replaced by double curtains; the flowery thick silken ones were in green and yellow, and the sheer was in a lined soft green. The sofa's upholstery had a silvery green hue that seemed to be in harmony with the ambience. The pink striped bed sheet and the red gladioli on a corner table with cream coloured tablecloth seemed to brighten the room. It suddenly occurred to him that no other woman in the house had been as thoughtful about decorating her bedroom as ma. And at a time when the couple was in early sixties, and in debt?

"Ma, I like your room. Whenever Sheila and I settle down properly, our bedroom would be exactly like this," he said.

Vaishali smiled. "Sheila would never approve of it."

He understood her thought process.

"I'll make sure that she never enters your room." He quipped and laughed.

During the first month of her departure, Sheila was regular in sending long e-mails; later her messages were short and sporadic. For the last two months there had been no news from her. His attempts to contact her on phone had also been futile. Initially, he was distressed, and later turned apprehensive and sad that he may never see her again.

From morning till night, Vivek was by his mother's side administering medicines, offering tea, water, massaging her head, talking to her about his project — ridiculing the robust politicians with overindulgent bellies and dour bureaucrats — reading the newspaper, stories and poetry. One night when he stole a wink of sleep and was about to roll over on the other side of the sofa, he was surprised that a hand reached out and steadied him.

"Sir, you can take some rest. I'll take care of ma'am."

Startled, he turned to find Julian standing just behind him.

"I'll manage," he said.

"I'm watching you for the last two-three days. You have hardly slept. Please sir, snatch some sleep and come back. In the meanwhile, I'll look after madam."

Already exhausted, Vivek did not protest. For the next few days, the process continued, and Julian gave him the respite for a few hours sleep at night, and he was thankful to her.

One night, he surprised her by bringing a tea- tray with two cups of tea, a few biscuits and salted snacks.

"You should have ordered me to prepare tea," Julian said.

He ignored the comment with a smile. Knowing about her past, he had turned more sympathetic towards her. After she had finished tea, collected the tray and was about to leave, she said, "You are very different from the other members of the house. Mothers are known to take care of their sons, but I have never known a son take care of his mother with such devotion."

"I am the worthless member who does nothing and has all the time."

"Prema ma'am has told me everything about you — your childhood, youth and what you do — and she is all praise for you."

"She is a good soul."

Julian nodded and left.

Nursed by her son, Vaishali recovered and could move around the house on her own. Vivek didn't need to remain awake at night. He was mildly amazed that he missed Julian's company. Within three -four weeks, Vaishali was in command of the house: a ship in turmoil needed the presence of their seasoned captain.

□□□

XV

Supriya

KP Tekriwal, popularly known as Kappu amongst his friends and relatives, had experienced more of loneliness in childhood, and adolescence than warmth and affection. Born to a Mumbai industrialist busy in expanding his financial empire, and a mother, a well-known socialite lost in her fashion world and late-night parties, Kappu was thrown in the company of nannies and au pair as a toddler. An only child, he had no concept of a family. He was hoping to find happiness and fulfilment with Supriya but was frustrated because of the crush she had on Deepak Chopra that had matured into a strong bond over the years.

"What do you find attractive in that old man?" He mocked her. "He is old enough to be your father."

"I can relate to him better." She was straightforward.

"Which you don't with me?"

"You are too busy in your business."

"But I come to you, I don't go to others."

"You do," she replied. "I am no fool; I am your wife and am aware of your activities. You are actually searching for a mistress in me. You never notice me except to satisfy your need. Have you cared to find out my needs, my likes and dislikes, my expectations out of life? I work in an office, am holding a senior position, and run into many problems. I am a woman — slightly capricious — but you have never pampered me. Neither have you cared for your children. Sometimes, I feel that you are more interested in the yarn of my nightie than in me. It disturbs you that it is not produced from the same yarn manufactured in your factories."

Kappu avoided other women. He tried to take interest in the family and give his children the love and affection he had missed out in his childhood. However, he found himself out of tune with them. His efforts invariably backfired. Maybe, Supriya was over possessive of the kids.

But as a family, they were at their best at social gathering. 'As happy as the Kappus,' was the epithet labelled to the family. Sincerely, they wanted to live up to the standards they had projected in the social circle and failed. "It is a sham," they told each other in the privacy of their home, and still did not want to break up the marriage for the sake of children.

Since a substantial part of the day was spent in Deepak's room — which she thoroughly enjoyed — it took its toll on her time. She had to sit late or take the files home. Unable to cope, she denied her husband physical pleasure for a few nights at a stretch, and it irritated Kappu.

"I hope —" he said looking into her beautiful eyes — "you are not making it with the old man."

"Oh, shut up!" she yelled at him. "Just because I am not up to it for the last three-four nights, you have to say such a nasty thing."

"You can go to other women if you want to," she added angrily.

Their relationship nosedived after the fierce exchange.

Immaculately dressed, Kappu was looking forward to an important business party, and was waiting for his wife. A formal party was an occasion to cajole her and show off his gallantry. He wanted to make up with her after the last bitter quarrel and had bought an antique piece of precious jewellery for her. Supriya was unable to get away from a high-level meeting chaired by the PM at his residence. Frowning, Kappu went to the party alone, something he detested.

After he was through with the business interactions over scotch — struck a lucrative deal and got a lukewarm nod for another with a Kannada tycoon, (which he would have clinched by throwing a hint of Supriya's granny, the powerful Home Minister of Karnataka if Supriya were present) — he was at a loose end. Bored after meeting the same professionals and businessmen over the last three-four hours, he moved to an isolated corner as it would have been impolite to leave the party before the Union Commerce Minister. These were the moments in the party where Supriya dazzled the most with her wit and charm, and made other women look almost ordinary.

"Are you the famous Mr. Kappu?" A young woman in early thirties accosted him.

"Famous or not, I'm Kappu alright." He scowled.

Gitanjali was not put off by his foul temper, and cheered him up with her crisp comments, Chanel perfume, and her beauty. As the GM of an upcoming on- line company she represented her boss who was mostly abroad. Earlier, she had pleaded with the Minister for tax rebates for on- line companies as the business were in its infancy. Weariness had stolen over her as she seemed to know no one, and she hung around him throughout the evening. Finally, when the party broke up after midnight, he felt a little sorry for losing out on her company.

Gradually, Supriya stopped going out with Kappu, and he did not miss her as Gitanjali made sure to run into him at all the parties. Often, he bedded down with her at her pad. Her presence in the office or late evening or at odd hours revitalized him. A product of I I M Kolkatta, her suggestions on financial matters were sound, and it helped him in business. Within a couple of months, he was able to persuade her to leave her company and join his enterprise as GM (Finance).

Gitanjali's influence harmonized his domestic life; he was more pleasant and considerate to his wife and children. The children adored him, and the two holidays the family had in Switzerland and the US were memorable. Encouraged, Supriya planned a holiday in Paris, booked the tickets, but a week before the departure, he backed out stating that he had an official meeting to attend in California that he could not afford to miss.

"Are you going with Gitanjali?"

"Of course, I need her officially."

"And personally too?"

Without a smile, he nodded.

"Do you want a divorce?" she asked.

"Not me. If you want it, let me know."

Supriya blamed herself. Her love for Deepak was an

invisible shadow in their relationship and didn't allow the marriage to bloom.

Kappu spent more time at Mumbai, Ahmedabad, and Bhilwara than at Delhi. Now, no one talked of the Kappus being a happy family.

(2)

One night when a storm howled, and rain lashed Delhi, Kappu arrived with Gitanjali from Bhilwara. Supriya was alone at home; the children had gone for a sleep-over to Kappu's cousin. Kappu was intoxicated, and the driver all but dragged the master to his bedroom. He insisted that Gitanjali should spend the night with him. Gitanjali refused as it would tantamount to insulting Supriya and wanted to flee; Kappu prevented her escape.

"Please go, I'll take care of Kappu." Supriya told the young woman.

"I am sorry ma'am, I really am."

"It is okay. Run away."

His legs staggering, Kappu stood in the doorway, not allowing his mistress to get away. He ordered the driver to go home. Not wanting to be a part of the family strife, he bolted.

"If you go tonight, you will be fired," he said threatening the mortified GM. His voice slurred, but his determination did not vacillate.

At the moment, Gitanjali was least worried about her job, unfortunately, she did not know how to circumvent the situation. Supriya showed her another exit door at the back; Kappu was too quick for Gitanjali and intercepted her.

A bizarre scene was enacted that night.

Fumbling on the doorsteps, he shouted at Supriya, "You

can go to your old man or any other place, but Gitanjali will stay here tonight."

Her body shaking with anger, Supriya slapped him. The slap resounded in the quiet house. Humiliated by his wife in presence of his mistress, Kappu lost his sanity. He ferreted out an old cane of his father's from the cupboard and caned Supriya. Pushing Gitanjali into his room, he forced himself on her.

"You are a bloody animal." Supriya shrieked at him when she heard the girl's screams.

"Drag me to a court." He bellowed at her. When she spit on him, he slapped her so hard that she fell down.

Though insulted and physically assaulted, she vetoed the thought of calling the police as the disgrace in public would be unbearable. Instead, she decided to quit. Seething in anger, she threw a few clothes in a briefcase and left hurriedly in her car. Before she sat in the vehicle, she had tried a few phone numbers, but could not contact any of her friends. No one answered in the state guest houses at that unearthly hour.

"It is I who should have left," Gitanjali muttered collecting her torn clothes. She called a taxi.

The storm was upon Supriya as she drove out of her husband's bungalow in Chankaya Puri. In utter confusion, she had picked up the wrong purse and didn't have adequate money, neither the credit cards to go to a respectable hotel. Unable to reach her aunt on the cell, she drove all the way to East Delhi and found her house locked. "I am stupid! I have made a mess of my life," she said to herself. To make matters worse, the cell battery dropped so low that she could not use it. She could not go to Kappu's cousin, not in such a state and such weather.

Her heartbeat went up as hers was the only car on the lonely roads flooded with water. The danger of water logging increased her anxiety as Delhi is notorious for it. She decided to gatecrash at a friend's who stayed at Motibagh C-II flats, though she was not intimate with her. "I am sure to shock her," she murmured.

While crossing the I T O underbridge, the car gave her some anxious moments as it waded through the rising waters. She avoided the India Gate hexagon, and took the route to Ferozshah, and Janpath roads. At the roundabout near the Meridian hotel, the car tyre hit the pavement near the turning; fortunately for her, the car continued to move without much damage. In a daze, she drove on. Suddenly, there was power failure, and it was pitch dark on the roads except for the light from the car headlights.

When she reached the big roundabout near 10, Janpath, she could not locate the Janpath Road leading towards Aurangzeb Road, and had two rounds of it, and was still unsure which way to go. In a flash, it occurred to her that she could try houses of two juniors in MS apartments on Kasturba Gandhi Marg. On seeing the headlights of a car coming speedily towards her she lost control and the car smashed into a tree protruding on the road and stopped running. "All along I feared this," she mumbled to herself. The car head lights had also conked out.

She felt lost.

Nonetheless, she opened the bonnet, but could not make out anything. An ignoramus about the car, she tinkered a little and gave up. In desperation, she kicked the car. "Damn you, Kappu! Damn you!" she shouted in the dead of the dark night with tears in her eyes.

Her kicking breathed fresh life in the battery, and miraculously the car headlights were switched on. In the car light, she noticed the sign board indicating Akbar Road. She thought of Deepak, her heart fluttered for an instant, yet she overruled her emotions. Taking an obligation from Vaishali was beyond her, not even in such dire straits.

Leaning against the car, she sobbed, and prayed. The daughter of a famous economist on deputation to IMF, the mother, a world-renowned danseuse, the late grandfather, a Chief Secretary of Karnataka, and her granny still one of the most powerful politicians of Karnataka who wielded enormous clout even in Delhi, and what a mess she had made of her life? Tears trickled down her cheeks and mingled with the pouring rain.

A car slowed down, and someone opened the door.

"Supriya? What are you doing here?"

Her eyes clouded by tears and rain; she could not place him. Kranti introduced himself.

"My car broke down," she said brushing away her tears.

He shook his head, as he was as much of a novice as she was. Still, he tried to be helpful, opened the bonnet, and said aloud above the noise of thunder and lightning, "It appears that some water has gone inside the engine. But I am not sure; I don't know anything about cars."

"Help me to get a taxi."

"Forget it. Our house is a few yards from here."

"No, drop me somewhere near a taxi stand, I'll go home." Supriya was emphatic.

"Not in such weather. I'll not allow it for anyone."

With a lot of empathy, he turned her face towards the

light of the car-beam, frowned, and said, "You have deep cuts on your forehead and head. Has someone bashed you?"

She coloured, and said, "I just fell down."

He didn't persist and checked each door of the Zen. All at once, he noticed the briefcase. Without a word, he picked it up, and gently catching her by the arm, led her towards his car.

Abruptly, he left her arm, and stopped. Surprised, she looked at him.

"I hope you trust me. I am a suspended cop, and do not have a good reputation these days."

Though Deepak had not confided much in her about the ongoing proceedings, or shouting of the women's organizations at his residence, she had missed little because of the wide coverage in the print media. She looked at him, caught his arm partly to assure him of her confidence in him, and more as her legs were tottering because of the physical and emotional upheaval she had undergone.

"I trust you; implicitly."

A speeding police car slowed down and pulled up beside them.

"Are you all right madam?" A policeman inquired.

"I am okay. Thank you."

"She is fine. She is with me. I am also a cop — Kranti Chopra."

Both the policemen alighted from the vehicle, saluted him, and asked if they could render any assistance.

"Look after madam's car, it has broken down."

The cops promised to tow away the car to the adjacent police station at Safdarjung, and Kranti gave the car keys

to them.
Tenderly, Kranti made her sit in the car, and drove down to his residence.

(3)

Supriya's presence at Deepak's house at about 2am in the morning disturbed the sensibilities of all the members of the Chopra household. It was as if Mt. Everest had suddenly shifted to Akbar Road!
"What is she doing in my house at this hour?" Vaishali reacted. Her voice was shrill, very unlike her own. She was surprised to find Supriya reclining on the divan, and Prema and Kanupriya fluttering around her as if she were a VIP. Kanupriya told Supriya to change, and despite her protests, took her to the bedroom.

Vaishali observed that the recently renovated divan, and the pastel-coloured cushions bought last month were ruined by the dripping water. She mumbled some thing, and controlled herself on noticing that Prema was listening to her.
"Why is she here?" Vaishali's imperious voice cracked.
Kranti explained the facts how her car had broken down.
"She must have done it on purpose." Vaishali concluded.
"No, ma, the car really broke down. She is in very bad shape. Probably, she has left her house."
"If so, why have you brought her here?" Vaishali's hostile tone unnerved Kranti.
"Ma, she didn't want to come, I virtually forced her to come."
"Is there anything you can do properly?" She hit back.
"Where could she go at such an hour? And in this storm? You do know that Delhi is not a safe place." Kranti answered.

"As a cop you should know —" Vaishali glared at her son — "no place is safe for a woman at this hour of the night, whether it is Delhi or Nongpoh!"

Kranti looked hard at his mother and left the room.

The room was charged, though the person responsible for it was changing her clothes in Kanupriya's room. Alone in the lounge with her mother-in-law, Prema felt uneasy. "I'll tell papa," she said.

Vaishali overruled her. "There is no need to disturb him at this hour; we will tell him in the morning."

But to her dismay, Deepak walked in; he had already been informed by Kranti.

"Where is Supriya?" he asked.

"Why don't you go and sleep?" Vaishali reproved her husband. "We women will look after your subordinate. Or is it that you don't trust us?"

Suddenly, everyone was quiet, and stared at Vaishali.

Kanupriya rose, caught her mother's arm, and said, "You are not well, ma. Go and catch some sleep."

At that very moment Supriya unbolted the door, and Kanupriya ran across the room, and brought her into the lounge. On seeing Supriya attired in Kanupriya's new nightie and gown, Vaishali's whole body revolted as if her daughter had purposely insulted her. The soft blue coloured gown suited her fair complexion, and ironically it fitted her better than Kanupriya. More composed than when she had arrived, Supriya carried herself with dignity though the injuries on her forehead had turned more prominent. In the white light, she appeared to be an angel who had lost her way on the earth and had been badly maltreated by the locals.

"Madam, sir," she said apologetically, "I am sorry for

making a nuisance of myself at this odd hour and disturbing all of you."

Vaishali was still fumbling for words when Deepak said, "I've known you for over two decades. Come on, you have a right to turn to us."

"Of course!" Vaishali endorsed her husband though her assurance was weak, reflecting her dilemma.

Kanupriya touched Supriya's hands, temples, and forehead, and predicted that she was turning cold. She massaged her hands, and feet. Julian brought a glass of hot milk with chocolate, and an aspirin. Prema brought a blanket, and covered Supriya. Deepak looked at her with love, and wanted to reach over to her, touch her, and give her courage. But how could he, surrounded as he was by his own kin?

Dr. Nirmala Misra who had been called by Kranti, walked in. Kranti thanked the doctor for her visit at such an odd hour. Vaishali was upset as she didn't approve of any flurry on Supriya's account.

The doctor examined Supriya, gave her two injections, and prescribed some medicines. When the doctor emerged from the room, Deepak asked, "How is she?"

"She will be better by morning. She has been beaten with a stick; there are deep marks on her body. She is lucky that no bones have been broken. It will take time for the wounds to heal." Glancing at Kranti, she said, "If you want to file a criminal case against the person who has thrashed her, I can give a certificate."

"There is no need." Vaishali interceded; she did not want anything to do with a criminal case, one was enough for the family.

"Doctor, that she will decide when she gets up in the

morning," Kranti said.

Kranti paid her visiting charges, and escorted the doctor to the patio where her car was parked.

Deepak was worried as to who would do such a thing to Supriya; she had never harmed a soul in her life.

"We need to take care of her, tonight." Kanupriya was concerned.

"Why are you indulging in theatrics, Kanu? It is a minor incident, the doctor has given her the sedatives, and she will be alright by morning."

"It is not me, but you who are overreacting, ma. Are you aware of the crap you have been talking for last one hour?" Kanu hissed at her. "I have been through it, and I know how it feels and hurts. You are fully aware that her husband has thrashed her with a stick and still you are being so naive."

Snubbed by her daughter, Vaishali went back to her room.

"You mean Kappu — that suave looking young man - has beaten our Supriya." Deepak was stupefied.

Kanupriya nodded.

Deepak's face hardened and turned red with anger. He rose, and said, "I would like to see her."

"Madam is sleeping; it is not advisable to disturb her, sir." Julian said politely. Kanupriya told her to go to her room.

The father and the daughter were the only two left in the drawing room. At Deepak's instance, Kanupriya narrated the details.

"I think Supriya has been badly beaten by her husband. I have gone through that trauma; I know how it feels. I have never seen ma act so bitchy."

"Beta, Vaishali is not well." Deepak looked at her with affection, and wondered how much she knew about his relationship with Supriya. "Go and sleep, you have to go to the office in the morning."

Without a protest, Kanupriya said "Good night" and gently placed her arm around his neck and left. Deepak kept on pondering about this new facet of Supriya's relationship with her husband as he had always considered them a happy, compatible couple.

"Are you still in mourning?" Vaishali said scathingly. She stood just behind his sofa. "You too have to go to the office tomorrow."

"Sit down, Vaishali."

"No, let us go to our room."

Reluctantly, he rose, and looked grimly at his wife. Weak and haggard, she led the way to the bedroom. Once inside the room, she bolted the door, and said, "Her rights are in the office, not at home."

He didn't answer her.

"I want to make it clear so that there is no confusion."

"Behave yourself Vaishali. You are acting mean and petty."

"Bitchy," she corrected him. "That's what Kanu told you."

He didn't dispute on a meaningless issue and wanted to move to the crux of it as he had often done in Cabinet meetings. "But why?"

"It's my home."

"Is anyone disputing it?"

"She had no business to come here. Throw her out in the morning."

She turned her head away closing further discussion on the subject.

(4)

Working in the kitchen, next morning, Julian said to Prema, "Ma'am, Supriya madam's husband is a real rascal.

I saw the marks on her body. The skin has turned blue at many places. All men are the same, they want to beat down their women with their physical strength. Why ma'am?"

Prema nodded without replying to the maid with whom her relationship had changed to that of a confidante in the last few months. So many women had suffered at the hands of men, she reflected. Kanupriya, Julian and now Supriya. The world was full of them.

Vaishali found her husband still glued to the paper, and absent- mindedly scanning the pages.

"Why are you not going to the office today?" Her tone was rude, and edgy.

"I'll go a little late."

"But don't you have an early meeting?"

"I have told Aggarwal to handle it. And mind your tone."

"What is wrong with my tone?"

"You are out to create a scene."

"Yes, I want that woman out of my house —."

Unexpectedly, Supriya walked into the lounge surprising the senior couple. She had not missed anything of the exchange between the couple and was fully dressed to go to the office.

"Get ready, sir, we will go to the office."

"Sit down, Supri. I want to talk to you," Deepak said.

"Not here," she whispered. "Let us go to the office. Please!"

Powerless and indecisive, he gave in to her request.

"Why are you both not taking breakfast?" Vaishali asked.

"Ma'am, there is a meeting at 9.30. I must be there before that. Sir can come later." Supriya replied.

To run away from his wife was Deepak's immediate need; he preferred to join Supriya and sat down in the staff car in a state of confusion. Supriya's unexpected refuge at his home had created turbulence in his life that he was unable to handle. Worried that the havoc should not rip through his life, Deepak reflected that everything ought to be in proper place: Supriya, Kappu, Vaishali and, he himself. Whenever anyone of them was in the wrong place at the wrong time, it created chaos. Relationships must flow in parallel lines, almost like parallel roads. The driver waited for his master's orders, but Deepak was lost in his thoughts. Supriya told the driver, "Chalo." When the driver turned left from Janpath towards UPSC, Deepak did not approve of the crossing of the roads and frowned.

Looking at the twisted face of her boss, she asked, "You don't want to go to the office?"

"I want to run away with you to some remote place," Deepak said, and resignedly added, "But let us go to the office. Your rights in my life are confined within the boundaries of the office only."

Unable to comprehend his thought process, Supriya felt he had gone nuts.

Comfortably settled in her favourite seat in Deepak's room, Supriya told him everything.

"The bastard!" he said. "I am really sorry. Your suffering is because of me."

He shook his head in dismay. "We must find a decent place for you to stay. A pretty woman like you can't stay in a hotel - you are vulnerable."

He put his PS on the job, and they attended the meeting. Four international conferences and a dozen national level meetings were scheduled in Delhi during the next 3-4 days. All the circuit houses, guest houses and inspection quarters were booked. Later, Deepak used his own influence, and failed. Even Kranti could not do anything. Supriya tried her contacts and failed.

(4)

When Supriya alighted from the car in the evening with Deepak, Vaishali gave her a dirty look. It made Supriya's skin crawl.

"Ma'am, I am sorry for imposing myself on you but unfortunately, I have not been able to get any circuit house or guest house. Within a day or so, I will surely move out."

"It's okay," Vaishali said condescendingly. "My only concern is that there are so many people in the house — sons, daughters-in-law, daughter, grandchildren — they are surprised that you are here instead of being at your house."

"Yes, ma'am. Actually, I would have preferred to stay put in the car rather than come here. It was my bad luck that Kranti spotted me."

"Don't talk like this, Supriya," Vaishali said realizing that she had crossed the unwritten line of decency. "You are most welcome, but we have our limitations — you should appreciate them."

"I do, ma'am," Supriya said.

Over tea in the lawn, Supriya blasted her mentor. "Why are you such a coward that I can't spend a few nights in your house with respect?"

Like a condemned criminal, he listened to her diatribe without responding to her various questions.

"I lost my heart to you more than two decades back at Mangalore beach when the sun was about to set. Every time I see you, I want to touch and hug you. I feel sorry that none of my children is through you. The way I feel for you, I don't feel for any other man or woman. And yet my love is so weak that I cannot spend even a night at your place with dignity."

She noticed Julian bringing another pot of tea and was quiet for a while. When she went back, he answered, "I'll talk to Vaishali. These days she is getting very edgy. First, it was Vinay, then Kranti."

"And now it is you." She spoke fiercely.

The quivering of her fingers jolted him. "Supri, please calm down."

She had a glass of water and clasped the arms of the chair to stop the trembling.

"Have I ever done anything of which you need to be ashamed of except for kissing you once? Why is your wife so intolerant of our relationship?"

"She feels threatened."

"Is her love so weak?"

"You are younger," he said looking at her, and added, "and are more beautiful. You give her a complex, and I don't blame her."

"Perhaps for the first time you have complimented me on my beauty though grudgingly."

"Vaishali has always felt insecure about you, when you were a probationer, or later as an under secretary."

"Oh, but you never told me."

He talked of his relationship with his wife including the vow, and how finally he had broken it.

"By and large, you have been a good husband, Deep."

"I don't know whether I am good at anything, but I am trying to keep my family together in all crises. I have succeeded so far but I may fail."

"You know how to balance - you follow the middle path," she said satirically. "I am sure you will succeed."

Her face a little contorted with rage, she rose.

"Sit down, Supriya," he said. "Vaishali is staring at us from her window. Be a little cautious and control your emotions."

He noticed that Vaishali had left her strategic corner near the window from where she kept a watch over the members of the household.

"You felt hurt that Kappu brought Gitanjali home. Vaishali also feels the same way. Her home is her little empire, which she guards fiercely. Your invasion has disturbed her confidence, she is apprehensive that she may be thrown out."

Sarcastically, she smiled. "Unlike Kappu, you don't have the courage to do it; that is why she is sure of herself."

"She has suffered a lot in life and made me also suffer, partly because of her stupidity and partly mine. She can handle the crises of her sons, but a slight encroachment on her rights in her own territory she will not tolerate."

"But you are all powerful. If you want, she will not misbehave."

"I am no Kappu, and she knows it," he said softly as he saw his wife walking towards them. Perhaps, Vaishali felt that she had given them adequate time to sort out their differences.

Supriya left her seat for Vaishali and went inside even though the latter had called the maid to get another chair. Once Supriya closed the door, she was mad as hell.

She called her granny. Three things happened.

When the Chopras had just finished dinner at about 10pm, a State Government car arrived, and MS Reddy, the Resident Commissioner, Karnataka, walked in tentatively. He went over to Supriya, apologized for his misconduct in the morning, and requested her to move to the Karnataka House where the Chief Minister's suite was thrown open for her. Supriya told him that it was rather late for a shift, and to send the car in the morning. "No, ma'am, I'll lose my job if you don't shift by tonight." Reddy had been extremely rude to her in the morning stating that even a driver's room was not available for her. Now, he folded his hands, and bowed down, almost like a minion in the Government, though he belonged to the IAS and was a year senior to her. Supriya was aware of the supreme power her granny wielded in Karnataka politics and was not surprised at the level to which the bureaucracy had been reduced there.

Supriya was ready in less than half an hour and was given a warm farewell by the entire Chopra household. "You are always welcome, Supri," Vaishali said salvaging her little pride though no one took her seriously. Ensconced comfortably next to the driver, Reddy wondered why the bitch had created so much of a ruckus when she was so happy with that family.

A couple of days later, there were a dozen income tax raids in Kappu's offices and home. The message was too loud for Kappu to ignore: Supriya's granny had unleashed her wrath on him. Kappu did not take the bureaucratic pin- pricks seriously but politicians, and especially from the south, never forgave you. The list of their enemies was well documented, perhaps even better than their accounts. He swallowed his pride, went to Karnataka House with an entourage that included his mother and other relatives, and almost fell on his knees asking for his wife's pardon. Showered with presents of expensive antique jewellery, Supriya was persuaded to go back home. Her return was triumphant.

Home was the place for her. With various individuals in their proper place, Deepak was at peace.

She was transferred from the UPSC to the Finance Ministry, a ministry of her choice; and snapped her relationship with Deepak Chopra.

But there was not a single day when Deepak and Supriya did not remember and miss each other. At times, Vaishali overheard him mutter Supriya's name in his sleep, and wept. The effervescence of sexual pleasure that had helped her experience the quintessence of life slowly faded away. And so did love. Without love, sex grew tepid, and degenerated into a routine, and later into insignificance. In less than five-six months, both distanced from each other, and went back to their old rooms. She wished she could turn back the clock and welcome Supriya to her home and give her the respect she had asked for.

XVI

Court Drama

When the trial recommenced, the courtroom was fully packed. The media had already condemned Kranti as a rapist before the trial began. He had lost sympathy of everyone except Vivek and Sudha. Backing those who were down and out or abandoned by society was a part of Vivek's attitude to life; he was the only one in the family who provided the emotional strength arising out of propinquity. Sudha stood like a rock protecting her former boss; her support was more tangible. She had arranged one of the leading criminal lawyers of the capital for him, who had promised not to charge anything.

"But why?" Kranti was puzzled.

"Because he is doing a favour to me," Sudha answered.

Kranti did not have the patience to probe; he had too many things on his mind.

Albert, Josef, Tony, Smith and Monty — all friends of Joe, were produced in the court by the Public Prosecutor, but all of them were exposed as established goons and criminals by Kranti's counsel, Prabhat Verma.

At the end of the day, Kranti and Sudha walked into Prabhat Verma's chamber, and Kranti lavished rich praise on his performance.

"It is too early to comment. It will get difficult as the trial proceeds," he replied.

Sudha was discomfited as Prabhat Verma's usual confidence was missing.

"Is something wrong?" she asked.

"Nothing is wrong." Prabhat drawled. "I am only being cautious - not pessimistic."

Disturbed, Kranti looked sharply at his counsel. "Do you think that the prosecution has a case?"

"None," he said. "But there is a catch. A protector of law getting involved in such a case is bad publicity." He looked at his client, and added, "Secondly, your wife has filed the case, now that is very unusual. Worse, you must be exonerated beyond any shadow of doubt if you have to keep your job."

"Do you think it would be difficult?"

"Yes, if you don't handle the media properly."

Kranti and Sudha were both quiet.

"A wife filing a rape case against her husband is lot of fodder for the media. They are going to love it. In the case of any ordinary person, no body would have noticed it, but a decorated police officer involved in such a case — it makes news. Considering your family background, it is sure to make headlines as the case progresses. And the judge is not going to like it."

"What is wrong with his family background?" Sudha said. "He has excellent credentials."

"That's exactly what is going to go against him. His

father: Chairman, UPSC and former Cabinet Secretary, his brother Vinay, a famous scientist and now a schoolteacher."

Kranti was crestfallen.

"Nothing will be allowed to pass off; everything would be scrutinized by the media. It would be a repeat of what the media covered 2-3 months back when the women's organizations were up against you; unless something more sensational dwarfs it."

Suddenly, Sudha's eyes lighted up. "Supposing —" she riveted her eyes to Prabhat — "supposing, we kidnap Julian."

"No." Kranti intervened. "No, it can backfire."

"No one will know; it will be a smooth operation."

"You are underestimating your Chief. Perhaps, Kulwant Singh is prepared for such a contingency. Whatever the outcome, I will be squarely blamed for it." Kranti clarified.

"I don't approve of such methods," Prabhat said. "If you are planning on such lines, you should find another counsel."

"Come on, Prabhat, we are discussing various possibilities. We can think of something less revolting to your sensibilities, but we do need to have a contingency plan."

"Ignore her suggestion, please," Kranti said to the counsel. "And do it your way."

A few minutes later, Kranti left.

Prabhat didn't approve of his client; he had taken up the case at Sudha's instance. He was in love with Sudha for the last two years and wanted to marry her. Sudha had not made up her mind.

Prabhat looked at her gravely. "Do you think he raped Julian?"

"No. Definitely, no."

Her emphasis disturbed him.

"He is brave and courageous, and would never stoop so low," she added.

"Sometimes, I wonder whether you are in love with him," he said.

She too wondered whether he was right; she hardly knew her emotions. Putting up a brave smile, she said, "No, I am not in love with him. But I do look up to him as my mentor in the police force. If you can get him acquitted, I'll marry you."

"And if I fail?"

"Then, I'll not marry you." Her eyes sparkled with mischief.

"And my fees?"

"That you don't get either way."

Her laughter cheered his drab office.

At Deepak's house, the dining hall was abuzz with excitement. Every witness was dissected including the performance and body language of the prosecutor, and Kranti's counsel. When Kranti walked in, a hush descended, only the clattering of the cutlery was audible. He stared absent mindedly at them. No one smiled.

"Sit down, Kranti." Vaishali ordered.

The uninviting glances made him turn towards his room.

(2)

Joe gave his testimony against Kranti. He narrated that on the fateful night, he and his friends were in a mood of revelry and had gone to Julian's house to wish her a happy Christmas. When they reached there, they were shocked to find a stranger raping Julian after tying her to a cot. They had tried to help, but the stranger fired at them. "All my friends ran away except me. Because of my deep affection for Julian, I challenged him, and the stranger shot at me and hit me in the leg. Since then, I am handicapped for life. My life has been ruined. On hearing the shots, the locals arrived. Due to a misunderstanding, they thought that I was responsible for raping Julian and beat me. But I did not lose courage and lodged an FIR against the stranger at the police station. That stranger is Kranti Chopra," Joe said, and identified Kranti.

P K Verma's cross examination was long and arduous; the judge and audience were bored and started yawning. However, Verma was methodical in exposing the criminal notoriety of Joe pointing out that he had over a dozen criminal cases against him in different courts of the north-east. The counsel also handed over a list of the large number of jails sentences he had undergone. "He is easily the most notorious criminal in the north-east, my lord." Verma concluded.

SN Biswas, Superintendent Police, Guwahati, confirmed that Kranti had taken the vehicle from him on that night. "Most probably, Kranti Chopra was the stranger referred to by Joe and others, but I am not sure." Neither could he say anything about Julian's rape as he was not present on the spot.

After the court broke up for the day, Trehan, the public prosecutor felt slightly sheepish that things were not turning in his favour. His face was slightly flushed when he told Julian and Prema, "Don't worry, I'll get that bastard hanged."

"What nonsense are you talking?" Prema reacted, her love for her husband getting the better of her.

Surprised by Prema's retort, he said angrily, "Make up

your mind on whose side you are. If you are with your husband, why have you lodged the FIR? You are wasting my time and that of the court also."

Speechless, she stared at him.

"How would you feel when he gets a seven-year jail? Make up your mind whether you want to go ahead or withdraw the complaint."

Unable to stand the plight of her mistress, Julian intervened. "We will withdraw the case, sir."

"No," Prema said. "We will go ahead; it was a momentary weakness."

Alone in her room at home, Prema wept. "Why do I love that swine?" she murmured.

A knock disturbed her thought process. She raised her head and found her husband inside the room.

"What do you want?" she asked rudely.

Ignoring her scowl, he inquired whether she was planning to withdraw the complaint.

"You have wrong information; I have no such intention."

"I was hoping sanity will prevail."

"I'm not seeing any signs of repentance either."

The verbal dual turned fierce and bitter.

"You are a rapist and should be in a mental asylum." Prema screamed.

But for the apprehension that Prema might file another case of physical assault against him, he might have hit her.

"Leave the room!" Prema shrieked at him.

The ferociousness in her body language mellowed him, and his anger evaporated.

He changed his strategy. "You still love me Prema, I can see it."

"If you can see that, why don't you appreciate my point of view, and apologize to Julian."

"I can apologize to you — but Julian, a whore — no, never."

"Please!"

"No." He shook his head vigorously.

"I'll never tell you to apologize again," Prema said in rage. He turned to go and was surprised to see Julian at the door.

(3)

Vaishali was excited to get a letter from Madhulika. Vinay had been able to win the hearts of the students and the teachers and was accepted by the missionaries. The letters arrived periodically and Vaishali was equally responsive.

Vinay was able to convince the Christian missionaries controlling the school, of his penitence, and begged for forgiveness. In his confession, he told all, and asked them to be merciful. Moved by his sincere apology, they embraced him, and appointed him as a senior teacher. His knowledge, commitment, and charisma in the school was so markedly superior to other teachers that he made them look puny and reduced them into almost insignificance. Many years later, he took over the school as its first Director.

Madhulika finally made it to the local college. With Bhavana, their little daughter, they had carved out a little world of their own. The fear of the media, the vituperation of the scientific community, their friends and relatives still haunt them. They never venture out of the district and want to remain in the confines of the familiar surroundings protected by the mighty Himalayas.

(4)

When Vaishali did not get her morning cup of tea, she searched for Julian all over the house. But she could not locate her: the maid had disappeared.

The news perturbed everyone. Both Kranti and Prema panicked. The gate man informed them that she had left alone in the late evening and had not returned.

Kranti called Sudha and broke the news. "Are you up to something?"

"No, but it is a great news. This calls for a celebration, sir."

"Are you sure that you are not involved in any way."

"I'm sure, sir."

Kranti was certain that the prosecutor would term it as a kidnap, blame him for it, and want an inquiry. Even Kulwant Singh would hold him responsible for it. Possibly, Prabhat could also lose interest in the case. But overall, it was beneficial for his case.

Prema held herself responsible for Julian's vanishing act. Yesterday's incident had once again exposed her fondness for Kranti, which had unnerved Julian, and she had bolted so that the case could be closed.

Prema called Trehan and briefed him.

"We need to put up Julian on the stand. Find her fast," he said.

He thought for a while, and added, "I do hope that you are not at the back of her disappearance."

"Of course not," she said forcefully, and banged the phone.

She tried all her resources, and still could not trace Julian. Frustrated, she didn't want to face Kranti at the breakfast table, but Kanupriya forced her. With puffy eyes, Prema settled for cornflakes and milk.

"It is bad news for you," Vaishali said with empathy.

Deepak pulled a long face, and added, "We are all sorry."

"Maybe, it is the best for the family." Vivek echoed the feelings of the family that they were trying to suppress.

"But not for me." Prema looked angrily at her brother-in-law.

Despite his anxieties, Kranti was relaxed. The circumstances were finally turning favourable. He had a two-egg omelette, four slices of bread, and a glass of milk. Cheerfully, he rounded off his breakfast with black coffee, and rose. Picking up an apple from the fruit basket, he said, "Bye, everyone." and left.

"Is he responsible for it?" Deepak cocked his eye.

"It's not past him but it's too dangerous. I don't think he can risk it." Vivek offered his opinion.

"Risk of any kind of danger has never deterred Kranti. At times, he can be quite stupid." Deepak opined.

"I think we are underestimating bhaiya. He will never make such a foolish move." Kanu defended her brother.

"But Sudha can." Vaishali voiced.

"It's neither of them." Prema spoke so confidently that it puzzled everyone. "On the extension, I overheard them talking to each other. Sudha was planning something big, but somehow it did not materialize."

All of them looked deprecatingly at her for her unseemly conduct. Only Vaishali defended her. "I don't blame her, after all it is war."

That silenced them.

Prema and her team strove throughout the day trying to track down Julian. She wanted to give herself a day before reporting the matter to the police formally. Joe and others at Nongpoh were alerted in case Julian turned up there. Help from other women's organizations was also sought, but the media was avoided.

Prema was confused why everything was going against her beliefs. How could nature err and help a rapist? She wondered whether there was any order in nature. Did poetic justice exist only in the minds of poets and thinkers? Was there no cause and effect in the cosmos conceived and created by God? Were the systems and philosophies evolved by man not in sync with the fundamentals of nature and its harmony? Or was it that she was in the wrong and her husband was actually as innocent as he was claiming to be. Utterly confused, she was clueless how she would be able to find Julian who, she was certain, had run away only to mitigate her (Prema's) suffering.

At night, she lay in the bed for a long time reflecting on the principles she had been taught by her father, the principles that were flouted by her own brother who had a flourishing practice in the High Court. Were her father's principles a hoax or were they outdated? Caught up in a vortex, she didn't have any idea where to trace Julian? Suddenly, her eyes lighted up. Kavita?

Prema called Kavita; she was shocked on hearing what Prema had done. "Somehow I feared it, that is why I didn't want Julian to stay with you," she said. Later, she gave addresses of two of Julian's friends.

A tip off was enough to charge Prema. Next day, when she was about to leave the house, she spotted Vivek lazing around in the lounge. "I need your help, come with me. We have a task on our hands."

Aware of her mission, Vivek hesitated. To him the rape of a whore seemed a ludicrous charge: a whore was meant for sex only. He felt that Prema was indulging in dramatics. Secondly, he had sided with Kranti as he was abandoned by everyone. Assisting Prema in her search for Julian seemed inappropriate.

"Helping me is not an act of betrayal to Kranti," she said appreciating his thought process. "Don't you see that because of him, my life has become so miserable?"

Vivek made no comment.

"He has a powerful ally in Sudha, but I have no one. I need you."

The expression of sadness in her liquid eyes made him change his mind.

"All right," he said taking the passenger seat. "But why are you gunning for him? You love him. `Kranti, Kranti' is written all over you."

Angrily, she pressed the accelerator, and raced the car towards Janpath Road. "Stop uttering his name. I hate him."

Furious, she lost control and rammed the car into a 3-wheeler taking a wrong turn, and damaged it. Her sharp tongue escalated the trouble. A dozen people collected, and some of the fellow 3-wheelers supported the victim. It took a long time for Vivek to wriggle out of the ugly situation; he had to shell out Rs500/. The altercation mellowed Prema, and Vivek took the wheel.

"Have you not taken on too much on your hands? You can't cope with all this."

Prema guided Vivek down the Ansari Road, Daryaganj, and said, "The reasons for my weakness are that I am too close to both my adversary and client. I am losing objectivity and am getting sentimental. It is bad for my case."

They parked the car in front of an old building. On the

second storey, a middle-aged couple from the north-east welcomed them when Prema told them the reason for their visit. They gave a long list of places where there was a possibility that Julian could take refuge. Vivek was disheartened, but Prema felt it was a break. They decided to go to Wazirabad, the northern end.

It took them a long time to reach Wazirabad. Prema took the opportunity of giving all the details of the heinous crime, Julian's molestation at home, and why she had filed the case.

"What you — and many — do not appreciate is that Julian was a college student and not a whore when she was raped. Her hands and feet were tied. And incidentally, how could Kranti have known her status? Whether she was a student, married or a whore?"

Before taking a U-turn, she looked at him, and said, "I am fighting for the dignity of a helpless woman."

Vivek offered no comment. He was grim.

On reaching the destination, they learnt that Julian was supposed to spend the night there but had changed her plans at the last moment. Rohini, Pritampura, Janakpuri, Dwarka, Vasant Kunj, Mehrauli.

"We have covered most of Delhi." Vivek was exhausted in the evening.

Saket was their last stop.

"Your brother has so many plus points — helpful to one and all, warm, affectionate, expressive, brave and courageous — almost fearless. But to unleash all that power on a helpless woman is so revolting that I have started detesting him. To take advantage of her tied hands and rape her!" She shook her head with bitterness. "Are all men so lecherous?"

"Prema, please!"

"I know that you don't like him for being pushy, arm twisting, and lacking in basic niceties, but he was such great a fun to be with. My entire future is ruined because of his lust for the fair ones."

It was almost twilight when Vivek pulled over at Press Enclave address at Saket. They went up the flight of stairs to the terrace. Their hearts missed a beat on spotting Julian staring at the new moon with her back towards them.

"Julian!"

Julian gave a start.

"Ma'am, how could you find me here?"

Prema explained how they had gone to different places in her search.

"You work very fast."

"NRK has taken up your case, I have no choice. I have a job to do. Let us finish it."

"No, ma'am. You love your husband, and your heart bleeds for him."

"You are mistaken. I hate that man and want him behind the bars. He has wronged you and must be punished."

Julian hesitated.

"Let us not get sentimental about it. There is no room for emotions in a court of law. A rapist is on the loose – he should be behind the bars. It is good for the society. It is in the interest of the women of the country."

Julian introduced them to the couple with whom she was staying. They pestered her for a cup of coffee; Prema refused, and hurriedly forced Julian into the car.

(5)

On the return journey, the car broke down near IIT,

Hauz Khas. Prema was upset; she wanted Julian within the safety of her house, but Vivek was cool. He told Julian to get the tool kit from the dicky, opened the bonnet, and tinkered with various screws for about 10-15 minutes. Prema was too exhausted to get up and kept a watch over her most important client.

"The battery points need to be cleaned," he said confidently. Prema spotted a tea kiosk across the road. Protecting Julian from the traffic by catching her arm, he crossed over and ordered three cups of tea, some biscuits and hot water. Julian carried the hot water tumbler, and Vivek cleaned the wax on the battery contact points with his hanky. When Prema switched on the ignition, the engine revved.

"You are a genius with the cars, sir," Julian said. She was amused when he told her that he had done a 3- month course in car repairing.

The boy from the tea stall brought tea, and they sipped it as Vivek regaled her with a story about how he had once helped a Minister from Rajasthan when his car broke down, and he was stranded in the tribal area of Banswara. "His eyes almost popped out of the socket when I told him I had done BA with a first class from St. Stephen's," he said highlighting it with his hand gestures and breaking into boyish laughter. "Of course, I didn't tell him about the 3-month course." Leaning against the car, Julian smiled, and sometimes broke into uninhibited laughter as Vivek fluttered around her, cracking jokes. Seated in the car, Prema looked at them, and studied Julian's emotional responses to Vivek's wit and charm. For the first time, she had seen Julian cackle with laughter.

"Has he told you that he has not only done a course in

car repairing but also in gardening and tailoring," Prema said. "He is an expert in many areas."
"Yes, I am good at many things except making money."
"He has all the credentials of being an excellent house husband," Prema added making them laugh. But as soon as she had uttered the words, she regretted her remark. She had no business to lead Julian up the garden path that didn't exist for her.
"Come on, let us hurry up," Prema said, distracting their attention. "Mummy will be getting worried."
Prema suggested that Vivek and Julian should sit in front as she wanted to steal a nap. Throughout the half hour drive in the peak hour traffic, Vivek tried to boost Julian's spirits. Pretending to be asleep, Prema listened attentively pondering whether he was flirting with Julian, or was it that Julian was enticing him, and throwing the bait as a professional.

When he parked the car in the foyer, and Julian had escaped into the privacy of her room at the back, Vivek said sombrely, "Your client is back and safe!"
"Thanks," she answered. Was Vivek playing a part? Was he more complex than what he projected? Prema kept on reflecting on it as she refreshed herself for dinner.

The Chopra household was not happy at Julian's return, though they showed signs of relief that a competent maid would continue to give them conveniences to which they were accustomed. "Good to have you back Julian," Vaishali said. "But where had you run away?"
"She had gone to a friend's so that we have peace and harmony at home." Prema replied on Julian's behalf.
Kranti scowled on seeing her and left the dining table early.

(6)

Prema used her influence and had the next date of hearing preponed. The public prosecutor put Julian on the stand. Attired in plain soft grey, her youth and beauty had an electrifying effect on the gathering, and the judge. Julian won their sympathy as the rape victim.

"Who were your parents?"

"They both died when I was very young. I don't remember them."

She told the court how she was brought up by her grandpa, who wished to fulfil her ambition of becoming a schoolteacher, the loans he took from Joe and his evil designs of marrying her, the incidents of Christmas night, how she was stripped, and tied to the bed by Joe, and his accomplices. She narrated about the arrival of Kranti with a pistol, how the goons had run away, and the injury to Joe. Instead of saving her, Kranti had taken advantage of the situation and raped her. She also mentioned how she was gang raped by Joe and his men four months later and turned into a prostitute.

In details, she explained the incident at Amit Bhardwaj's party and her reaction. She was grateful to Jean Simpson, Amit and Kavita Bhardwaj, Prema ma'am and the entire Chopra family for giving her protection in their house.

"My entire bitterness, my lord, is against Kranti Chopra who was supposed to protect me. I didn't expect any mercy from Joe and his men. They are goons and have this notorious reputation. I know of many girls who have been raped by them and sold to brothels in Kolkata. But Kranti Chopra, a protector of law, betrayed his duty, his uniform. He is the son of Chairman, UPSC, formerly a Cabinet Secretary. Kranti Chopra belongs to a decent, noble family but is a rapist. He is a devil incarnate. He should be sent to prison or a mental asylum otherwise even his own daughter will not be safe from him."

She had quoted the words often used by Prema. When spoken in fury in the court, they had a great impact on everyone including the judge. Those who felt earlier that there was no substance in the charges were now convinced by Julian's testimony. The judge too betrayed an emotion of sympathy.

Back home from the court, Julian told her mistress, "I'm going to be the most talked of prostitute in the country."

On the next day (a Saturday), a battery of reporters from the media barged in, ignoring the loud protests from the gatekeeper. They wanted to interview Julian. Deepak overruled their suggestion but found it difficult to contain the volatile journalists who refused to leave the premises. Deepak was aware that he could not be running to the Principal Secretary to the PM all the time, he had to face it. He also realized that as his tenure in the UPSC was ending, he was getting weak and unsure. The confidence on which he had prided himself all his life was slipping away.

"I don't like this," he told Prema.

A nervous Prema answered, "Neither do I." She inquired whether she should call the police.

"No, no, we will face it," Deepak replied. "But it is disturbing the peace and harmony of our home."

If Kranti were not suspended, there would have been no difficulty in handling such a trivial situation. Deepak shook his head absent mindedly and continued to mutter. Rattled by his mumblings, Prema said, "I am sorry papa.

Do you want Julian and me to leave the house?"
"You are too hasty in your conclusions." Vaishali rebuked her. "Deepak has never mentioned it."
She looked at Prema's flushed face, and added, "And my dear, where can you go?" She called her bluff. "Except to be with us."
Caught on the wrong foot, Prema felt ashamed. "You are right, I can't go to daddy, and I have no other place to go to. I have to be with you only."
"I have never wanted you to go anywhere, Prema." Deepak assured her, and gently placed his hand on her shoulder.
"Papa, I don't know whether I am right or wrong."
"Believe in yourself." Deepak said.

The journalists squatted in the lawns and ruined them; Kranti was itching to thrash some of them, Vaishali controlled him. Deepak could not take it beyond a point and called the Police Commissioner.
"I am sending the police force, sir," he said. "But it is all your son's doing. The journalists also have a job to do."
Shaken, Deepak closed his eyes. A truck load of policemen arrived after an hour and drove away the journalists.

On Sunday, it was the turn of women's organizations once again, and they shouted slogans against Kranti and Deepak.

Frustrated, Deepak bolted the door, and switched on the TV. Unfortunately, Kranti's case was being discussed on news channels, and his house was shown live.

(7)

Julian's cross examination was long and gruelling.
"Why didn't you recognize him in the first instance at Amit Bhardwaj's house?" PK Verma questioned her.
"When he raped me, there was no light in the guest

house. It was almost dark - the coal fire was the only source of dim light. I recognized him at the party as the surroundings were similar. There was a power break down, and the only source of dim light in the big hall were the three candles I had lighted. I recognised him primarily from his dress and general body language."

"If somebody else were dressed in black trousers and red shirt and was of the same height, could you have mistaken him for Kranti Chopra?"

"Definitely, no."

"If Kranti Chopra were dressed in white, would you have recognized him?"

For an instant she hesitated, and then said,"I would have recognized him in any dress."

PK Verma hammered it repeatedly that it could be some one else instead of Kranti Chopra, but Julian didn't waver.

"I am definite that it was Kranti Chopra and no one else."

"It beats me that a woman sees a man many times but does not recognize him and then in a party, suddenly, she is able to recognize him when there was no electricity. Her motives appear mala fide, my lord." PK Verma concluded.

Next day, he asked her, "If you had not been raped by Kranti, would you still have been a prostitute?"

"Yes. If Kranti Chopra had not arrived unexpectedly on that Christmas night, I would have been gang raped by Joe and his men the same night and sold to the brothel in Kolkata four months earlier. Kranti's raping me did not change my future."

"Why didn't you scream when Kranti raped you?"

"When Joe and his friends were assaulting me, I had screamed and shouted in the dead of the night, but no one came to my rescue. I had accepted my fate when Kranti raped me for I was sure, no one would come." She thought for a while and added, "Actually, when Kranti came, I thought that god had sent him to protect me. I was so shocked when he raped me that I could not even scream."

Her tears and candidness won everyone's heart.

Late in the evening, Prabhat Verma, Sudha and Kranti discussed the day's proceedings in Verma's chamber. A little agitated, Kranti said, "She was born to be a whore."

Prabhat and Sudha made no comment.

"She is so bitter against me and not against Joe and his friends though I was the one who helped her."

"Yes, that's our stand," Prabhat said curtly. Unable to stand the contemptuous look of his own counsel, Kranti left abruptly.

"Somehow, I feel sorry for Julian," Prabhat said looking minutely at Sudha. "I hope you are not backing the wrong horse."

"I hope not," she said uneasily. "But I'll find out."

"When will you find out?" he said angrily, "when the case will be over. You are aware that the judge has decided to give top priority to this case."

Apologetically, she replied, "Soon."

"But for you, I would never have taken this case. These sons of bureaucrats are a spoilt lot; they feel they can get away with anything. And senior cops by themselves are much worse. In Kranti, we have both. It is a deadly combination."

"I have known him for the last four years. He has not taken any interest in me or made any pass. Not even a remote hint."

Irritated, he said, "But you are no Julian!"
The snub lowered her esteem. Why was he being rude purposely?
Prabhat apologised for his comment. A little later, he said, "A fair, nude woman tied to the bed in a lonely place can make anyone lose one's head."
"Then why blame him even if he has done it."
"Who am I to blame? It is Julian, the victim, who is blaming him. And the case has been filed by the organization founded by Kranti's wife."
"Would you have done what Kranti has done?"
"No." He was categorical. "But you have to understand my background. I have five sisters and am the only brother. In fact, I am the only male member in the house as my father died about fifteen years back. In my family, making a lewd comment against a woman is sacrilege. A rape is worse than murder, and punishable with nothing less than death."
"I have chosen the wrong counsel," she murmured.
Prabhat laughed. "Don't worry; your ex-boss is in safe hands. I don't confuse my cases with my personal feelings. But my convictions are deep rooted. If I am convinced that Kranti has actually raped Julian, I will not fight the case."
"I like your honesty. My former boss has less of it."
"But you love him."
"No. I never loved him though I respect him. How can one love a married man? And I want to settle down."
Understandingly, he nodded.

(8)

Kranti was upset by the attitude of his counsel; it appeared to him that Prabhat suspected his bona fides.

Despite Sudha's faith in him, he explored the possibility of finding another counsel, and called a legal friend to Connaught Place for discussion. Parking the car in the lot opposite the Bata showroom, he was almost shocked to see Kanupriya walking with a middle-aged man having a military bearing, his arm on her shoulder. He wanted to interrogate his sister right there; unfortunately, both slipped inside the Zen restaurant. Ironically, it was the place of Kranti's rendezvous with his friend. Realizing that he would be making a fool of himself, and embarrassing his sister also, Kranti hesitated. Already in trouble, he did not want to multiply his problems. He waited for his friend outside Zen and escorted him to United Coffee House instead.

When he reached home, he found Kanupriya in the lounge humming a tune of '70s, her face beaming with smiles.

"Who was the man with you in CP?" Kranti questioned her roughly.

Kanupriya was tongue - tied as if caught immediately after a successful steal. Angrily, Kranti asked again. But there was no response.

"Why don't you answer?" he shouted.

"Lt. Col. Jayant Saxena," she mumbled.

"Where does he work?"

"At army headquarters."

"Is he married?"

"I — don't think so," she said uncertainly. "But bhaiya, I am not sure."

"How long has this been going on?"

By now, Kanupriya realized that her brother was bullying her.

"It's none of your business."

"If the man is married, it becomes my business."

"First, look at yourself, bhaiya. Look at your actions and where you have landed yourself. You are under suspension!"

"Shut up!" Kranti bellowed.

"You are a rapist!" She hit back angrily.

He slapped her.

The slap resounded in the house. On hearing it, Vaishali dashed from the kitchen.

"Mom, he slapped me!"

"How dare you raise your hand on Kanu?"

"I am sorry, ma," Kranti said apologetically and explained how he had seen her with a married man. "I got carried away. But I was only concerned for her."

"This is no way to behave with your sister. She is not a ten-year-old girl but thirty plus."

The noise alarmed Deepak, and he rushed in. Kanupriya briefed him about Kranti's misdemeanour.

"You seem to have lost all rights, son. Whatever you do is wrong now."

"But papa, at least you should appreciate my intentions. I was genuinely concerned for her."

"I do, son. But you should also appreciate that because of you, my house is on fire." Deepak said. "My first priority is to extinguish the raging fire."

"You are acting like a mad criminal." Vaishali rebuked Kranti. "Now, the time has come when you are going to face the consequences of your ugly actions. Don't take it out on Kanu. You have to suffer it yourself. And all alone."

Deepak, Vaishali and Kanupriya left the lounge. With his head in his hands, Kranti sat alone, his eyes closed.

"Oh, god!" he muttered.

Prema and Julian had returned from the prosecutor's office and listened to the family strife. Gesturing Julian to go to the kitchen, Prema touched Kranti on the shoulder. "The Sword of Justice has yet to strike you."

His face streamed in tears, he said, "You have ruined me, Prema."

"Not yet."

"What do you want me to do? Commit suicide." He spoke harshly.

Prema was perplexed. This was a new manifestation of Kranti, with which she was unfamiliar.

Without a word, she went to her room, and closed the door. She was aware that she had kindled the fire ravaging this home — the fire to which her father-in-law had alluded while snubbing Kranti. This was what she had been wanting for the last many months: to crush her husband's overbearing pride and arrogance. But she was not sure whether he would still apologize to Julian. Neither was she happy with the result. Kranti symbolized hauteur, honour, and fearlessness. But she had found him weak, timid and behaving almost like a coward.

She wept.

The heated exchange between the brother and sister that had blown out of control because of his stupidity was the last straw for Kranti. Strangely, of all her brothers, Kanupriya loved him the most. In the dead of the night, he packed his belongings, and left the house. Vaishali found his short note on the dining table next morning.

When Vaishali showed it to Deepak, his face was grim as he tore it into shreds. "It was overdue," he said, his throat choked. "I don't know where we are heading."

Kanupriya blamed herself for Kranti's departure. Prema showed signs of anxiety, and nervousness: the children would miss their father.

Kranti shifted to the BSF guest house and applied for government accommodation.

□□□

XVII

Downfall

Krandhikar was an idealist, all the time searching for truth even if he had to ferret it out from mounds of husk by meticulously winnowing or threshing it. An avid reader of Hercule Poirot's exploits since his childhood, he would have liked to remove the layers of mystery, one by one, under which the major cases relating to murder, rape or kidnapping were shrouded. Like his hero, the motive for the crime was more important to him than the associated frills, and he tried to understand the psyche of the criminal before the charge sheet was filed in the court. But Poirot had all the time at his disposal and was not accountable to anyone (except his reputation), whereas Krandhikar was required to get results, and often soon. The delicate unravelling of the mystery was set aside, and forceful, brutal methods were adopted. It happened not infrequently that in order to appease the political bosses and get immediate results, a wrong person was fixed. His heart bled on such occasions;

his anger increased when he watched the drama in the court. He continued working on his own with his few confidantes, and sometimes was able to save the person wrongfully punished. Once, when he was able to get the life sentence verdict changed to exoneration in respect of a septuagenarian held responsible for the murder of his son (the son's wife had actually committed the murder), the old man had touched his feet and Krandhikar had wept with him. He considered those moments as the most precious in his life.

A chronic bachelor, he stayed alone and bestowed all his affection on his younger officers. Kranti and Sudha were his favourites. An upright bureaucrat, Krandhikar was a role model for police officers. For the last five years, his niece, a divorcee, and a practising lawyer in the session court, was staying with him along with her seven -year- old son.

Krandhikar was on leave at Chennai to nurse his ailing elder brother. He was surprised to read the news about an NGO filing a FIR of rape against Kranti and decided to talk to him after his return to Delhi. As soon as he joined the CRPF, he bagged a UNDP assignment for one year in Kazakhstan. The biting cold in the country forced him to curtail the deputation and return to India. With assembly elections approaching in four States, Krandhikar was busy marshalling his CRPF units, and was not aware that the NGO responsible for filing the FIR against Kranti was founded by Prema.

It was his niece who brought it to his notice over dinner. He refused to believe it. Whatever he had known of Kranti, he had always considered him as a straight officer with no kinks. His fault if any was that he tried to

emulate him in all respects: over ambitious and equally short tempered.
"A wife filing a FIR against her husband is serious, Chachu?"
"I concede," he said, a little confused.
He remembered the cheerful couple whenever he had met them at the parties or functions.
"Wasn't he one of your favourites?"
"Yes," he muttered. "I treated him like my son."
"Perhaps, you are getting old, and your judgement is getting warped. The talk amongst the lawyers is that he raped the girl." Looking at his thick grey hair, she added, "The fact is that we can never understand human nature." Catching the arm of her son, she left the room.

Jolted, Krandhikar continued to sit for a long time. Studying human nature was the key to his attitude in solving the serious cases. It surprised him how he could have misjudged Kranti?

He had not taken the FIR against Kranti seriously, neither his suspension. He considered it as a corollary of the police report. He was certain that Kranti was innocent and would come out unscathed. But his niece's assertion that everyone amongst the lawyer fraternity considered that Kranti had actually raped the girl: was too serious to be dismissed. He also refused to accept that he was getting old and senile.

Though he had left the Delhi Police, he kept a watch over the happenings there. If he had continued in Delhi Police, he would have been responsible for Kranti's case. Then he would have gone after Kranti hammer and tongs. Why did Kranti do it? he wondered.

He decided to find out the truth. The first thing in the

morning, he called Sudha, and invited her for lunch.

A luncheon invitation by the former Chief meant it was serious business though she was completely at sea about its context. Sudha had enjoyed a special relationship with him, and she wanted to retain the bonding even after his promotion.

Krandhikar was straight forward as before and told her what had bugged him the whole night. "Do you think he really raped the girl?"

"I think not," she answered tentatively. "But Prema's filing the FIR and all the women of the household going against him worries me." She looked at him, and added uncertainly, "Maybe, he did it."

Without any mental reservation, she told him all she knew. He too, shared his niece's opinion.

"I want to know the truth," he said.

This was the moment she feared when she had to choose between her loyalties for Kranti and Krandhikar. In a dilemma, she avoided his eye contact.

Prabhat had also wanted her to find out the truth.

"I know how you feel for Kranti, but would you not like to know the kind of man he is?" Krandhikar asked.

"Now, it is outside the area of your official business," she said coldly.

Krandhikar frowned and nodded thoughtfully. Sudha was committed, and a daredevil. Only she could discover the truth, and no one else.

"Sudha, you know me too well. There is a bee in my bonnet, and I have to get to the bottom of it. I can't be wasting my affections on a rapist. And I know that you are the only one who can help me in finding the truth."

He forced her to take another roti, and added gently,

"Give it a thought before rejecting my proposal."
"Yes, sir," she said, and enjoyed the 'Shrikhand'.

At night, she mulled over the discussion. Earlier, she had not given any thought to the issue raised by her former Chief. Her emotions regarding Kranti were vague and nebulous. Of late, she had been considering the remote possibility that whatever the outcome of the court case, Kranti and Prema's relationship was going to get fractured. Possibly, then she had a little chance of marrying Kranti, though she knew Kranti had no emotions for her. Prabhat's assessment that she was nothing in comparison to Julian - a fair one - could not be wrong, and Kranti cared only for the fair ones. Why should he settle for another dark one like Prema? No, she had no future with Kranti.

Throughout the night, she kept on tossing and turning. Though she had expressed her opinion before Krandhikar that Kranti might have raped Julian, she had never believed it for an instant. Suddenly, it flashed across her that maybe he had actually done it as the girl had said in her testimony. The thought was so disturbing that she opened the side door and paced in the lawn. It was a moonless night, and the sky was bursting with stars in the chilly December night.

If Kranti really did rape a helpless girl, why should she have any feelings for such a criminal or think of ever settling with him? Krandhikar was so right: if he didn't want to waste his emotions on a rapist, neither did she.

Discovering the truth was risky. Kranti was dumb in some respects but was at his best when dealing with criminals. If she had to get the vital piece of information, she could not be straight forward and had to act in a surreptitious manner. So long as he did not get an inkling of it, and treated her like a younger colleague, she was safe. Aware that she had the spunk to carry out the operation, all she needed was a bit of luck. If she got caught, she had it.

It was almost dawn when she decided to take up the challenge. Krandhikar was relieved to hear her positive response; he had already told the Commandant of the CRPF unit stationed at Guwahati to dig up some information.

(2)

The prosecutor introduced Madam Katrina, the owner of the brothel, as a witness, but she denied Julian's sale to her. According to her, Julian had approached her as she was in acute poverty and needed money. Joe was one of her clients and visited the brothel regularly; however, she had no other commercial dealings with him. She was cross examined by Prabhat Verma and Joe's lawyer.

A few days later, the prosecutor produced Prema on the stand. Her testimony as the President of NRK was of little consequence, and Prabhat Verma did not cross examine her. Kranti did not appreciate the strategy of his counsel and had doubts about his having joined hands with the prosecutor. When Kranti called Sudha and confided his doubts in her, she invited him for dinner. Surprised at the odd gesture - they had never socialized after office hours - nonetheless, he accepted the invitation though it bugged him all through the afternoon.

Sudha opened the door, and Kranti found that the house was unusually quiet. She told him that her aunt who stayed with her, had gone to Pune to meet her son, and the servant had left early as her child was sick. Somehow, it made Kranti uneasy. After the FIR, he had grown a little wary of women especially when he interacted with them alone. Attired in a soft blue sari, with her long-permed hair, and an unusual sexy appearance, Sudha looked very different from the way she dressed for the office or at the few parties she attended. The soft blue sofa set, the matching divan, and the overall ambience had a soothing effect on him. The only glamour in the room was provided by the floral chintz curtains. She offered him a peg of Vodka, took a glass of red wine for herself, and sat down on the sofa next to him.

Kranti was in a foul temper; he had an altercation with Krandhikar when he had called upon him in the afternoon. The Vodka fired his spirits, and he sniped at everything she spoke. Finally, he told her about his row with the former Chief.

"He does not trust me, and I have done so much for him." Kranti complained. "When the crunch came, he talks of morality."

"Why doesn't he trust you?"

Her tone was crisp, and a little defiant; Kranti glared at her. She wanted to say something nasty to him, however, discipline, and habit took over.

"Forget it, sir. Relax." She placed her hand on his shoulder. He jerked it, startling her.

"A suspended officer, charged with rape! How can I relax, Sudha?"

Tense, he looked at her as if he would snap. She looked at the tautness of his face, and asked gently, "Do you have any choice?"

"No." He was brusque, and his tone rude.

"We are not in the office. You are at my home, and I am the hostess." She reminded him.
"Are you teaching me manners?"
"No. I am trying to tell you that your conduct is hurting me, and you are not behaving like a dignified guest."
It dawned on him that he was no longer her boss.
"I'm sorry, Sudha."
He caught her hand and looked at her. She was slightly taller than Prema, and a shade fairer than her. With a lithe figure, she looked sensual and pretty. He pulled her closer, she didn't resist him. Bringing her head closer, he kissed her violently.
"There is something of Prema in you."
"I am dark like her," she said.
The telephone ring disturbed them. Sudha picked up the receiver; it was Krandhikar.
"Is Kranti with you?"
"No, sir." She lied.
"Today, I was a little rough to him, especially when he needed me. Be nice to him when you meet him next."
"I will, sir," she answered putting down the phone.
Sudha told him about Krandhikar.
"After all, he is human," Kranti said.
"Despite his temper, he is a very decent human being."
About to hurl a volley of abuses on the old man, he abruptly stopped. "Are you fond of him?"
"Of course. Whatever I am today, I owe it him. He was a friend of my papa's and motivated me to join the services even before I filed for divorce."
Her simple admission made him uncomfortable.
"Let us have dinner," she suggested, and warmed the dishes in the microwave. He didn't offer to help her and

watched her assured movements. Within 20 -25 minutes, she invited him to come over to the table.

Dinner was an unusually quiet affair. His confidence had taken a beating, and he felt restless in the unfamiliar sedate atmosphere of her home. He had seldom seen her in a place other than the office, where he was in complete command. Now, he felt, she had controlled him, his body and mind.

"What are you thinking, Kranti?"

It was the first time she had used his first name. Somehow, he was not completely taken by surprise; it seemed the most natural next move by her.

"I have made a mess of my life, Sudha."

"Like all bad things in life, it will also pass."

"But I'll never be the same again."

"With each day, a part of us changes, Kranti. I am very different from the girl who met you 4-5 years back though you have never noticed me earlier."

It was so true. He realized that he had hardly ever noticed her as a woman. She was dark, and not worth a second look. The thought made him a little nervous as if he had committed another crime.

Dinner over, she caught his hand, and moved to the bedroom. He acquiesced in her as if he had no choice. Except for the light pink bed cover, the room was draped in shades of white. A soft lilting tune filled the room.

But she did not move towards the bed as he expected, and instead sat down on the 3-seater sofa in the room. Uncertainly, he stood there for sometime appreciating the small Kashmiri carpet.

"Come, come, sir," she whispered.

He sat down next to her wondering what she was up to.

Instead of relaxing he was turning edgy.
"Tell me what happened at Nongpoh about eight years back, Kranti," she said placing her hand on his arm. "Unburden yourself."
"So, Julian lay nude, tied to the bed — what happened next?"
She was patient and persuasive.
The burden of hiding the truth had given him so much psychological stress and tribulations for the last few months that he was close to breaking point. The soothing lights, the background music, a slightly mysterious seductress, and the heady atmosphere of romance made him throw caution to the wind. Kranti told her everything and hid nothing.
He felt light and free. As free as when he was paragliding in the Grindlewald valley in Switzerland many years ago.

Her heart twisted; an emotion on the fringe of love that she had nurtured for the last two-three years was crushed.
A light touch on the mobile, and as if pre-arranged, the landline phone rang.
"Yes, Nandini," Sudha asked.
"I'm waiting for your call for last one hour. Remember you had to give me some information."
Sudha apologised, took out a folder from the cupboard telling Kranti that she would take about thirty-forty minutes.
He understood and slipped away.
The next day, Sudha handed her former Chief, an audio CD.
"But where is the video?" he asked.
"Somehow, it got spoiled. This is the best I could manage,"

she answered, and left hurriedly.

A week later, Sudha walked to Prabhat Verma's office early in the morning, and told him, "I have done a lot of research during the last one week, I am confident that Kranti is innocent."

"What did your research cover?"

"Interrogating him, his family, and friends."

"I did not know that you took me so seriously."

"Come on Prabhat? How can I take you casually?" she said handing him a list of names that puzzled him.

"You are competent." He remarked and smiled. "Are you planning to marry me or not?"

Tersely, she replied, "Engagement — next month."

Taken by surprise, his jaw dropped.

"You have really pulled the carpet from under my feet though I have been waiting to hear this news for months."

"Are you reconsidering?" she asked.

"Oh, no," he said, rose from the chair, and embraced her. "This calls for a celebration. Which place?"

"Ashoka." She decided.

"So be it," he said dropping a kiss on her inviting lips.

(3)

On listening to the audio CD, a gamut of emotions hit Krandhikar. He felt a stab in his heart that he had treated a rapist as his son. But ironically, most of the glory he had earned in Delhi Police, he owed to Kranti. Krandhikar ruminated over the years he had spent with Kranti, and how he had brought fame and honours to Delhi Police. Sudha must have skated on thin ice to get the CD, he reflected. The thrill of digging out the ugly truth was lost in the maze of the past, and the confusion about Kranti's future. Producing the CD in the court was akin to ordering the war hero to be thrown before a death squad.

The CD was a vital piece of evidence and could not be withheld from the court. As a cop he was morally and legally duty-bound to produce it in the court, otherwise it could go against him. He could not take shelter under the pretext that he was not involved in the affairs of the Delhi Police. Some courts did not consider a CD as evidence, whereas others accepted it. Whatever the outcome, the CD would swing the case against Kranti. He debated whether to hand it over to Kulwant Singh, who disliked Kranti, or to adopt some other strategy. Indecisive, he kept it in his office safe.

After dinner, he got a call from his nephew at Chennai that the condition of Krandhikar's elder brother had turned critical. He was on deathbed, and desired to see him. Krandhikar's private secretary was able to book a seat for him in the night flight reaching there at 3am but was unable to pass on a message to Chennai Police. There was no one to receive him at the airport. The storm and blinding rain caught him unaware, but without getting ruffled, he took a taxi. To his dismay, the driver was tipsy. Though he bawled at the driver and threatened to throw him out of the taxi and take over, the driver was past caring and shouted back at him. Forcibly, Krandhikar tried to stop the car, but the driver pressed the accelerator shouting "Hurray!" He lost control, crossed the yellow line, and rammed into a truck.

The driver was killed instantly. Krandhikar was unconscious, and by the time the police were able to identify and rush him to the hospital, crucial time was lost, and he slipped into a coma.

(4)

Kranti's departure in a fit of pique had saddened everyone, yet strangely it brought peace and harmony in the house. It was as if the only discordant note in the family was deleted or muted though its effects reverberated for long in the house and would continue in the lives of Prema and the children for the rest of their lives, if Kranti divorced her.

On return from Banswara, Vivek was quite excited about the new project he had established there. Of late, he had developed the art of rhetoric, and made others listen to his grandiose plans. In a house torn by conflict arising out of the court case, it was a welcome distraction. Consciously, they talked and talked of it, as if the setting up of the new project would change the lives of millions overnight. Losing their eldest son to Darjeeling, and Kranti — their emotional backbone for last many years — to the court case, now Deepak and Vaishali centred their hopes on the youngest son. The most useless son became all important. Everyone was concerned about what he did and thought. Neither of the parents thought of pinning their future on Kanupriya, their bright daughter, for they were sure that she would remarry soon. The frequency of Vivek's visits increased, and he talked to Julian on the pretext of getting updated about the court proceedings. Often, Vaishali saw them together, and was worried.

About two-three months back, Vivek had got a mail from Sheila stating that she had met a guitarist from Argentina and had liked him. She hinted that she had no intention of returning to India. Like Vivek, the guitarist was a broke, and her life was going to be as tough as it was with him. The mail had broken his heart as he had had great times with her. Stoically, he accepted it and moved on in life.

On learning about Kranti's departure, Vivek was upset for the sake of Prema and her children. He met him during the trial, and asked him to return home, but he refused. "So long as that whore is in the house, I'll never go back," he said.

Vaishali grew more sentimental about the house as Deepak's retirement approached nearer. She examined the trees, the ferns, the leaves, bushes, hedges and plants minutely. She was amazed that there were many plants she was admiring perhaps for the first time. "I'll miss all this," she murmured.

In the last week of January, she asked Deepak to have a round in the garden at night, but he refused. Despite the biting cold, she moved through the trees towards her favourite spot. By the side of three imposing neem trees, she had planted a few imported plants gifted by a friend of hers settled in the UK. A Blue Jacaranda, an American tropical tree, a foxglove called Paulownia tomentosa, and several silvery ferns. Later, she added a willow, a chestnut maple and a pine. All these had taken roots, thanks to Vivek who had sound arboreal knowledge. He had guided the gardener to plant them under the canopy of the trees so that they were protected from the blazing May and June sun. In the first summer, Vivek had personally put-up thick tarpaulin sheets. Her favourite seat also provided a view of an old eucalyptus tree slightly leaning towards a younger one.

She was appalled on hearing the whispering of a couple. How could any one dare enter her garden, and indulge in romance? To avoid the rustling of leaves, she moved slowly. When she reached closer, she recognized the voices of Vivek and Julian. Her heartbeat wildly; she had to support herself against a tree otherwise her legs might have given way.

Julian was sitting on Vaishali's seat, and Vivek was removing some thorns embedded into her feet.

"To be merciful is the most sacred tenet of the Bible, which you — a good Christian that you are — seem to have forgotten. Remember, Christ offered the other cheek to the man who slapped him. Christ came to me in my dream yesterday and told me to warn you to be merciful otherwise —." Vivek spoke in his sweet resonant voice.

"What would happen if I disobeyed?"

"He will shoot these thorns into your feet," he said, and laughed.

"You see — it is a sign of God. So be merciful."

"But why didn't God come in my dreams?" she asked.

"Because you are not prepared for it. The soil must be well prepared to receive the seed."

With a mischievous smile flickering on her lips, she nodded.

"But now I will send him to you, and I am sure he will come in your dreams too," he said removing the thorns.

The whole ambience seemed surreal to Vaishali : the full moon in all her glory, the moonlight filtering through the foliage and dancing on the leaves as they swayed in the gentle breeze, the silvery beams falling on the young couple accentuating their innocence as if they were exposed to love for the first time in their lives, the irregular shadows in the backdrop, the hollows of darkness where moonlight was unable to penetrate, and an all pervading quiescence settling down on the night and enveloping them. Almost like a dream.

It was one of the most romantic scenes Vaishali had ever witnessed in her life, and it overwhelmed her. But the lover was her son, and the woman her maid, and a former whore.

"You have not met Sheila, but you have heard about her. Do you know that she had a live - in relationship with a scientist in US? He came to India to meet his parents, and never went back. Sheila came to India in search of her fiancé and learnt that he had married and even had a child. Sheila forgave him."

"I didn't know," Julian said.

Neither did Vaishali.

He looked at Julian, and gently kissed her hand. "So should you."

Vaishali's eyes turned moist. She wondered whether her son was serious in flirting with Julian, or it was a pretext to persuade her to forgive Kranti.

Slowly and cautiously, she turned, and retraced her steps. Deepak was asleep, and she slipped inside the quilt beside him.

(5)

Prabhat Verma's short list of witnesses was focussed on proving Kranti's character and integrity. The prosecutor questioned Kranti for a long time, but he did not deviate from the story he had told Prema and others in which he emerged as a hero rather than a criminal. All the attempts of the prosecutor failed to shake him. However, the prosecutor did not question him on his career as he had an impeccable record.

In the closing arguments K.K. Trehan, the senior

Public Prosecutor stated that he was able to prove that Julian was raped by Kranti. P.K. Verma, Kranti's counsel said that the state had no case, and it was a trumped-up charge. It appeared ludicrous that a competent, decorated officer was dragged into a rape case of a notorious whore of Kolkata. It was unfortunate that a family squabble was brought to the court to tarnish the image of his client.

Krandhikar was no longer in coma, and had been shifted to a room; however, the CD could not be produced in the court. On learning about the accident, Sudha had flown to Chennai and met him.

Everyone was apprehensive of the judgement: Julian, Prema, Kranti, his family members, the media and the women's organizations. Sending ripples in the media, the judge fully exonerated Kranti, Joe and five others because of lack of credible evidence. Overcome by emotions, Kranti embraced his counsel, and Sudha. Deepak, Vaishali, Kanupriya and Vivek beamed at him, and he waved to them with almost tears in his eyes. Prema was disappointed, but at heart she was greatly relieved that her intuitions had proved wrong. Pushing through the journalists, Prema went up to Kranti, and congratulated him. He placed his arm around her shoulder and hugged her lightly as if all the discord generated by the trial was swept away by the judgement.

Disillusioned by the judicial system, Julian was shaken. She also felt that Prema had been making a fool of her when all along she had wanted her husband to win the case.

"Will you go back to your husband now, madam?" A TV journalist asked Prema.

Without a comment, she looked at her husband, and

everyone knew the answer from her ravishing smiles.

Acquitted by a judge known to be a feminist, Kranti was given a warm reception by the family when he returned in the evening. Vaishali was so happy at the vindication of the family honour that she applied a tilak on his forehead and did the 'aarti'. Julian locked herself in the room and refused to come out. When Vaishali went to her room to cajole, she screamed at her, "But madam, he raped me."

It rattled Vaishali though she didn't allow the thought to mellow down the jubilations. "She cannot take the judgement gracefully," she muttered to herself. "She is losing her sanity." But Julian's words continued to rankle.

A little later, Julian informed that she wanted to quit. Vaishali told her to continue till she was able to find a suitable replacement.

(6)

At the instance of the Department of Personnel, the UPSC was to take up an exhaustive review of the efficiency of officers in paramilitary establishments like CRPF, BSF etc. and the corresponding amendment of recruitment rules. The two - day seminar was inaugurated a day before Deepak's retirement. The Home Minister paid rich tribute to Deepak Chopra for his services to the nation, and his contribution to the administrative services. "Men like Deepak Chopra are like a light house; unfazed, they weather all storms and keep on guiding the ships that pass by. The coming generations would wonder that we had a man of his kind in the administrative services." The Minister of State for Personnel also lauded his achievements.

Krandhikar had been discharged from the hospital,

and after 2-3 weeks was able to move around with a stick. He made it a point to attend the seminar as he was looking after CRPF. He also felt it necessary that Deepak Chopra ought to know the truth about his son.

During the tea break when both the Ministers had left, Krandhikar tacitly escorted Deepak to a corner. "I used to adore your son like my own but now I am ashamed of him."

"He has been exonerated by the court," Deepak said acidly.

"There were no independent witnesses, and perhaps the prosecutor was won over."

"What nonsense are you talking?" Deepak lost his control. "Once the court has acquitted him, you have to accept it."

Confidently, Krandhikar continued, "I am a cop. I have spent thirty-two years dealing with such cases. There is no doubt in my mind that Julian was raped by him."

"Do you have any proof?" Deepak's hand trembled slightly.

"Yes, I have a CD." Krandhikar said softly, in fact so softly that he had to repeat on Deepak's request.

"I want to see it."

"Sir, please control yourself. Let us go to your room."

He escorted him to the room and closed the door.

"The video was spoiled but the audio is quite clear. And it is not doctored, I have got it checked. If you want, I'll bring the player from my car, the CD is with me."

Deepak nodded, had some water, and ordered coffee.

He was more composed when Krandhikar returned. The cop closed the door and switched on the player.

"The bastard!" Deepak muttered after about twenty-five minutes. "Being over smart with me!"

He looked at the senior cop. "Why didn't you produce the CD in the court?"

Krandhikar told him about the accident.

"Oh, I am sorry," Deepak said. He thought for a while, and said, "Could I have the CD? I want Kranti to tell me the truth."

"Yes, it is for you. But if you would not mind, in certain areas, I know your son better than you. He will dupe you. I would like to be present when the CD is played. I will be behind the scenes."

Deepak appreciated that perhaps the cop was right; Kranti could outwit him, not Krandhikar.

Agitated that he was going to engulf the house of one of the most respected bureaucrats in a crisis on the eve of his retirement, Krandhikar tiptoed out of the room. But in the broader principle for which the grand old man stood, it had to be done.

Deepak called Kranti and asked him to meet him at five. He rose and peeped outside the window. At the end of February, the garden was barren. It was a conspicuous reminder of Supriya's absence who looked after these trivial things that were close to his heart. Reluctantly, he went back to the seminar, and slumped into a back seat, his brain feverishly charged by the shocking revelation.

As predicted by the Met. Department, the westerly disturbances brought dark clouds accompanied by lightning and thunder. Kranti, who had been reinstated, knocked before five, and entered. "What foul weather?" He scowled throwing the raincoat on one of the chairs.

"You wanted me, papa?" he said glancing around the room.

"Yes, son, I want to have a chat with you."

"Here, in the office," he said. "It is very unusual of you."
"We are amidst unusual circumstances, are we not?"
Kranti didn't answer; he was worried that it had something to do with him.
"I want you to tell me the truth about what happened at Nongpoh about eight-nine years back."
Self-assured, Kranti smiled and said, "Papa, you are at it again. I have already told you earlier, and now even the court has exonerated me."
"The court had no independent witness and perhaps you were able to influence the prosecutor, if not the judge," Deepak said quoting Krandhikar.
"If there is no case from where will independent witnesses spring up? And I have no influence over the prosecutor or the judge. Both hate me."
"But Kranti, I want the truth. What you have been telling the court and all of us is a bunch of lies."
"Papa, Prema and Julian seem to have influenced you with their sob story. I have told you my story truthfully — that is the truth." He rose from the seat. "You are busy with the seminar and tomorrow you are retiring. You have to attend so many farewells and parties. I also have to run around to ensure my posting in Delhi."
"Sit down!" Deepak thundered as he had never spoken with any of his sons earlier. "I didn't realize that any of my sons could lie blatantly before me."
His entire body shaking with rage, he said, "I'll give you the proof."
Suddenly, Kranti was scared. Deepak went over to the record player and pressed the knob. Kranti's own voice resounded in the room.
"The bitch!" Kranti murmured. "I feared it. But I could

not imagine she was working for you."

Kranti felt as if the lightning that had flashed outside had struck him. He sank into the seat.

Suddenly, he had a brain wave. He rushed towards the record player, stopped it, pressed another knob, and took out the CD.

"I am sure, papa, the CD is doctored. It is the handiwork of my enemies."

"I want you to tell me the truth. What actually happened?"

"You are behaving like a judge rather than my father. What do you propose to do if I do not obey you?"

"I'll do something which will shock you. I'll get the entire case reopened based on this."

"The court does not acknowledge the CD as evidence."

"But if the person who has recorded, and the person at whose instance it was recorded, give their evidence - any court will accept it."

"You will not do anything of this kind, papa." Kranti spoke confidently, and with a swish of his fingers snapped the disc into small shards.

"Is there any other proof?" His tone was aggressive and bordered on hostility. With an abrasive gesture he again rose. "Papa, you should appreciate that I am a cop and not an amateur."

"I considered it, son." Deepak said grimly. He was extremely unhappy at the way his son was misbehaving. "It was a copy. The original is safe."

"It is safe with me," Krandhikar said appearing from the ante room used by Deepak for taking lunch.

"So, you are at the back of this operation!" Kranti stared angrily at him.

Krandhikar nodded. "We both want to know the truth

from you."

Cornered, Kranti took the coffee that had arrived by now, and told his story. Exactly the way it had happened.

Krandhikar had taken the precaution of video recording the whole proceedings right from the time Kranti had entered the room including his fresh confession.

"Good, son," Deepak said after half an hour. "Now, I want you to apologise to Julian in presence of all the family members."

"Why are you doing it to me?" His eyes full of tears, he looked weak and helpless. "Papa, you know I can't do it, she was a whore."

"A human being, nonetheless," Deepak answered. "And she was a college girl and not a prostitute when you raped her."

"I was not responsible for turning her into a whore."

"No, you were not. But she was helpless and tied to the bed when you raped her."

Kranti was quiet.

"You will apologise to the woman," Deepak said sternly, "otherwise I'll have the case reopened."

Kranti tried another strategy. "Do you want me to commit suicide, papa?"

"I am willing to pay any price."

That silenced Kranti.

Deepak thanked Krandhikar and reached home with his son.

(7)

The mist that had settled down on the Akbar Road bungalow with the arrival of Vinay and Madhulika in November 2000, and had turned into thick smog with Kranti's trial, had finally lifted with his exoneration.

Raucous laughter of the women resounded not only inside the rooms, but spilled over into the garden, shrubs and trees.

A close colleague of Deepak had invited him and the entire family for dinner; everyone was getting dressed when Deepak reached home with Kranti at about 8pm. Prema had worn a red sari and looked resplendent when she looked at herself in the mirror. That her husband was free from the stigma of rape, and she was pardoned by him for her act of transgression, was a great feeling. The magical spell of his love and passion entranced her. For the last two weeks, she and Kranti were in a state of bliss as if they were newly married and had planned a week's holiday in the Mauritius islands.

"I want to talk to the entire family," Deepak told a cheerful Vaishali attired in a maroon sari. "And call Julian also."

At the mention of Julian, Vaishali's smile faded. Kranti had slipped away to the toilet to regain his composure.

Slowly, the entire family walked in. Julian stood far away, a little perplexed.

"Notwithstanding the court judgement, there are certain facts which have not come to light so far. Kranti will tell all the facts as they happened," the family patriarch said.

The air was charged with apprehension. They were all scared of the harsh, repulsive truth which they had been avoiding to face: the court judgement had helped them to distance themselves from it.

Bravely, Kranti told all. His countenance was grim and severe. Finally, he concluded, "It is true that I raped Julian. I am sorry."

"Julian," Deepak called her.

In a trance Julian walked up to him escorted by Kanupriya.

"Kranti, I want you to ask for her forgiveness." Deepak's sonorous voice rang in the room.

With tears in his eyes, Kranti said, "I apologize. Please forgive me."

Julian could not believe such a moment in her life. Shocked by the turn of events, she stared at her rapist like a statue, unable to utter a word.

Vivek went over to her, and said, "Do you forgive Kranti for what he did to you eight-nine years back?"

Julian still did not respond.

Bending down a little so that he could look into Julian's eyes, Vivek said again, "We all want to hear your reply, Julian. It is important to all the family members."

All along these years, Julian had wished to stab the man who was now begging for forgiveness. But seeing him in tears confused her.

"Your decision is very important to all of us." Vivek was patient. He touched her lightly on the shoulder. "Do you forgive him?"

Dumbstruck by the strange turn of events, her eyes brimming in tears, Julians' throat was choked. She nodded, moved closer to Kranti and slapped him hard. She turned and bolted.

"I feared this all along. I am ashamed of you." Vaishali spoke fiercely, her eyes welled with tears.

"You swine, you cheated me." Prema cried and dashed away to her room.

"Do you also have to say something?" Kranti looked sadly at Kanupriya.

"No, you have suffered a lot," she replied, and scooted behind her sister-in-law.

Mission accomplished, Deepak felt jittery on seeing

his son withered, and lifeless on the sofa. Where was the glow, the spring, the swagger and the chutzpah associated with him? Deepak did not have the courage to go up to him and ameliorate his grief; he blamed himself for humiliating his own son and reducing him to nothingness. But it had to be done.

Vaishali returned with a tea tray for her husband, and son. Neither of them had it. Uncertain whether it was the denouement on Kranti's case or not, she placed her arm around Kranti's shoulder; he jolted it away. Disgraced, Kranti had to make an effort to stand on his own legs. Nonetheless, he rose, and without looking at either parent staggered into the darkness.

THE END

Epilogue (About five and a half years later)

Kranti never went back to the Akbar Road bungalow and moved to a government accommodation. The media limelight Prema had attracted during the court case enabled her to start her own private practice. Along with Julian, she finally left the protective umbrella of her in-laws. Julian completed BA, B. Ed, and with a little help from Deepak Chopra, took up a teaching assignment in a convent school.

In time, Kranti's anger subsided, and he called upon his parents once or twice a month.

Vivek spent the next five years in Rajasthan collecting accolades from the State Government and the locals. But gradually, he became restless and wanted to move out to some other place. He selected Odisha, hoping to uplift the poverty-stricken masses in the tribal region.

It was the month of August, the overcast sky burst into rain when Deepak, and Vaishali boarded the Air India flight for Bengaluru. After many years, Vaishali had insisted to accompany her husband to Mysore where he had to deliver the valedictory address at the university convocation. While Deepak was busy placing the handbags in the cabin in the first class, Vaishali spotted Supriya sitting in the first row, and moved towards her. Now Additional Secretary in the Ministry of Agriculture, Supriya was going to Bengaluru to attend a conference.

"Hi, Supriya," Vaishali said.

Surprised, Supriya rose; she wondered why she had not listened to her fluttering heart. Vaishali embraced her and whispered, "The last time when we met, I was very unfair to you. I'm sorry."

Without a word, Supriya pressed her hand gently.

Vaishali informed her about Kanupriya's marriage, and how Kranti had rescued a dozen children held hostage by terrorists in Srinagar and was awarded the President's medal for exceptional bravery. Grievously injured, he was in the hospital for a month, and was lucky to survive.

Supriya turned her head and broke into a broad smile on seeing Deepak.

"How are you sir?" she said offering her hand. Supriya knew that he had missed out on the Padma award as well as the governorship. Unable to control his exuberance, he hugged her as if cocking a snook at the world at large.

"I have missed you Supri," he muttered.

"So have I, sir."

Her heart bounced, and she blushed. With her hand in his, he kept on chatting, and she continued to nod her head admiring him. A little later, she went back to her seat.

Filled with frisson after the fortuitous meeting with Supriya, Deepak felt rich and full. When Vaishali leaned against him, he quietly placed his arm on her shoulder, something he had not done in years.

Appendix

Stella And Vinay's Research

Stella had a sound background of symmetries and super symmetries — her father had been a professor of mathematics for twenty years at Princeton — and her Chinese professor Tse Tung was also famous for his research in astrophysics. When Stella joined him, he had already moved to particle physics.

In physics, a fundamental particle is a particle that is not made of other particles. All fundamental particles are either fermions or bosons. The electron, proton, neutron etc are fermions and have half integer spin, whereas bosons have integer spin. An example of a boson is photon. Over the decades, scientists have developed a Standard Model of Physics consistent with the latest developments in quantum physics and relativity.

Symmetry of a physical system is a physical or mathematical feature of the system that is preserved or remains unchanged under some transformation. The most important example in Physics is that of the speed of light which has the same value in all inertial frames of reference. The principle of symmetry, also known as the invariance principle, controls the laws of nature in the cosmos. Just as events are controlled by the laws of physics, the latter are controlled by the principle of symmetries. The Standard Model of Physics must be in consonance with the principle of symmetry. The breaking of symmetries is equally significant and explains many secrets of nature.

Based on symmetries controlling the interaction between fundamental particles, many of these particles should not have any mass i.e., they should be massless, though actually we know they have a definite mass. This was a major puzzle for physicists for decades and it was not consistent with the Standard Model of Physics. The problem was solved by six physicists in the 1960s by postulating the presence of a particle, now called the Higgs particle, and its associated field termed as the Higgs field, which pervades everywhere and has a nonzero value. With the existence of this field, electroweak symmetry breaking was possible, and it is responsible for the masses of fundamental particles such as elementary fermions and massive W and Z gauge bosons.

The Higgs particle was supposed to be a scalar boson with zero spin, even parity and zero charge. It was highly unstable and therefore not detectable in nature.

The existence of the Higgs particle was finally confirmed by Large Hadron Collider at CERN in 2012 -2013. The mass of Higgs particle is 125 GeV/c2.

Another problem which bugged the scientists was that of the nature of dark matter.

The matter which is visible to us through telescopes constitutes only 4.9% of the known universe, 26.8% is dark matter and 68.3% is dark energy. The existence of dark matter was hypothesized because of the difference between the mass of large astronomical objects determined from their gravitational effects and the mass calculated from the observable matter (stars, gas, and dust). The 'missing mass' was noticed for the first time in the orbital velocities of stars in the Milky Way by Jan Oort in 1932 and again in the orbital velocities of galaxies in clusters by Fritz Zwicky in 1933 and confirmed by Vera Rubin in 1960-70s using galaxy rotation curves.

The consensus of cosmologists is that dark matter is composed of uncharacteristic subatomic particles and the search for this particle is on.

What cosmologists know is that dark matter is the main source of gravity holding every galaxy together; it binds galaxies together in clusters, and it warps space around galaxy clusters creating a lensing effect. The dark matter has no electrical charge, and it passes through baryonic matter, which contains neutrons and protons. It does not emit or absorb light and does not interact with electromagnetic radiation. The only way its presence is felt is through gravity and weak interactions.

Jane Oldfield and Graham Stole were common friends of Stella and were doing research in astrophysics at Washington Observatory. Both were committed researchers but their data on a cluster of galaxies in the Milky Way was considered erroneous by other physicists, and they were lampooned in a conference. Frustrated, they left for an unknown adventure in Alps, were swept away by an avalanche, and died.

Stella was stunned by this tragedy. Aware how dedicated they were to astrophysics; she wanted to redeem their honour. She also felt that something was amiss in the conclusion of the physicists at that conference. She collected data from a galaxy cluster where the dark matter was abnormally high and compared it to another set of data where the dark matter was extremely low. It surprised her that the value of the Higgs particle was different in the two data. Suddenly, it dawned on her that there was nothing wrong with the data collected by her friends, but perhaps the laws of physics with which physicists were familiar, did not apply in dark matter. She worked hard on it for months with her Chinese professor and was able to prove mathematically that dark matter was a different world where different laws needed to be propounded.

Stella dared to postulate in her doctorate thesis at the end of 1991 (the Higgs particle existence was confirmed only in 2012-13) that the Higgs field did not exist in dark matter and instead another field was hypothesized by her. The new particle was a scalar boson and lighter than the Higgs particle but slightly more stable.

In her thesis, Stella established a relationship between dark matter and dark energy and was able to calculate the rate at which dark matter and dark energy were increasing.

Stella's untimely death robbed her of all the glory. When Vinay planned to declare her research as his own, he gave the new particle his name. Sending shock waves in the world of physics, Vinay postulated mathematically his thesis of the Vinay particle and its associated field, and how it was more relevant than the Higgs particle in dark matter. Later, Vinay collected data from many other galaxy clusters and gave it universality.

Acknowledgements

I am extremely grateful to Mr Vishnu Saxena for his words of encouragement and sound advice. Many thanks to LK Puri and his daughter Namita for scribbling copious comments that were of immense help; Devika Kumar for going through the manuscript line by line and painstakingly suggesting changes; and Anju Chibber for her suggestions. Prof. Vijay Gupta, my class fellow, for vetting the research done by Stella and Vinay.

My daughter Shikha for giving me her moral support. Sushma, my wife, for getting deeply involved into skin of the characters and criticising them ruthlessly. Along with me she has experienced their joys and pains. And for her repetitive editing that helped the novel take its present shape. Many thanks my life partner!

Thanks to Dr A Gupta and his team; and special thanks to Dr Atul Jain.